Robert Godda[...]mbridge. His first novel, [...] his books have captivated readers worldwide with their edge-of-the-seat pace and their labyrinthine plotting. His first Harry Barnett novel, *Into the Blue*, was winner of the first WHSmith Thumping Good Read Award and was dramatized for TV, starring John Thaw.

Robert Goddard can be found on the web at **www.robertgoddardbooks.co.uk**

Also by Robert Goddard

In order of publication

PAST CARING

A young graduate starts to investigate the fall from grace
of an Edwardian cabinet minister and sets in train a bizarre
and violent chain of events.

'A hornet's nest of jealousy, blackmail and violence. Engrossing'
DAILY MAIL

IN PALE BATTALIONS

An extraordinary story unfolds as Leonora Galloway strives to solve the
mystery of her father's death, her mother's unhappy childhood and a
First World War murder.

'A novel of numerous twists and turns and surprises'
SUNDAY TELEGRAPH

PAINTING THE DARKNESS

On a mild autumn afternoon in 1882, William Trenchard's life changes
for ever with the arrival of an unexpected stranger.

'Explodes into action'
SUNDAY INDEPENDENT

INTO THE BLUE

When a young woman disappears and Harry Barnett is accused
of her murder he has no option but to try and discover what led
her to vanish into the blue.

'A cracker, twisting, turning and exploding with real skill'
DAILY MIRROR

TAKE NO FAREWELL

September 1923, and architect Geoffrey Staddon must return
to the house called Clouds Frome, his first important commission,
to confront the dark secret that it holds.

'A master storyteller'
INDEPENDENT ON SUNDAY

HAND IN GLOVE
The death of a young English poet in the Spanish Civil
War casts a shadow forward over half a century.

'Cliff-hanging entertainment'
GUARDIAN

CLOSED CIRCLE
1931, and two English fraudsters on a transatlantic liner stumble
into deep trouble when they target a young heiress.

*'Full of thuggery and skulduggery, cross and
doublecross, plot and counter-plot'*
INDEPENDENT

BORROWED TIME
A brief encounter with a stranger who is murdered soon afterwards draws
Robin Timariot into the complex relationships and motives of the dead
woman's family and friends.

*'An atmosphere of taut menace...heightened
by shadows of betrayal and revenge'*
DAILY TELEGRAPH

OUT OF THE SUN
Harry Barnett becomes entangled in a sinister conspiracy
when he learns that the son he never knew he had is languishing
in hospital in a coma.

'Brilliantly plotted, full of good, traditional storytelling values'
MAIL ON SUNDAY

BEYOND RECALL
The scion of a wealthy Cornish dynasty reinvestigates a 1947 murder
and begins to doubt the official version of events.

'Satisfyingly complex...finishes in a rollercoaster of twists'
DAILY TELEGRAPH

CAUGHT IN THE LIGHT

A photographer's obsession with a femme fatale
leads him into a web of double jeopardy.

*'A spellbinding foray into the real-life game
of truth and consequences'*
THE TIMES

SET IN STONE

A strange house links past and present, a murder,
a political scandal and an unexplained tragedy.

'A heady blend of mystery and adventure'
OXFORD TIMES

SEA CHANGE

A spell-binding mystery involving a mysterious package, murder and
financial scandal, set in 18th-century London, Amsterdam and Rome.

'Engrossing, storytelling of a very high order'
OBSERVER

DYING TO TELL

A missing document, a forty-year-old murder and the Great Train
Robbery all seem to have connections with a modern-day disappearance.

*'Gripping...woven together with more
twists than a country lane'*
DAILY MAIL

DAYS WITHOUT NUMBER

Once Nick Paleologus has excavated a terrible secret from his
archaeologist father's career, nothing will ever be the same again.

*'Fuses history with crime, guilty consciences and human fallibility...
an intelligent escapist delight'*
THE TIMES

PLAY TO THE END

Actor Toby Flood finds himself a player in a much bigger game when he investigates a man who appears to be a stalker.

'An absorbing display of craftsmanship'
SUNDAY TIMES

SIGHT UNSEEN

An innocent bystander is pulled into a mystery which takes over twenty years to unravel when he witnesses the abduction of a child.

'A typically taut tale of wrecked lives, family tragedy, historical quirks and moral consequences'
THE TIMES

NEVER GO BACK

The convivial atmosphere of a reunion weekend is shattered by an apparent suicide.

'Meticulous planning, well-drawn characters and an immaculate sense of place... A satisfying number of twists and shocks'
THE TIMES

NAME TO A FACE

A centuries-old mystery is about to unravel...

'Mysterious, dramatic, intricate, fascinating and unputdownable'
DAILY MIRROR

FOUND WANTING

Catapulted into a breathless race against time, Richard's life will be changed for ever in ways he could never have imagined...

'The master of the clever twist'
SUNDAY TELEGRAPH

LONG TIME COMING

For thirty-six years they thought he was dead...
They were wrong.

*'When it comes to duplicity and intrigue,
Goddard is second to none'*
DAILY MAIL

BLOOD COUNT

There's no such thing as easy money.
As surgeon Edward Hammond is about to find out.

*'Mysterious, dramatic, intricate,
fascinating and unputdownable...
The crime writers' crime writer'*
DAILY MIRROR

NAME TO
A FACE

Robert Goddard

CORGI BOOKS

TRANSWORLD PUBLISHERS
61–63 Uxbridge Road, London W5 5SA
A Random House Group Company
www.transworldbooks.co.uk

NAME TO A FACE
A CORGI BOOK: 9780552164993

First published in Great Britain
in 2007 by Bantam Press
an imprint of Transworld Publishers
Corgi edition published 2008
Corgi edition reissued 2011

A CIP catalogue record for this book
is available from the British Library.

Addresses for Random House Group Ltd companies outside the UK
can be found at: www.randomhouse.co.uk
The Random House Group Ltd Reg. No. 954009

The Random House Group Limited supports The Forest Stewardship Council
(FSC®), the leading international forest certification organisation. Our books
carrying the FSC label are printed on FSC® certified paper. FSC is the only forest
certification scheme endorsed by the leading environmental organisations,
including Greenpeace. Our paper procurement policy can be found at
www.randomhouse.co.uk/environment

Typeset in 11/15pt Giovanni Book by Falcon Oast Graphic Art Ltd.
Printed and bound by CPI Group (UK) Ltd, Croydon, CR0 4YY

2 4 6 8 10 9 7 5 3 1

NAME TO A FACE

PROLOGUE

They will never ignore him again. They will never patronize him as they have too often of late. Nor will they ever forget him. They will not be allowed to. Fame and scholarly acclaim will see to that; fame – and a place in history. They will not be able to refuse him a fellowship now. They will offer him one. They will beg him to accept one. They will come crawling. And for all their slights and condescensions . . . he will pay them back.

Godfrey Shillingstone smiles to himself and sips his brandy. He gazes contentedly into the dying fire that has warmed the room where he is taking his solitary ease and reflects that he could hardly be more obscurely located or more thoroughly disregarded than he currently is. But soon, very soon, that will change. His certainty on the point has made these past days of waiting bearable. Several more must elapse before he can be on his way. Those he can also bear, savouring as he does the thought of what awaits him in London. When his discovery becomes known, his circumstances will be transformed. His life will at long last become what it should be. His labours will be rewarded. His ambitions will be fulfilled.

He drains his glass and rises from his chair. The clock in the hall strikes the half-hour as he does so. The house is otherwise silent, save for the smouldering sputter of the logs in the grate. He moves the fire-guard into position and takes up his candle. There is no sense in waiting for his host and hostess to return from their engagement. They will have nothing of the slightest interest to report. What passes for society at this intellectually impoverished toe-end of the kingdom holds no appeal for Godfrey Shillingstone, the soon-to-be-widely-celebrated antiquarian.

This, though, was no more the reason he declined to accompany the Revd Dr and Mrs Borlase to the Treweekes' supper party than the one he disingenuously offered up: a migrainous headache. The truth was quite otherwise, as he is happy to acknowledge, albeit only to himself. He recoiled from the notion of being separated by any appreciable distance from the great treasure he has recently laid hands upon. As far as the Borlases are concerned, it is a crate of geological specimens that he has lodged under lock and key in one of their outhouses, pending shipment to London, and he has no intention of disabusing them of the notion. Its true nature will be revealed when the time and place are right. Its true nature will be his to unveil when – and only when – he is ready to do so.

Shillingstone steps out into the hall, closes the drawing-room door behind him and turns towards the stairs. Then he stops. A breath of air before bed, perhaps? A reassuring tug on the chain securing the outhouse door? The idea is suddenly irresistibly appealing. The children and their maid are asleep. There is no one to remark his coming or going. He sets down the candle on the table beside the clock and heads towards the front door.

The night is breezy and mild; a fullish moon flits between fast-moving clouds. An owl hoots in the woods above the house as he pulls the front door softly shut behind him. The whisper of the wind in the trees makes for a soothing sound. The world about him is at peace. All is as it should be. He feels happier than he can ever recall feeling. And he suspects that in the weeks and months that lie ahead he will feel happier yet. He smiles to himself. He walks along to the corner of the house and on round the circular lawn at the head of the drive towards the stable-yard.

He is halted abruptly before he is halfway to his destination by a noise that is neither bird nor breeze. His smile yields to a frown of puzzlement. There is the noise again: the creaking of a hinge somewhere in the yard ahead of him. And another noise follows it: the clink of a horse's harness. His puzzlement turns to anxiety. He strides hurriedly forwards.

The scene reveals itself as he passes through the gateway into the yard. He is pulled up short by his own incredulity. The door of the outhouse where he has stored his great treasure is open; a lamp burns within. A man he does not recognize – short, thin, meanly dressed – stands by a horse, clutching its bridle, in front of the open doorway. Two other figures can be seen beyond in the lamplight, stooping over an object Shillingstone *does* recognize, very clearly – all too clearly.

'Stop,' he cries, recovering himself and plunging across the yard. 'Stop at once.'

The man by the horse looks round at him, his face in shadow. The horse whinnies. The animal is wearing a pack-saddle. They have come prepared. There can be no doubt of their intentions. It is the fulfilment of a fear Shillingstone has considered irrational – until now. The two men within stand upright. One of them releases his hold on the rope fastening the crate and steps forward, letting the lamplight fall upon his face, deliberately, as it seems to Shillingstone in that moment, boldly, brazenly.

'Tozer.' The stupefaction audible in Shillingstone's voice is not to be wondered at. Jacob Tozer is the estate steward, who dwells with his wife and children in the cottage adjoining the yard. His assurance several days ago that there was only one key to the padlock he supplied to secure the outhouse was obviously a lie. He possessed a second key all along and must even then have been planning to use it.

'Mr Shillingstone,' Tozer responds, his gaze open and unabashed, his tone drained of all his customary subservience. 'You ought to be abed at this hour.'

14

'Who are these people? What is the meaning of this?'

'The meaning's clear, I should've reckoned. As for my friends here, they're folk you took no heed of when you'd have been wise to. They've come to take back what you should never have formed the godless purpose to steal in the first place.'

'I stole nothing. I had formal sanction from Lord Godolphin to—'

'There's a mightier lord than the noble earl whose business we're about, Mr Shillingstone. And we mean to carry it through. You shouldn't have come out here.' Tozer shakes his head in evident regret. 'You really shouldn't.'

'Unhand my property this instant or I'll see you all hanged as common thieves.'

Tozer and his two mute companions do not move. Shillingstone glares at them each in turn, clinging to the hope that he can browbeat them into submission while stifling as best he can the growing conviction that for them there is no turning back.

'Give this up now, Tozer. Send these men away. Leave the crate where it is. Lock the door and give me the key. Then perhaps I'll consider saying nothing to Dr Borlase of your conduct tonight.'

'You'll *consider*?'

'Yes. I will.'

'No need to trouble yourself so far, Mr Shillingstone. No need at all.'

There is the faintest nod of Tozer's head in the direction of the man holding the horse. Then, too swiftly and too darkly in the jumbled shadows for Shillingstone to forestall, the man moves, in a darting lunge. The blade of a knife gleams fleetingly in a shaft of lamplight, then strikes home, the force of the blow and the weight of his assailant's body behind it flinging Shillingstone against the open door of the outhouse. As it swings back behind him, he falls.

He is on the ground, the cobbles hard and moist beneath him, before the realization that he has been stabbed forms as an organized thought in his brain. And Tozer's hand, rough and hard-sinewed, has clamped his mouth shut before he can cry out for help. There is no pain yet, but something hot and liquid is flowing between his skin and his shirt, something he knows, though can barely believe, is his own blood.

'This is your doing,' rasps Tozer, staring down at him. 'Yours, not ours.'

Shillingstone tries to raise himself on his elbows, but already he is as weak as a kitten and cannot seem to draw breath. He is helpless in Tozer's grip, helpless to do other than look blearily up into the shadow-wreathed face above him. He does not know where the other two men are now. He scarcely knows where he is himself.

'What did you hope for from this, Mr Shillingstone? Fame and fortune? A page to yourself in the history books? It's not to be. No one will ever know what you tried to force the world to hear. Or why you had to die tonight at our hands. No one will care. You'll be forgotten. And so will we. But we don't mind. You do, but

16

we don't. There's the difference between us. Your secret is safe with us. You have my word on that. My solemn word.'

Blood is filling Shillingstone's lung. Death is tracing its cold, mocking fingers around him. He cannot breathe. He cannot move. He cannot think. He can sense only loss – and encroaching darkness. The glory he so keenly anticipated is beyond his grasp. The life he aspired to is out of his reach. The world leaves him as he leaves the world – without a word.

Tozer lowers Shillingstone's head to the ground, closes the dead man's sightless eyes, crosses himself and stands up. He turns to his companions. 'Hurry,' he urges them, pointing to the crate. 'There's much to do.' Then he glances down at Shillingstone's body. 'More now than ever.'

ONE

Few of Jardiniera's clients lived in Monaco, for the simple reason that few residents of the principality possessed a garden. The high-rise apartment blocks jostling for a tax-free footing on its expensive square kilometre of the Côte d'Azur left little room for the landscaped riots of greenery to be found in the grounds of villas to east and west.

An exception to this rule was, however, one of Jardiniera's best clients. Barney Tozer was in fact rather more than a client, having bought himself a slice of the company and with it the implicit right to prompt attention whenever he required it. He had also bought himself, at a price Tim Harding should only have been able to guess at but actually knew to the last eye-watering zero, the penthouse apartment in one of the most prestigious blocks in La Condamine. Thanks to the sheerness of the rock face against which the block had been built, the penthouse came complete with its own garden, perched at the level of the next road above, commanding a fine view of the yacht-crammed Port de Monaco and the sparkling blue vastness of the Mediterranean.

An electronically operated shutter-door set in the high stone rear wall of the garden gave access to a double garage, sparing its owner the need to squeeze his four-wheel-drive giant into the communal garage in the block's basement and allowing Harding to drive his Jardiniera truck in off the road after entering the four-digit code he had been trusted with on the number-panel attached to the entryphone.

Harding was a well-built, broad-shouldered man in his late forties, brown hair bleached blond enough by the sun to camouflage the streaks of grey, skin so deeply tanned that his blue-grey eyes sparked brightly, frown- and smile-lines more or less equally pronounced on his evenly featured face. Gardening for a living had kept him physically fit, but something in his gaze, something wounded and wary, suggested that people had always been a greater mystery to him than plants.

He parked the truck on the hardstanding in front of the garage and climbed out into the cool, clear, light-filled air as the shutter-door completed its well-lubricated descent behind him with a reassuringly solid clunk. Harding was dressed for work, in jeans, boots and skiing jacket, although he happened to know that no soil would be turned or shrub pruned this morning. He happened to know, but was obliged to pretend he did not. Which was only one of the reasons for the discomfort he felt.

The morning was fine but chill. Winter and spring were still taking turns this early in the year, even on the Riviera, where the locals seemed to regard anything other than warm, settled weather as a personal affront. It was a quiet time for Jardiniera. Many of their clients were away. Most of the gardens they tended were ticking over gently, with little need of anything beyond routine maintenance. Harding knew he would be unable to plead pressure of work as an objection to doing what was going to be asked of him. He knew, in fact, that he would be unable to raise an objection of any kind. Even though some instinct he suspected he ought to heed told him he should.

Barney Tozer was on the terrace beyond the swimming pool, leaning back against the balustrade that guarded the drop to the roadway far below. He was in the middle of a phone conversation and did no more than raise a hand to acknowledge Harding's arrival. This was no surprise. He was a man who spent so much time on the phone that his right shoulder was permanently lower than his left, giving his whole body a slightly skewed, misshapen appearance. He was about the same age as Harding, but did not look so well on it, a substantial paunch filling out the loose sweater he wore above baggy trousers and deck shoes, his thinning hair cropped short, a second chin wobbling beneath his jaw as he spoke. But the obese and gleaming watch lolling on his wrist hinted at the other kind of pounds he had acquired an excess of over the years, not to mention the euros, dollars, yen and Swiss francs.

He was, Harding needed no reminding, a seriously wealthy man.

There was a vagueness about the source of this wealth. Barney Tozer's company, Starburst International, dealt in timeshare properties and the luxury end of the holiday market, but Harding had always found it difficult to believe that such business could yield profits on the scale its chairman and managing director's lifestyle suggested it did. Harding was no expert, of course. He knew that. And he knew there were other factors complicating his relationship with Barney. One of those was that he actually liked the guy. Barney was a generous, affable, garrulous, down-to-earth Cornishman who hardly fitted the tax-exile stereotype. He and Harding had become drinking buddies over the last couple of years – friends, for want of a better word, though there were in truth too many secrets between them to make it quite the right word.

Harding crossed the modest but manicured lawn and made his way slowly round the pool to where Tozer was standing, scanning the lemon trees and hibiscuses as he went to confirm that they were looking well, even though he knew his host would be unlikely to notice their condition unless they shed their leaves and died in front of him. The phone call was ending in murmured farewells. By the time Harding reached the terrace, it was over.

''Morning, Tim,' said Tozer, slipping the phone into his pocket and smiling broadly. 'Hope you haven't had to make too much of a detour to fit me in.'

'Not at all. There's a villa on Cap Martin I'm going to visit this afternoon. I might be in line for quite an ambitious landscaping job there.'

'Your speciality.'

'Well, it's supposed to be.' So it was, although general care and maintenance accounted for more and more of Jardiniera's business. 'Anyway, what can I do for you, Barney?'

'Come inside. We can talk over coffee. Unless you fancy something stronger.' Tozer winked over his shoulder at him as he headed towards the patio doors leading into the apartment.

'Coffee's fine, thanks.'

'Have it your way.'

But Harding was not going to have it his way. That he already knew. Forewarned was not in this case forearmed.

'Carol's at the beautician,' Tozer explained as they traversed the huge, modishly furnished lounge en route to the kitchen. 'Seems to spend more and more time there. Says that's a sign of middle age. Could be a sign of covering up for torrid sessions with a gym-freak toy boy, of course. How's a husband to know?'

'I expect she really is at the beautician, Barney.'

'Yeah?' Tozer smiled back at Harding. 'You're probably right.'

He *was* right. There was no doubt about it. The real doubt surrounded the question of whether Barney knew why Harding could be so certain on the point. And that doubt seemed to have been growing recently, to a degree guilt alone could not explain.

'Black, no sugar?' They had reached the kitchen, fitted out like the lounge in the very latest style and its most expensive version.

'Please.'

Tozer flicked a couple of switches above the slate worktop. A kettle roared into life. A grinder devoured a hopperful of beans. In less than a minute, the coffee was brewing. Tozer lit a cigarette during the interval, not troubling to offer one to Harding, a confirmed non-smoker.

'Planning something new for the garden, Barney?'

'Hardly. That's Carol's province.'

'I just thought—'

'I didn't ask you round to discuss bloody pot plants.'

'No. I guessed not.'

'I bet you did.' Tozer looked thoughtfully at him through a plume of cigarette smoke. 'What's old Barney up to now, hey? What bee has he got in his bonnet?' He chuckled, pushed down the plunger on the cafetière and poured their coffees, adding sugar to his own. 'Let's sit down.'

They settled round a corner of the large table at the far end of the room. Harding sipped his coffee, which was as excellent as ever – Colombian, he reckoned. Tozer flicked ash into a wooden ashtray the diameter of a dinner plate and glanced at his watch. There was in the movement the first hint of nervousness on his part.

'I'm ever so slightly pushed for time, actually, Tim. Tony's due in an hour. We're off on a 'forty-eight to Abu

Dhabi.' Tony Whybrow, who had occasionally and somewhat half-heartedly joined them on their periodic boys' nights out, was Starburst's finance director and the only other representative of the company Harding had ever actually met. 'Work, work, work, hey?'

'But money, money, money.'

'Yeah. Anyway, like I say . . .' Tozer took another puff at his cigarette and started on the coffee. 'Fact is, I need to ask you a favour.'

'Go ahead.'

'Thing is . . . Have I ever mentioned my brother?'

Had he? Harding had asked himself exactly that question during the drive from Villefranche. 'Well, I know you have a brother, so . . . either you or Carol . . .'

'Humphrey. Humphrey and Barnabas, hey? Bloody stupid names. But Barney's OK. Suits me, so I've been told. As for Humphrey, I used to call him Humpty when we were children. He's five years older than me. I couldn't get my mouth round the sound, see? And then there was the nursery rhyme. So, I thought Humpty was . . .' Tozer shrugged. 'Funny.'

'Where does Humphrey live?'

'Humph. That's what I settled for in the end. He's still stuck in Penzance.' Tozer's roots in west Cornwall had definitely been mentioned to Harding, more than once. 'Have you even been to Penzance, Tim? I can't remember if I've asked you.'

'Neither can I. But, yeah, I have. For what it's worth. A family holiday in Cornwall when I was ten. We stayed near Land's End. Sennen Cove. Must have gone through

25

Penzance, but all I can recollect is a view of St Michael's Mount. Does that count?'

'Bet it rained a lot.'

'It did, as a matter of fact.'

'No surprise there.'

'So, this favour . . . has to do with . . . Humph?'

'Yeah. A narrow-minded misery-guts if ever there was one. But . . .' Tozer gazed past Harding into some unfocused vision of his childhood. 'He is my flesh and blood.' His face creased into a rueful smile. 'Worse luck.'

'And . . .'

'He's asked for my help. My . . . personal help. That's some kind of world record, so I don't want to disappoint him. But it would mean I'd have to go to Penzance. Right away.'

'And you have business in Abu Dhabi?'

'Oh, that could be postponed. No, no. That's not the problem. It's a . . . tax thing.' Tozer lowered his voice, as if, despite the fact that there was no one else in the apartment, he was worried about being overheard. 'I've used up my ninety-one days in the UK this fiscal year. I can't set foot in Penzance, or anywhere else in the old country, before April sixth. It's a no-no. An absolute no-can-do. But Humph'll just think I'm making an excuse if I turn him down because of that.'

'You will have to turn him down, though, won't you?'

'As it stands, yeah. But . . . there's such a thing as cushioning the blow. What I really need . . . is for someone to go in my place.' Tozer smiled cautiously at Harding. 'Know anyone who might be available?'

Harding returned the smile. 'You mean me?'

'It'll only take a few days. A week at most. I'll cover all your expenses. You can even bill me for your time at garden maintenance rates. It's the quietest time of the year for you anyway. Look on it as a second Cornish holiday. You might get better weather this time round.'

'I can't just drop everything and—'

'Come on. You're always singing young Luc's praises. I'll bet he could cope without you for a month, let alone a week.'

That much was undeniable. Luc could always be relied upon and would probably relish the extra responsibility. 'Well, maybe. But you haven't told me what Humph wants help *with* yet.'

'It's no big deal, believe me. It just needs . . . handling properly.'

'Wouldn't Carol be a better choice?'

'She can't stick Humph at any price. And vice versa. It'd be better to turn him down flat than send Carol. But it has to be somebody I can trust, obviously. And you'd be surprised how few of my so-called friends I *do* trust. But there is you, Tim.' Tozer stubbed out his cigarette and looked Harding in the eye. 'You should be flattered.'

'Well, I am, of course. But . . .'

'I still haven't told you what's involved.' Tozer grinned. 'Have I?'

TWO

'You're going, then?' said Carol, breaking the post-coital silence into which they had descended. Sex had failed to distract her for long from the subject of the strange mission Harding had agreed to undertake on her husband's behalf. It was in Harding's mind also as he lay in bed with her at his apartment in Villefranche late that afternoon. It could hardly not be.

Theoretically, of course, he could have joined Carol at the penthouse after Barney's departure for the Gulf. In some ways, it would have been more convenient, as it might often have been in the past, given the frequency of Barney's absences. But some scruple neither cared to put into words had always deterred them. The apartment in Villefranche was their territory. And they did not stray from it.

'I thought you might be able to talk your way out of it.'

'Not a chance.'

'How hard did you try?' Carol propped herself up on one elbow and squinted slightly as she stared at him. Her face was still faintly flushed from their exertions and her highlighted brown hair tousled, but the lubricious twinkle he had been pleased to notice in her eye earlier had turned to a steely gleam.

'As hard as I could in the circumstances. You know there was no way I could turn him down.'

'I suppose not.' Carol sighed and flopped back down on the pillow. 'And what *exactly* does he want you to do?'

'I've already told you.'

'Told me some of it, you mean. I want to hear the whole thing.'

'OK. His uncle – their uncle, Barney and Humph's – died just before Christmas.'

'I know. Uncle Gabriel. Lived in Penzance in a house full of junk.'

'Junk – or valuable antiques. Take your pick. The locals will be able to next week when the contents are auctioned. It appears Barney's uncle specified in his will that's how his possessions were to be disposed of. No bequests to relatives. No opportunity for them to help themselves to a memento of the old boy. Just . . . everything to the highest bidder. Proceeds to charity . . . or somesuch.'

'Nice.'

'There was a feud between him and Barney's dad. You know about this too?'

'Not really. Their dad died before I met Barney. And he

doesn't say much about him. Or his mother. Anyway, what family doesn't have its feuds?'

The question reminded Harding how little he really knew about Carol. Not to mention how little *she* knew about *him*. Their affair was sustained by need and habit. Neither had ever used the dreaded L word and they were unlikely to start now. 'Well,' he pressed on, 'feud there was, over the usual sort of stuff. Gabriel was the younger brother. He never married. Barney's dad—'

'Arthur,' Carol interrupted matter-of-factly. 'His name was Arthur. And Barney's mum was called Rose.'

'Right. OK. Arthur and Rose. They started out their married life in Arthur's parents' house, which they took over completely when the old folks died. At that point, Gabriel asked Arthur for something their dad had supposedly promised him but hadn't actually left him in his will. Arthur didn't believe any such promise was made. He refused to hand it over, causing a lot of bad blood. And then . . . it went missing. Stolen by Gabriel, according to Arthur, though Gabriel denied it. There was no proof he'd taken it. It was hardly the sort of thing Arthur could go to the police about. Result? They fell out big time. Never exchanged another word, at any rate not a civil one. Gabriel didn't even attend Arthur's funeral. Went on denying theft, perhaps because he didn't regard it as theft. But he *had* taken something. That's certain. Because Humphrey's spotted it among the lots to be auctioned.'

'And what is it?'

'Barney said he'd let Humph fill me in.'

'You mean you don't get to find out unless you go.'

'That's one way to look at it. Humphrey wants Barney to supply the cash to make sure he can buy back whatever it is, no matter what he has to bid for it. Humphrey's poor as a church mouse, apparently.'

'Poorer. You should see where he lives. Barney's tried to help him, but . . . they're another pair of brothers who don't get on.' Carol rolled over and propped her chin on Harding's shoulder. She gazed at him, her brow furrowed in thought. 'Barney's told me nothing except he needs you to go to Penzance to sort something out with Humph for him. Why the secrecy, I'd like to know. I mean, why does some old argument about a family heirloom matter so much?'

'I'm not sure it does. Barney's happy enough to stump up the cash. He just wants me to nursemaid Humphrey during the auction and make sure he doesn't do anything stupid beforehand.'

'Such as?'

'Try to steal the thing back, I suppose.'

'Well, he's crazy enough for that. I wish you luck.'

Harding grinned. 'Thanks.'

'There's something funny about it all, though. Why's Barney so set on *you* going?'

'He said you can't abide Humphrey.'

She nodded ruefully. 'That's true.'

'And he said he could trust me.'

'Did he?' Carol closed her eyes. 'Oh shit.'

'Don't let it get to you.' Harding raised his head and kissed her. 'It's a good thing he does, you know.'

'Yeah.' She opened her eyes again. 'I know.'

'I'll go, make sure Humphrey's on his best behaviour, hold his hand at the auction, then leave him beaming over the spoils and jet straight back here.'

'Sounds easy.'

'No reason why it shouldn't be.'

'Maybe not. But . . .' She chewed her lip as her mind dwelt on the evident mystery of her husband's thought processes. 'How did Barney react when you told him you'd been to Penzance in August 'ninety-nine?'

'He didn't bat an eyelid. But, then, why should he? It's just a coincidence that I paid my first visit to the town since childhood the same summer you floated into his life. It's not even a very big coincidence. Lots of people visited Penzance in August 'ninety-nine to see the eclipse. And it wasn't there he met you, anyway, was it?' As Harding knew, Carol had been running a café in the Isles of Scilly when she had first encountered Barney Tozer in the summer of 1999, with life-changing consequences. Meanwhile, Harding's wife, Polly, had been dying slowly of cancer. Their journey to Cornwall to witness the total eclipse on 11 August that year had been her last journey of any kind before the final decline. The day after the eclipse, they had taken a helicopter trip to the island of Tresco. But Carol's café had been on its larger neighbour, St Mary's. Coincidence stretched only so far.

'It's strange, though, isn't it?' Carol mused. 'The idea that you and I could have met then, in Cornwall, rather than four years later and a thousand miles away.'

'Not quite a thousand. And nearer five years than four.'

Carol sighed heavily. 'Do you have to be so literal?' She pushed back the sheet, sat up on the edge of the bed and stretched. 'I'm going to take a shower.'

Harding watched her cross the room, rubbing a muscle in her back as she went. He called to her as she reached the open doorway. 'Hey.'

She stopped and looked over her shoulder at him, frowning slightly. 'What?'

'You're beautiful, you know.'

'Oh yeah? All over? Or just in parts?'

'Do a few slow pirouettes and I'll give you a part-by-part assessment if you like.'

'Fool,' she said, laughing lightly as she headed on towards the bathroom with a sashay of her hips.

Harding stayed where he was, staring up at the ceiling, across which the lowering sun cast a golden triangle of light. He listened to the hiss and spatter of the shower and wondered if he had been right to deceive Carol as he had. It had been as much as anything an instinctive lie. To have told the truth would have raised too many questions openly between them. Why had he not mentioned the August 1999 trip to Barney? Why had Carol so evidently not mentioned it either? And why was she so bothered by the prospect of him going to Penzance now, at her husband's bidding?

Harding did not really know why he had held the information back. It had something to do with Carol's reaction the first time the subject had cropped up. It had disturbed her. There was no doubt about it. The co-incidence – slight as it was – had troubled her. And it still did.

It also had something to do with Polly and his eagerness to suppress the active recollection of their final few years together. He would never have returned to the scene of their last holiday of his own volition. But it was a chance to come to terms with his past, to prove he could cope with the memories the trip was bound to revive. He had moved to France to escape those memories. And he had succeeded. Now he would discover how complete his success really was.

THREE

Harding flew to England two days later. Luc drove him to Nice Airport in time for the early-morning flight, assured him coping in his absence would be *'pas de problème'*, then roared away in the Jardiniera truck at a speed that suggested he for one would be enjoying the interlude.

Harding had not told his parents, siblings or any of his friends back home that he was going to be in the country. Already, for reasons he could not properly analyse, there was something faintly furtive, if not secretive, about the trip.

The flight was two hours, shorn to one on the clock by the change of time zones. But a coach ride to Reading, a long wait at the station and a train journey to the far end of the West of England main line swallowed most of the rest of the day. It was five o'clock on a dull and windless Friday afternoon when the train pulled into Penzance.

Harding had already adjusted by then to the thinness of the light, the altogether greyer tone of his homeland compared with the crystalline brilliance of the Côte d'Azur. He and Polly had driven down from Worcestershire, so there were no reminders of their trip in the manner of his arrival. But his first glimpse of St Michael's Mount out in the bay as the railway line curved to meet the shore a couple of miles short of Penzance was the first of what he knew would be many tugs at his memory.

They had stayed in a b. and b., which Harding was not sure he could find even if he wanted to. This time, with Tozer covering his expenses, he was putting up at the Mount Prospect. It was a short taxi ride to the hotel's lofty perch up a narrow side street on the eastern fringe of the town. And there again, in the view from his room, was St Michael's Mount, afloat in the grey plane of the bay.

Unpacking took no more than a few minutes. He was travelling light, physically at any rate. He phoned Carol and they talked so warmly and casually that he could almost believe he had imagined her anxiety about the trip. She said she was missing him already, which could not really be true, given how irregular their assignations were. Barney was due back the following morning. She said nothing about missing him.

'Met Humph yet?'

'No. I'm going round there now.'

'Brace yourself. He's not what you'd call the sociable type.'

36

It was a warning Harding had already absorbed. He consulted the street map of Penzance he had bought at the station and set off.

On his way through reception, he spotted a copy of the local weekly paper, *The Cornishman*, lying on the counter. He took it into the deserted lounge and leafed through the property supplement to the auctions page. There it was, as he had anticipated, prominently advertised.

ISBISTER & SONS
AUCTIONEERS AND VALUERS
HOUSE CONTENTS SALE
TUESDAY 21ST FEBRUARY – 10AM
Viewing: Saturday 18th February 10am – 4pm
and Sunday 19th February 12 Noon – 4pm
At HEARTSEASE, POLWITHEN ROAD,
PENZANCE
We are favoured with instructions to SELL by
AUCTION as above
CHINA, GLASSWARE, JEWELLERY, BOOKS,
PAINTINGS, STAMPS, COINS, BANK NOTES,
TOYS, MODELS, FURNITURE, LINEN AND
GENERAL HOUSEHOLD EFFECTS

The summarized list of items filled the entire column. Gabriel Tozer had evidently been a formidable hoarder, accumulating more crockery, cutlery, wine-glasses, clocks, watches, cufflinks and old books than any single man could plausibly need. The tin soldiers and 00-gauge train sets hinted at a childhood collecting mania which the first-day covers and Georgian guineas implied had been carried on into adulthood. But had he really wanted to give a mob of strangers the pick of his gramophone records and walking sticks and the run of his house while they made their choices and marked up their catalogues? The answer, baffling as it was, appeared to be yes.

It was dark by the time Harding left the hotel, and colder than he had expected. He turned up the collar of his coat, descended to the shore road that ran alongside the railway line and followed it through the fumes of sluggish traffic to the roundabout where it met the bypass at the eastern edge of town. The adjacent superstore was doing a brisk trade. The weekend was taking its customary British shape.

Beyond the roundabout lay an industrial estate and the heliport from which he and Polly had flown to Tresco. Wedged in among the warehouses was a jumble of stark, white-rendered, low-rise flats and maisonettes. A more dismal contrast with a penthouse in Monaco could hardly be conceived. Such were the widely different domiciles of the brothers Tozer.

Humphrey had a first-floor flat overlooking the heliport, reached by a flight of wooden stairs. There was a light showing through the tissue-thin curtains, but a response to Harding's stab at the doorbell was a long time coming.

The man who eventually opened the door was faintly

recognizable as a relative of Barney Tozer, but only because Harding knew him to be a relative. Humphrey Tozer was several stones lighter than his brother, gauntly thin and grey-skinned, with lank, greasy hair and a sad, sullen gaze. He was wearing decrepit horn-rimmed spectacles and a drab outfit of darned sweater, frayed shirt and trousers worn to a grubby sheen. His head twitched slightly to an irregular rhythm as he stared at Harding, breathing audibly and exuding a sharp, sour reek.

'Mr Tozer?' Harding ventured.

'I'm Tozer, yeah.' The voice was low and gruff and hesitant.

'Barney sent me.'

'Barney?'

'Your brother.'

Tozer's lip curled into a sneer. 'I didn't ask him to *send* someone.'

'He couldn't come himself.'

'Why not?'

'Tax problems.'

The sneer became a strange, twisted little smile. 'That's a good one.'

'Can I come in?'

'What for?'

'To talk. About the auction.'

Tozer contemplated the idea for ten or twelve slow seconds. Then he said, 'All right. Since you're here.'

Tozer led the way down a short hallway and into the lounge. It was a small room and would have been cramped if it had contained even a reasonable quantity of furniture. As it was, Humphrey Tozer's domestic comforts amounted to one armchair, a pouffe, a television, a table with two hard chairs and a bookcase of largely empty shelves. A clock stood on the mantelpiece above the unlit gas fire, but there were no ornaments and just one picture on the wall, over the clock: a framed Constable print. A rumpled copy of *The Cornishman* lay on the table, next to a jumbled stack of what looked like several months' worth of the paper's back copies. It felt colder to Harding inside the flat than it had out. He doubted if refreshment, or even a seat, was likely to be offered him.

'Who are you, then?' Tozer asked, frowning at him from the middle of the room as Harding lingered in the doorway.

'A friend of Barney's. Tim Harding.'

'A friend? Not an employee? Not a . . . dogsbody?'

'As it happens, I'm here to help.'

'How are you going to do that?'

'Barney's told me all about the auction and why you want to buy one of the lots.'

'*All* about it? I doubt that.'

'Enough, then. He's been in touch with the auctioneers and opened a credit account. We can bid whatever we need to.'

'*We?*'

'Like I said, I'm here to help.'

Tozer took a step towards Harding. His gaze narrowed. 'I might have known Barney would find some way of wriggling out of his responsibilities.'

'He's hardly doing that. He's effectively giving you a blank cheque.'

'Giving his old school chum Clive Isbister one, you mean. I asked Barney for more than money. I asked for his presence, here, in his home town. And even he'd have to admit I've never asked him for—' Tozer broke off and gave a contemptuous snort. 'I'm like the dog at the banquet, aren't I? I'm supposed to be grateful for whatever scrap gets tossed my way.'

'Look, Mr Tozer, I—'

'Don't want to be here? I'll bet you don't. Doing Barney a favour, are you? Or just doing what he tells you to do? He's always been good at controlling people. But that's you and me both, I suppose.'

Harding let the silence that followed grow until it had drawn some sort of line under Tozer's resentful rant. Then he said quietly, 'Do you want my help or not? Whether you succeed in buying this . . . whatever it is . . . doesn't really matter to me, you know.'

'Huh.' The grunt was accompanied by a faint softening of Tozer's stance. 'All right,' he murmured, his gaze shifting evasively. 'You've made your point.'

'Why don't you tell me what we'll be bidding for?'

'Barney held that morsel back, did he? Typical.'

'If you say so. But what is it?'

'It's in the catalogue. Under the paper.' Tozer pointed to the table. 'Lot six four one.'

Harding slid *The Cornishman* to one side, revealing Isbisters' catalogue for the auction, folded open at a late page. He picked it up. Lot 641 was at the top of the page, circled in red ink.

> A Georgian 18ct gold ring, set with an emerald and eleven cushion-shaped diamonds, London 1704, presented in a starburst-patterned ebony and ivory-inlaid box, *c.* 1870, 2½in (6.5cm) wide, £2,000–3,000. (May be bid for as separate lots if desired.)

It was the description of the box rather than the ring that seized Harding's attention. 'Good God,' he said before he could stop himself. 'Starburst-patterned.'

'That's where he got the name for his company from,' said Tozer, sidling closer. 'He remembers it as clearly as I do. All of it.'

'All of what?' Harding asked, looking up at him.

'All of the things . . . I don't discuss with a stranger.'

'Fair enough.' Harding dropped the catalogue back on the table. 'But you do believe this . . . heirloom . . . was stolen by your uncle.'

'That proves it.' Tozer jabbed a forefinger at the red-circled entry. 'I'm going to see the ring tomorrow. For the first time in nearly forty years.'

'As long as that?'

'Oh yes. Uncle Gabriel clung to it for as many years as he could eke out his life. And now he hopes to cheat me of it from beyond the grave.'

'Where did he steal it from?'

'Our house in Morrab Road. Grandfather's old—'

Tozer broke off, seeming suddenly to sense he had said too much. He peered suspiciously at Harding, who had not failed to notice his use of 'me' rather than 'us' but tried to give no sign of it. 'You don't need to know any more.'

'Do you want me to come with you ... to Heartsease?'

'No.'

'I'd like to see the ring – and the box – for myself.'

'Then go. But later in the day. I'll be there when they start. At ten.'

It was an explicit warning-off. Harding had no choice but to accept it. 'All right. I'll wait till the afternoon.'

'You do that.'

'I'm staying at the Mount Prospect.'

'Barney's seeing you all right, then.'

And you, you miserable sod, Harding thought but did not say. 'You can contact me there or on my mobile,' he said emolliently. He picked up the red ballpoint lying by the catalogue and wrote his number at the foot of the page. 'I ought to have your phone number as well.'

'I'm in the book.'

'OK.'

Tozer's gaze drifted to the catalogue. 'The ring and the box ... mustn't be parted.'

'Well, they're not going to be, are they?'

Tozer looked up at Harding. 'No,' he said quietly but firmly. 'They're not.'

Harding did not wait to be asked to leave. Fresh air was what he needed after the rancid chill of Humphrey

43

Tozer's flat. Fortunately, there was plenty of that billowing in from the bay as he made his way back to the Mount Prospect. He phoned Carol again after his solitary dinner in the hotel's restaurant, but elicited little sympathy.

'I told you he was bad news.'

'You never mentioned his hygiene problem.'

'I've done my best to forget it.'

'Well, at least I won't have to see much of him. He's made it obvious he wants me to keep my distance.'

'Do as he asks, then.'

'I will, believe me.'

'The sooner you're back here, the happier I'll be.'

'Me too. By the way, did you know Barney got the name Starburst from the box that contains this ring Humphrey wants so badly?'

'No. What does it mean – starburst?'

'It's a pattern of some kind. I'll see it at Heartsease tomorrow. But it's odd, don't you think? Barney using the name, I mean.'

'Not really. It probably just popped into his head at the time.'

'Yeah. I suppose so.' But that was not what Humphrey thought. He thought it proved the box – and the ring – meant as much to his brother as to him. And though he did not say as much to Carol, Harding was beginning to think so as well.

FOUR

Harding had explored the historic heart of Penzance and was walking aimlessly along the promenade late the following morning, heading towards the fishing harbour of Newlyn, when the call came he had been expecting since breakfast.

'Hi, Tim. How's it going?'

'Fine, thanks, Barney. How was Abu Dhabi?'

'Dry. What's it like in the old home town?'

'Overcast. If you really want to know.'

'What I really want to know is how you got on with Humph.'

'As well as could be expected. I wouldn't say there was an outburst of gratitude, but he seems . . . happy enough.'

'Good.'

'He's going to Heartsease this morning. I plan to take a look this afternoon at the ring *and* the famous starburst box.'

'Carol said you'd spotted the connection.' Harding

45

had agreed with Carol that she would mention his call – one of his calls, at any rate. 'Dad was always going on about it when we were kids. The name just stuck in my memory, I suppose.'

'The ring's three hundred years old, Barney. Has it been in your family all that time?'

'Doubt it, old son. Dad never actually said which ancestor first laid hands on it. Probably didn't know. And it certainly doesn't matter. Just keep an eye on Humph till the auction and wait to see if he cracks a smile for the first time in decades when you plonk the bloody thing in his paw straight afterwards.'

'OK, Barney. Leave it to me.'

Heartsease was in a tree-shaded road lined with large family homes that looked to date from the inter-war years. It was a big, inelegant pile of a house, with timbered gables, squat chimneys, irregular dormers and uneven bays, dankly flanked by limp palms, overgrown evergreens and a spectacularly feral camellia.

The neighbourhood was probably quiet as a rule, but Isbisters' advertisement had brought double-parked cars and a steady stream of bargain-hunters to Polwithen Road. Harding trailed behind several of them up the drive to the side-door, taking the route prescribed by a sign out on the pavement. He reflected that Humphrey had been wise to come early. A chance to inspect the belongings of Gabriel Tozer (deceased) and to prowl round his house was evidently the high spot of quite a few people's Saturday.

The auctioneer had put the conservatory adjoining the entrance into service as a cloakroom, where coats and bags had to be left. Catalogues were on sale at a fiver a throw, but Harding kept his money in his pocket. His interest, after all, was confined to one lot and one lot only.

As he was waiting for the ticket for his coat, he was suddenly jostled to one side by a burly, scruffily dressed figure, demanding the return of a bag he had deposited. The man was middle-aged, with grey-shot black hair cut in a rudimentary short-back-and-sides. His jowly face was flushed and pockmarked and sheened with sweat. And there was a smell of whisky on his breath.

'Leaving so soon, Mr Trathen?' the cloakroom attendant enquired as he passed Harding his ticket and the other man a bulging Co-op carrier-bag.

'I've seen enough,' Trathen replied, jostling Harding still further as he took his leave.

'Doesn't take long to see enough when you're seeing double,' the attendant murmured. 'Sorry about that,' he said, smiling at Harding. 'Probably shouldn't have let him in. I don't think he was here as a serious buyer. As any kind of buyer, come to that.'

'No?'

'Bit of a sad case, Ray Trathen. But you don't want to know about him, believe you me.'

Harding moved on into the house, having established that Lot 641 was to be found in bedroom 2. He paused in the large, square hallway at the foot of the stairs, up and down which his fellow punters were coming and going. Doors stood open to the drawing room, dining room and kitchen. Only one door, beneath the stairs, was marked PRIVATE. Everywhere else they were free to roam.

The interior of Heartsease was a stolid, spacious family abode, with a lot of handsomely burnished wood, well-proportioned rooms and stained-glass flourishes in several of the windows. Solitary occupant as he was, Gabriel Tozer had done a good job of filling it with possessions rather than people. Cabinets, book-cases, bureaux and tables groaned under the weight of his meticulously catalogued belongings, every chair, every lamp, every doorstop, every jug, every spoon, every neatly stacked run of *Country Life* and the *Illustrated London News*, every rug across which the punters moved, every humdrum object they picked up and put down again, bearing its telltale numbered tag.

It was the same upstairs as down. If anything, the concentration of material was even greater, with toys, models, train sets, coins, banknotes, stamps, postcards, cigarette cards, wristwatches, pocket watches, musical boxes, snuffboxes, cameos, figurines, compasses, candlesticks and yet more accumulated back copies of magazines – *Reader's Digest*, *The Countryman*, *Punch* and journals too obscure to be remembered – filling glass-fronted cabinets in all four bedrooms or standing in dusty stacks on the broad landing.

But only one cabinet, in only one bedroom, inter-ested Harding. It contained tie-pins, cufflinks, signet rings, a couple of silver cigarette cases, a baffling number of hourglasses and . . . a small box decorated with radiating panels of black and white, the lid standing open to reveal its contents, nestling on a bed of satin: a gold ring with an emerald set within a circle of diamonds.

'Nice, isn't it?'

Harding looked round to find, standing close beside him, a representative of the auctioneers, identified by a badge pinned prominently to his lapel. He was a big, bluff, tweed-suited fellow with thinning fair hair, beetling eyebrows and a broad, yellow-toothed grin. And according to the badge he was none other than Clive Isbister, auctioneer-in-chief.

'I can open the cabinet if you want to take a closer look.'

'That's all right. Don't bother. I, er . . . see you're Clive Isbister.'

'For my sins, yes.'

'I'm a friend of Barney Tozer. I gather—'

'You wouldn't be Mr Harding, would you?'

'Yes. Tim Harding.' They shook hands. 'How did you—'

'I spoke to Barney on Wednesday when he set up an account for the auction. He mentioned a Tim Harding would be attending on his behalf. Then there was his brother Humphrey paying that particular ring a lot of attention earlier today. And now you, sporting a tan that clearly isn't the product of a Cornish winter. Elementary, my dear Watson.'

Harding laughed. 'Going well, is it – the viewing?'

'Bit of a nightmare in some ways, to be honest, but it's much the best way to stimulate interest.'

'I think I might know what you mean about nightmares. I met a bloke called Trathen on my way in.'

'Ray Trathen?' Isbister winced. 'Bad luck. I'm sorry for Ray, of course. He and I were at school together. But he's his own worst enemy.'

'You were at school with Barney as well, weren't you?'

'Yes. That's right. I expect that's why Barney gave Ray a job a few years back. For old times' sake. It didn't work out, I'm afraid. Most things don't in Ray's life. Excuse me, will you? One of my colleagues is waving rather frantically at me. Probably another breakage. Just as well there's so much here, hey? I don't think you'll have any serious trouble getting the ring, by the way. It's a lovely piece, but sadly not fashionable. And fashion is all in this business, as in most others. See you on Tuesday, no doubt.'

Harding had been tempted to ask Isbister how much he knew about Gabriel Tozer's alleged theft of the ring. Yet perhaps, he reasoned, it was best he had not had the chance to do so. It did not really matter, after all, given the apparent confidence of all concerned that it would not be leaving the Tozer family.

Looking at the ring, its emerald and surrounding diamonds glittering in the light of the overhead lamp, switched on so that the contents of the cabinet might be seen to their best advantage, Harding could not help but feel it was too small and trifling an object to justify a feud of several decades' standing, however valuable it might be. But a ring could have a symbolic as well as a monetary value. So could a starburst box, come to that. There was something about this ring in this box that mattered to Humphrey Tozer and *had* mattered to his Uncle Gabriel. As for Barney, Harding was unsure. The indifference could have been sham, the willingness to delegate responsibility a ploy of some kind.

Not that it really mattered. Harding had agreed to do Barney this favour and it would not take much to see it through. He had promised to keep an eye on Humphrey, but proposed to do the bare minimum in that direction. He *would* bid as high as he needed to to secure Lot 641 at the auction, however. And then, he told himself, he would fly home and forget all about it.

After a mooch round the other bedrooms, Harding felt he had seen enough. Spectating at the avaricious mass scrutiny of a dead man's belongings rapidly palled. He sensed that Gabriel Tozer had been an obsessively private man. It was strange, then, and faintly obscene, that his goods and chattels should be priced and tagged and fingered by dozens upon dozens of strangers. Harding headed downstairs.

He was most of the way down when he noticed a young woman crossing the hallway from the direction of the conservatory. She was conspicuous because she was wearing a short, belted mac, had a small rucksack slung

51

over one shoulder and was also carrying a well-filled canvas bag. She was petite, almost elfin, with boyishly cropped dark hair, and still darker eyes set saucer-like in a delicate, heart-shaped face.

Harding stopped dead at the sight of her and she glanced up at him as he did so, then slipped a key out of the pocket of her mac, unlocked the door marked PRIVATE and stepped through out of sight, closing it behind her.

Harding leant back against the newel post behind him as other people moved past. There had been no recognition in the young woman's glance; not so much as a flicker. But *he* recognized *her*. There was no doubt of that in his mind. He recognized her, even though, for the moment, he could not place her, could not fix her in his memory, could not put a name to a face he felt disablingly certain he knew very well.

FIVE

Harding drifted from one ground-floor room to another, paying the sale lots no attention but probing his memory for the identity of the young woman he had just glimpsed. The answer was bound to come to him soon, he reasoned. But it refused to. It hovered tantalizingly at the very edge of his mental vision, out of focus and reach. It was there, but he could not grasp it.

Tiring of his own unaided efforts, he went out to the conservatory and asked the cloakroom attendant who she was.

'That's Hayley Winter,' the man replied. The name failed to jog Harding's memory. 'She's the late Mr Tozer's housekeeper. She lives in the basement.'

'I thought Gabriel Tozer lived alone.'

'I believe he took her on a year or so ago. Needed help around the place as his health began to fail, I suppose. Anyway, she's staying on until the house is sold, as far as I know.'

'How would I . . . get to speak to her?'

'There are steps from the patio down to a separate entrance. Just . . . ring the bell.'

Harding had not noticed the existence of a basement on his way in, though its windows were obvious enough when he left the house and headed round to the rear. He passed the garage on his way, where yet more lots were on display – lawn-mower, gardening tools and a big old Mercedes. The garden itself was overgrown and neglected, ornamental shrubs engulfed by straggling thorns and rampant weeds. These had colonized much of the patio as well. It certainly did not look as if Gabriel Tozer had been in the habit of taking tea there on sunny afternoons.

Steps led down, as promised, to a narrow, deeply shadowed basement area. As he descended, Harding felt nervous as well as puzzled. The name Hayley Winter meant nothing to him. Yet he knew her. He was certain of that. But how? Still his mind could not fix upon the answer.

The paint was peeling on the basement door. Dust layered the hexagonal frosted-glass window set in it. He hesitated for a second before prodding at the bell-push.

A few moments passed, then the door opened and Hayley Winter gazed cautiously out at him. Close to, she seemed even smaller than she had looked from the stairs, plainly dressed in jeans and sweater, her face barely made-up. The familiarity of her face struck him more acutely than ever. But still he could not place it.

'Can I help you?' she asked, frowning.

'I . . . saw you upstairs. I . . .'

'I'm nothing to do with the auction.'

'No, but . . . haven't we met? I mean, don't we . . . know each other?'

'I don't think so.'

'My name's Tim Harding.'

The frown deepened. 'I don't know anyone by that name.'

'You're Hayley Winter, right? The auction people told me.'

'Did they?'

'Yes,' he replied. Her voice, light and accentless, meant as little to Harding as her name. But he had looked into her wide, dark eyes before. He had no doubt of that. 'I know this must seem odd, but, although you don't recognize my name and I don't recognize yours, we *have* met. Honestly. We know each other. Somehow.'

'I don't think so.'

'Do you come from round here?'

'No. I moved down from London last year. What about you?'

'No. I . . . live abroad. I haven't been to Penzance for . . . six or seven years.'

Hayley Winter's frown was suddenly tinged with curiosity. 'Which is it?' she asked, bizarrely. 'Six or seven?'

'I was here – briefly – in August 1999.'

'August 1999,' she repeated.

'Yes.' Harding shaped a smile. 'Is that important?'

55

'Is this . . . something to do with the accident?'

'What accident?'

'I've told Ray Trathen. It's nothing to do with me. It's all in Isbister's hands.'

Harding shook his head. 'I'm sorry. I don't understand. I bumped into Ray Trathen upstairs. Literally. He used to work for Barney Tozer, apparently. I'm over here on Barney's behalf, actually. But—'

'You're the guy he sent for the ring?'

'Yes. How did—'

'Mr Isbister mentioned it. I know about the ring, of course. Gabriel told me. Look . . .' She pressed her hands together in a strange, almost prayerful gesture. 'Do you want to come in? I've just made some tea. It'll probably be stewed by now, but . . . you're welcome to a cup.'

'OK. Thanks.'

The basement was a haven of neatness and order after the cluttered chaos of the rest of the house. Harding was shown into an antiquely equipped but spotlessly clean kitchen, glimpsing a simply furnished lounge and bedroom through open doors along the way. He found himself wondering how old Hayley Winter was. A lot younger than he was, certainly, but maybe not as young as she looked. There was something bemusingly mature yet childlike about her, something weathered but vulnerable.

She poured the tea, in cups and saucers rather than the mugs he might have expected. As she moved to the fridge to fetch the milk, he noticed just how slightly built she was. He tried to stop actively searching his memory for a trace of her. The recollection would come to him eventually, he felt sure. They stood either side of a large, bare, scrubbed table, sipped their tea and looked at each other.

'It's quite a scrum up there,' said Harding.

'I'm trying to keep out of the way.'

'Good idea.'

'We really have never met, you know.'

'Not even in . . . August 1999?'

'I wasn't here then.'

'But the date struck some kind of a chord with you.'

'Only because that's when the accident was.'

'What accident was that?'

'It's only what I've heard. Barney's never mentioned it to you?'

'Was Barney involved?'

'Oh yes. He was there. He was very much involved. According to Ray Trathen, that's why he—' She broke off, frowning again, more suspiciously than before. 'Barney hasn't told you?'

'No. He hasn't. Why don't you?'

'I don't know. I mean, it's common knowledge. Pretty common, anyway. But . . .'

'I won't tell anyone I heard about it from you, Hayley. If you don't want me to.'

'I don't mind. Why should I?' She bridled at the implication, then looked slightly abashed. 'Sorry, I didn't mean to . . . You really don't know?'

'Not a thing.'

'But you're a friend of Barney's?'

'Friend. Employee. Bit of both. But the employee part's strictly freelance. I'm doing him a favour where the ring's concerned, that's all. My day job is garden maintenance. Barney's one of my clients.'

'Has he ever explained to you why he left Cornwall?'

'People move to Monaco for one reason and one reason only. To dodge the taxman.'

'I wouldn't know about that. Gabriel reckoned he left because of the accident. And Ray Trathen will tell you the same.' She sat down at the table. Harding took the hint and sat down opposite her. 'It's none of my business, of course. None at all. It's only what Gabriel said. It was a diving accident, off the Scillies, in August 1999.' Harding's ears pricked up. The Scillies, in the summer of 1999, was where Barney had met Carol. 'Barney was diving with a girl called Kerry Foxton. They were exploring a wreck. Anyway, there was some problem with Kerry's oxygen supply. They got separated and she somehow became trapped underwater. By the time they'd found her and brought her to the surface, she'd stopped breathing. She was resuscitated, but had already suffered brain damage. She never recovered.'

'She died?'

'Some time later, yes. I don't know the details. But a lot of people blamed Barney, apparently. He left for good not long after. Gabriel didn't seem to think tax was the reason. Neither did anyone else. Officially, no one was blamed. But fingers were pointed. You know how it is. A tragedy like that has to be laid at someone's door.

58

And Barney was the more experienced diver. So . . .'

'Was Kerry Foxton from round here?'

'I'm not sure. Like I say, I don't know the details. Ray Trathen's the man to ask about that.'

'What makes him such an expert?'

'Well, he was—'

Hayley was cut off by the bleeping of Harding's phone. Cursing himself for having left the thing switched on, he pulled it out of his pocket, spotted the caller's number as Carol's and switched it straight to voicemail. 'Sorry. You were saying?'

'Just that Ray Trathen was on the boat they dived from.'

'He was?'

'I guess he didn't drink so much then. And he was still working for Barney, of course. Though not for much longer.'

'Are you saying that's why Barney sacked him? Because he was a witness to what happened?'

'I'm not saying anything. But it's what Ray says to anyone who's willing to listen.'

'But surely, if Barney was culpable in some way, and Ray knew it, that would be a reason for *not* sacking him.'

'You're right. It would.' Hayley smiled faintly. 'The guy's not strong on logic.'

'What did you mean earlier when you said you'd told him everything was in Isbister's hands?'

'Well, it is. The auction, I mean. All Gabriel's . . . things. Have you seen how much there is?'

'I've taken a look round, yes.'

'Did you spot the videos?'

'I . . . don't think so.'

'In the drawing room. There's a corner cupboard stacked with them. Hundreds, I should say. All unlabelled.'

'What's on them?'

'Old documentaries. Gabriel loved that kind of thing. Global warming. Ancient civilization. Life on Mars. He'd watch stuff like that for hours.'

'What's that to do with Ray Trathen?'

'It's why he's been round here so often lately making a nuisance of himself.' Hayley sighed, as if weary of the subject she was about to embark upon. 'Ray claims he lent Gabriel a video a couple of years ago. He got it back. But then, recently, when he played it, he found what Gabriel had actually returned to him was, well, wouldn't you guess, an old edition of *Horizon*.'

'Gabriel had recorded over it?'

'No, no. He never recorded over anything. That's why there are so many. Ray claims Gabriel deliberately gave him back the wrong video so he could hang on to the one Ray had lent him.'

'Why would he want to do that?'

'Because of what was on it, I guess.'

'And what was that?'

'Ray's not saying. Something important, apparently, something he badly wants back – but isn't going to get unless he buys the entire collection at the auction. Assuming his video really is among them, of course. Assuming he hasn't imagined the whole thing.'

'Do you think he has?'

'How would I know? It's like the family feud about the ring. The likes of you and me are never going to find out what the truth is, even if we want to.'

'And do you want to?'

'Not really. I'm more concerned with finding another job. And somewhere to live when this place is sold.'

'Will you go back to London?'

'Not if I can help it. All the reasons I left . . . are still there.'

'Maybe that's where we met. I used to live in London. When I was first married.'

'It's a big city.' Hayley went swiftly on. Perhaps, Harding thought, she wanted to forestall a discussion of where in that big city they might plausibly have met. 'Is your wife over here with you?'

'No. She died . . . a few years ago.'

'Sorry.' And a look of genuine sorrow did indeed cross Hayley's face.

'That's OK. I'm used to it now.'

'Do you ever get used to something like that?'

'No,' Harding admitted at once, feeling strangely happy to be caught out in the pretence. 'As a matter of fact, you don't.' She knew as much herself, he sensed, quite possibly from personal experience. Maybe bereavement was one of the reasons for her flight from London. 'Well,' he said, swallowing the last of his tea and standing up, 'I'd better be going.'

'It's been nice talking to you,' she said, smiling up at him. 'Even if we don't know each other.'

'But we do, of course.' He returned the smile. 'Somehow.'

'Are you sure?'

'Yes.'

'I'm sure we don't.'

'Quite a stand-off.'

'How could we settle it?'

'We'd have to . . . compare notes, I suppose. About our lives. Our pasts. That kind of thing.'

'Yeah.' Hayley frowned thoughtfully. 'I suppose we would.'

'I'm . . . at a loose end until the auction,' said Harding. 'Maybe you'd like a . . . break from the circus upstairs. It'll be going on again tomorrow.'

'I know. In fact, I was already planning to make myself scarce.'

'Really?'

'There's a Turner exhibition on at the Tate in St Ives. I was thinking of going up there tomorrow. If you want, you could come along . . . and have another go at convincing me we've met before.'

'I'd like that.'

'Good.' Her smile acquired a sheepish edge. 'So would I.'

SIX

The cupboard stacked with unlabelled videos was attracting little attention when Harding returned to the drawing room after leaving Hayley's basement flat. The note on the lot-number tag – SOME BETAMAX – might have gone a long way towards explaining why. If Ray Trathen really meant to buy them up in search of the one that supposedly belonged to him, Harding reckoned he was unlikely to face fierce competition.

First a ring in a starburst box. Now a switched video. Gabriel Tozer had apparently been determined to auction several secrets along with a lifetime's worth of possessions. The minor mysteries wrapped round them would have intrigued Harding even without the personal interest he had in some of the questions they raised. Why had Carol never mentioned the diving accident? Where had he met Hayley before? What did all the contradictions and coincidences amount to? Something? Or nothing?

'Ray Trathen's the man to ask about that,' Hayley had told him, meaning the accident. But maybe there was more Trathen was an expert on. Maybe a lot more.

Harding went back upstairs and tracked down Clive Isbister in one of the bedrooms.

'Still here, Mr Harding?' Isbister asked, looking surprised to see him again.

'Just leaving, actually. But I wondered if you could . . . help me with something.'

'Happy to. If I can.'

'Do you know where Ray Trathen lives?'

'Taroveor Terrace. I'm not sure of the number. But . . . why do you ask?'

'Oh, I . . . just wanted to check if he'd be . . . bidding against me at the auction.'

'Unlikely, given the state of his finances. Plus his' – Isbister smiled – 'interest in another lot.' The smile faded. 'I don't think you need worry about Ray.'

'I'm just trying to . . . cover all bases.'

'Well, it's up to you. I expect he's in the phone book. But you might do better to try the Turk's Head in Chapel Street around six. I believe he starts there most evenings.' The smile returned. 'A creature of habit, our Ray.'

Harding had wandered through the subtropical haven of Morrab Gardens earlier in the day. He returned there after leaving Heartsease and listened to Carol's voice-mail message while sitting on a bench near the bandstand.

* * *

Barney's playing golf, so I thought I'd give you a call. What are you doing? Treating Humph to a cream tea? It'd be wasted on him. He doesn't appreciate the good things in life. But I do. Our afternoons together are very good, Tim, very, very good. Shall we pencil one in for Thursday? You'll be back by then. And I'll be . . . well, you just wait and see. Call me before five if you can. Otherwise, I'll call you. Take care. And take it easy. I want you firing on all cylinders. Know what I mean? Of course you do. 'Bye for now.

It was gone four o'clock, gone five in Monaco. He was surprised at how relieved he felt not to have to respond to the message. He had been in Penzance for less than twenty-four hours, but already the Côte d'Azur seemed a long way away. He was aware that something more than déjà vu had infected his encounter with Hayley Winter. His inability to recall where and when they had previously met was only part of the reason he had suggested they spend the following day together. The other part he did not care to examine too closely. But its existence he did not doubt. Though as for what it amounted to . . . only time would tell.

It was not yet six when he entered the Turk's Head, but Ray Trathen was already installed at one end of the bar, puffing at a cigarette between gulps of bitter, a tightly rolled copy of the auction catalogue parked by his elbow.

Harding ordered a pint and turned to look at Trathen,

whose bleary gaze suggested he had visited several other pubs since leaving Heartsease. Perhaps that was his normal Saturday routine. Or perhaps this had been a particularly trying Saturday.

'We met at Heartsease this afternoon,' said Harding, smiling warily. 'You're Ray Trathen.'

'Yeah.' Trathen frowned. 'I am. But I don't . . .'

'I'm Tim Harding. Quite a place, that house, don't you think?'

'How did you . . . know my name?'

'Clive Isbister told me. He said . . . you know all there is to know about the Tozer family.'

'He did?'

'Can I get you another?' Harding nodded at Trathen's glass.

'Yeah. Thanks.' A moment later, the glass was empty. 'Wouldn't say no.' And, a few moments after that, it was full again.

'I gather you used to work for Barney Tozer.'

'I did, yeah. You know him?'

'Sort of.'

'That's how a lot of people know him.'

'He lives in Monaco now, right?'

'Yeah. Tax exile. Exile, anyway.'

'I'm surprised he hasn't come over for the auction.'

'I'm not. He's afraid to show his face round here.'

'Because of the diving accident?'

'Accident? That's not what I'd call it.'

'No?'

Trathen shaped another frown. 'Why are you so interested?'

'Well . . .' Harding lowered his voice theatrically. 'Truth is, Barney's offered to put some money into my business. And I'm just wondering if he's the sort of bloke I should get mixed up with. Financially – or in any other way.'

'Take a long spoon.'

'Sorry?'

'You'll be supping with the Devil.'

Harding smiled. 'He can't be that bad.'

'You can find out the hard way if you want. Or you can take my advice. Give Barney Tozer a wide berth.'

'Why?'

'Because, sooner or later, he'll shaft you. Take my word for it. What sort of business are you in, anyway?'

'Landscape gardening.'

Trathen emitted a derisive grunt, though whether at the expense of Harding's choice of occupation or Tozer's suitability as a partner in it was hard to tell. 'Barney likes to dabble. No question about it. He'd just moved into fish farming when he took me on to handle his PR. But that all went by the board when he vamoosed to Monte Carlo. And my job with it.'

'Was he already in the timeshare game then?'

'Oh yeah. That and a few other games as well. Not all of them strictly kosher. As Kerry Foxton found out. To her cost.'

'She's the girl who died in the diving accident?'

Trathen looked woozily surprised. 'Clive really has

been shooting his mouth off, hasn't he? He's not normally so . . . free with info.'

'I didn't get her name from Isbister. I've been . . . asking around.'

'So it seems.' Suspicion was taking lumpen shape in Trathen's mind, but Harding was prepared to bet he was too drunk to be restrained by it. 'Kerry was a nice girl. Just too inquisitive for her own good.' He sighed. 'But I suppose that goes with the territory.'

'What territory?'

'Well, she *was* a journalist.'

'Was she?'

'I should know, shouldn't I? I fixed it for her to meet Barney. I thought he'd get an ego-stroking profile in one of the Sunday supps out of it. Instead, he got a load of very bad publicity and she got . . .' Trathen's voice trailed into silence.

'It *was* an accident, wasn't it?'

'So the inquest said. When they finally had one. She was a long time dying.'

'You were there when it happened?'

'Yeah.' A jag of painful memory twisted Trathen's features into a grimace. 'I was on the boat.'

'So, was it an accident?'

'Maybe. Maybe not. Who knows why Kerry's oxygen supply malfunctioned? All by itself? Or with a little encouragement?'

'You're suggesting . . . she was murdered?'

'I'm suggesting that delving into Barney Tozer's affairs can be an unhealthy activity. *Terminally* unhealthy.'

'Come off it. You don't mean that.'

'Don't I?' Trathen's gaze switched suddenly to a figure behind Harding. He raised a hand in half-hearted greeting. 'Evening, Darren.'

'Hi, Ray.' A gangly, carrot-haired young man in jeans and garishly logoed zip-top hovered at Harding's elbow. 'Got a light?'

Trathen obliged with a light for Darren's roll-up. Leaning forward to accept it, Darren, who was clearly not having his first drink of the day either, contrived to slop lager from his crookedly held glass down Harding's jacket.

'Shit, man, I'm sorry,' Darren slurred, grabbing a bar-towel to mop up the spillage.

'It's OK,' said Harding, smiling grimly as he repulsed the heavy-handed dabs of the towel. 'I'll be fine.'

'There's not that much really.'

'*I'll be fine.*'

'OK, man. Cool.'

'Why don't we sit over there?' Trathen jerked his head towards a table by the window facing on to the street. 'We'll be out of harm's way.'

Darren made a wavering peace-be-with-you gesture with his cigarette hand as they went, then plonked himself on a bar-stool next to someone else he knew.

'Sorry about that,' said Trathen when they had settled.

'Never mind.'

'Where were we?'

'You were telling me you think Kerry Foxton was murdered because she knew something to Barney

69

Tozer's disadvantage about his business activities.'

'I was telling you I thought it was possible. Distinctly possible. There were sides to Starburst International I knew nothing about – except that it was best to know nothing about them. Only Barney and that slimeball Whybrow know how it all fits together. See . . .' He leaned forward, his eyes gleaming with delight in the intricacy of his conspiracy theory. 'Kerry said she'd been sent down to do a piece for the *Sunday Times* on how the Cornish were dealing with the rush of visitors for the eclipse. But that was bullshit. I checked with them after the accident. Like I should have checked before. They hadn't sent her. She'd freelanced for them in the past, but her Cornish trip was nothing to do with them. It was all her own idea. I think the eclipse story was cover for her to get close to Barney and learn some of his secrets. And I think she may have succeeded. Worse luck for her.'

'How did this . . . diving expedition . . . come about?'

'It was Barney's idea. I thought he was out to impress Kerry. He seemed to be having a hard time keeping his hands off her. Can't say I blamed him. She was quite something. Anyway, I assumed the trip was intended to boost his action-man credentials. He fixed it with another old school chum of ours, John Metherell. Kerry was certainly keen on the idea. Maybe she thought she could hang another piece for the papers on it. The *Association* story's always a good one to rehash.'

'The what?'

'Scilly's most famous wreck. HMS *Association*.

Flagship of Admiral Sir Clowdisley Shovell. Foundered on the Gilstone rock and lost with all hands in 1707. Never heard of it?'

'Don't think so.'

'There was quite a hoo-ha when they located the wreck back in the nineteen sixties. Divers have been exploring it ever since, though all the valuable stuff was brought up years ago. John Metherell lives on St Mary's. He's a real *Association* buff. Supposed to be writing a book on the subject. Due out next year, for the three hundredth anniversary. Well, it *was* due out then. Maybe he's gone off the idea since the accident. I wouldn't know. We don't exactly keep in touch. Anyway, he organized the trip and went along for the ride, like I did. He even videoed it.'

'There's a video of what happened?' Harding tried to sound only mildly curious on the point.

'Not exactly. John was too busy trying to help to do any recording once we knew something was seriously wrong. Not that there was much we could do. We got her breathing. Well, Alf Martyn got her breathing. He was the only one who knew any first aid. But it was obvious she was in a bad way. She never actually spoke. I'm not sure she knew where she was.'

'How did this . . . Alf Martyn . . . come to be on board?'

'It was his boat. He makes a living out of ferrying tourists round the islands. He had his brother with him as well.'

'But it was just Barney and Kerry who dived to the wreck?'

'Yeah. John and I stayed on the boat with Kerry's friend, Carol Janes.'

'Carol *who*?'

'Janes. The future Mrs Tozer.' Trathen took a deep swallow of beer. 'Funny how things turn out, isn't it?'

SEVEN

'Funny how things turn out.' Ray Trathen was right on the money there as far as Harding was concerned. Carol had been on the boat when Kerry Foxton met with her fatal accident. And Carol had been Kerry's friend before she became Barney Tozer's wife. She had never mentioned any of this to Harding. She had never breathed a word to him. Maybe she had reckoned he was unlikely to hear of it. Maybe Barney had as well, though he had certainly tempted fate by asking him to go to Penzance. Whatever their calculations, Harding had heard of it *now*.

Extracting as many details as he could from Trathen had been a delicate exercise. He had not wanted to admit why he was so interested in the part Carol had played in events. Nor had he wanted to reveal Hayley's role as his informant for fear of causing trouble for her. That consideration had prevented him from probing the question of the switched video. It was hard to imagine it contained anything other than the material

Metherell had recorded on the day of the accident. But it was evidently not the original. Trathen had referred in passing to that still being in Metherell's possession.

So, what was the long and short of Trathen's account of the accident and the background to it? Harding asked himself that question as he walked back to the Mount Prospect through the soft, dank Penzance evening. Kerry Foxton, freelance journalist, proclaiming an interest in the total eclipse of 11 August 1999, arrived in Cornwall from London a couple of weeks beforehand. She spent half her time with her college friend, Carol Janes, on St Mary's, where Carol was running a café in Hugh Town, and the other half on the mainland, mostly in Penzance, where Starburst International maintained an office – later closed when its fish-farming interests were disposed of. Barney Tozer was at the time living in a big house near Marazion with a succession of short-stay girlfriends, though he was as often as not abroad on business. Kerry contacted Trathen, then on the Starburst payroll, to suggest profiling his boss. Trathen recommended the idea to Tozer, who agreed and immediately took a shine to Ms Foxton. She already knew the *Association* story and he had the means to arrange a dive to the wreck. John Metherell obtained the necessary permit and hired a boat and crew for the trip. Though no diver himself, he was keen to go along in order to visit the stretch of ocean where the subject of his book had gone down.

The party set off from Hugh Town, St Mary's, in ideal weather, on Friday, 6 August. They cruised out to the

Western Rocks and stopped at the dive site near the Gilstone. Metherell videoed the preparations, then Tozer and Kerry went down. None of those left on the boat thought there was anything wrong until Tozer surfaced, saying he had become separated from Kerry and was worried she was in difficulties. He went down again, returning about ten minutes later, holding Kerry limp in his arms. They hauled her aboard and found she was not breathing. Tozer could not say how long she had been in that state. He had found her half in and half out of the wreck. Alf Martyn got her breathing again, but she was still unresponsive. There was a lot of panic. Trathen had only a confused recollection of the fast and bumpy ride back to St Mary's. Martyn radioed ahead for help. There was an ambulance waiting for them when they reached Hugh Town. They stood on the quay, watching it speed off to the island hospital. Kerry was flown to Derriford Hospital in Plymouth later that day. Trathen for one never saw her again.

The police made desultory enquiries, but never seemed to think it was anything other than an accident. Kerry's air-supply hose had been pierced, presumably by contact with the wreck, draining her oxygen cylinder before she could surface. The equipment belonged to Tozer, who claimed it was in good condition. But then he would, as Ray Trathen saw it. The whole venture was risky, according to local divers, who reckoned twin cylinders with separate hoses a must for wreck penetration. Tozer countered by saying penetration had never been the plan. They were just going to take a look.

Kerry must have decided to go in alone, knowing he would try to stop her. Ultimately, that was the coroner's conclusion. In effect, it was all her own fault.

Trathen never went along with that and, to hear him tell it, his doubts on the issue were why Tozer eventually sacked him. Harding suspected he had voiced those doubts only *after* being sacked. Tozer wanted out of Cornwall. Trathen was just part of the baggage he discarded in the process.

As to Tozer's relationship with Carol Janes, there too Trathen was sceptical. He thought it might have begun *before* the accident. Maybe Carol was an accomplice in sabotaging Kerry's equipment. The hose could have been tampered with, causing it to blow under pressure. If Carol did aid and abet her friend's murder, her reward was a marriage of convenience and a share in Tozer's fortune. Trathen had no evidence to back any of this up, of course. It was just the kind of slanderous nonsense an aggrieved former employee – and alcoholic to boot – would come up with. He claimed EU auditors had started asking awkward questions in the months before the accident about the use Starburst had made of lucrative development grants. But he could not prove Kerry Foxton was on the trail of the scandal, if scandal it was. The auditors were still sniffing around when Trathen was sacked. What they subsequently uncovered, if anything, he had no idea.

Trathen admitted the police had studied Metherell's video without noticing anything suspicious. He did not mention his interest in Gabriel Tozer's video collection, however. Nor did Harding. Neither was being completely honest with the other.

Carol's abrupt transition from Kerry Foxton's friend to Barney Tozer's wife left a bad taste in Harding's mouth, though, there was no denying it. She had always said they had met when Barney strolled into her café in Hugh Town one day. That now looked at best a distortion, at worst a lie. They had married in Cannes only a few months later, while Kerry was still lingering on life support in a hospital bed in England. The Foxton family had insisted on keeping her alive long after all hope of recovery had faded. According to Trathen, she had finally died some time in 2003. The inquest had been held in October of that year.

Harding was already acquainted with the Tozers by then, although his affair with Carol had not yet begun. Barney's fleeting return to Penzance to give evidence had presumably been camouflaged as yet another business trip. Nothing had been said about its real purpose, least of all to Harding. It was as if it had never happened.

Talking to Carol again after suddenly learning so much about her that he had never known before was a daunting prospect. Harding had turned off his phone before entering the Turk's Head and found himself hoping there would not be another message from her when he turned it back on.

There was not. For a simple reason, as he discovered halfway back to the Mount Prospect: his phone was no longer in his pocket.

* * *

It was not being kept for him behind the bar at the Turk's Head. No one had handed it in. Recalling his encounter with the supposedly drunken Darren, Harding started to feel queasily certain that it had been stolen from him. Darren was long gone, of course. His surname was Spargo, according to the barmaid. He stacked shelves in one of the supermarkets on the edge of town. Tesco or Morrison's. She could not remember which. Neither could any of the locals. Trathen had moved on too, perhaps, it was thought, down the road to the Admiral Benbow.

But Trathen was not in the Admiral Benbow. And Harding doubted it would have helped a lot if he had been. The dismal truth was that tracking down Darren Spargo was unlikely to achieve anything. Harding could not prove he had stolen his phone. Maybe young Darren was in the habit of topping up his weekend drinking and clubbing fund with the odd opportunistic phone theft.

Or maybe, which was a far more disturbing thought, it had not been opportunistic at all.

EIGHT

Harding was woken by the bedside telephone early the following morning.

'Call for you from a Mrs Tozer, sir,' the receptionist announced. 'Will you take it?'

'Sure. Put her through.'

'Tim?'

'Carol. Hi.'

'What the hell's going on? Your mobile seems to be permanently switched off.'

'Ah. Does it?'

'Well?'

'I'm afraid it was stolen last night. Some pickpocket helped himself to it in a pub.'

'*What?*'

'Simple as that. I'm sorry to say.'

'But I left—' Harding heard her sigh. 'Couldn't you have been more careful?'

'I wish I had been.'

'How am I going to keep in touch with you now?'

'Call me here. You'd better tell Barney that as well. Say *I* phoned *you*.'

'When were you going to, exactly?'

'Soon, of course. I suppose I was hoping . . .' He rubbed his eyes, which were still not focusing properly. 'Never mind.'

'Has anything else gone wrong?'

'No. I've seen the ring. Nice-looking piece. There'll be no problem. I'll fly home on Wednesday, as planned. I got your message about Thursday.'

'And?'

'I'll be all yours.'

Harding had surprised himself by the extent to which he was prepared to mislead Carol. Staring at his reflection in the bathroom mirror as he shaved, he acknowledged the deceit inherent in just one of the phrases he had uttered. *'There'll be no problem.'* In truth there already was a problem. Indeed, there were several. And they seemed to be multiplying.

He was paged during breakfast. *Mr Tozer* was on the telephone now. He took the call in reception.

'You want to watch those Cornish,' chortled Barney. 'They've had to diversify since wrecking went out of fashion.'

'I'm glad you're amused.'

'Other people's misfortunes are always a hoot. Lose your wallet as well, did you? What about your passport?'

'It was just the phone.'

'Oh, well, not so bad, then. How's it going at Heartsease?'

'Fine. Your friend Isbister doesn't seem to think there'll be much competition for the ring. It should be a doddle.'

'And Humph's happy to let you deal with it?'

'Content, certainly.' Strictly speaking, Harding supposed he should have checked on Humphrey's state of mind since his visit to Heartsease. But, then, why should the man *not* be content?

'Plain sailing, then?'

'Looks like it.'

'Take the day off from my family, Tim. Relax. Pretend you're a tourist.'

'Yeah. Good idea.'

Unaccountably, Harding *did* feel relaxed as he made his way down to the railway station later that morning. Patches of blue were breaking through the grey, hummocked clouds. It was almost warm when the wind dropped. He had been to St Ives with Polly, of course. It had been an obvious place to go from Penzance. But he did not feel remotely morbid about returning there. Hayley's company – and the intriguing question of where and when they had met before – would keep his memories of that day at bay.

She arrived a few minutes after he had bought the tickets, wearing a lightweight parka over a sweater, a loosely pleated skirt and soft pinky-grey boots. She looked as pleased to see him as he felt to see her.

'I can't describe what a relief it is to be out of the house today, Tim,' she said as they boarded the train. 'I know this auction is what Gabriel wanted, but it still seems indecent somehow.'

'It'll soon be over.'

'Yes. And then Heartsease will be an empty shell. With just me left in it.'

'Any idea yet what you'll do when it's sold?'

'No. Like I told you, I don't want to go back to London. But I may have to.'

'D'you have family there?'

She laughed. 'Is this the start of a softly-softly interrogation to find out when we might've met?'

He laughed too. 'Sort of.'

'Then we'll have some rules. As far as life stories go, you start.'

Harding's potted autobiography was over by the time they had reached St Ives. It would have been over sooner, but for Hayley's disarming line in probing questions. These were not about the feasibility of some chance meeting they might both have forgotten, which she clearly did not believe had happened, but homed in rather on a subject Harding was far from comfortable with: the emotional journey his life had taken him on.

'Do you blame yourself at all for your wife's death?' she asked at one point.

'No. Of course not.'

'It's just that I have the sense . . .'

'What?'

'Well, that you . . . feel guilty about it in some way.'

It was true. Though how Hayley had sensed it Harding could not imagine. 'When she was dying,' he said in an undertone, 'it got to the stage when I just wanted it to be over. For her sake, so I told myself. But it was for my sake as well. I've always reproached myself for that. In the end, I was willing her to die, to release me, if you like, to . . . make it easier for me.'

'That was only natural.'

'Or plain selfish.'

'It's how you coped, that's all. And regretting it since . . . is part of the process.'

'Is it?'

'I think so, yes.'

'Then how come no one else has ever guessed that's how I felt?'

'Most people don't have much of an imagination, Tim. And a few, like me' – she smiled – 'have too much.'

St Ives. The wind was stronger than on the south coast, ripping and eddying along the narrow picture-postcard streets. But the cloud was thinner. Sunlight deepened the blue of the sea and gilded the lichened roofs of the town. They walked out from the station to St Ives Head, where they were battered by the wind, and soon doubled back to the Sloop Inn on the quayside for lunch.

It was there that Hayley finished a brisk summary of

her life. Born in Colchester in 1971, the youngest of three daughters of chartered accountants, she was expensively educated, took a degree in music at Durham and pursued her dream of playing the harp for a living until an imprecisely diagnosed wrist disorder intervened. Her long-standing relationship with a concert violinist foundered on his ill-disguised belief that the disorder was psychological in origin. London readily became a hateful place to be for a newly single ex-harpist the wrong side of thirty. She remembered the passage in *A la recherche du temps perdu* in which Proust conjured up the magical appeal of the rail route from Paris to the far west of Brittany and impulsively took the train from Paddington to the far west of Cornwall.

'A man reading *The Cornishman* joined the train at St Erth. He left the classifieds section on the seat when he got off at Penzance. I picked it up. And there was Gabriel's ad for a live-in housekeeper. Pure chance. Or maybe you'd call it fate. If you believe in fate.'

'I think I might.'

'But have you ever been to Colchester?'

'Not that I recall.'

'Or Durham?'

'Once.'

'When I was a student there in the early nineties?'

'No. Not then.'

'What about the brasserie in the Park Lane Hilton when I was playing the harp? Or when *anyone* was playing the harp?'

'No.'

'So you see, Tim, if fate has brought us together, it isn't for a second time.'

'Maybe not. But I can't—'

He had glanced out through the window they were sitting by as he spoke. Suddenly, his attention was seized by a familiar face among the passers-by on the quay. His gaze was met, coolly and cockily, by Darren Spargo.

Harding jumped up and made for the door. The pub was busy, a Sunday lunchtime crowd milling at the bar. By the time he had forced his way through and made it outside, Spargo had vanished. Harding looked along the quay and the main shopping street. There was no sign of Spargo. The winding, twining back streets and alleys that led off in all directions offered a wealth of escape routes. Pursuit was not merely futile but impossible.

'Sorry about that,' he said to Hayley as he made a shamefaced return to their table in the Sloop.

'What happened?'

'You wouldn't believe it.'

'Try me.'

Harding sighed. 'I saw someone who I'm more or less certain stole my mobile yesterday. At the Turk's Head in Penzance.'

'Really?'

'His name's Darren Spargo.'

'*Darren?*'

'You know him?'

'Oh my God.' Hayley's eyes widened. 'I'm sorry, Tim. I'm *really* sorry.'

'Why?'

'Darren's my problem. But now it looks as if . . . he might be yours too.'

NINE

Hayley had met Darren while shopping at Morrison's. He had broken off from shelf-filling duties to chat her up and ask her out. She had found him instantly and profoundly resistible and had turned him down. But Darren had not taken no for an answer, then *or* later. He had become first a nuisance, then a plague on her life, haunting the route she walked into town, materializing in her path when she emerged from a shop and now, it appeared, harassing any man he deemed to be a rival for her affections.

'He must have been at Heartsease yesterday afternoon and seen you come and go from my flat, then followed you to the Turk's Head.' Via Morrab Gardens, Harding silently calculated. 'I can only imagine he stole your phone to see if there were any messages from me on it.'

'He'll have been disappointed, then.' Or maybe not, Harding reflected grimly. What use might Spargo seek to make of evidence, as he saw it, that Harding was two-timing Hayley?

'Unfortunately, seeing us together today will only make him more suspicious, however little he learnt from your phone.'

'Has he followed you before like this?'

'Not quite like this, no.'

'Have you reported him to the police?'

'No.'

'Maybe I will.'

'You can't prove he stole your phone.'

'What do you suggest I do, then?'

'The same as me. Ignore him.'

'How long have you been ignoring him?'

'Quite a while.'

'Maybe it's time to try something different, then.'

'Like what?'

'Do you know where he lives?'

'Yes.' Hayley looked solemnly at him. 'But I don't think I'm going to tell you.'

'Why not?'

'I don't want to be responsible for anything . . . extreme.'

'You wouldn't *be* responsible.'

'Let me talk to him. Ask him to see reason. Return your phone. Leave me alone. Call a halt to this before it gets out of hand.'

'Seems to me it already is.'

'Let me *try*.'

Harding sighed. 'All right. But if it doesn't work . . .'

A ghost of a smile crossed her lips. 'Then I'll tell you where he lives. Meanwhile . . .' Her smile strengthened. 'I have a question for you that may take your mind off Darren. Did you speak to anyone while you were at the Turk's Head – such as Ray Trathen?'

It was Clive Isbister who had alerted Hayley to Harding's interest in Ray Trathen. She had spoken to him at the end of viewing and he had mentioned Harding's enquiries about where Trathen could be found. There seemed no point in denying it, nor in holding back anything Trathen had told him. Hayley had probably heard it all before anyway. She certainly did not react as if any of it was a revelation. She did warn him not to trust Trathen, however, a point she returned to later in the afternoon.

They had visited the Turner exhibition at the Tate by then and retreated to the gallery café for tea. Harding had found it impossible to focus his mind on art and was surprised to discover Hayley had been similarly distracted.

'I didn't take much of that in,' she freely admitted.

He grinned ruefully. 'Neither did I, to be honest.'

'I'm not sure Ray Trathen isn't a bigger pain than Darren.'

'You don't mean that.'

'Conspiracy theories are self-replicating, you know. They're like a virus. That diving accident's become Ray's private little Paris underpass, with Kerry Foxton standing in for Princess Di.'

'Maybe so. But I can't pretend I wouldn't like to take a look at Metherell's video.'

'Ray's got you hooked. First the video. Then some other titbit. You'd do better to trust your instincts. For example, is Barney Tozer capable of murder?'

'I imagine we all are. In the right circumstances.'

'You really believe that?'

'Yes. I think I do.'

She nodded solemnly. 'You'd better ask Metherell to show you the video, then. And see what you make of it.'

The afternoon was turning towards evening by the time they left St Ives. They had seen no more of Spargo. Hayley's conclusion was that he had been frightened off by being spotted spying on them. Harding was far from convinced, though he did not say so. It seemed to him that the young man posed more of a threat than Hayley thought. He did not share her confidence that she could, as she put it, 'handle Darren'. But he could hardly reveal why he was so doubtful. The theft of Harding's phone gave Spargo the means to meddle painfully in his life. Whether he would was another question.

Harding sensed Hayley was similarly holding back her reservations about his declared intention of probing the circumstances of Kerry Foxton's diving accident. She thought he should leave well alone. That was clear. But she never actually said so. It was his decision. And she was happy to let him take it.

It was a more complicated decision than she could know, of course. There was more to whet Harding's curiosity than Barney and Carol's conspicuous failure ever to have mentioned the incident. There was the need Harding was beginning to sense to arm himself against the unexpected – to learn as much as he could about two people he evidently did not know as well as they had let him suppose. Leaving well alone was not an option.

He and Hayley parted outside Penzance railway station. During the train ride back from St Ives, he had decided to ask her to dine with him at the Mount Prospect the following evening. He was surprised how disappointed he felt when she turned him down. But his disappointment did not last long.

'I can't tomorrow. But how about Tuesday? You're not leaving until Wednesday, are you?'

'Tuesday's fine.'

'The auction will have come and gone by then. It'll all be over.'

'I suppose it will.' Somehow, though, Harding doubted it.

'Until then, you'll be careful, won't you?'

'You think I need to be?'

'We all need to be.' She kissed him lightly on the cheek. 'Thanks for today, Tim. I enjoyed it – despite Darren.'

'So did I.'

She smiled and nodded faintly. 'Good.'

There was only one Metherell in the directory with an Isles of Scilly address. Harding sat on his bed at the

Mount Prospect, concocting a cover story even as he punched the numbers into the bedside phone.

A woman answered. 'Mercer House.'

'Could I speak to John Metherell, please?'

'Who's calling?'

'My name's Hardy. But he . . . doesn't know me.'

'Hold on.'

Harding heard her call 'John' and waited through a brief, muffled conversation before a gruff male voice came on the line.

'John Metherell speaking. What can I do for you, Mr Hardy?'

'It's a . . . delicate matter. I was wondering if I could come and talk to you about . . . Kerry Foxton.'

There was a pause, during which Harding thought he heard Metherell sigh. 'Oh yes?'

'I gather you have a video . . . shot on the day of the accident.'

Now there definitely was a sigh. 'What's your interest in this, Mr Hardy?'

'Kerry was a friend of mine. We lost touch. I only heard recently of her death. I've been . . . trying to understand what happened.'

'What happened was a tragic accident. I don't know that there's anything more to be said. Especially not after all these years.'

'It would really help me if you could . . . at least let me see the video.'

'It won't tell you anything.'

'Maybe not. But—'

'Where are you phoning from?'

'Penzance. I've come a long way, Mr Metherell. If you could just see your way clear to—'

'All right.' A note of brisk compliance entered the man's voice. 'I don't object to discussing it. Or showing you the video, come to that. If you're willing to go to the trouble of flying over here.'

'I am.'

'Very well, then. When were you thinking of?'

'Tomorrow?'

Metherell clicked his tongue thoughtfully, then said, 'Tomorrow it is.'

TEN

The Isles of Scilly were a subtropical archipelago set in an aquamarine ocean beneath a cloudlessly blue sky. That, at any rate, is how they appeared in the posters adorning Penzance Heliport. As Harding viewed them during the helicopter's descent to St Mary's on a grey, chill, wintry Monday morning, they were wind-lashed outcrops of rock in an angry, spume-flecked sea. His summertime visit to Tresco with Polly felt half a world and rather more than seven years away.

There was another and more substantial reason for his glum mood. Earlier, just before leaving the Mount Prospect, he had taken a phone call in his room. The caller had told the receptionist his name was Tozer and Harding had expected to hear Barney's voice when he was put through. But instead . . .

'That you, Harding? This is your new buddy, Darren.'

'What do you want?'

'I want you to lay off my girl. Hayley.'

'She's not *your* girl.'

'Isn't Carol Tozer enough for you?'

'Now, listen. I—'

'No, *you* listen. Lay off Hayley, or Barney gets to hear the message his missus left on your phone. I don't think he'll like it, do you? What d'you think he'll do about it? He's not someone you want to cross, man, that's for sure. Carol could end up like that friend of hers, Kerry Foxton. So could you. It could get seriously nasty. Know what I mean? But it doesn't have to. It's up to you. Stay away from Hayley.'

Exactly how his life had become so complicated in the course of a single weekend was a mystery Harding pondered as he disembarked from the helicopter at St Mary's Airport. It had seemed such a simple errand at the outset. But at every step he had uncovered a disturbing secret. And he sensed his visit to Scilly would be no different. It was too late to turn back, though. He had to find out what was at stake. He had to give himself the advantage of knowing the truth.

'Mr Hardy?' A tall, stout, bearded man wearing a flat cap, Barbour and corduroys moved forward from the vehicles parked behind the small terminal building. He unzipped a broad grin and extended a hand. 'I'm John Metherell.'

They shook. 'How did you recognize me?' Harding asked, more than slightly perturbed by the possible answers that occurred to him.

'Easy. You're the only solitary male aboard I *don't*

recognize.' Metherell nodded to a couple of departing passengers he evidently knew. 'Tourists are thin on the ground in February.'

'You didn't say you were going to meet me.'

'Spur-of-the-moment decision. Plus I thought it might be useful if I showed you what the diving expedition was all about. *Before* you saw the video.'

'How are you going to do that?'

'Wait and see. Hop in.'

They clambered into a battered white Honda and set off. 'So, you knew Kerry Foxton?'

'Yes.'

'But . . . you lost touch.'

'I, er, went abroad. Lost touch with everyone. You know how it is.'

'Can't say I do, actually.'

'Anyway, when I heard she'd died, I . . . wanted to find out as much as I could.'

'How well did you know Kerry?'

'Very. For a while.'

'I don't remember her father ever mentioning you.'

'I never met him.'

'Right.' Metherell paused to watch for traffic at the end of the airport access road, then pulled out. 'Who put you on to me?'

'Ray Trathen.'

'Ah. Good old Ray. Was it he who told you about the video?'

'Yes.'

'Then I'm puzzled. He has a copy himself as far as I know.'

'Mislaid.'

'Really?'

'So he says.'

'Well, he's capable of mislaying anything, I suppose. Still peddling his murder theory, is he?'

'Yes.'

'With sufficient conviction to make you think it's just possible Kerry's death *wasn't* an accident?'

'Exactly.' Harding was treading carefully and could only hope *how* carefully was not apparent from his tone. His cover was thin and could easily be blown. He had chosen to use a pseudonym on an impulse he now regretted. He should have deliberated longer and harder before contacting Metherell. But he had not, and now here he was, with Spargo's squeakily menacing voice still echoing in his ear, risking exposure as an impostor with every word he spoke.

'It's balderdash, I can assure you. Ray's just working off a grudge against Barney Tozer. Although he probably drinks enough to believe his own fantasies. I'll give him that. I dare say he's convinced himself by now that Barney really did murder Kerry.'

'But he didn't?'

'No. He may have neglected to check the equipment he and Kerry were using as thoroughly as he should have. That's certainly what the coroner implied. So, you could argue he was partly responsible for what happened, although Kerry made things worse for herself by entering the wreck, but at the end of the day . . . it was just bad luck.'

'Where are we going?' Harding glanced round at the high-hedged fields of daffodils to either side of the road. His grasp of the island's geography was just sufficient to tell him that they were not heading for Hugh Town, where Metherell lived.

'I thought a word with our skipper that day might put your mind at rest.'

'Alf Martyn?'

'Correct. He and his brother Fred grow daffodils when they aren't ferrying tourists round the islands.'

'And they were both on board?'

'They were. This is their place just coming up. Pregowther Farm.'

Metherell turned right into a hedge-screened farmyard. A four-square granite and slate farmhouse stood in front of them, flanked by corrugated-iron-roofed outbuildings in various stages of disrepair. Broken ladders, gates, fence-rails and rusty harrows filled one corner, while chickens were pecking and bobbing in the long grass that encroached at another. A track led out of the yard into a daffodil field, beyond which several more daffodil fields sloped down and away towards the sea. A crudely written sign declaring BULBS FOR SALE had been propped against the doorpost of one of the barns. But of sales staff there was no sign.

'The Martyns are one of Scilly's oldest families,' Metherell remarked as he turned off the engine and they climbed out. 'A Robert Martyn settled here in the fourteenth century.'

'Ray mentioned you're something of an historian.'

'Hard not to be, living here. Everything's closer on a small island. Even the past.' Then he added, apparently as an afterthought: 'Perhaps especially the past.'

They walked to the front door of the farmhouse. A drift of pop music, distorted by a slightly off-signal radio, reached them from within. It cut off as soon as Metherell rapped the knocker.

The door was answered a few seconds later by a frizzy-haired, moon-faced, scarlet-cheeked young woman dressed in cropped trousers and a smock top stretched round a distended stomach. She looked at least six months pregnant and was breathing heavily.

'Hello, Josie,' said Metherell.

'Hi, Mr Metherell,' Josie panted cheerily in reply.

'Alf in? Or the father-to-be?'

'No. They're both at the boatyard. They lavish more care on the *Jonquil* than they ever do on me.'

'I'm sure that's not true.'

'You ask Fred and see if he doesn't blush when he denies it.'

'Maybe I will.'

Josie laughed. 'Well, if you want to catch them, they'll likely be there till tea-time.'

'OK. Thanks. Mind if we leave my car here and walk down through your fields to the beach?'

'Be my guest.'

* * *

'There's something on the beach I want to show you before we drive over to the boatyard,' Metherell explained as he led the way at an ambling pace along the track that formed the edge of the Martyns' daffodil fields. It led down through a succession of open gateways towards a broad and rocky bay, into which the sea was rolling and foaming. 'You might as well see it while we have the chance.'

'It's the video I was really interested in,' Harding tentatively objected, fearing that he was being ever so subtly sidetracked.

'What did Ray tell you about the *Association*?' Metherell pressed on.

'That it sank among the Western Rocks in, er . . . 1707.'

'Correct. The bay ahead of us is Porth Hellick, where a lot of the bodies were washed up.'

'Really?'

'Including that of Admiral Sir Clowdisley Shovell. I'm writing a book on the disaster.'

'So Ray said.'

'It's as good as finished. Due out in October of next year, for the tercentenary. It's a tricky business, though, judging when you can safely sign off on a project like that. There's always the possibility that some new discovery might be made.'

'After three hundred years?'

'That's the thing with the *Association* story. It seems to have tendrils that keep on growing. Shovell was in command of a fleet of twenty-one men-of-war returning to Portsmouth from operations in the Mediterranean. It was the primitive navigational methods of the time that did for him. Principally the impossibility of accurately measuring longitude at sea. Three other ships went down that night. About fourteen hundred men were drowned and a fortune in gold and silver coin was lost. The disaster prompted the Government to put up a prize for a solution to the longitude problem.'

'Won by John Harrison with his marine chronometer.'

'Bravo, Mr Hardy. You evidently know all about this.'

'Far from it. I read a book about Harrison once. But I must have missed the *Association* connection.'

'Well, there it is. The disaster was to have historic consequences, little comfort though that would have been to the fourteen hundred who drowned. The wreck of the *Association* was finally located in 1967. Cue rival teams of divers swarming all over it in search of treasure. Lots of headlines. Lots of interest. Which naturally I'm hoping will be revived next year. New revelations would do my book no harm at all.'

'Do you expect any?'

'You never know, Mr Hardy. You never know.'

They had reached the last field before the beach. No daffodils were being cultivated here and there was no hedge beyond it to break the wind that met them full in the face. The bay was a deep scoop out of the coast, the surf surging in round craggy black arms of rock.

'Porth Hellick is a natural sump for wreckage blown in on a sou'wester,' said Metherell. 'Imagine what it must have looked like here the morning after the disaster, with bloated corpses dotted across the sand. Sir Clowdisley's among them, of course. There's a stone marking the spot where he was found.'

Metherell pointed to a rough granite block set on a plinth at the edge of the beach. They walked across to it and Harding looked down at the inscription.

THIS STONE MARKS THE PLACE
WHERE THE BODY OF
ADMIRAL OF THE FLEET
SIR CLOUDESLEY SHOVELL
WAS WASHED ASHORE
AFTER HIS FLAGSHIP H.M.S. ASSOCIATION
WAS WRECKED ON THE GILSTONE ROCKS
ON THE NIGHT OF 22ND OCTOBER 1707

'There's a rather gruesome legend concerning the discovery of Sir Clowdisley's corpse,' said Metherell.

'Oh yes?'

'The story goes that a local woman was first on the scene. Taking a fancy to a ring the admiral was wearing, she tried to steal it from the body, couldn't dislodge it and so cut off the finger along with the ring.'

'A ring?' Harding looked round at Metherell, whose smile had suddenly acquired a mischievous tinge.

'Yes. A rather fine emerald ring, apparently. Set with diamonds.'

ELEVEN

'Why don't we put our cards on the table?' Metherell's smile broadened as he propped one foot on the plinth of the Shovell monument and held Harding's gaze. 'Your name's Harding, isn't it, not Hardy? You're the chap Clive Isbister tells me Barney Tozer's sent over to buy a cherished family heirloom at tomorrow's auction. Lot 641. An emerald-and-diamond ring in a starburst box, hallmarked 1704.'

'All right.' Harding summoned some kind of smile himself. 'You've got me. I'm Tim Harding.'

'The question is: why are you interested in Kerry Foxton?'

'Well, I, er . . .'

'Would I be right in surmising you were disturbed by the rumours of foul play that reached your ears in Penzance and decided to find out if there was any substance to them?'

'Yes.' Further denial seemed pointless. 'You would be right.'

'I quite understand. Barney might not approve. Hence the alias. Well, don't worry. He won't hear of our meeting from me. He's a man even his friends find hard to trust completely. A bit of a chancer, to be brutally honest. But not a murderer.'

'I'm glad to hear it.'

'As for the ring, you needn't worry about that either. I shan't be bidding against you.'

'Do you really think it's the same ring that was stolen from Shovell's body?'

'No. As a matter of fact, I don't. Put simply, it can't be. I'll explain why not as we walk back.'

They began to retrace their steps from the beach along the track through the Martyns' fields. Harding, feeling as relieved as he was embarrassed, listened humbly as Metherell outlined the history of Admiral Shovell's ring.

'There's quite a lot we know for certain and a good deal more we can safely infer. The Admiralty sent a man called Edmund Herbert to the islands in 1709 to investigate the possibilities of salvaging the lost vessels. He accomplished little on that score, but his subsequent report did detail the known circumstances of Sir Clowdisley's death. The ring was certainly missing when the body was found by a search party from one of the surviving ships. Lady Shovell later offered a reward for its return, to no avail. There's no evidence of an amputated finger, however. The bodies of the captain of the *Association* and two stepsons of Sir Clowdisley who'd been serving aboard the ship were found nearby. They were buried in Old Town Church, just round the coast from here. But Sir Clowdisley's body was taken to Plymouth for embalming, then on to London for a full fig state funeral in Westminster Abbey. Nothing more was heard of the ring for nearly thirty years. Then, according to a letter written in the seventeen nineties by Lord Romney, Sir Clowdisley's grandson, an elderly widow resident on this island confessed on her deathbed to the theft of the ring and asked the parson to return it to the Shovell family, which he duly did. Romney says it was later refashioned as a locket. Its current whereabouts are unknown. But you'll appreciate it can't be in that cabinet at Heartsease. And yet the Tozers' ring does match the description of Sir Clowdisley's and dates from the right period. It's quite a conundrum. One which I'll naturally be exploring in my book.'

'Any idea who the widow was?' Harding asked hesitantly.

'Her name wasn't Tozer, if that's what you're getting at. The Tozers have no Scillonian connections.'

'You've checked, have you?'

'Yes. I've checked.' They went on in silence for a moment, until the roof of Pregowther Farm came into view ahead of them. Then Metherell added, 'It wasn't Martyn either. In case you're wondering.'

* * *

'How's Carol?' Metherell asked during the short drive to the boatyard.

'She's, er . . . fine,' Harding responded guardedly.

'It surprised me, Barney and her getting together. Not that I knew her very well, but even so . . .'

'How long did she live on the island?'

'A few years. I used to drop in to her café from time to time. That's where I first met Kerry. She was very interested in the *Association* story from the word go. Fatally so, as it turned out.' Metherell sighed. 'Some people reckoned Carol taking up with Barney after what happened to Kerry was, well, wrong in some way. You can imagine the gossip. Only after him for his money. Not bothered about her friend. That kind of thing.'

'What did you think?'

'Me? Oh, I took the view that it proved Carol had no doubt it *was* an accident. She's hardly likely to have pursued a relationship with Barney if she suspected him of murder, now is she?'

'I suppose not.'

'The truth is that everyone who was aboard the boat, Ray Trathen apart, is convinced it was an accident. The Martyns will tell you the same. Like a lot of tragedies, there's no one to blame. It really is as simple as that.'

Several vessels were being worked on in the boatyard. The *Jonquil*, a handsome blue and white craft propped up on stakes, was receiving attention to its paintwork from two strikingly similar-looking men in dusty boiler-suits. The Martyns were both short and broadly built, balding and bearded, with bony, sharp-nosed faces and dark, deep-set eyes. Harding's impression during Metherell's round of introductions was that Alf, the greyer and more heavily lined of the two, was the older by quite a few years. He certainly did most of the talking, while Fred stood half a step behind his shoulder and contributed little beyond nods to confirm his brother's remarks.

Metherell trotted out Harding's cover story without apparent compunction and Alf expressed their evidently genuine regrets over what had happened.

'First and last time, touch wood, we've ever lost a passenger. A real shame. Miss Foxton was a nice girl, really nice. Ain't that so, Fred?' Fred nodded. 'Well, you don't need me to tell you that, o' course, you being her friend. Sounds like Mr Metherell's given you all the facts. There's not a lot more to be said. We'd played it by the book. Salvors' permission. Harbourmaster and coastguard notified. Equipment on the boat in good working order. And the weather was as near perfect as you could wish for. The sea was like a millpond that day. Weren't it, Fred?' Fred nodded. 'But it's when you least expect trouble you get it. We can't answer for the kit Mr Tozer brought with him. Divers we know reckon spotting signs of wear and tear on hoses is real tricky. You've got to be that particular. Anyhow, worn or not, Miss Foxton's hose probably snagged on part of the wreck, which she had no business getting into in the first place. We'd have refused to let her dive from our boat with just the one oxygen cylinder if we'd known

107

that was her game. Single air supply inside a wreck is just *so* risky. Ain't that right, Fred?' Fred nodded. 'You dwell on something like that. Take my word for it. You ask yourself what you could've done to stop it going wrong. Not a lot, in this case. That's the honest answer. But you go on asking yourself. You can't help it. You can't ever forget it. Even if you could, there'd be folk to remind you. No offence to you, Mr Harding. But there it is in a nutshell.'

'Well, thanks for going over it again,' said Harding.

'You're welcome.'

'And congratulations.' Harding looked at Fred, who frowned bemusedly back at him. 'Your wife. She's expecting, isn't she?'

For a moment, Fred did not seem to understand. Then he gave a gap-toothed grin and giggled. 'So she is.'

'How long to go?'

'Ten weeks,' Alf replied, apparently more knowledgeable on the subject than the father-to-be.

'Do you know if it's a boy or a girl?' asked Metherell.

'It'll be a boy,' Alf declared. 'The Martyns always have sons.'

Mercer House was part of a Georgian terrace facing the public park in the centre of Hugh Town. The Metherells ran it as a high-class b. and b. in the season. Mrs Metherell was out when they arrived and Metherell showed Harding straight into his study at the rear.

It was a book-lined sanctum looking out on to a walled garden. A large desk supported a computer and a mass of paperwork. A framed antique map of the Scillies was hung above the fireplace, decorated with frolicking mermaids and seahorses. Circled depictions of four wrecked ships immediately drew Harding's attention. They were, he saw as he peered closer, the *Association* and the three others that had gone down on the night of 22 October 1707: the *Eagle*, the *Firebrand* and the *Romney*.

'That's the Gostelo Chart,' Metherell explained. 'The original's in the British Library. Tantalizingly undated, but more or less contemporary with the disaster. The dedication to the Governor of Scilly, Sidney, Earl of Godolphin, proves that.' He tapped the elaborately scribed caption. 'The governorship was a hereditary perquisite of the Godolphins. Sidney was the first earl. He died in 1712. So, the chart can't be later than that.'

'It was a big thing, wasn't it – the loss of Shovell and the *Association*?'

'Very. But it's a more recent and less historic loss you're interested in, isn't it? So, let me show you the famous video.'

A TV set, DVD player and VCR were housed in a cabinet in the corner. The video was evidently already in the machine. Metherell sat down at the desk and waved Harding towards an adjacent armchair, then rummaged among his papers, flourished a pair of remotes and aimed them at the TV.

'Don't get too excited,' he cautioned as the screen lit up. 'It's just people on a boat. I'd stopped shooting long before we realized there was a problem.'

It was immediately obvious that Metherell's description – *'just people on a boat'* – was exactly right. The first shakily captured footage was of Carol relaxing in the stern with Ray Trathen. Carol was wearing denim shorts, flip-flops and a dramatically low-cut T-shirt. Ray, beer bottle in hand and looking rather more than seven years younger than the man Harding had met over the weekend, was clad in shapeless casuals. He rolled his eyes at the camera when he realized Metherell had caught him ogling Carol's cleavage. The sea beyond them was, as Alf Martyn had said, millpond flat.

The camera panned slowly, taking in a lighthouse in the middle distance. Then the fo'c'sle of the *Jonquil* came into view, with Fred Martyn at the wheel and Alf standing beside him in the cockpit, squinting into the lens.

Barney Tozer and Kerry Foxton were standing amidships, between Metherell and the Martyns. They were wearing their wet-suits, but had not yet donned the rest of their diving kit. Kerry had her back to the camera. She was a small, slim, dark-haired young woman, slight enough of stature to be dwarfed by Barney, phocine and massive in black matt rubber. He winked at Metherell and said something to Kerry, gesturing for her to turn round. She obliged, cocking her chin and beaming theatrically as she did so.

Harding gasped at the first sight of her face. Metherell froze the frame and looked round at him. 'Is something wrong?'

Harding stared at the blurred image of Kerry Foxton, short hair tousled, eyes bright, mouth parted in a smile.

He had seen those eyes and that smile before. The resemblance was as uncanny as it was undeniable. Was something wrong? Yes. Definitely. Something was very wrong.

TWELVE

The divers, fully kitted up now, their faces obscured by wet-suit hoods, goggles and breathing apparatus, stepped off the boat, Barney taking the lead, into the stretch of sea adjacent to the buoy the Martyns had deployed earlier. Barney vanished first, then Kerry, the wake of her dive fading rapidly. She was gone. The video cut out.

'Want to see any of it again?' asked Metherell.

'No, thanks.'

'OK.' Metherell switched off the TV and set the video to rewind. 'As you see, it doesn't tell you much. There's no clue as to what followed.'

It was true. The video contained nothing either suspicious or remarkable. Unless, like Harding, you were acquainted with Hayley Winter. 'Did you ever . . . meet Kerry's family?' he asked, his gaze still fixed on the screen.

'I met her father. He came down and asked a few

questions of those involved. Those he could get to speak to, anyway. A nice man, as I recall, though nothing like as flamboyant as Kerry's personality had somehow led me to expect. Small, inoffensive, quietly spoken. And crushed. Yes. Crushed is how he seemed.'

'No other relative?'

'Not that I recall.'

'Did she have any brothers? Or sisters?'

'I'm not sure. I don't think so. I mean, she may have, but . . . I never met them.'

'Didn't the family show up at the inquest?'

'No. Her parents were dead by then, of course.'

'They were?'

'Yes. It's why—' Metherell broke off, waiting until Harding had turned to look at him before continuing. 'It's a sad story right to the finish. The doctors in Plymouth soon gave up on Kerry. Evidently, you don't come out of the sort of coma she was in. Her parents refused to accept that. They moved her to a private hospital in London. Then to some clinic in Munich that had a reputation for working miracles with coma cases. They commuted over to see her. I don't know if any progress was made. Not enough, obviously, because, when they were killed in a pile-up on the M4 driving home from Heathrow Airport after yet another visit to Munich, whoever was left to make the decisions . . . pulled the plug on Kerry.'

'I see.'

'Do you? I have the impression something's . . . troubling you.'

'Have you ever met Gabriel Tozer's housekeeper at Heartsease?'

'Can't say I have. I didn't even know he had one.'

'What about Clive Isbister, then? Or Humphrey Tozer? Would they ever have met Kerry?'

'I don't know. There's no reason why Clive should have. The same goes for Humphrey, I assume, though I scarcely know the man myself. Why do you ask?'

'That leaves Ray Trathen, then. He must have noticed.'

'Noticed *what*?'

'The resemblance.' Harding looked back at the blank and unrevealing TV screen. 'The quite startling resemblance.'

When Harding left Mercer House, he still had several hours at his disposal before the four o'clock helicopter back to Penzance. Metherell had obligingly offered to drive him to the airport, so it was agreed he would return to Mercer House around three fifteen. He lunched, on Metherell's recommendation, at the Mermaid, down by the quay, then walked out round the walls of the old Elizabethan garrison at the western end of the town.

It was also the western end of the island. The dark grey finger of the Bishop Rock lighthouse stood out on the horizon, hemmed in by the other jagged rocks it gave warning of. Somewhere out there lay the wreck of the *Association*, scene of the disastrous diving expedition of 6 August 1999.

The date was both a tease and a lure. Harding had

arrived in Penzance with Polly the following day, by which time Kerry Foxton was in hospital in Plymouth, in a coma from which she would never wake. He could never have met her. Not in Penzance, at any rate. Her photograph might have appeared on the front of *The Cornishman*, of course. He *might* have seen that. But it was not enough, not nearly enough, to account for his strong sense of familiarity.

And what of Hayley? How was it she so closely resembled Kerry Foxton? Was she aware of the similarity? It was too striking to be a matter of chance. Somehow, somewhere, there was a reason for it.

Harding glanced north towards Tresco, distinguishable from the other islands by its central belt of woodland. His memories of exploring the famous Abbey Gardens there with Polly were distinct yet distant, as if he were recalling the experiences of another life, another man. His past was numb, like a frozen limb, his present a labyrinth of contradictions.

Judith Metherell, a briskly mannered woman whose taste in clothes made her look a decade older than Harding suspected she really was, greeted him when he returned to Mercer House. She surprised him by apologizing for mishearing his name over the phone, then went to extricate her husband from his study.

'Glad you made the effort to come over?' Metherell asked as they drove out of town.

'Glad isn't quite the right word.'

'Kerry Foxton wasn't murdered, Mr Harding.'

'I'm happy to believe it.'

'But there's something else you're *not* happy about.'

'True.'

'A passing resemblance that Gabriel Tozer's house-keeper bears to Kerry.'

'More than passing.'

'Maybe that's why he chose her.'

'How do you mean?'

'The old boy always had a mischievous streak. He liked to get under people's skin.'

'Did he really?'

'Yes. And it seems to me he's still doing it. From beyond the grave.'

It was a twenty-minute flight to Penzance, nothing like sufficient for Harding to decide what his next step should be. Carol's friendship with Kerry; Kerry's resemblance to Hayley; his own conviction that he had met Hayley or Kerry – or both, for that matter – before: he was beset on all sides by the inexplicable and the unresolvable.

One problem he no longer had any patience with was Darren Spargo. He did not like being threatened. He did not like it at all. He felt, in fact, very much in the mood to do some threatening of his own. And Morrison's supermarket was only a short walk from the heliport.

But he was out of luck. The woman at the information desk informed him that Darren no longer worked there. And if she knew where he lived, she was not telling.

* * *

Ray Trathen was the obvious source to tap for information about Spargo and much else besides. Harding decided to try the Turk's Head at Trathen's usual time. That left him an hour or so to freshen up back at his hotel. Hayley had declined his invitation to dinner and he wondered now if that was because she had known what he would discover during his day trip to Scilly. But he wondered also if that was one suspicion too many. He wanted, he needed, to give her the benefit of the doubt.

None of which was any kind of preparation for the news that awaited him at the Mount Prospect.

'You're a popular man, Mr Harding,' the receptionist said as she handed him a note with his key.

'Sorry?'

'All these phone calls.'

'Ah.' He glanced at the note and ran his eye down the list of callers. Clive Isbister at 10.38. Barney Tozer at 11.21. Isbister again at 12.08. Barney again at 14.10. Carol at 14.58. Humphrey Tozer at 16.11. And Isbister yet again at 17.02. The message was the same in each case. Please call as soon as possible. He *was* popular. Or *un*popular. What was going on? What could they possibly all want with him?

He phoned Isbister first, judging he might not be available on his office number much longer. And the man himself answered promptly.

'Mr Harding. At last. Where have you been?'

'Out of town.'

'All day?'

'Yes. Since you ask.'

'Sorry. None of my business, really. I gather from Barney you've lost your mobile, so perhaps you haven't heard what's happened. Unless you've spoken to him since your return, of course.'

'I haven't spoken to Barney.'

'Ah. I see.'

'What *has* happened?'

Isbister sighed. 'There was a burglary at Heartsease last night, Mr Harding. A very specific burglary. Just one thing taken. And I expect you can guess what it was.'

'Not . . . lot six four one?'

'The very same.'

THIRTEEN

Gabriel Tozer had had a burglar alarm fitted at Heartsease some years previously, though he had economized by having movement sensors fitted on the ground floor only. Isbister had set the alarm personally on leaving the house at the end of Sunday's viewing. It had been triggered shortly after nine o'clock that evening. Hayley had phoned the police and been advised not to stir until they arrived. In the event, the police had been unable to find anything amiss, bar an unlatched window in the dining room. They had detected no signs of a break-in.

'It took us some time to notice what had happened ourselves,' Isbister went on. 'I thought it prudent to give the house the once-over this morning in view of the alarm going off. We finally discovered the lock on the cabinet containing the ring had been forced, but the doors had been wedged together with a matchstick so it wasn't immediately obvious. The ring, along with the starburst box, was missing. But nothing else.'

'Nothing at all?'

'We checked exhaustively. It was just the ring he came for.'

'Via the unlatched window.'

'I think that's how he left, certainly. I'm not sure it's how he arrived, though. He may have unlatched the window while mingling with the crowds earlier in the day. But he couldn't have been sure we wouldn't spot that while locking up. So, another possibility is that he sized up the alarm system, hid somewhere – in the airing cupboard, maybe, or a wardrobe, or even under one of the beds – and waited till it was dark and everything was quiet before helping himself to the ring and leaving through the dining-room window. Going downstairs set off the alarm, of course, but by then it didn't matter. He had what he wanted.'

'Is that what the police think?'

'They favour the first theory: unlatch the window and come back later. I have the impression they also think it's possible the ring was stolen during viewing hours and the thief returned during the evening for some more goodies, only to leg it when he set off the alarm. They obviously have a poor opinion of our powers of observation. I can tell you *that* didn't happen.'

'Do they have any suspects?'

'I don't know. Frankly, I doubt they're entertaining high hopes of finding the culprit. Half of Penzance left their fingerprints around Heartsease over the weekend. Nobody actually saw the burglar. Miss Winter very wisely lay low. A tough case to crack, I'd say.'

'Do *you* have any suspects?'

'No. You don't want to confess, do you?'

'*Me?*'

'Just joking, Mr Harding. You could have bought the ring tomorrow, for a price Barney can readily afford, I'm sure. On the face of it, you're the last person who'd steal it.'

'Who's the first person, then?'

'Someone who badly wanted it, but didn't have the money to pay for it.'

'And who might that be?'

'Your guess is as good as mine. Better, I hope, for your sake, if Barney's still in the mood he was when I spoke to him this morning. He doesn't like to have arrangements he makes interfered with. He doesn't like it at all.'

Isbister was, if anything, understating Barney's anger at being cheated of the ring, as Harding soon realized when he phoned him.

'What the bloody hell's going on, Tim?'

'I don't know. The ring's been stolen. That's all I can tell you.'

'Well, it's not enough. You promised to make sure everything went smoothly.'

Harding was tempted to contradict Barney on that point, but opted for something less inflammatory. 'I wasn't to know this was going to happen.'

'Who took the bloody thing?'

'I haven't a clue.'

'Well, find out. Get it back. I'm not going to let some sneak thief put one over on me.'

'I don't really see what I can do.'

'Talk to this housekeeper Clive's told me about. See if she knows anything.'

'All right.' That at least presented Harding with no difficulty. As it happened, he had rather a lot to discuss with the housekeeper already.

'And try to calm Humph down. He tells me he's seen neither hide nor hair of you since Friday.'

'I didn't know he needed to.'

'Well, you know *now*. For God's sake, Tim, this was supposed to be a piece of cake.'

'It's not my fault it isn't, Barney. There's obviously more going on here than you gave me to understand.'

'What do you mean by that?'

'The ring was targeted. That's obvious. I've no idea who by or why. Have you?'

'No, I bloody haven't.'

'Are you sure?'

'Of course I'm sure. Maybe Humph knows of someone. You'd better check that. And buy yourself a phone so I can keep in touch. You've been incommunicado all day.'

'OK. I'll do that.'

'I want to know who did this.'

'So do I, actually.'

'You could try putting the squeeze on a former

employee of mine, now I come to think about it.' Barney's tone had softened considerably. 'Name of Ray Trathen.'

'I met Ray at Heartsease on Saturday.'

'You did?'

'He certainly bears you a grudge.'

'You can't believe a word he says.'

'I don't. But there *was* a diving accident in August 1999, wasn't there?'

Barney groaned audibly. 'Is Ray still going on about that?'

'Oh yes.'

'I guess I should have warned you.'

'Maybe you should.'

'All right.' There was silence for a moment, then Barney resumed, almost contritely. 'I'm sorry, Tim. By rights, it ought to be me sorting this out, not you. But as it is . . . you'd be doing me a big favour if you . . . gave it a go.'

'I'll see what I can do.'

'Thanks. I owe you one.'

Harding congratulated himself on how he had handled Barney, who was back now where Harding needed to have him: in his debt. It was a fragile advantage, though, with Harding's phone – and Carol's incriminating message – in Darren Spargo's possession. He could not afford to rest on his laurels.

Nor could he spare the time to visit Humphrey. A phone call would have to suffice.

123

'You've resurfaced, have you?' was the elder Tozer's less than genial conversation-opener.

'Barney's asked me to look into the theft of the ring.'

'Has he now?'

'Do you have any idea who might have taken it?'

'No. I don't.'

'I imagine . . . the news came as a nasty shock to you.'

'It did. Though perhaps it shouldn't have.'

'Sorry?'

'I ask Barney to send me money. Instead he sends me you. I ask him to help me retrieve something Uncle Gabriel stole from us. Instead, what happens? It gets stolen all over again.'

'What are you saying?'

'I'm saying the ring's further out of our reach than ever. And I don't think you're capable of doing anything about it.'

Humphrey Tozer's vote of no confidence mattered little to Harding. The theft of the ring meant his business in Penzance would not be concluded at tomorrow's auction. It had, in fact, given him more time to probe the mystery of Hayley's resemblance to Kerry Foxton and his sense of a previous connection with one or both of them. Perversely, he was almost grateful for the opportunity it had handed him. But he had to tread carefully. With Spargo on the loose, he was in a vulnerable position. Finding Spargo, indeed, was far more important to his welfare than laying hands on the Heartsease thief. He set off into the Penzance evening knowing that had to be his first objective.

He found Ray Trathen *in situ* at the bar of the Turk's Head, unaware, as far as he could judge, of the burglary at Heartsease.

'Still here, then?' Trathen greeted him, woozily cocking one eyebrow.

'I've just got back from St Mary's.'

'What took you there?'

'John Metherell.'

'Oh yeah?'

'The video, Ray. I've seen it.'

'What did you make of it?'

'I saw no evidence of murder. Not a shred.'

'There's none so blind . . .'

'I wasn't blind to one thing. Kerry Foxton and Hayley Winter. They're so alike.'

'I didn't know you'd met Hayley.'

'Briefly, yes.'

'Well, you're right. She looks a lot like Kerry.'

'How do you account for that?'

'I don't.'

'It must have struck you as odd.'

'Yeah, well, Gabriel Tozer was an odd man.'

'You think he chose her specially?'

'Wouldn't put it past him.'

'But she came down from London of her own volition. He couldn't have—'

'Review her CV during this "brief" meeting, did you?'

Harding took a deep breath. 'I happened to ask what had brought her to Penzance.'

'And you believed her explanation?'

'Why shouldn't I?'

'Because of how close in looks she and Kerry are. They could almost be twins. Sisters, at all events. Coincidence? I think not.'

'Are you suggesting they're related?'

'I don't know. Why don't you ask her?'

'Maybe I will.'

'You could ask her what happened to my copy of Metherell's video while you're about it.'

'You think Gabriel Tozer tricked you out of it?'

'Somebody did.'

'That lad who spilt his drink on me last time I was here.' Harding noted with grim satisfaction the confusion his sudden change of subject had clearly caused Trathen. 'Darren Spargo.'

'What about him?'

'Do you know where he lives?'

'No. I see him in here off and on. That's it. What d'you want with him?'

'It's a—'

'Did you say you're looking for Darren Spargo?' put in a man standing next to them at the bar.

'Er, yes.'

'Can't imagine why.' The man laughed. 'Bit of a pillock, if you want my opinion.'

'I wouldn't disagree with you.'

'He lives out at Treneere, if you want to know, next door to my aunt. Worse luck for her.'

It was a cheerless walk out to Treneere, a large estate of council housing on the northern edge of the town. The Spargo residence blended drably but durably with its neighbours. There were lights at the windows. Rock music thumped from an upper room. Two bicycles lay where they had fallen next to the front path. Harding cast a leery eye about him before pressing the doorbell.

A child with Marmite smeared round her lips opened the door and stared up at Harding. Then a bustling, broad-hipped woman with tired eyes and a wary expression took her place.

'Can I help you?'

'Is Darren in?'

'No. He won't be back for hours yet, I shouldn't think.'

Harding had half-expected something like this and was uncertain how to proceed. But he did not have to consider the problem for long.

'Is your name Harding?'

'Yes,' he cautiously admitted.

'Darren said you might look round.'

'He did?'

'Left this for you.' She stepped briefly back, then re-appeared . . . with Harding's mobile phone. 'Picked it up by mistake, he said. Is that right?'

Harding smiled despite himself. 'Sort of.'

She handed him the phone. 'No harm done, then.'

FOURTEEN

Harding had been sitting at the top of the steps leading down to the basement flat at Heartsease for what felt like several hours, but was actually less than one, when he heard footsteps on the drive at the side of the house and the faint rattling of a bunch of keys.

'Hayley,' he called, standing up and crossing the patio into the nearest shaft of lamplight. 'It's me.'

'Tim.' She was wearing her short raincoat over jeans and trainers and had added a bandeau round her head that made her look younger and smaller than ever. She was carrying the canvas bag he had seen her with on Saturday and was leaning slightly to one side to bear the weight of whatever it contained. 'Thank God it's you.'

'Sorry if I startled you.'

'You didn't. Not really. I guess I was expecting you.'

'I heard about the burglary.'

'But you'd have come anyway. Once you'd seen the video.'

'Is the video why you put me off tonight?'

'No. I've been to my judo class. I go every Monday.' She smiled uncertainly. 'Come inside, Tim. We've a lot to talk about.'

She offered him coffee and he accepted. They sat either side of the kitchen table, waiting for the kettle to boil, staring at each other wordlessly, both equally unsure how to begin.

Harding took his phone out of his pocket and laid it on the table. 'I got this back,' he said quietly.

'Good. Darren promised to return it. He's got a part-time job at the snooker club now. Morrison's sacked him for absenteeism, apparently. Anyway, I spoke to him at the club this afternoon. He seemed to see reason.'

'Are you sure about that?' It had occurred to Harding that Spargo could easily have recorded the message Carol had left on the phone; Harding was not necessarily off that particular hook. 'He didn't sound very reasonable when he phoned me at the hotel this morning.'

'That was before he realized how much trouble I could cause him.'

'What sort of trouble?'

'If the police knew he'd been hanging around the house, they might suspect him of the burglary. I convinced him I could make *sure* they suspected him.'

'You play rough.'

'When I have to.' The kettle began to whistle. Hayley

129

rose and filled their cups. She placed one in front of Harding and sat down again with the other. 'Ironically, the burglary gave me the means to get Darren off my back. And yours.'

'Do you think he might have done it?'

'Why should he?'

'Why should anyone?'

'There's a reason. There has to be.'

'I think there has to be a reason for everything, Hayley. Including your resemblance to Kerry Foxton.'

'You're right. There *is* a reason.' She took a cautious sip of the coffee, and leant back in her chair, bracing one knee against the edge of the table. 'Ray Trathen has the crazy idea Gabriel chose me as his housekeeper *because* of the resemblance.'

'But he didn't?'

'No. Someone else did that.'

'Who?'

'Nathan Gashry. An old boyfriend of Kerry's. He never got over being ditched by her. He never got over her at all. I knew nothing about Kerry when I met Nathan. This was eighteen months ago. He seemed like—' She flinched as if in pain. 'He seemed like the answer to my prayers. He worshipped me. So I thought. What he actually worshipped, of course, was a likeness of Kerry. I found out later he'd trawled through hundreds of pictures, probably thousands, on Internet dating sites, looking for her . . . doppelgänger. Eventually, he found her: *me*. My life was a mess around then. The wrist problem. The rejection by Roderick – the violinist I told you about. For a while, quite a while, I believed Nathan was my salvation. But the longer we were together, the more he talked about Kerry. And the differences between me and her – the things you can't see. Then I met a previous girlfriend of his. Veronica. He'd persuaded her to have cosmetic surgery to make her look more like Kerry. She was in a bad way. It frightened me. I persuaded Nathan's sister to tell me the truth. Ann told me the whole story in the end. The Foxtons lived near her, in Dulwich. That's how Nathan came to meet Kerry, through Ann. He was always too clingy for her, according to Ann. I could believe that. Kerry broke it off. Nathan refused to accept it was over. He convinced himself he'd get her back, sooner or later. Then came the accident. Nathan was devastated. He was forever visiting her in hospital, talking to her for hours on end. He never got a response, of course. Ann reckoned he finished up preferring Kerry comatose to Kerry conscious. She was unable to send him away; incapable of severing their connection. Kerry's parents sent her to a specialist coma clinic in Munich. Nathan followed. Then the Foxtons were killed in a car crash.'

'And Kerry was taken off life support.'

'Yes. There were no other close relatives. It was a clinical decision. Nathan had no say in the matter. And no way of coping with it – other than to remake someone else in Kerry's image. First Veronica. Then, because I looked so much more like Kerry than her without the need of any surgery, me.'

'What did you do when you found out?'

131

'I dyed my hair blonde.' She shook her head slowly and sipped some coffee. 'Isn't that ridiculous? I dyed my hair. To prove I wasn't Kerry.'

'How did Nathan react?'

'Badly. As you'd expect. Crazily. Dangerously. He threatened me . . . with a kitchen knife. I managed to calm him down. I convinced him I'd never do anything else to . . . ruin his image of me.'

'And then?'

'Then I left. While he was at work. Incredibly, through all this . . . madness, he managed to hold down a succession of surprisingly well-paid jobs. Anyway, the day after the knife incident, I fled.'

'Where to?'

'Here.' She smiled faintly, acknowledging his look of surprise. 'That's right. That's when I had my moment of inspiration. But it wasn't Proustian. I came here because of Kerry. She'd been a big part of my life, though for a long time I hadn't realized it. I had nowhere to go, no one to hide with from Nathan. He knew where my parents lived. And my sisters. He'd soon have tracked me down if I'd gone to any of them. I decided to follow Kerry to Cornwall instead. Strangely enough, Nathan wasn't interested in what had happened to her. He didn't care *why* she'd ended up in a coma. His obsession was all about her and him. Nothing else mattered. So, this is the last place he'd expect me to run to.'

'Did you really see Gabriel's advert in a discarded newspaper on the train?'

'No. I'm sorry, Tim. I had to edit some of the facts.

132

When I arrived, I booked into the cheapest guesthouse I could find. Ann had told me about Barney Tozer's part in the accident. I first came to see Gabriel out of curiosity – to see what he knew about it. He claimed to know nothing and promptly turned the tables by persuading me to tell him why I'd left London. He could be charming when he wanted to be. And he was very . . . perceptive. The curmudgeonliness was an act. He offered me this flat. He did need a housekeeper, when all was said and done. I settled in. It was just the safe haven I needed. But then Gabriel died. And it stopped being safe, bit by bit. First there was Darren. Now this burglary. I have to leave anyway, sooner or later. Maybe it should be sooner.'

'You surely wouldn't go back to London.'

'No. Both of my sisters would take me in, at least for a while. And neither of them lives in London, so . . .'

'But I thought you said Nathan would be able to find you if you went to them.'

'Yes. But he's stopped looking for me. I'm still in touch with Ann, you see. According to her, he's taken up with Veronica again. I feel guilty about that. I wish I could do something for her. But in the final analysis . . . you have to look after yourself.'

Harding smiled. 'I expect the judo helps.'

She smiled back. 'It's certainly given me more confidence. Darren doesn't worry me anything like as much as he thinks he does.' Her face changed then. A shadow seemed to pass across it. She drew herself up to the table and leant towards him. 'The burglary worries me, though. A lot.'

'Whoever it was only wanted the ring.'

'Yes. But why? Gabriel never told me he had it, you know. He kept it locked away. I only realized it was here when Isbisters started cataloguing the contents. It isn't hugely valuable. And the only people known to have an interest in it, Barney and Humphrey Tozer, were set to secure it at the auction.'

'Somebody else obviously wanted it for themselves and couldn't afford to outbid Barney. Does it really matter who that was?'

'It might. Ann told me things . . . about Kerry . . . that I didn't take seriously. I'm starting to take them seriously now, though.'

'What things?'

'It was Ann who first got Kerry interested in the *Association* story in general and Admiral Shovell's ring in particular. Ann thinks Kerry's work on that story may have led her into danger. In other words, that what happened to her *wasn't* an accident. But it had nothing to do with Barney Tozer's dodgy business practices. Instead, it was all about the ring.'

'Why should anyone care so much about a three-hundred-year-old ring?'

'I don't know. I can't imagine. That's why I thought Ann was wrong about the accident. But the burglary . . . makes me think she was right all along.'

'I don't see how. The ring stolen last night never even belonged to Admiral Shovell. Metherell put me right on that. The admiral's ring was looted by a local woman when his body was washed up on St Mary's. She owned up to what she'd done on her deathbed years later and the parish priest returned the ring to the Shovell family. It can't possibly have ended up with the Tozers.'

'Oh, but it can. Metherell obviously doesn't know the full story.'

Harding's curiosity was aroused. 'Doesn't he?'

'Ann's a keen genealogist. She researched the life of one of her ancestors, Francis Gashry, who was some kind of civil servant back in the eighteenth century. In the process, she turned up something about Shovell's ring. She told Kerry what it was. That's why she came down here. One of the reasons, anyway. And Ann believes it may be the reason why she met with a fatal so-called accident.'

'What did Ann find out?'

'Basically, that Shovell's ring and the Tozers' ring are one and the same.'

'How can that be?'

'I don't know. I was never interested enough to try and get Ann to tell me. I didn't think it mattered. Until now.'

'Do you think she knows who stole the ring?'

'She might. Who had cause to steal it, at any rate.' Hayley finished her coffee and set the empty cup down, staring across at Harding as she did so. 'But you ought to understand this. She promised me she'd never do anything that risked alerting Nathan to my where-abouts. And she's a woman of her word. She won't tell

135

you a thing – she won't even speak to you – unless I ask her to.'

'And would you be willing . . . to ask her?'

'I'm not sure. I'm really not. But . . .' She pressed her hands together in a gesture he recalled from their first meeting. 'I'll think about it while I'm taking a bath.' She smiled. 'I need one. You're welcome to stay. We can talk again afterwards. Unless, of course . . .' Her look grew hesitant. 'Unless you feel you have to go.'

'No,' he said, noting the sudden lightening of her gaze. 'I'm happy to stay.'

FIFTEEN

It was not what he had expected. Not exactly, anyway. She had asked him to stay. She had not wanted to be alone. Nor had he. At first she had only asked him to hold her and he knew enough about her past to do no more than that. Soon enough, though, they had made love, once in the small, still, silent hours, then once again as dawn crept in greyly around them.

It did not feel like a betrayal of Carol. Indeed, it set his affair with her in its proper context. Sex by appointment, during engineered afternoons, at his apartment in Villefranche, had never been like this. He wanted to cradle Hayley in his arms, he wanted to caress and protect her, far more than he wanted to savour the moment when she stared up into his eyes and he could hold back no longer. This he remembered and recognized as the beginning of love.

'I can trust you, can't I, Tim?' she asked as they lay together in the serenity of early morning.

'You can, yes,' he assured her.

'Why does this feel so right?'

'Because it is, I suppose.'

'A lot's gone wrong in my life.'

'I know.'

'I need that to change.'

'Maybe it just has.'

'You won't let Nathan find me, will you – you won't lead him to me?'

'Of course not.'

'And you won't go looking for him while you're in London?'

'No. I won't.'

Late the previous evening Hayley had called Ann Gashry and asked if she would meet Harding and tell him whatever he wanted to know about the ring. Ann had agreed, while making it clear to him when he had taken the phone that she was doing so for Hayley's sake, not his. She had sounded precise and calm and cautious – the ideal person to keep a secret. They had made an appointment for five o'clock the following afternoon, Harding reckoning it would take him most of the day to travel to Dulwich. But he was no longer sure now that he wanted to go at all.

'I won't go near him, Hayley. I promise.'

'Good.' She kissed him. 'You're still going to London, though, aren't you?'

'I think I have to.'

'Is it really the ring you're looking for? Or is it Kerry?'

'I told Barney I'd do my best to find out what's going

on. So, I have to speak to Ann Gashry. It's as simple as that.'

'Is it?'

'Yes.'

'You must have wondered, though. If the person you're certain you've met before isn't me, but Kerry.'

'How would I have met her?'

'If the diving expedition hadn't ended in disaster, you might have bumped into each other in Penzance in August 1999.'

'But it did. And we didn't.'

'Are you sure? I was reading a book recently about the latest ideas in cosmology. *The Universe Next Door*. Part of Gabriel's library. Strictly speaking, it should be in the auction. Technically, I stole it. Anyway, cosmologists apparently think there's an alternative universe out there somewhere for every alternative reality. Which means, in one version of this world, you did meet Kerry. Perhaps that's what your mind's trying to tell you.'

'By that rationale, there's a version in which you and I met before as well.'

'And one in which we never meet at all.'

'I guess so.' He looked into her eyes. 'But let's not go there.'

He left reluctantly and hastily, while it was still too early for Isbister's crew to arrive and start preparing for the auction – an auction from which Lot 641 would now be omitted. The postman was making his rounds, but no one else was about as Harding hurried along Polwithen

Road through a chill grey morning, with the taste of Hayley's farewell kiss still lingering on his lips and the joys of the night still alive in his mind.

He spent no longer at the Mount Prospect than the few minutes he needed to pack his bag and the few more minutes it took to check out. He should have phoned Barney, of course, and told him what he was doing. But he phoned no one. Neither Barney nor Carol would be able to contact him now, since they had no way of knowing he had recovered his mobile. And that was how he wanted it. Whatever the future held, the present was a tangle of unanswered questions and conflicting obligations. He believed his life was better for what had happened between him and Hayley, but he knew it was no easier. Far from it.

Pursuing the possibility that Ann Gashry knew who had stolen the ring was partly an evasion. Harding acknow-ledged as much to himself as the train pulled out of Penzance station and began its five-hour journey to London. It meant he could be said to have done his best by Barney, if scarcely by Carol. It spared him the need, at least for a while, to confront the consequences of his actions. When he eventually returned to the Côte d'Azur, he would not be going back to the life he had lately been leading there. That was over. What would take its place was unclear. He and Hayley would have to decide that between them. They would have to discover what they really meant to each other. And then . . .

He booked himself into the Great Western Hotel for the night when the train reached Paddington, knowing it was unrealistic to think of returning to Penzance until the following day. He phoned Hayley and left her a message reporting his arrival. She had said she would make herself scarce during the auction, so he was not surprised by her absence. He had been surprised, however, to discover she possessed no mobile, but it was only one of the many oddities that made her the bewitchingly elusive person she was. Comfortably on schedule for his appointment with Ann Gashry, he headed down to the Tube.

A steely rain was falling in Dulwich, inducing a premature dusk. Harding made his way along Bedmore Road, a broad, straight thoroughfare of robust inter-war family homes, wondering which house the Foxtons had lived in, before arriving at Ann Gashry's door.

The interior felt more Victorian than twentieth-century, with lots of heavy curtains and ponderously ticking clocks. He was admitted by a small, round rubber ball of a woman and led into a fustily decorated drawing room, accompanied along the way by a mildly curious King Charles spaniel. The woman called up the stairs for Ann, made him an offer of tea, which he accepted, then vanished, her status in the household – servant, companion, relative – left unclarified. The dog followed her at a leisurely pace.

Harding had only a minute or two in which to

inspect various silver-framed photographs on the mantelpiece before Ann Gashry arrived. She looked remarkably similar to a Flapper-era woman whose picture he had just been studying, though the similarity did not extend to dress. His hostess was kitted out in twinset, pearls and calf-length skirt. A Home Counties bob and librarian glasses completed the dowdy effect, but her piercing, damson-eyed gaze hinted that he should not judge her by her appearance.

'Mr Harding.' They shook hands. 'Did Dora offer you tea?'

'Yes, she did.'

'Good. Shall we sit down?'

'Thanks.' They settled either side of the fireplace. 'And thanks for seeing me.'

'As I explained on the phone, Mr Harding, you have Hayley to thank for that. The way my brother's behaved towards her . . .' She shuddered. 'I sometimes find it hard to believe Nathan and I are the same flesh and blood, but there it is. Our parents divorced and I stayed with Father while he went with Mother, so we've had . . . different upbringings. He's a good deal younger than I am as well. But even so . . .'

'It can't be easy for you. Holding out on him about Hayley.'

'I hardly ever see him, actually. It really isn't that difficult.'

'The Foxtons lived nearby, I gather.'

'Just a few doors away. I miss them. Such nice people.'

'What happened to Kerry was . . . tragic.'

142

'Indeed. She had such . . . charisma. Her death was an irreparable loss to all who had the good fortune to know her. A tragedy, as you say. Also a mystery. And I believe it's the mystery rather than the tragedy you've come to discuss.'

'Yes.' He smiled. 'It is.'

'But I don't quite understand your interest in the matter. Hayley said you were acting on Barney Tozer's behalf.'

'I *was*.'

'And now?'

'I want to find out the truth. For everyone's sake.'

'A noble but perilous ambition.'

'Why perilous?'

'I don't know. But you have Kerry's sad example to tell you that it is.'

'It might have been an accident.'

'I don't think so. Nor does Hayley, does she?'

'Not since the burglary, no.'

'Ah, yes. The burglary.' She looked round, catching some noise from the hall. 'Here's Dora with the tea, I think.'

It was indeed Dora. Ann switched adroitly to a recommendation of the latest exhibition at Dulwich Picture Gallery while tea was delivered, lingering on the subject until Dora was long gone and they both had a cup in their hand. Then she swiftly reverted to the question of the ring.

'I'm both surprised and unsurprised by news of its theft. Surprised because such an act seems, on the face of it, inexplicable. Unsurprised because its history is riddled with similar incidents.' She sipped her tea and paused to order her thoughts, then said, 'As you shall hear.'

SIXTEEN

'My involvement in this – and hence Kerry's – began with my researches into my most, indeed only, eminent ancestor, Francis Gashry, a Member of Parliament for twenty years in the mid-eighteenth century. He was born in London in 1702. His parents, original name Gascherie, were Huguenot refugees from La Rochelle. Most of my information about him came initially from the archives of the Huguenot Association. His political career had its roots in his appointment in 1728 as secretary to Admiral Sir Charles Wager, recently retired from the sea and a member of the Admiralty Board. Wager became First Lord of the Admiralty in 1733. That made Gashry a significant person in the Admiralty without being an official member of staff, though he was later to become one – Commissioner of the Navy, no less.

'But I digress. The crux of the matter is that as Wager's right-hand man and a semi-detached civil servant,

Gashry was the natural choice to tackle a sensitive problem that presented itself in February 1736.

'As you know, nearly thirty years previously, in October 1707, Admiral Sir Clowdisley Shovell's flagship, HMS *Association*, had gone down off the Scillies, with the loss of all hands, including Shovell. Shovell's body had been washed up on the coast of St Mary's and, at some point prior to the arrival of a search party, a precious emerald-and-diamond ring had been stolen from his finger. Attempts to recover it had failed, despite a large reward offered for its return by Lady Shovell. She died in 1732, with the fate of the ring still unknown.

'In February 1736, however, that changed, with the arrival at the Admiralty of two letters passed on to Wager by Lord Godolphin, hereditary – and absentee – Governor of Scilly. The first letter was from the Reverend Richard Symons, parish priest for the islands. It reported that one of his parishioners, an aged widow, had made a dying confession to the theft of the ring, which she had kept hidden ever since but now wished to be returned to the Shovell family. Symons explained that he was arranging this through a gentleman called Godfrey Shillingstone, who was in the Scillies at the time conducting antiquarian research, with Lord Godolphin's blessing, and was due to leave shortly, bound for London, where he would deliver the ring to His Lordship, for onward transmission to the Shovells.

'This would have been excellent news, especially for Wager, who had served under Shovell as a junior officer, but for the contents of the second letter. It was from the

146

Reverend Dr Walter Borlase, Vicar of Madron, near Penzance, a living controlled, like most others in the area, by Lord Godolphin. Shillingstone had stayed with him for a few nights on his way to the Scillies and had done so again on his way back. Borlase was a magistrate and alderman as well as a priest. He must have been mortified to have to report to his patron, who had previously asked him to assist Shillingstone in any way he could, that the unfortunate antiquarian was dead and the ring missing once more.

'Borlase recounted that he and his wife had been dining out one evening shortly after Shillingstone's arrival. Their guest had opted not to join them and had remained at their home, where a burglary had occurred prior to their return. The servants had heard nothing. Shillingstone had gone outside, for whatever reason, and been knifed to death. And the ring had been stolen from a desk drawer in Borlase's study, where Shillingstone had previously lodged it for safe keeping. The lock on the drawer had been forced. Nothing else had been taken. But the ring was gone.

'This would have been quite bad enough, but, to make matters worse, Lord Godolphin had already alerted Shovell's eldest daughter, Lady Hyndford, to the recovery of the ring and was at a loss how to explain to her that it had been stolen yet again. To get himself off the hook, he argued that the whole problem was Admiralty business, which he was happy for them to deal with as they saw fit.

'Perhaps out of loyalty to his old commanding

officer, Wager took the matter on and dispatched Gashry to Penzance with instructions to investigate the circumstances of Shillingstone's murder and, if possible, recover the ring. Gashry later wrote a full report of what he accomplished, which is how I know about his mission. The report mouldered in the archives until 1964, when the Admiralty was absorbed by the Ministry of Defence and there was a clear-out of old documents. A junior civil servant called Herbert Shelkin kept a lot of stuff that would otherwise have been destroyed, including the Gashry report, which he was particularly interested in because the Shelkins, original name Schulkin, also come from Huguenot stock. He wrote an article about Huguenot MPs, mentioning Gashry, in the Huguenot Association journal about ten years ago. That's what put me on to him. He's a rather eccentric individual, afraid officialdom might yet accuse him of stealing the documents he removed and cancel his pension. But I was able to persuade him to let me read the report. And a fascinating read it was too.

'Gashry spent several weeks at Castle Horneck, Borlase's residence on the outskirts of Penzance. He questioned every member of the household and under-took extensive enquiries in the neighbourhood. He made himself a thorough nuisance. But I imagine he knew this was a task he had to take seriously. His career might have been badly compromised by failure.

'Complete success was nevertheless beyond him. He was suspicious of the servants, but could prove nothing against any of them. A pair of strangers had been seen in the area on the day of the murder who matched the description of two men seen in the nearby village of Ludgvan the day before that. This was significant, because Walter Borlase's younger brother, William, was Rector of Ludgvan. There could easily have been confusion between the two. William Borlase was an antiquarian in his own right. Shillingstone had originally intended to stay with him, but building work at the rectory meant he was put up at Castle Horneck instead. Someone, Gashry reasoned, had been looking for Shillingstone – and the ring. The burglary had been carefully planned.

'Gashry tried to establish who knew where the ring was being kept. It appeared that the only person other than Borlase and Shillingstone who *might* have known – and he denied it – was Borlase's steward, Jacob Tozer. Yes, the Tozers enter the story at this point. They enter, never to leave.

'Was there a connection between Tozer and the two strangers? If so, what was their joint motive for stealing the ring? It had to be a powerful one, given their willingness to murder Shillingstone in the process. Yet the example of the widow on St Mary's showed that the ring was too notorious to be easily sold for profit. Why did they want it, then?

'At some point, Gashry hit on a possible answer. Perhaps the theft of the ring was camouflage. Perhaps the murder of Shillingstone was the real object of the exercise. But, again, why? What had Shillingstone done?

He had returned from the Scillies with several crates of geological specimens, which were still in an outhouse at Castle Horneck. He had been awaiting the next sailing of the tin-ship for London to transport them to the capital. Borlase had paid the specimens no heed before *or* after Shillingstone's death, so his assertion that only the ring had been stolen was questionable, given his uncertainty over how many crates there had originally been, not to mention what they actually contained. Those remaining were opened and found to hold un-remarkable mineral samples. Undaunted, Gashry formed the hypothesis that Shillingstone had been murdered after interrupting the theft from the outhouse of one or more of the crates in which something else altogether was being transported. The theft of the ring had then been staged to distract attention from the true purpose of the crime.

'Jacob Tozer became Gashry's prime suspect. He knew when the Borlases would be out, he could be presumed to have discovered where the ring was being kept, and he also had a key to the outhouse where Shillingstone had stored his crates. But Borlase had complete confidence in his steward and Gashry could unearth nothing in the way of solid evidence against him, despite a snap search of the cottage adjoining Castle Horneck where Tozer lived with his wife and children. Tozer certainly didn't crack under the pressure. Gashry described him as "infuriatingly imperturbable".

'However tireless his investigations may have been, Gashry was no closer to recovering the ring. He decided to travel to the Scillies in order to find out more about the aged widow and Shillingstone's antiquarian researches.

'His first objective, after what seems to have been a nightmarish crossing, was soon accomplished. The Reverend Symons informed him that the woman's name was Mary Mumford. She was a native of St Mary's and had lived all her life in a cottage close to the bay where Admiral Shovell's body had been washed up.

'Gashry's achievements in respect of his second objective are, sadly, a mystery. According to Shelkin, several pages were missing from the report when he came across it and he was never able to find them. The report resumes with Gashry back in Penzance, the search for the ring abandoned and preparations for his masterstroke under way. Based on descriptions of the ring provided by Symons and Borlase, he proposed to have a replica made and presented to Lady Hyndford as the real thing. She'd only been a child at the time of her father's death and had no reason to challenge its authenticity. A line would be drawn under an affair Gashry described as "toilsome and intractable".

'So you see, the ring stolen from Heartsease almost certainly *is* the genuine article, kept hidden by Jacob Tozer after his theft of it from Castle Horneck and passed on as an heirloom in his family, to be squabbled over by later generations.

'As for who stole it from Heartsease, only one name springs to mind. After I'd told Kerry all this, she asked me to arrange for her to meet Herbert Shelkin. In his retirement, he runs a dubious kind of genealogical research agency, in Lincoln. I accompanied her when she went up there to speak to him. What soon became obvious under Kerry's gentle grilling was what I should have guessed at the outset. He had the missing pages from the Gashry report all along. He didn't want anyone to know what they contained. He was keeping one secret back for his very own.

'Eerily, in view of what was to happen later, he warned Kerry not to enquire into the matter further. He said it was dangerous ground – his exact words: *dangerous ground*. He declined to explain. Indeed, he declined to say very much at all, at least of substance. The man's happy enough to blather irrelevantly for hours at a stretch. What's beyond dispute is that he knows the true history of Tozer's ring, as very few others do. As soon as Hayley told me about the burglary, I thought of Shelkin. Why he should have stolen it I don't know. But there'll have been a reason. And he'll have thought it a good one.'

SEVENTEEN

'I suppose you'll go to Lincoln now and see what you can learn from Herbert Shelkin,' said Ann Gashry, eyeing Harding over the rim of her teacup. 'If you're set on finding out what's behind all this, it's the obvious thing to do.'

'Yes,' said Harding thoughtfully. 'It is.'

'But I must warn you that extracting information from that man – information you want, at any rate, as opposed to whatever double-talk he's in the mood to serve up – is no easy matter.'

'Think it'd be a waste of time to try?'

'I wouldn't go that far. Kerry and I agreed after our meeting with him that it was clear he had the missing pages. She swore she'd find a way to get a look at them and maybe she succeeded. Our trip to Lincoln was actually the last time I saw her. It's possible she had another crack at Shelkin before going to the Scillies. Probable, I'd have to say, given how determined she always was to accomplish whatever she set her sights on. I knew her from childhood as a very strong-willed person.'

'Was she born here in Dulwich?'

'Yes. Her father worked for British Telecom. He and his wife were a very sedate couple. Kerry was anything but, of course. It was always a pleasure to see her when she whirled back, from wherever her glamorous career had taken her, to visit them.'

'And to visit you, no doubt.'

'Well, the connection with Nathan meant we kept in touch, I'm glad to say. Of course . . .' Ann set her cup in its saucer and drew herself up, as if in preparation for some important announcement. 'Nothing good came of Kerry's interest in Shelkin's secrets, Mr Harding. It destroyed her and, indirectly, her parents. It turned Nathan into . . . what he became. And it caused Hayley a lot of suffering. Admiral Shovell's ring is, in the final analysis, just an un-remarkable piece of Georgian jewellery. Bearing that in mind, my advice to you is to go home and forget all this.' She smiled. 'But you won't, of course.'

When Harding left, he had in his pocket not merely a note of the address and phone number of the Herbert Shelkin Genealogical Research and Advice Service, but the one-man band's actual business card. 'I won't be needing it,' Ann Gashry had coolly remarked. The readiness with which she had handed it over encouraged Harding to chance his arm in another direction, though he instantly regretted it.

'Does your brother live far from here, Miss Gashry?'

Her expression grew glacial. 'Near or far shouldn't concern you, Mr Harding. I advise you not to contact Herbert Shelkin. But I *forbid* you to contact Nathan. Hayley's free of him and must remain so.'

'Of course. I only—'

'Thought of taking a look at what kind of a man he is?'

'Well . . .'

'A poor sort. Take my word for it.'

Harding had never been to Dulwich before. Nor even to Lincoln. Gazing through the drizzle-blurred lamplight along the cloned house frontages of Bedmore Road, he detected no cross-overs between his life and Kerry's, just as he had detected none between his life and Hayley's. On whatever level he had met either of them before, it hardly seemed to lie in the world of the everyday. Still regretting his parting question to Ann Gashry, he headed for the station.

On the train back to Charing Cross, he called Hayley again. But she had not yet returned to Heartsease. Nor had she left a message on his phone, as he had hoped she would. He thought of calling Barney and/or Carol, but soon thought again. He still had no clear idea of what he should say to either of them. Impulsively, he tried Shelkin's number, but got only an answering machine and a wheezily enunciated message from the man himself. *'Leave your name and number and I'll be sure to get back to you.'* Harding left neither. He needed to think before committing himself where Shelkin was concerned. He needed to think about everything.

Before Harding had done much of that, Hayley called. He was on the concourse at Charing Cross at the time, wondering what he should do with an empty evening in London. He did not realize it was her at first, the call originating from a mobile number he did not recognize.

'It's me, Tim.'

'It's good to hear your voice, Hayley. I was beginning to worry about you.'

'No need. I'd have rung earlier, but I didn't want to interrupt when you were with Ann. I've just spoken to her.'

'Does that mean you know about Herbert Shelkin?'

'Yes. Are you going up to Lincoln to see him?'

'Looks like it. No sense giving up halfway on this, I suppose. Much as I'd like to.'

'You don't mean that.'

'Part of me would like nothing better than to get on the sleeper tonight back to Penzance – and you.'

'All of me would like that, Tim. But . . .'

'Exactly. Duty – of a sort – calls. Now, what's with the mobile? I thought you didn't have one.'

'It's Jeanette's. She's in my judo class. I was moaning to her about being stuck at Heartsease with the auction going on around me and she suggested I stay with her tonight. She has a cottage in Mousehole. I'm there now. Sounds like I could be staying tomorrow night as well,

156

if you're going up to Lincoln. I don't really want to be alone at Heartsease. Since the burglary . . .'

'Do you know how the auction went?'

'No. But it'll have gone smoothly, I'm sure. Which means they'll already have started stripping the place.'

'I'll be back on Thursday whatever happens, Hayley. Even if I can't see Shelkin tomorrow. That's a promise. To you *and* me.'

'OK. Thursday.'

'Did Ann mention . . .' Harding hesitated. But he knew it had to be said. 'Did she mention I asked her . . . where Nathan lives?'

'Yes,' Hayley answered softly. 'She did.'

'I don't know why I asked. It was stupid. I wish I hadn't. She was never going to tell me anyway. And the truth is . . . I don't really want to know.'

'Yes, you do. But . . . I know what you mean.'

'I won't ask again.'

'Good. And, Tim . . .'

'Yes?'

'Thanks for telling me.'

'That's OK. I don't want there to be any . . . secrets between us.'

'There aren't. There are just . . . things we haven't got round to telling each other yet. But we will. Starting on Thursday.'

'Yes. We will.'

'I'll call you this time tomorrow.'

'OK.'

''Bye, Tim.'

''Bye.'

'Love you.'

He stood where he was, asking himself, amidst the babel of passing voices, whether she had really spoken those last words. He had echoed them, too late for her to hear. And now he repeated them under his breath, amazed by the thought that they might actually be true.

He consumed a pizza supper to stave off hunger, sat through a film at one of the Leicester Square cinemas to pass some time, then headed back to his hotel.

He could have waited till morning before trying Shelkin again, but something prompted him to leave a message for him that night. To his astonishment, however, the answerphone had been switched off. And the call was taken by a living, heavily breathing human.

'Herbert Shelkin.'

'Mr Shelkin. Good evening. I . . . I'm surprised to get you. I was going to . . . leave a message.'

'I work a good deal at night. Who am I speaking to?'

'My name's Harding. I was hoping to . . . consult you.'

'On a genealogical matter?'

'Yes.'

'Concerning your own family?'

'Not as such, no. It's . . . complicated.'

'That's in the nature of the subject, Mr Harding. I pride myself on being an expert in complexity – and its resolution.'

'Right. Good. Well, could I . . . come and see you?'

'Certainly. I offer a free half-hour of advice before any fees arise.'

'Fine. How about . . . tomorrow?'

'That should present no problem. Are you coming far?'

'From London.'

'Then we'd better make it the afternoon. Would two thirty suit?'

'Yes. I should think so.'

'And you have the address of my office?'

'Yes. It's . . . on your card.'

'Ah. My card. Did someone recommend me, Mr Harding?'

'Yes. I'll, er . . . explain when we meet.'

'Excellent. I'll look forward to that.'

EIGHTEEN

Lincoln was a step further back into winter compared even with London. A pall of gunmetal-grey hung over the city and an east wind chilled Harding to the bone as he climbed the hill towards the cathedral. A guilty conscience about his failure to contact Barney or Carol, especially Carol, was also gnawing at him, but there was little he could do to ward that off either. He had phoned Luc before leaving London to tell him his return would be delayed, news the young man had greeted with his customary sangfroid, undented even by an instruction to deny he had heard from Harding if questioned by Barney. Luc's casual *'D'accord, d'accord'* had made such tactics sound so trivial and reasonable that Harding could almost believe they were. But only almost.

Harding had time for a sandwich and a pint in a pub before his appointment. The Herbert Shelkin Genealogical Research and Advice Service was housed in a first-floor room above a gift shop. The threadbare stair carpet and damp-stained wallpaper suggested running costs were kept to a minimum. The office itself was chilly, cramped and cheaply furnished, the air laden with stale cigarette smoke.

Shelkin was a concavely thin man of seventy or so, his skin matching the grey of his shabby clothes and improbably luxuriant hair. His features had a blood-hound look to them, thanks to oversized nose and ears and frown-lines heavily entrenched around his mouth. Even his eyes were those of a lugubrious tracker. He was sitting at his desk, tapping at a computer, when Harding entered, though stacks of files and papers ranged across the floor and a phalanx of filing cabinets along one wall suggested he made as much use of old technology as new.

'Mr Harding,' he said, removing a nearly expired cigarette from between his lips as his gaze swung up from the screen. 'Come in.' He stubbed out the cigarette in a butt-filled ashtray and half rose. They shook hands. 'Take a seat.'

Harding sat down on the rickety chair facing Shelkin across the desk. 'Thanks for seeing me,' he said, with what he hoped was an ingratiating smile.

'No problem. I do most of my business through this thing these days.' Shelkin waggled a bony finger at the computer. 'Personal consultations have become a rarity.'

'Well, thanks anyway.'

'Now, you said you aren't enquiring about your own family.'

'Correct.'

'Pity. Harding's an Old English name. Literally, son of a herdsman. Solid yeoman stock. You wouldn't have Huguenot blood on your mother's side, would you?'

'I'm afraid not.'

'Only, Huguenot lineage is my speciality.'

'So I believe.'

'Ah yes. You also said I came recommended. Who by, may I ask?'

'A friend of a friend. The thing is—'

'Ann Gashry.' Herbert Shelkin smiled thinly in the silence that followed, then reached for the pack of cigarettes at his elbow, flipped up the lid and proffered it to Harding. 'Smoke?'

'No, thanks,' Harding murmured, as his mind raced to cope with the realization that somehow Shelkin had rumbled him.

'I was lucky enough to get out of the Civil Service before the healthier-than-thou brigade forced the likes of me to skulk on the street.' Shelkin lit up and waved the match until it was extinguished, then snapped it between his fingers and dropped it into the ashtray. 'I find tobacco helps me think. People don't travel hundreds of miles to see me, Mr Harding. I'm good at what I do. It's given me a purpose in life since I retired. But I don't have clients flocking to my door from all corners of the country. It just doesn't happen. So, your visit has to have some deeper purpose than an idle interest in your family tree.'

'Yes, well . . . it does.'

'Indeed. And since it comes in the same week as the theft of an emerald-and-diamond ring from the late Gabriel Tozer's house in Penzance, I thought I knew what it was even before you arrived. Your reaction to my mention of Miss Gashry's name confirms it.'

'How did you . . . hear about the theft?'

'There are no secrets in cyberspace. Isbisters' catalogues are accessible on-line. The abrupt withdrawal of Lot 641 from yesterday's auction didn't go unnoticed.'

'I can't believe they broadcast the reason for its withdrawal over the Internet.'

'They didn't. But I have my sources. One of them tells me a man called Harding was due to buy the ring on behalf of Barney Tozer, Gabriel's expatriate nephew.'

Harding could not suppress a sigh of resignation. The game appeared to be up. 'I see.'

'I'm glad you do.'

'Who is your source?'

'That would be telling. And I think it's your turn to tell. Why are you here?'

'I'm trying to find out why the ring was stolen, Mr Shelkin. And who stole it.'

'Did Miss Gashry accuse me, perhaps?'

'Certainly not.'

'You're a poor liar, Mr Harding.' Shelkin drew deeply on his cigarette. 'But that's no bad thing. Let me see if I've understood your predicament. You're in hock in some way to Barney Tozer.'

'No.'

'You owe him a favour, then. Something of the sort, at any rate. The favour was to represent him at the auction and buy the ring. But the ring's been taken from under your nose. You've heard the sad tale of Kerry Foxton and you think there's a connection. You've gone to see Ann Gashry and she's told you . . . what? All about her ancestor, Francis Gashry?'

'Yes.'

'All she knows, anyway. I should never have shown her the report. She convinced Miss Foxton I had the missing pages. Perhaps she's convinced you too. It isn't true. They were missing when I found the document, forty-two years ago, lying neglected in the Admiralty archives. My curiosity was aroused at once. There's nothing like a gap in the record to whet the appetite.'

'And has your curiosity ever been satisfied?'

'No. It hasn't.'

'Who could've taken the pages?'

'Anyone with access to the archives, in theory. But it seems more likely to me that the pages were removed when the report was submitted – or shortly after.'

'Who'd have done that?'

'The man it was submitted to is the most obvious candidate. Sir Charles Wager, First Lord of the Admiralty. A Cornishman, as it happens. Born West Looe, 1666. Acquired a large estate nearby in later life, Kilmenath, bought with some of the colossal fortune he obtained in prize-money from the capture of a Spanish treasure fleet. Also the local MP. A man of substance. A man of few words. A man of mystery.'

'Why should he have removed part of the report?'

'Who can say? But Francis Gashry's career started to take off straight after his mission to Penzance. He was Assistant Secretary to the Admiralty within two years. Within five he was Commissioner of the Navy, MP for *East* Looe and husband of the wealthy young widow of Wager's nephew, through whom he ultimately inherited Kilmenath. Not bad for the son of a penniless Huguenot refugee. Not bad at all.'

'What are you suggesting?'

'Wager all but adopted Gashry as his son and heir, buying his lifelong loyalty – and silence, on whatever subject it was required.'

'Why should it be required where Godfrey Shillingstone's Scillonian researches were concerned?'

'I don't know, Mr Harding. But if Gashry's theory was correct, the theft of the ring from Castle Horneck was intended to disguise the theft of something else. Something Shillingstone had brought back with him from the Scillies. Something more than geological specimens.'

'What could that have been?'

'I can only repeat myself: I don't know. As I told Miss Gashry and Miss Foxton when they came to see me seven years ago.'

'But that's not all you told them. You warned Kerry off. You described the subject as "dangerous ground".'

'Did I?' Shelkin frowned. 'I don't recall.'

'Come off it. You recall everything.' Harding leant across the desk. He sensed he might be able to gain the upper hand after all. 'What makes it dangerous ground?'

Shelkin's lips tightened into a pout. He played for time by flicking ash off his cigarette and taking a long drag on it. Then his expression softened appeasingly. 'There's no danger that I know of. My warning was a clumsy attempt to discourage Miss Foxton from prying further into a puzzle I still had high hopes of solving. She was a journalist. I didn't want all my painstaking work scooped by her.' He shrugged. 'It's a bitter irony that she subsequently died in circumstances Miss Gashry interpreted as proving there was substance to my warning. But there wasn't. How could there be?'

'You tell me.'

'It can't possibly matter to anyone today what Shillingstone was up to, Mr Harding. It's interesting, but inconsequential. Historically speaking, it's a byway of a byway.'

'How come your "painstaking work" has never got to the bottom of it?'

'Simple lack of evidence. I've explored every avenue. They've all turned out to be cul-de-sacs.'

'Tell me about some of them.'

'To what purpose?'

'To convince me they really were cul-de-sacs.'

'Good God, this is intolerable.' Shelkin angrily stubbed out his cigarette, the modest effort of which sparked a coughing fit. He braced himself against the edge of the desk as the fit slowly subsided, along with

166

his indignation. There was a long pause as he recovered his breath. Then he started speaking quickly, in a clipped, matter-of-fact tone. 'Shillingstone's exchange of letters with Lord Godolphin, in which he's given carte blanche to delve where he likes on the Scillies, yields no hint of what he hoped to find there. The second earl was a notoriously incurious man and seems to have granted permission largely because of Shillingstone's persistence. Shillingstone's papers were donated after his death to his old college at Oxford, but were destroyed in a clear-out in the nineteenth century. William Borlase's *Cornish Antiquities*, published 1754, refers to Shillingstone's work on the Scillies as "unprofitable" without elaboration. And my extensive explorations of later generations of the Shillingstone family have turned up precisely nothing. Need I say more?'

'Is there any more to be said?'

'Oh, one thing, yes.' Shelkin sighed heavily. 'You may as well know. I sense you won't be satisfied until you do. Miss Foxton came back to see me, on her own, a few days after her visit with Miss Gashry. She demanded to know what justification I had for warning her off. I was in no position to give her a satisfactory answer, of course. The post had just arrived that morning and was lying here on my desk, opened but unread. I offered her a cup of coffee in an attempt to lighten the mood. I keep the kettle over there.' He gestured towards the last filing cabinet in the row, on which stood a tray bearing cups and saucers, coffee jar and milk bottle, next to an electric kettle. 'While my back was turned, she stole one of the letters. It must have caught her eye while we were talking. And she must have moved very quickly.' He sighed. 'Never trust a journalist.'

'How do you know she stole it?'

'Her father returned it to me. He'd found it amongst her possessions. He naturally had no idea how she'd come by it. Borrowed, he assumed. But no. It was stolen. And that morning when she came here has to have been when it happened.'

'Who was the letter from?'

'A man called Norman Buller, whose ancestor the Reverend William Buller was executor of Francis Gashry's will. Mr Buller had come across my article in the Huguenot Association journal mentioning Gashry while researching his family tree on the Internet. The Reverend Buller's brother John was joint MP with Gashry for East Looe – multi-seat constituencies were common in those days – and hence a close political associate. Mr Buller had a cache of papers left by Gashry at his death and preserved by his executor. He wondered if I wanted to look through them. Obviously, I did. They might conceivably have included a complete version of Gashry's report on the Shillingstone affair. There would have been two copies, one for Wager's personal attention, one for the file. Wager's copy could plausibly have wound up in Gashry's possession. So, I hastened to Mr Buller's door. Miss Foxton had been there before me, as I feared, passing herself off as my assistant. The papers were humdrum stuff: letters from John Buller about constituency management and details of Gashry's subscriptions to government loans. Hardly anything related to his Admiralty career. There were a great many documents, however, and Mr Buller didn't claim to have read all of them. From which followed, of course, the dismal conclusion that he couldn't be sure Miss Foxton hadn't removed any during her visit. She'd been left alone with the papers for an hour or more, apparently. He insisted he'd have noticed any attempt on her part to remove some of them, but I wasn't convinced.'

'If she *had* taken something, surely it would have been discovered amongst her possessions, like Buller's letter.'

'My thought exactly. But her father insisted there was nothing else and his distressed condition discouraged me from persisting with my enquiries. I did contact an amateur historian who'd been with Miss Foxton at the time of her accident, but—'

'John Metherell.'

'Yes. You know him?'

'I've met him. He's writing a book about the wreck of the *Association*.'

'So I believe. Anyway, he couldn't help me. Miss Foxton's discussions with him had been limited to the *Association* story. The friend Miss Foxton had been staying with on St Mary's said Mr Foxton had taken everything of his daughter's away with him. It was a dead end.'

'You gave up?'

'I had to. Just as you'll have to give up trying to find

the Tozers' ring. Eventually.' Shelkin lit another cigarette and inhaled cautiously. 'When the time comes, you'll know. Believe me. I speak from experience.'

NINETEEN

'I often attend evensong at the cathedral, Mr Harding. I did so on Sunday. And I spoke to the dean afterwards. So, I think you'll agree I have an unimpeachable alibi for the night of the burglary at Heartsease. Even supposing I need one, which, in the absence of any credible motive, I don't suppose I do, do you?'

Shelkin's parting shot had hit home. Standing on the platform at Newark North Gate station waiting for the connecting train to London late that cold afternoon, Harding asked himself what, if anything, he had gained from his trip to Lincoln. Considering he had not really wanted to go in the first place, the answer was dismally little. He did not believe Shelkin had either the Tozers' ring or the missing pages from the Gashry report. Kerry Foxton *might* have stolen a complete copy of the report from Norman Buller, but it was much more likely she had not. Besides, as Shelkin had said, the contents of those missing pages could hardly matter now, all of two hundred and seventy years later.

Hayley rang as the train was nearing King's Cross. And Harding made no effort to conceal his pleasure at hearing from her.

'I'm going to come down on the sleeper, even if there isn't a berth. Sitting up all night's no hardship if I get to see you in the morning.'

'I'll find out what time it gets in.'

'Early would be my guess. You don't have to meet me at the station.'

'But I want to. So, that's settled. Learn anything useful in Lincoln?'

'Not really.'

'No fresh leads?'

'None I need to follow. Which is a blessing, really. It means I can stop dashing around the country on Barney's behalf and start . . .' He hesitated, unsure how to continue, for the simple reason that he had no clear idea of what was to happen next in his life.

'Start what, Tim?'

'We're going to have to talk about that.'

'Yes. I guess we are. And you know something? I'm looking forward to it.'

'So am I.'

'Until tomorrow, then.'

'Yes. Until tomorrow.'

''Bye.'

''Bye, Hayley.'

'Love you.'

'Love you too.'

The sleeper rolled out of Paddington just before midnight. There had turned out to be plenty of vacant berths and Harding had a cabin to himself. To his subsequent surprise, given the many problems he was beset by and the many more likely to be created by allowing himself to fall in love with Hayley, he slept like a baby.

It was a grey, damp morning in Penzance. Harding could not see Hayley waiting for him on the platform as he left the train, but he was at first undismayed. She might easily have overslept. He checked the station buffet and wandered up and down by the taxi rank. The other sleeper passengers had mostly dispersed by now. Anxiety began to creep over him.

Then a woman called his name. '*Tim*.' She was moving towards him from the direction of the car park. Harding did not recognize her. She was slimly built, with straw-coloured hair tied in a ponytail and an open, smiling expression. She wore a raincoat over the sort of uniform suit worn by staff in a bank or building society. 'You're Tim Harding?' she called as he drew closer.

'Yes.'

'Jeanette Taylor. Hayley asked me to meet you.'

'Ah. Right.' He smiled. 'She's been staying with you, hasn't she?'

Jeanette did not return the smile. She looked puzzled.

'No,' she said, with a tight little shake of the head.

'You're in her judo class.'

'Yes. But she hasn't been staying with me.'

'She phoned me . . . from your cottage in Mousehole . . . on Tuesday evening.'

'No, no. I drove her up to Newquay Airport on Tuesday. By the evening, she'd have been on her way to Spain.'

'*Spain?*'

'On holiday. A spur-of-the-moment thing, she said. She asked me to meet you here this morning and apologize for letting you down. You were hoping to see her while you're here, apparently.'

'*Hoping to see her?*' Harding repeated incredulously.

'She asked me to give you this.'

Jeanette handed him an envelope. His name was written on it in broad capitals. *TIM*. He tore it open and stared in stupefaction at the note inside. *Sorry. Truly. H*. It occurred to him, with hopeless irrelevance, that strictly speaking he could not be sure she had written it. He had never seen her handwriting. But Jeanette was not lying. He felt leadenly certain of that – if of very little else.

'Can I give you a lift somewhere?' came the chirpy enquiry.

He asked to be taken to Heartsease, pointless though he knew returning there was. The house was silent and empty. Shortly after Jeanette had driven away, leaving him staring in at the blank basement windows, an

Isbister & Sons van pulled up. Four men had arrived to finish the clear-out. They knew nothing about Hayley and suggested he phone their boss, Clive Isbister, which he did – to little purpose.

'Good morning, Mr Harding. I'm afraid I've heard nothing from the police about the ring. I must say, even though it wasn't part of the auction, I was surprised you didn't—'

'Forget the ring. I'm looking for Hayley.'

'Miss Winter? I saw her briefly on Tuesday morning. She said she was going away for a while. Can't say I blame her, after the burglary.'

'Did she say when she was coming back?'

'No. But I don't suppose she'll be gone long. At least, that's the impression I got. Why?'

'Never mind.'

She must have regretted letting him stay the night. She must have decided to end their relationship before it had properly begun. But why, in that case, had she phoned him in London, twice? Why had she encouraged him to believe she was waiting for him in Penzance when, in reality, she had fled to Spain? It made no sense. To change her mind was one thing. To deceive him like this was something else again. And it did not fit with his reading of her character. It did not fit with anything.

He walked aimlessly towards the sea after leaving Heartsease and found his way to the churchyard at the bottom of Chapel Street, where he sat on a bench among the graves and gazed out despairingly into the grey, cold, unconsoling ocean.

He had to find her. He had to persuade her that it could not end like this. But how? According to Jeanette, she had been tense and largely silent during the drive to Newquay and had conspicuously failed to say where in Spain she was going. She had been catching a plane to Gatwick. Her destination beyond that was anyone's guess.

When Harding's phone rang, he thought for a crazily hopeful moment that it was Hayley, calling to say it had all been a terrible misunderstanding. But it was not Hayley. Instead, he heard the smooth, familiar voice of Starburst International's finance director.

'Tim? This is Tony Whybrow.'

'Tony?'

'Where are you?'

'Penzance.'

'Really? According to the Mount Prospect, you checked out two days ago. Trying this number was a last throw of the dice. Barney said you'd lost your phone. But he might have got confused. He's not thinking straight at the moment.'

'Isn't he?'

'Anyway, thank God I've got you. You have to come back, Tim. Right away.'

'Come back?'

'I guess it'll take most of the day for you to get up to Heathrow from Penzance. But it can't be helped. I'll book you on the eight p.m. flight to Nice and meet you when you arrive.'

'What are you talking about?'

'We need your help to sort this mess out. If it *can* be sorted.'

'What mess?'

'Sorry. Getting ahead of myself.' He paused. 'There was a break-in at the penthouse last night. Carol was alone at the time. An intruder threatened her with a knife.'

'My God.'

'Don't worry. Carol's unharmed. Physically, at any rate. Fortunately, she was able to talk the intruder into putting the knife down and leaving peacefully. She's badly shaken up, though, as you can imagine. And Barney's spitting blood. He wanted to call the police in immediately. But I recommended we get your input first.'

'My . . . input? What—'

'The intruder was Hayley Winter, Tim. And you and I have a great deal to talk about.'

TWENTY

It was eleven o'clock local time when Harding's plane touched down in Nice. He retained little awareness of the journey that had filled most of the day. The train to Reading; the coach to the airport; the long wait in the terminal; the evening flight across France; they had been a blur somewhere at the margin of his thoughts, barely impinging on his consciousness.

Whybrow had declined to elaborate on his stark report of Hayley's mercifully aborted attack on Carol. *'I'll give you all the details when we meet.'* That had left Harding prey to as many dreadful speculations as his imagination could conjure up. Yet none was more dreadful in its way than the frightening realization that he had understood nothing as it truly was. He had been deceived. He had been manipulated. He had been made a fool of. And just how big a one he suspected Whybrow was going to explain with unsparing clarity.

* * *

Whybrow was waiting outside the customs hall. He appeared, as ever, cool and elegant, dressed in a dark suit and open-neck shirt. He was carrying a slim brief-case in one hand and a rolled copy of the *Financial Times* in the other. He had the fluent carriage of an athlete and the disconcertingly direct gaze of a powerful thinker. He kept his thinning hair bristlingly short and his chin baby-smooth. For all his undemonstrative, quietly spoken manner, there was something narcissistic about him, something faintly scornful of others. Whenever he had made up a drinking threesome with Harding and Tozer, he had always finished the soberest of them by some way, with the least about him-self revealed. Happiness was control in the world of Tony Whybrow.

'Bad business, Tim,' he said, tapping Harding on the elbow with his newspaper in greeting. 'You don't look so good.'

'I don't feel so good. Think I'll feel any better when you've told me exactly what happened?'

'No point pretending that's likely.'

'Are we going to Barney's now?'

'No. It's late. And he's been hitting the bottle. Go and see them in the morning. He'll be more rational then. And Carol will be calmer. I hope.'

'It must have been a terrible experience for her.'

'Yes. It was.' Whybrow glanced in the direction of the exit leading to the car park. 'I'll drive you to your place. We can talk on the way.'

'OK. But—'

'Let's go, shall we?' Whybrow cut him off, with a hint of impatience. There was much to say. But the time to say it had not quite come yet.

'You're sure it was Hayley who did this, aren't you, Tony?' Harding asked as they settled into Whybrow's Lexus. 'I can't really believe she's capable of threatening anyone with a knife.'

'How well do you think you know her?' The car started almost inaudibly and glided out of its parking bay with little apparent intervention from its driver. 'You can't have met her more than a couple of times.'

'I haven't,' said Harding defensively. 'Even so . . .'

'Here's the deal, Tim. I only learnt the identity of Gabriel Tozer's housekeeper after Barney had talked you into going to Penzance on his behalf. I wouldn't have allowed the situation to develop as it has if I'd known sooner. There were simply too many risk factors. As events have resoundingly confirmed.'

'Hold on. Are you saying you knew Hayley . . . before?'

'Knew of her, yes. I'll come to that later. Barney and I are in the midst of some particularly delicate negotiations at present. I may have taken my eye off the ball where his family problems are concerned. He certainly did so himself. Hence the impossible position he put you in.'

'Why was it . . . impossible?'

'Because you didn't know all or even most of the factors that were in play. Before I explain them, though,

I'd better tell you how last night unfolded.' They were clear of the car park now, heading for the main road into Nice. 'Hayley rang the penthouse around seven. The phone had rung a couple of times before and Carol had answered, but the caller had hung up. Only when Barney answered did she speak. She introduced herself and confessed straight out to stealing the ring from Heartsease.'

'She said that?'

'She did. She also said she regretted what she'd done and was willing to hand the ring over to Barney and explain why she'd stolen it. She wanted him to meet her in Menton later that evening. He agreed. It was a nicely judged decoy. She said she'd be waiting for him on the promenade near the casino at eight o'clock. He set off, telling Carol he was meeting me to discuss some business emergency. Perhaps if he'd told her the truth, she'd have been more on her guard, though I doubt it. Anyway, while Barney was in Menton, stooging around the sea front as eight o'clock came and went, Hayley was in Monaco. She'd been there when he left, hiding in the shadows near the back gate. As he drove out and the shutter-door came down, she'd wedged a bar under it to stop it closing. Barney's not the type to wait to make sure the door's completely shut every time he leaves. You know that. Well, it looks like she did too.'

'So, she got in by rolling under the door?'

'Yes. It wasn't difficult. And it was even less difficult to get inside the apartment. The patio doors were unlocked. I expect she had some other way in planned,

181

but that made it real easy for her. She crept into the kitchen and took a knife from the block on the work-top. Carol was in the lounge watching television. She never heard a thing. Suddenly, there was a knife at her throat. She thought she was going to be killed. There and then.'

'Poor Carol.' Harding shut his eyes for a second, imagining how she must have felt in the moment when she realized her life might be about to end. 'What did she do?'

'She was paralysed by fear. Probably just as well. But she wasn't struck dumb. So, she talked, pleading for her life. At first, she didn't know who her attacker was. Hayley stayed behind her. Carol reasoned with her as best she could. It was a monologue, apparently. Hayley never said a word. Then, suddenly, she threw down the knife and fled. It was only at that point that Carol recognized her.'

'But she's never met her before.' It was a feeble objection. Hayley's resemblance to Kerry Foxton made some form of recognition inevitable. As Whybrow emphasized in his own way by ignoring the point.

'Carol was in shock. She can't properly account for what she did afterwards. Instead of calling the police, she locked herself in the bathroom, fearing Hayley might come back. She didn't, of course. She was prob-ably long gone by then. Meanwhile, Barney was starting to worry. He phoned home and got no answer. Then he worried some more. He didn't want to head back in case Hayley was simply late for their appointment. So, he phoned me and asked me to call round. Carol was still in the bathroom when I got there. I had to do quite a lot of talking just to get her to open the door. I'd searched the apartment by then and was certain no one was hiding anywhere. The bar was still propping open the shutter-door when I arrived, by the way. Hayley hadn't bothered to remove it. Or maybe she'd been too distraught at her loss of nerve to think of it.'

'How do you know she lost her nerve? Maybe she'd only ever intended to threaten Carol. Though why I can't imagine.'

'She left something in the kitchen that convinced me she was planning to murder Carol. A pocket recorder, with a tape in it. I listened to the tape while waiting for Barney to drive back from Menton. I'd phoned him, but not the police. I don't believe in acting hastily. And this is a good example of why that's always a sensible policy.' Whybrow pressed a button on the dashboard. The radio and hi-fi panel lit up. A tape engaged in the player. And Carol's voice echoed in the car.

Barney's playing golf, so I thought I'd give you a call. What are you doing? Treating Humph to a cream tea? It'd be wasted on him. He doesn't appreciate the good things in life. But I do. Our afternoons together are very good, Tim, very, very good. Shall we—

Whybrow's finger hit the off switch. Silence reclaimed the foreground. Harding could not suppress a groan as he gazed out through the passenger window into the

183

blackness of the Mediterranean. 'That's quite enough of that, I think, don't you?' said Whybrow softly.

'Has Barney heard this?'

'Not yet. And there's no reason why he needs to. As long as we can agree how to handle the ... ramifications.'

'What exactly do you mean?'

'I believe Hayley's plan was to frame Barney for Carol's murder, leaving the tape to be found by the police when they responded to the anonymous 112 emergency call she obviously intended to make after killing Carol. She'd arranged for him to have no alibi that would bear examination, whereas I assume she had one standing by for herself. The tape would have supplied the perfect motive. It could plausibly have been obtained from your phone by some private detective, employed by Barney to check up on Carol. It was a good plan. We can only be grateful she couldn't bring herself to go through with it. Barney's denials wouldn't have counted for much. I don't know how I could have got him off. The beauty of it, from Hayley's point of view, was that Barney would have understood very clearly who'd framed him and why, without being able to do a damn thing about it, except tell the truth and have it universally disbelieved. Sweet revenge, in Hayley's mind. Better than murdering Barney, she'd have murdered his beloved wife and ensured he'd spend the rest of his life in prison contemplating that fact.'

'Barney might have understood. But I don't. What would Hayley have been avenging?'

'Her sister's murder – as she sees it.'

'What?'

'Her name isn't Winter, Tim. It's Foxton. She's Kerry Foxton's twin sister.'

TWENTY-ONE

'I wasn't with the company back in the summer of 1999,' said Whybrow. His soft, sussurant voice was the only sound that reached Harding through the dark blanket of the night. 'If I had been, things might have been very different.' They were parked in a lay-by just round the headland from Nice, no more than a couple of kilometres from Villefranche. 'I think I'd have questioned Kerry Foxton's credentials – and her motives – sooner and more searchingly than I gather Ray Trathen did. But that wouldn't necessarily have made any difference. There's no legislating for accidents. And an accident is what happened to her on that diving expedition.

'I made enquiries about the Foxton family at the time of the inquest. It seemed prudent to establish whether there were any surprises in store for Barney. That's when I first heard about Hayley. Barney really should have told me sooner. He'd heard from Carol, of course. Kerry had confided in her that she had a twin who'd suffered from depression since her mid-teens. Her parents were embarrassed by the contrast between the two girls and never mentioned Hayley. After a spell in hospital and a sequence of recoveries and relapses, Hayley cut herself off, living alone in Birmingham, where she held down various temporary jobs when she was well enough to work. Kerry kept spasmodically in touch with her, but the accident put a stop to that. Her parents told Hayley nothing about it, apparently for fear the news would only make her illness worse. She didn't hear about their deaths until long after the event.

'She'd become content to have no contact with her family. Self-imposed isolation is quite common in such cases, I'm told. She must have supposed Kerry and her parents had abandoned her. Then, at some stage, almost certainly *after* the inquest, she found out what had really happened to them. I don't know how and it doesn't much matter now. The point is that she did find out.

'You'd think learning a thing like that might be the last straw for someone with a history of mental trouble. Not so in Hayley's case, though. At the time of my original enquiries, I arranged to have a confidential word with a psychiatrist who'd treated her while she was still living in London. It transpired he'd had doubts about the diagnosis of depression all along and had come to believe the real problem was rooted in feelings of inferiority to her twin – something he never mentioned to the family. When I asked him what effect her twin's death might have had on her, he answered in one rather surprising word: liberating.

'You never suspected Hayley was mentally ill, did you? Why not? Because Kerry's death means she's no longer crushed by her inability to match her sister's achievements. More than that, it's given her a way to surpass those achievements, by becoming her twin's avenger.

'Who can say what she hoped to gain by latching on to Barney's uncle Gabriel? Barney's convinced she tried to persuade the old man to leave her Heartsease and all his money. It's possible. That would have been a kind of revenge. If so, the plan failed. Gabriel was far from a soft touch. But the family feud over the ring came to light as a result of his death and she began to plot a direct move against Barney, having been encouraged by the likes of Ray Trathen – and maybe even Gabriel too – to believe he'd murdered Kerry. Whoever stole your phone must have been put up to it by Hayley. She was presumably looking for anything she could use against Barney. And, boy, did she strike lucky.

'Don't feel you have to admit or deny anything, but it's occurred to me you may have got closer to Hayley than was good for you. The tape proves you and Carol are lovers. I've known that for quite a while, by the way, though happily Barney doesn't have a clue she's been unfaithful to him. Valuable information for Hayley. But was it also unwelcome information? Was jealousy part of the mix? You tell me. If you want to. Or not, if you don't.

'I've advised Barney not to call in the police. Hayley's arrest and prosecution would only tempt the media, especially Fleet Street, to reopen the Kerry Foxton story. Then they might start digging into Starburst International, which we don't need at any time, but especially not at the moment, with a particularly juicy deal about to be finalized involving the sort of people who'd run a mile if the press started sniffing around.

'What we really need to do is to find Hayley and persuade her to submit herself to professional care so this kind of thing can't happen again. We'll see she has the best treatment available. Barney will pay. The fact she didn't go through with her plan suggests to me she knows she needs help. We're willing to supply it. I think she may be willing to accept it, especially if it's offered by the right person. I see you as that person.

'I imagine you must have found out enough about Hayley at least to know where to *start* looking for her. We'll cover your expenses. Do whatever is necessary to find her. Quickly. I doubt Carol will sleep soundly in her bed until you do. She doesn't know about the tape, incidentally. She was still locked in the bathroom when I came across it. So, that's between you and me. Which is how it can stay as far as I'm concerned. I don't want to sully Barney's rosy vision of his marriage.

'I can't predict how he'd react if he learnt the truth about your afternoons with Carol. His volatile temper and the stake he has in Jardiniera suggest to me it would work out badly for you. And for Carol. So, for all our sakes, let's avoid that, shall we?'

Harding did not immediately respond. He sat still, staring straight ahead through the windscreen towards the faint, twinkling lights of Villefranche. But there was no stillness in his mind, where more grim realizations and queasy suspicions than he could keep track of jostled and collided.

He was being blackmailed. That was clear, however subtly Whybrow had phrased his proposition. Harding did not need to be told how disastrous it would be if Barney heard the tape of Carol's message. He had no choice but to do what was asked of him. Or at least to try.

Finding Hayley, if she did not wish to be found, would be far from easy. She would surely not return to Penzance. Ann Gashry could well know where she was. It was certainly apparent that Ann had lied about Hayley in virtually every particular. Nathan had not been her brutal Svengali. Nathan, indeed, might not even exist. Some explanation for Hayley's likeness to Kerry had been needed to distract Harding while the plot against Barney Tozer was set in motion. Feeding him titbits about Francis Gashry and sending him to see Herbert Shelkin had served the same purpose. And then there was the night he had spent with Hayley. Had that just been another way of blinding him to the truth?

He wondered if Ann had tracked Hayley down in Birmingham and told her her parents and twin sister were dead. If so, it implied they had been co-conspirators ever since. He wondered also if Whybrow could be right about Hayley's mixed motives for attacking Carol. Either way, Hayley knew about his affair with Carol and had done even before they slept together. Darren Spargo had not been stalking her. Rather he had been acting a part, scripted and paid for by Hayley.

There was one consolation worth clinging to. She had not taken her plot against Barney to its logical, murderous conclusion. Carol was traumatized but unscathed. Barney was outraged but at liberty. The situation was not beyond redemption. Maybe Whybrow's solution to the problem was the best all round.

And maybe it was too good to be true. The reasons he had given for avoiding police involvement were not entirely convincing. Harding knew what Ray Trathen for one would say was the real explanation. Barney did not want Hayley's belief that he had murdered Kerry to be examined in court – not to mention the newspapers – because she was right: he *had* murdered Kerry.

If that was true, Barney's reluctance to see Hayley prosecuted was reinforced by guilt. He did not know how she had planned to frame him for Carol's murder, of course. As far as he was concerned, she had only intended to do to him what he had done to her: take the life of a loved one. Maybe he saw the justice in that and had no wish to punish her for it – an interpretation that only rendered Whybrow's calculation more impenetrable.

In the final analysis, it did not really matter. A peace offering was on the table. And Harding was to be its broker. Willingly or not.

'I'm asking a lot of you, I know,' said Whybrow, breaking the long, heavy silence. 'But I wouldn't if I thought you weren't equal to the task.'

'Is that so?'

'You'll do it?'

'I don't appear to have much option.'

'I'm sorry you see it like that. Truth is, this is in everyone's interests.'

Oddly, Harding felt that probably *was* the truth. He sighed. 'There are leads . . . I could follow.'

'Good.'

'When would you want me to start?'

'As soon as possible.' Whybrow ejected the tape from the dashboard player and handed it to him. It was a cynical, mocking little gesture. There would be another copy. There would always be another copy. 'There's no time to be lost.'

TWENTY-TWO

Harding barely slept that night. In the small hours, just as he was finally slipping into unconsciousness, he was jolted fully awake by a realization that had long lain dormant in his mind. It was Whybrow's account of Hayley Foxton's life story, as opposed to Hayley Winter's, that had set his memory searching once more. Suddenly, sickeningly, he knew where he had seen her before. He knew for a virtual certainty, though he could not render the certainty absolute without returning to England – and reopening a door he would have preferred to leave closed.

It was one more parcel of unwelcome knowledge for his overburdened mind. Mentally and physically weary, he set out on the drive to Monaco next morning hardly knowing what to expect from his encounter with Barney and Carol. So much had happened since their last meetings. So much that he had been unaware of had intruded into his life.

*   *   *

He assumed both of them would be waiting for him. Whybrow had said they would be expecting him at 10.30. As it was, Barney was alone when he arrived, prowling the terrace like a wounded bear, downcast and unshaven, his trousers and shirt so crumpled he might have slept in them.

'Carol's still out for the count,' he explained, leading Harding into the lounge. 'She took some pills to help her sleep. They packed a punch.'

'How's she coping with . . . what happened?'

'Pretty well. She has a lot of inner strength. More than me, I sometimes think.' He gave an all-purpose shrug. 'What can I tell you, Tim? Wednesday night isn't an experience I'd want to repeat in a hurry.'

'It must have been awful.'

'Yeah. But more awful for Carol than me. When something like that happens, without warning, it . . . knocks you sideways.'

'I'm sorry I couldn't give you any warning. I never had the slightest inkling Hayley was planning anything of the kind.'

'Why would you? You didn't know whose sister she was, did you?'

'No. I didn't.'

'Want a coffee? I just made some.' Tozer picked up his mug from the glass-topped table and took a slurp. 'Help yourself. You know where it is.'

The expedition to the kitchen gave Harding a minute or so to ponder the question of whether Carol's

194

no-show was down to sleeping pills or some evasion tactic she had devised. The question was still open when he returned to the lounge, coffee in hand. Tozer had lit a cigarette now and was slumped in one of the soft leather armchairs that faced the wide-windowed view of the office towers and apartment blocks of Monte Carlo, with a broad blue chunk of the Mediterranean shimmering beyond. Harding sat down next to him.

'I blame Humph as much as anyone,' Tozer growled. 'He should have told me Uncle Gabriel had a housekeeper who was the spitting image of Kerry Foxton. Of course, he never actually met Kerry. But he must have seen her picture in the paper. Then again, he didn't know she had a twin sister. Not an identical twin, but one close enough in looks . . . Well, maybe no one's to blame. Except Hayley Foxton, that is. She put the fear of God into Carol.'

'But, in the end, she didn't harm her.'

'No, thank Christ. But she planned to. Oh yes. She very much planned to. Even when Tony told me a couple of days ago who the housekeeper was, I never saw anything like this coming.'

'It's a pity you didn't tell *me*.'

'I would have done if I'd had the chance. But you dropped out of touch, remember? Even though, as it happened, I actually only had to call you up on your not-so-lost phone if I'd wanted to talk to you.' A suspicious glint had appeared in Tozer's eye. 'What was with all that?'

'It *was* lost. Stolen, I assumed. But it got handed back

in at the Turk's Head. A customer took it by mistake, apparently.'

'OK. But then you left Penzance, without letting me know where you were going.'

'Sorry. I got . . . sidetracked.'

'*Sidetracked?*'

'Hayley sent me off on a wild-goose chase to London, looking for the ring. She must have been playing for time at that stage. And she had an accomplice to help her do it. Ever heard of Ann Gashry?'

'Don't think so.'

'Or Nathan Gashry?'

'No. Who are they?'

'Neighbours of the Foxtons in Dulwich. Well, Ann was, certainly. Nathan . . . I'm not so sure about.'

'But this woman . . . led you up the garden path at Hayley's say-so?'

'Yes. Elaborately – and convincingly.'

'Then she might know where Hayley is. Hell, Hayley might have gone to ground *with* her.'

'It's the first thing I'll check.'

'Starting when?'

'Tonight. Tony's booking me on the seven o'clock flight back to London. I'm turning into quite a commuter.'

'And all on my behalf.' Tozer groaned and sat forward in his chair, massaging his forehead. 'Thanks for doing this, Tim. You'd be justified in telling me to get stuffed after I let you find out about Kerry Foxton the hard way.'

'It certainly might have been better if you'd filled

me in on the background before I went to Penzance.'

'Don't think I don't know it. Bloody stupid of me to think all that stuff wouldn't crop up. Truth is, I was just trying to get Humph off my back the easiest way I could. As to whether the ring rightfully belonged to Dad or Uncle Gabriel . . . I couldn't give a toss. Anyway . . .' Tozer took a deep pull on his cigarette. 'I don't want to see Hayley banged up. I didn't murder Kerry. Christ, why should I have? But . . .' Another pull. 'I should've checked our gear more thoroughly. There's no dodging that. I didn't know Kerry was planning to enter the wreck, but even so . . . I wasn't meticulous enough. Which makes me partly responsible for everything that happened. Then and after. Including this latest . . .' He shook his head. 'Bloody hell. I don't know what I'd do without Carol. Meeting her was the best stroke of luck I've ever had. Just a pity it coincided with the worst, hey? Funny thing, life. And death.'

'Funnier than you know.' Harding winced at the un-predictability of Tozer's reaction to what he was about to say. 'I was in Penzance a few days after the accident, Barney. With Polly. We went down to see the eclipse.'

'You did?' Tozer frowned. 'Why didn't you mention that when I asked you to go over?'

'Not sure. I guess I didn't want you to change your mind. I saw the trip as a chance to gauge how well I could cope with returning to places she and I had been together. Especially towards the end.'

'And how did you cope?'

'Fine. But, then, there was plenty to keep me occupied, wasn't there?'

Tozer gave a rubbery grin. 'Thanks to me, yeah.' He slapped his knee. 'Looks like we've both been holding out on each other, Tim. We'll have to put a stop to that. So, any gen on Hayley, you let me know pronto. Deal?'

'Sure. Though . . .'

'What?'

'Tony seems to think he's in charge of the operation.'

'He'd like to be in charge of everything. But I'm top dog and that isn't about to change. Anyhow, it doesn't matter which one of us hears from you first. We're eye to eye on this. If Hayley gives the ring back and signs up for some proper treatment, I'll pay her shrink's bills *and* pretend Wednesday night's . . . escapade . . . never happened.'

'That's big of you.' Harding and Tozer swivelled round simultaneously at the sound of Carol's voice. She was standing in the doorway that led towards the bedrooms, dressed in a grey tracksuit and fluffy pink mules. There were shadows under her eyes, her hair was flat and matted and there was something abnormal in her breathing. 'Really big of you. Considering it was *my* throat she nearly cut.'

'I know, princess, I know,' Tozer began, jumping up and hurrying towards her, right arm curled as he advanced in preparation for a hug. 'But we talked this through yesterday. You agreed then we'd regret getting the police involved.'

'Did I?' The hug engaged, but it was not reciprocated.

Carol's gaze met Harding's over her husband's shoulder. There was hurt and anger in her eyes, but also distrust, though distrust of whom he could not tell for certain.

'Come and sit down,' Tozer urged her.

'All right. Can you get me a coffee?'

'Sure. Coming up in the next bucket.'

Tozer bustled off to the kitchen. Carol advanced into the room. Harding stood up and moved across to her. He cleared his throat. 'How's it going?' he asked, his voice barely rising above a whisper.

'How d'you think?' she responded, at the same pitch, her eyes fixed on him.

'I don't—'

'You're going to go looking for her?'

He nodded affirmatively.

'When?'

'Tonight.'

'We can meet this afternoon, then. Barney's going into the office.'

'That could be difficult. I have to see Luc. Sort a few things out.'

'Fort de la Revère. Three o'clock. Be there.'

'I'm not sure I can—'

'*Be there.*'

TWENTY-THREE

The car park in the shadow of the walls of the old fort of La Revère up on the ridge of the Grande Corniche was more or less halfway between Monte Carlo and Villefranche. Harding had often met Carol there when she could not spare the time to come to his apartment. Sometimes they had eaten a picnic lunch together, sitting on one of the nearby benches, gazing across at the *village perché* of Eze and drinking in with their wine the heady panorama of the Riviera coast. Sometimes they had strolled out along the footpath towards La Turbie and laughed at the queue-jumping antics of the drivers approaching the motorway toll station far below. Or sometimes they had simply sat in one of their cars and talked and kissed and held hands.

Their rendezvous that afternoon was different from any that had gone before. The air was clear and cold; the sea and sky were deep, dazzling shades of blue. All appeared much as it ever did. But something else, something invisible but instantly detectable, had altered. Harding sensed it as soon as he pulled into the car park and saw Carol waiting for him. She was leaning against the wing of her Alfa Romeo, smoking a cigarette, the collar of her fleece turned up against the chill. The outsize sunglasses she was wearing meant he could glean nothing from her gaze as she looked up. But there was no trace of a smile as she threw the cigarette to the ground, stubbed it out and moved in his direction.

Her coolness towards him had been evident that morning at the penthouse. She had recounted her ordeal at Hayley's hands grimly and factually, almost as if Harding was some stranger with a professional interest in the matter. Even Barney had appeared puzzled by her attitude. Harding had tried to tell himself she was overcompensating to repress any hint of their secret intimacy. But he had not been convinced. And now, as she opened the passenger door of his car and climbed in beside him, he was certain she held him in some form of suspicion.

There was a moment when they should have embraced and kissed. The moment passed. A shadow fell between them. Silence blossomed. Then she said, quietly and simply, 'You slept with her.'

He did not know whether to be alarmed or relieved by the accusation. But he did know he could not deny it. 'I'm sorry,' he murmured.

'You bastard.'

'Did she tell you?'

'Not in so many words.'

'But you talked to her?'

'Oh yes. While she held the knife to my throat. I begged her not to kill me. But it wasn't the one-sided conversation I described this morning. She said quite a lot, actually. Some of it was about you. Mostly it was about Kerry.'

'You should have told me about Kerry yourself. Before I went to Penzance.'

'Maybe I should. Think I owe you an apology, do you?'

'No. I don't think that.'

'Kerry was my friend as well as Hayley's sister. I was devastated by the accident. I couldn't believe it had happened. Kerry always seemed so . . . invulnerable. But you move on, don't you? You have to. Like you and Polly. You put it behind you. Barney and I . . . helped each other. I didn't go after him because of his money, despite what so many people seem eager to believe. He was fun to be with. Still is, when he *is* with me. But he leaves me alone too much, thanks to Tony bloody Whybrow and his round-the-world deal-making. And I get bored easily. As you know.'

'Is that what I've been for you, Carol – an antidote to boredom?'

'I suppose so.' She gave a brittle little laugh. 'Sometimes I think the secrecy's more thrilling than the sex.'

Harding sighed and turned to look directly at her. 'Is there any chance you could take those sunglasses off?'

'Sure.' She plucked them from her nose. 'Satisfied?'

Her eyes were red and full. 'I talk harder than I feel, Tim. As you should also know. But clearly don't.'

'This morning, you said you'd never seen Hayley before. Was that true?'

'Yes. Why should I lie about it? At first, I had the crazy idea she was actually Kerry, come back to life. Her voice. What I could see of her face. It would have been frightening even without the knife. Then I remembered the loopy twin. And it all made terrifying sense. But no. I'd never met Hayley before. Kerry barely mentioned her. How often she thought about her – or visited her in Brum – I don't know. More than she let on, I expect. Twins are twins. You can't imagine being one. And they can't imagine not being.'

'What did she say to you?'

'That Barney murdered Kerry. That I must have been in on it. That we encouraged the clinic in Munich to let Kerry die. And made sure she wasn't told about the accident until it was too late. You know. The full paranoid works. She's a serious head case, if you want my opinion. All in all, a bad choice of partner for casual sex, I reckon, don't you? High risk of nasty consequences. And I don't mean a sexually transmitted disease.'

'You're angry.'

'You bet I am.'

'I had no idea she—'

'*You had no idea.* I wouldn't argue with that. You were only there for a few days, Tim. You'd agreed we'd meet after you got back. For Christ's sake. Couldn't you just have . . . kept your hands off her?'

'Maybe I would have . . . if you and I . . .'

'Loved each other. Oh, shit.' Carol put a hand to her face and briefly closed her eyes. 'That's what Hayley asked me. Did we – you and I – love each other? I mean, how could she know about us unless you told her? And why should she care anyway? Why should it matter to her?'

'What did you tell her?'

'The truth. It comes easily in situations like that, believe you me. And I have a horrible idea it's what saved me. Because that's when she said, "I can't do this," and threw down the knife and ran out. So, maybe I should thank you. Maybe you saved my life by seducing a madwoman.'

'She isn't mad, Carol.' It was strange, he fleetingly reflected, that he neither wished nor needed to be told unequivocally what answer Carol had given to Hayley's question. 'Just . . . mixed up.'

'Yeah? Well, she's not the only one. What exactly have you and Barney and Tony cooked up between you? After I'd got over the shock, I wanted to put the police on to her. The trauma of losing her sister doesn't excuse what she did to me in my book. But no. Suddenly we're all softly-softly touchy-feely. Barney's an old-fashioned sort of guy. He should want to nail her arse. Instead, he's falling over backwards to be reasonable, tolerant, *understanding*. Why?'

'Tony's persuaded him Hayley's arrest and trial would be bad for business.'

'You believe that?'

'Why not? Business is Tony's number one, two and three priority.'

'What's your excuse, then? Why are you running after her at their say-so?'

'I feel . . . partly responsible . . . for what happened to you.'

'So you should. But that can't be all there is to it.'

'No. It isn't.' The moment had come. She had to know. The hold Whybrow had over him could equally well be exerted over her.

Harding avoided Carol's gaze as he told her about the tape of her phone message to him and how it had come into Whybrow's possession. He spoke slowly and calmly, willing her to understand the intractability of their position. Their affair might be over. But it was not over *with*.

'I didn't tell Hayley about us, Carol. I didn't need to. She already knew. And now Tony knows as well. I have no choice but to go after her. Otherwise . . .'

'Jesus,' said Carol softly. She lit a cigarette with trembling hands and wound down the window. 'This puts Tony in control. Of you *and* me.'

'You could always . . . confess to Barney. Tony wouldn't have any control then. Over either of us.'

'I can't do that. I'd lose everything.'

'I'd lose quite a lot myself. But maybe it would be worth it.'

'Barney would tear you limb from limb.' She looked at him, eyes wide, nodding to confirm her seriousness. 'And me.'

'I'd better do as Tony says, then, hadn't I?'

'Yeah. But it won't stop even if you nab Hayley and lock her away in a Swiss funny farm. Once Tony gets his claws into someone, he never lets go. Not that I believe for a minute you intend to hand Hayley over to the men in white coats if you *do* track her down.'

'No?'

'No. You're half in love with her, aren't you?'

'I don't know what you—'

'Maybe more than half. Don't deny it, Tim. There's no point.'

He looked at Carol for a long, silent moment, then said, 'To be honest, I don't really know what I feel about her. I suppose that's another reason why I need to find her.'

'You'd better find something else while you're about it, then. Something we can use to shake off Tony.'

'What sort of something do you have in mind?'

'The truth.' She let the ambiguity as well as the significance of her answer sink in before continuing. 'I've been thinking. Maybe the real reason Barney and Tony want to hush up what happened on Wednesday night is that Hayley's right: Kerry *was* murdered.'

'You don't mean that.'

'Don't I? I'll tell you this. Kerry was on the scent of a big story in the weeks before the accident. She never breathed a word to me about it, but she dashed up to London for a couple of days and she was making lots of phone calls before and after that to someone called Shep. Short for Shepherd. I'd heard her mention him

206

before. Some old journalist, long retired. Sort of a mentor.'

'What were the calls about?'

'Dunno. She'd get choosy with her words and ring off if I came into the room in the middle of one. Besides, whatever Kerry thought, I wasn't interested. She was always chasing a story of some kind. I had the sense this was bigger than most, but . . .' She shrugged. 'I've only thought about it since. Mostly over the last thirty-six hours.'

'Where could I find this . . . Shep?'

'No idea. But I can give you a lead to someone who *might* know. Hayley mentioned him. She said she knew about his deal with Barney. It was her instant response when I tried to convince her Kerry hadn't been murdered. I can still hear her voice, hissing in my ear. "Save it," she said. "I know all about Barney's deal with Nathan."'

'*Nathan?*'

'One of Kerry's old boyfriends. I met him a few times. Bit of a hunk. But way too bland for Kerry.'

'Nathan Gashry.'

Carol frowned. 'How'd you know his surname?'

'I met his sister in London. Ann Gashry. Neighbour and friend of the Foxtons.'

'Well, well. She's who I'd have suggested you ask where Nathan hangs out these days.'

'Oh, I'll ask her. You can be sure of that. But Barney denied all knowledge of them only this morning.'

'Then either he's lying or Hayley is. And she sounded sincere enough to me.'

'What would the deal be?'

'Who knows? I'll do some digging this end. Find out as much as I can. It won't be easy. I've never shown the slightest interest in Starburst business. Barney'll think it odd if I start quizzing him.'

'You've genuinely never had any doubts about the accident before?'

'No. Why should I?'

'I don't know. But you weren't planning to tell me any of this today, were you? You've only opened up now because you're worried about Tony having a hold on you.'

'Do you blame me? I thought you'd sold out.'

'Are you happier now you know I'm actually being blackmailed?'

'*We're* being blackmailed, you mean.'

'Yes. That *is* what I mean. But what if we weren't, Carol? What if you could just wash your hands of this thing we had going? Would you do any digging then? Or would you just let the doubts die – and the questions go unanswered?'

'Do you know the biggest difference between us, Tim?' she countered. 'I'm a realist and you're not.' She inhaled deeply from her cigarette and flicked a quarter-inch of ash out through the window. 'The dead are dead. You can't bring them back. And you can't avoid joining them sooner or later. In the meantime, what's there to do but try to enjoy yourself? So, would I be rocking the boat if I wasn't afraid someone might be about to throw me out of it? No. Marriage to Barney has given me the kind of life I could only have dreamt of. I'd be willing to make a lot of compromises to hang on to it. But dancing to Tony Whybrow's tune isn't one of them. I don't need to know the truth about Kerry's death for her sake. I need to know for *my* sake.'

'Do you really believe she was murdered?'

'I believe it's possible.'

'Then you must believe you may be married to a murderer.'

'Yeah. Nice, hey?' She took a last drag on her cigarette and tossed it out through the window. Her other hand was closer to his at that moment than at any time since she had got into the car. Habit prompted Harding to fold his fingers around hers. She neither responded nor pulled away.

'Last week we were lovers, Carol. What are we now?'

'Allies.' She looked at him levelly. Her eyes had dried. Necessity had conquered sentiment. 'Of a sort.'

TWENTY-FOUR

Harding had phoned ahead and booked himself back into the Great Western Hotel at Paddington. After travelling in from Heathrow, he paused only long enough to check in and dump his bag, then headed for Dulwich. It was late for unannounced house calls, but that did not trouble him. Ann Gashry had to expect there to be consequences to the lies she had told.

It was gone ten by the time he reached Bedmore Road, but the drawing-room windows at Ann Gashry's house were still lit. With Dora presumably long gone, he reckoned she might be reluctant to answer the door at such an hour, so he gave the bell several lengthy and well-spaced pushes before adding a rap of the knocker for good measure.

The hall light came on. The frosted porch window revealed movement within. 'Who's there?' came the querulous call.

'Tim Harding.'

He heard her engage the chain before inching the door open and peering out at him. 'It's late, Mr Harding. What do you want?'

'The truth. As opposed to that hogwash you served up on Tuesday.'

'I don't know what you mean.'

'I'm short of time *and* patience, Ann. There was an intruder at the Tozers' apartment in Monte Carlo on Wednesday night. Hayley. She threatened Carol with a knife.' A flicker of alarm crossed Ann Gashry's face. 'Fortunately, that's all she did: threaten her. Otherwise you could be an accessory to murder.'

'*What?*'

'I'm doing my best to restrain Barney from calling in the police. I won't be able to do so indefinitely unless you come clean with me. It's up to you.'

Ann stared pensively at him, then quietly closed the door. A couple of seconds passed. He was on the point of rapping the knocker again, when he heard the chain being released. The door opened wide. 'Come in, then,' she murmured.

She was encased in an ankle-length dressing gown, which somehow made her look smaller and feebler than when they had first met. Harding steeled himself not to be taken in by this, however. He knew her to be sharp-witted and highly intelligent – as well as deceitful.

'Perhaps you'd like to tell me exactly what Hayley is alleged to have done,' she said as she closed the door behind him.

'There's nothing *alleged* about it.'

'There is to me.'

'The game's up, Ann. I'm not sure if you knew what she was planning. But you knew she was planning *something*. Sending me on a fool's errand to Lincoln was part of it. As was backing up her explanation for so closely resembling Kerry. The true explanation's altogether more straightforward. Kerry had a twin sister, didn't she? Called Hayley.'

Ann allowed herself the merest flinch. 'Come into the drawing room,' she said, leading the way.

Logs were burning down in the grate. Chamber music was playing on an invisible hi-fi. A tray, bearing the remnants of a supper, sat on a low table beside an arm-chair in front of the fire. A hardback novel, tasselled bookmark neatly inserted, lay next to the tray. Ann Gashry's evening looked to have unfolded in orderly and contemplative fashion. Until now.

'So.' She cocked her head slightly as she looked at him. 'What do you claim Hayley's done?'

'Are you sure you need me to tell you?'

'Yes.' Her expression gave nothing away. 'I am.' She lowered herself into her fireside chair, inviting Harding with a gesture of her hand to take the other.

He set out the events of Wednesday night in as much detail as he could afford to. He made no mention of the tape, of course, fervently hoping Ann did not know about that. The other facts spoke for themselves anyway. There was no doubt what Hayley had done and very

212

little doubt why. As he made clear by adding as much as he knew of her true life story.

Ann did not interrupt. Her only reaction was to look ever more pensive as he proceeded. When he had finished, she allowed herself a sigh that might have signalled nothing more than fatigue. 'Would you like a drink?' she enquired. 'I believe I would. There's whisky and brandy in the cabinet. Brandy for me, I think.'

The cabinet was in the corner. Harding poured generous measures for both of them. Cognac for her, Glenfiddich for himself.

'Thank you,' she said as he handed her the glass. 'Oh, could you put some more wood on the fire please? I'm feeling a little chilly.'

He shot her an eyebrow-arched glance as he tonged a couple of logs out of the well-stocked basket, letting her know that playing for time was futile. But the goose pimples visible on her wrist and forearm as she sipped her brandy suggested she really did feel cold. Or afraid.

Flames licked up instantly round the added logs. Harding sat down and gazed across at her, expectantly and insistently. 'Anything else?'

'No, thank you.' She took another sip of brandy.

'Well?'

A long, calming sigh escaped her. She closed her eyes for a second or two, then looked directly at him. 'I'm not about to apologize to you, Mr Harding, if that's what you think. You're right, of course. My brother Nathan hasn't spent the years since Kerry's accident in obsessive pursuit of women who resemble her. Nor did

213

he haunt her hospital bedside. In point of fact, he's always seemed indifferent to her fate. Perhaps that's why I considered him fair game in the fiction Hayley and I devised between us to mislead you. Because I've never been indifferent to what happened to Kerry. I believe she was murdered by Barney Tozer. He may protest his innocence as much as he wishes. This show of charitable reluctance to report Hayley to the police only confirms his guilt in my mind. It was I who traced Hayley after the inquest and told her all that had happened. You could say I set her on the course that led to her attack on Carol Tozer. She didn't tell me what she proposed to do. But you're correct in supposing I knew she'd soon do something. Again, I make no apology. I became very fond of those girls as they grew up. Too fond, my stepmother used to say, in her spiteful, in-sinuating way. I couldn't bear to see Kerry die a lingering death and Hayley languish in lonely obscurity after wit-nessing the wonderful, blossoming promise of their childhood. To stand by and allow all that to be snuffed out and forgotten? I couldn't do it. I *won't* do it. Someone's responsible. Someone is answerable. As far as I'm concerned, that someone is Barney Tozer.'

'But not Carol,' put in Harding.

'No.' Ann bowed her head. 'No, indeed.' She swallowed some more brandy. 'Perhaps that consider-ation is what stayed Hayley's hand. I pray so. I'll be honest with you, Mr Harding. I'm dismayed by what you've told me.' Her tune – and her demeanour – had suddenly if fractionally altered.

'You could've fooled me.'

'Well, as you know, I *can* fool people. I'm actually quite proficient at it. And I was well aware that Hayley intended to wreak some kind of vengeance on Barney Tozer. But I never for a moment envisaged that it would take such an extreme form. I can't imagine why Hayley should wish to harm Carol, let alone think of actually killing her.'

'How about because she wanted Barney to experience some of what she felt when you told her Kerry was dead?'

'I suppose . . . that's possible.'

'Which is what you wanted too, isn't it?'

'Yes, but—' She broke off and drew herself up defiantly. 'He deserves to be punished for what he did. But not punished in kind. I couldn't condone that.'

'It hardly matters what you could or couldn't condone. You aided and abetted it. As I'll make sure the police appreciate, if and when they're called in. But it's *when* unless you help me find Hayley. *Before* she does anything else like this.'

'I'm sure that won't happen. She's obviously realized violence isn't—'

'*Where is she?*'

Ann started at the barked question, but instantly regained her composure. 'I don't know. I haven't heard from her since Tuesday. She said she was going away. She didn't say where or for how long.'

'And you didn't ask?'

'I've never pressed her to tell me more than she wishes to.'

'How very considerate of you.'

'Her trust is hard to win, Mr Harding. And her soul is troubled. Ask more of her than she's able or willing to give and you lose her. I've tried to bear that in mind. It's a pity her parents never understood her well enough to do the same.'

'It also gives you a useful excuse for whatever she does, of course. *You weren't to know.*'

'That's not how it is.'

'Well, I'll have to take your word for that.'

'Misleading you was a regrettable necessity. Hayley said she needed time. I helped her buy some and I told you as much of the truth as I dared. I invented nothing where my ancestor Francis Gashry's concerned, as Herbert Shelkin must have confirmed to you. It's merely that it has . . . no direct bearing on what happened to Kerry.'

'For which you and Hayley both blame Barney?'

'Yes. I've no doubt in the matter. Nor has Hayley.'

'She might have now, for all you know.'

'I don't think so,' said Ann severely, as if the notion was absurd.

'When do you expect to hear from her again?'

'I couldn't say. I imagine, after coming so close . . . to doing such a dreadful thing . . . she'll need time to think. Time to reflect.'

'Spent where?'

'I don't know. I truly don't.'

'I'm not sure you quite understand the position you're in, Ann. Barney's prepared to stay his hand for as

216

long as it takes me to find Hayley and resolve this situation. But if I *don't* find her . . .'

'I can't tell you what I don't know.'

'No. But you could promise to alert me as soon as she contacts you.'

'*If* she contacts me.'

'I'll settle for that.'

Ann set down her brandy glass with exaggerated care. Several wordless moments passed as the clock on the mantelpiece ticked sonorously and the fire crackled. Then she said, 'Very well. I dare say it's . . . in everybody's best interests. Perhaps I . . . shouldn't have encouraged her.'

'Perhaps not.'

'She said you seemed . . . an honest man.'

'I am.'

'You have my word, then. If I hear from her, *you'll* hear from *me*.'

Harding stretched across to the Canterbury that stood a few feet from his chair and pulled out a newspaper: the *Daily Telegraph*, folded to display the crosswords on the back page. Ann had completed the quick as well as the cryptic, without a single crossing-out. He jotted his mobile number at the foot of the page and handed it to her. 'I'll be waiting.'

'Thank you,' she said, laying the paper down on the table.

'I need some information to be going on with.'

'I've told you all I can.'

'What do you know about Shep?'

'Who?' She looked genuinely puzzled.

'Shep. Short for Shepherd. Kerry's journalistic mentor.'

'I'm afraid I've never heard of him.'

'According to Carol, they were often in touch.'

'I'm afraid I've still never heard of him.'

'Do you think Nathan might have?'

'It's possible. I . . . couldn't say.'

'I'll ask him myself, then. If you don't mind giving me his address and phone number.'

'Must we involve him? I doubt he'll be able to help you.'

'Only one way to find out.'

A tremor of unease, mixed with distaste, crossed Ann's face. She cleared her throat nervously. 'I wouldn't want Nathan . . . to learn how I've . . . misrepresented him.'

'I'll do my best to steer round the subject.'

'Your best?'

Harding shrugged. 'It's all I can offer. And frankly . . .' He paused, forcing her to meet his gaze before he continued. 'It's more than you deserve.'

TWENTY-FIVE

Saturday morning dawned grey and cold, the high-rise Thameside apartment block where Nathan Gashry lived adding a vortical gale to the prevailing bleakness. Harding felt bizarrely elated as he approached the push-button entryphone panel, however. He felt, for once, that he was ahead in whatever game was being played, that the decoys were done with, that the trail he was following would lead him to whoever his quarry really was.

'Yeah?' came the gruff, belated response to Harding's triple prod at the button for flat 228.

'Nathan Gashry?'

'That's me.'

'Can I come in? We need to talk. My name's Harding. Tim Harding.'

'Who?'

'Harding. We've never met. I'm a friend . . . of Barney Tozer.'

'*Tozer?*'

'That's right.'

'Did he . . . send you here?'

Harding debated how to answer for a split-second, then opted for, 'Yes.'

'What the hell for?'

'It'd be easier to explain if you let me in.'

'Shit. This isn't . . .' A pause for thought. 'Oh, all right, then. Come up. Fifth floor.'

The door release buzzed. Harding was in.

The man who opened the door of flat 228 had the same probing, dark-eyed gaze as Ann Gashry, but was otherwise unrecognizable as her brother. Lean, chestnut-haired and unshaven, he was wearing espadrilles and a short, orientally styled bathrobe. He looked as if he was many years younger than Ann and inhabited a very different world from hers. The flat was all pared-down furniture and pale, empty space, with high-windowed views along the river towards Westminster.

'What's this about, mate?' he demanded, letting Harding in no further than the hallway.

'I'm trying to locate Hayley Foxton.'

'*Hayley?*'

'Barney reckoned you might be able to help.'

'Well, he reckoned wrong. I haven't a clue where she is.'

'Pity. Only, she was in Monte Carlo a few days ago. She broke into the Tozers' apartment and threatened Carol with a knife.'

'You're having me on.'

The light reaching them from the lounge altered fractionally. Harding turned to see a young woman standing in a doorway on the far side of the room, frowning at him. She was short and slim, with straight dark hair falling to her shoulders and slender, shapely legs visible from the thighs down beneath the hem of what looked like one of Nathan's T-shirts.

'Who's this, Nathan?' she asked uneasily.

'I'll tell you later,' Nathan replied. 'It's nothing for you to worry about. He won't be here long.'

'OK.' She did not sound entirely convinced. 'I'm going to take a shower.'

'Right. I'll have breakfast waiting for you.'

The young woman slipped out of sight. A door closed somewhere behind her. 'Is that Veronica?' Harding asked casually. But the response he got was far from casual.

'How d'you know her name?'

It was a good question. An even better one was how Hayley had known. 'I need to find Hayley, Nathan. Can you help me?'

'No. I haven't seen her in years. But—'

'That's not how she tells it.'

'You what?'

'We have to track Hayley down before she does anything like this again. For her sake as well as everyone else's. You do see that, don't you?'

'There's nothing I can tell you.'

'I think there is.'

'Well, you're wrong. OK, mate? *Wrong.*'

'You may have some valuable information without even knowing it.'

'That's it. You're leaving.' Nathan moved past Harding to the front door of the flat and pulled it open. But Harding kicked it instantly shut, leaving Nathan to stare at him with a mixture of fear and indignation.

'What the fuck d'you think you're—'

'Listen to me, *mate.*' Harding spoke quietly but intently, staring deliberately into Nathan's eyes. 'This is the story Hayley fed me and a few others besides. You've been trying to turn her into a recreation of her dead sister. Taking up with one twin where you left off with the other. Messing with her head as well as her body. And encouraging her to believe Barney murdered Kerry.'

Nathan's mouth sagged open. His brow furrowed. He seemed incapable of articulating a reaction. Which prompted Harding to press home his advantage.

'Crazy, right? But then she is, isn't she? As you know. Which is why I haven't mentioned it to Barney. Luckily for you. If he got the idea into his head that you were responsible for what Hayley's done . . . Well, I wouldn't want to be in your shoes, that's for sure.'

'I don't know where she is,' Nathan murmured.

'Tell me as much as you can. That's all I ask. Starting with exactly what kind of deal you struck with Barney.'

'Deal?'

'Hayley said you and he had some kind of . . . understanding. In relation to Kerry, I assume.'

Nathan's face was a picture of bafflement. 'Hayley . . . knows about that?'

'Evidently.'

'Hold on.' Nathan's powers of reasoning were slowly reasserting themselves. 'If you're a friend of Barney's, why don't you . . . ask him?'

'Because I'm not sure he'll want to tell me.'

'Well, maybe I don't want to tell you either.'

'Maybe not. But you should bear in mind it's not only Barney who'll cut up rough if he hears what Hayley says you did to her. I guess Veronica might take it badly as well. There's something of the Foxtons' looks in her, isn't there? I suppose that's what attracted you to her. Another substitute for Kerry.'

'It's not like that.'

'I'm sure it isn't. But it's a question of how it *looks*, isn't it?'

'Fucking hell.'

'What was the deal?'

'I should never have . . .' Nathan chewed his lip for a pensive moment, then quietly closed the door leading to the lounge and pointed towards the kitchen. 'We can talk in there.'

The kitchen was narrow and windowless, fitted out with an excess of marble and brushed steel. The pristine condition of most of the culinary gizmos on show suggested cookery was not one of Nathan's pastimes.

'Who are you?' he asked, squinting at Harding in the harsh overhead light.

'Someone you can get off your back with the answers to a few simple questions.'

'There's never been anything between me and Hayley. I swear it.'

'I believe you.'

'But it isn't . . . years . . . since I last saw her.'

'No?'

'Did she give you Veronica's name?'

'She might have.'

'Shit.' Nathan soft-landed a punch on the door of the Smeg fridge. 'I must have . . . let it slip.'

'Hayley came to see you?'

'Yeah. This was . . . a few months ago. Veronica and me had just . . .' He rubbed his forehead. 'Never mind. You don't need to know about that.'

'What *do* I need to know about?'

Nathan sighed heavily. 'OK. You may as well hear it. Not much point keeping it secret now. Hayley had done some digging. She'd found out I'd paid Kerry's bills at the Horstelmann Clinic in Munich.'

'*You?*'

'I told her parents I wanted to do everything I could to help Kerry recover. The Horstelmann was supposed to be the biz in coma cases, but a bed there didn't come cheap. Fortunately, I could cover her costs because I'd landed one of those fat City bonuses you read about in the papers.' Nathan shrugged. 'I wish.'

'You're saying . . . *you* didn't pay?'

'No. 'Course not. Why would I – even if I could afford to? Kerry had ditched me months before her accident.

We were finished, as she'd made crystal clear. I was just the front man.'

That was the deal, of course. It was obvious now. 'For Barney?'

'Yup.'

'Why didn't he want the Foxtons to know he was paying?'

'He made it worth my while not to ask. But if I was to guess, I'd say it was because he was afraid people might suspect he had a guilty conscience.'

'D'you think they'd have been right to?'

'Dunno. What do *you* think?'

'Maybe he was worried the Foxtons wouldn't accept the money if they knew it came from him.'

Nathan allowed himself half a smile. 'Yeah. Right.'

'But you let Hayley go away believing it confirmed Barney's guilt, didn't you?'

'Don't try to lay what she's done on me, mate.' Nathan braced his shoulders pugnaciously. 'I gave her the facts. What she made of them . . . was up to her.'

'You knew from Kerry she'd had psychiatric problems.'

'So?'

'That makes your . . . openness with her . . . a tad irresponsible, don't you reckon?'

'She'd already guessed who I was covering for. There was no point denying it.'

'You must have wondered why she wanted to know so badly.'

'I assumed she was keen to make sure she wasn't in

225

my debt. She didn't like me, you see. Never had. The one time I met her – with Kerry – she didn't leave me in any doubt what she thought of me.' Nathan chuckled mirthlessly. 'Which was pretty much what Kerry ended up thinking of me, as it happens. That's twins for you, I suppose.'

'Do you know what story Kerry was working on in Cornwall?'

'No. Like I told you, we'd split by then.'

'She might have been working on it *before* you split.'

'Might have. Might not. She wasn't big on sharing stuff. Y'know? Never had been. And I never pressured her to, anyway.'

'Jealous of her glamorous career, were you?'

Nathan stared at him levelly. 'Fuck off.'

'I will, if you'll answer one last question. Who's Shep?'

'Christ.' Nathan rolled his eyes. 'You're not going to tell me that old tosspot's mixed up in this.'

'Who is he?'

'Who *was* he's more like it, considering his state of health when I met him, which must've been at least eight years ago. Jack Shepherd. Kerry's editor on the first paper she worked for, down in Kent. The *Messenger*. The *Mercury*. Something like that. She kept in touch with him after she'd moved on to bigger and better things. Went to see him every now and then. Took me along one time. He'd retired from the paper and was living in Deal.'

'Got an address?'

'Why would I have? He was Kerry's friend, not mine.'

'Could you find where he lived if you went back to the town?'

'Maybe. But I'm not about to, am I?'

'Not if you can describe it well enough for me to trace, no.'

Nathan sighed. 'Will that get rid of you?'

'Yes.' Harding nodded emphatically. 'It will.'

TWENTY-SIX

'A *poky ground-floor flat facing Deal Castle, near the sea front.*' Such had been Nathan Gashry's succinct description of Jack Shepherd's retirement abode. There were, as Harding had expected, several J. Shepherds listed in the phone book covering Deal. But only one had an address in Deal Castle Road.

'Hello?' The man who answered the phone sounded old and wary but reassuringly alive.

'Jack Shepherd?'

'Yes.'

'Former editor of the, er . . . *Messenger*?'

'*Mercury. Kentish Mercury*. Part of the *Kent Messenger* group. Not the same thing.' Reassuringly sharp, too.

'Right.'

'What can I do for you, Mr . . .'

'Harding. Tim Harding. I'm phoning about . . . well, in connection with . . . Kerry Foxton.'

'Kerry?' There was an edge of something in Shepherd's voice: regret, maybe; or loss; or nostalgia. 'You were a friend of hers?'

'No. I'm a friend of her sister, Hayley.'

'Ah. Kerry's twin.'

'That's right. Do you know her?'

'No. We've never met. But ... I recall Kerry ... mentioning her.'

'Did Kerry mention Hayley's psychiatric problems?'

'Yes,' Shepherd replied cautiously.

'I'm trying to help her get over them. The thing is, could we meet, Mr Shepherd?'

'To what purpose? As I say, I've never met Hayley, so—'

'It's Kerry I want to talk to you about.'

'Really?'

'The loss of a twin is a hard thing to get over.'

'I'm sure it is. But—'

'I could explain myself much better in person. I'm in London at the moment. I could come down to Deal on the train this afternoon, if that's convenient.'

'It isn't. I have my daughter coming over. With my grandchildren.'

'This is very important. More important than I can get into on the phone.'

'My grandchildren are important too, Mr Harding.' A silence ensued, during which Shepherd's thoughtful breaths fanned the receiver. Then he said, 'Come tomorrow. If you catch the first train, you can be with me by eleven. I'll expect you then. But let me warn you: I don't discuss my friends with strangers, even when they're dead. You'll have your work cut out shifting me from that principle.'

Shepherd sounded as if he might be a hard nut to crack. Harding had no means of forcing him to disclose what Kerry had been phoning him about in the days and weeks before the accident. He could only rely on his powers of persuasion. Even if they proved sufficient, the answer might be of little help in his search for Hayley. And he would have to kick his heels until Sunday before he could even hope to find out. Which left him with no excuse for failing to do what he had known he would have to do, sooner or later, since waking in the small hours of Friday morning.

His destination was close to Hanger Lane Tube station, out towards the western end of the Central line. He had realized he would have to go back there one day. A settlement with the past could not be postponed for ever. But this was sooner than he had expected – sooner than he was ready for. When his phone rang shortly after the train had emerged from the underground part of the line, several stops short of Hanger Lane, he caught himself hoping the call, whoever it was from, would prevent him completing his journey.

'Hello?'

'Hiya. It's your good friend Darren here.'

As surprises went, this was a big one. Harding was struck momentarily dumb.

'Knock, knock. Anyone at home?'

Anger rushed in to swamp Harding's astonishment. He found his voice. 'What the hell do you want?'

'Any idea where Hayley's taken off to, man?'

'No, and even if I had I—'

'Wouldn't share the news with me? I know. I guess you've figured out by now she hired me to pull a few moves on you.'

'Yes. Ring to apologize, did you?'

'Nothing to apologize for, the way I see it. It was just a bit of business. No hard feelings, hey? Thing is, we could do a bit of business ourselves, you and me. Know what I mean?'

'No. I don't. And we couldn't.'

'Don't be so hasty. Hayley quit town owing me money, see.'

'Your fee, no doubt. For stealing my phone.'

'That and the other things. Point is, I don't like being left in the lurch.'

'Who does?'

'So, if someone else – you, say – picked up the tab, I'd be willing to tell them what I know about the burglary at Heartsease.'

'What do you know?'

'Who stole the ring. I was there, see, keeping an eye out. I saw who took it, man.'

'Perhaps you took it yourself.'

'Nah. Not me. Someone else. You'll never guess who. You'll need me to tell you.'

'In exchange for what Hayley owes you.'

'Yeah.'

'Which is?'

'A grand.'

'Come off it.'

'Barney can afford it. He'll see you right. You think it over, Mr H. Or clear it with your multi-millionaire boss. Whatever. I'll give you a bell Monday to fix the details. It'll have to be a cash deal, so you and me'll have to meet up. Nice to have the excuse, hey?'

'Now, just—'

'Catch you later.' The line went dead.

Harding had his doubts about whether Hayley owed Spargo any money at all, far less a thousand pounds. But it did not really matter. If Spargo knew the identity of the Heartsease burglar, Barney would be happy for Harding to pay him that and more to be let in on the secret. The devious Darren was on to a good thing. And he probably knew it.

Consulting Barney about Spargo's proposition would have to wait. The phone call had, after all, done nothing to deflect Harding from his destination: a storage depot near the Hanger Lane roundabout on the A40. His only other visit had been six years ago, at the wheel of a hire van loaded with such contents of the house in Worcestershire he had shared with Polly as he could not bring himself to sell or throw away after her death.

They were all still there, boxed and stacked in a small, securely locked, CCTV-monitored room, where, as far as

232

Harding knew, no one had set foot since he had closed the door on its hoard of tangible reminders of Polly and their life together.

Now, in eerie silence halfway along a gantried corridor, he was reopening the door, in search not of Polly, but of Hayley, and her particular place in his past.

The overhead light flickered into life. Harding stepped into the room. The air was fresh enough, thanks to the ventilation gaps between the walls and suspended ceiling. There was only the thinnest layer of dust on the crates. He glanced from one to the other of them, noting the words he had scrawled on their sides to indicate what they contained. *BOOKS. CLOTHES. MUSIC. ROCKY.* Ah yes. Rocky the rocking horse, treasured by Polly since childhood. Tears sprang into Harding's eyes. Suddenly the years that had passed dissolved to nothing. He leant forward, hands on knees, breathing deeply to compose himself. A minute or so passed. Then he was in control again.

The box he wanted was one of three marked *PICTURES.* Polly had been a talented painter, though not talented enough to make a full-time living as one. She had sold a few pictures in her time, however. Those she had hung around the house, along with others that had slowly accumulated in her makeshift studio, were stored here, apart from some that friends had asked to take as mementoes. And Harding was certain the picture he was looking for had stayed with the rest.

After a few minutes, he located the right box and hauled it out into the centre of the room. Beneath *PICTURES* he had written *Art Therapy*, a reference to the period when they lived in Harrow-on-the-Hill and Polly had worked as an art therapist at various clinics and day centres around west London. She had painted some of the patients she had met. He remembered these anguished, expressive portraits of people who possessed none of Polly's own robustness of mind, which had served her so well – if Harding less well – in the end.

He ripped off the strip of brown tape and opened the box. He was close now. He knew it. He had only to see it again to be absolutely certain. He began lifting out the pictures to examine. No. No. No. No. *Yes*.

There she was. Younger, angrier, weaker, but instantly recognizable nonetheless, something of her essence captured along with her features. He turned the picture round. On the back, Polly had written *Tooting, November 1994*. She would not have been so unprofessional as to record the subject's name. But Harding did not need her to have done so. He knew Hayley Foxton when he saw her. He had all along – without realizing it.

Did Hayley know? he wondered. There was no reason why she should remember a fleeting encounter with Polly from twelve years ago, far less connect it with Harding's uncanny conviction that they had met before. For they had not met, except vicariously. He had seen her face long before he had set eyes on her in person. She had gone as far as suggesting he might have known Kerry in another life. But nothing so fanciful lay at the heart of his unreciprocated sense of familiarity. He had often looked at the picture and pondered the enigma of the troubled young woman Polly had depicted, about whom, as he recalled, she had claimed to know virtually nothing. Never would he have imagined, never in a million years, nor even an alternative universe—

The trilling of his mobile sliced through his thoughts. He slid the picture back between the two others he had been holding apart and pulled the phone out of his pocket.

'Hello?'

'Mr Harding?'

'Ann?'

'Yes.' She sounded uneasy. There was a faint tremor in her voice. 'You asked me to call . . . if I heard from Hayley.'

'And you have?'

'Yes.' There was a moment of silence, followed by a whisper of static. Then she said, 'I know where she is.'

TWENTY-SEVEN

'Let's go through what she said again.'

Harding was sitting with Ann Gashry in a café just round the corner from Victoria station. She had agreed to travel in from Dulwich to recount in person the details of Hayley's out-of-the-blue phone call. The change of venue had diminished Ann. The noisy, crowded, grubby purlieus of Victoria were not her natural domain. Just as telling Harding everything Hayley had told *her* was evidently not something she relished having to do.

'I need to be clear about this. She was definitely phoning from Munich?'

'So she said,' Ann replied, in a voice so subdued it seemed she was afraid people at nearby tables might be listening in on their conversation.

'Where in Munich?'

'That she didn't say. Just that she'd flown there from Nice on Thursday. She assumed I'd heard what she'd done in Monte Carlo and wanted me to know she was as horrified by her behaviour as everyone else. She emphasized that I wasn't to blame myself. Her exact words were "It's all down to me". I asked why she'd gone to Munich. "Kerry died here and I have to come to terms with her death. There's nowhere better to start." Again, her exact words. I asked if she was alone and she said, "I'm getting help, Ann. You don't need to worry about me." Then she rang off.'

'Just like that?'

'Well, no. She said, "I'll call again." *Then* she rang off.'

'Who is she getting help from?'

'I don't know.'

'The Horstelmann Clinic, perhaps.'

'Perhaps.'

'Is Kerry buried in Munich?'

'I believe she was cremated.'

'But in Munich?'

'Yes. As far as I know. There was certainly no funeral in Dulwich. With her parents dead, there were no close relatives left. Apart from Hayley, of course.'

'And nobody bothered to let her know.'

'I only heard of Kerry's death after the event. I would have contacted Hayley if I'd been given the chance. I should have enquired what was to happen to Kerry after her parents were killed, of course. I should have done more to help Hayley. I realize that. If I had, this might never have happened.'

'But you believe Barney murdered Kerry. So nothing happening wasn't really an attractive option for you, was it, Ann?'

Ann flushed. The accusation that she had encouraged Hayley to avenge her sister's death hung unrefuted between them. 'I never meant it to go so far,' she murmured.

'Then let's hope we can stop it going any further.'

Harding had promised to alert Barney as soon as he had any news of Hayley. He phoned him from the concourse at Victoria station after seeing Ann Gashry off on her train back to Dulwich. Barney's initial reaction was predictable enough, though Harding's discovery that he had paid Kerry's medical expenses made even the predictable seem faintly suspicious.

'Munich? What the hell's she doing there?'

'Mourning her sister, I think, Barney.'

'What are we going to do?'

'I'd better go after her.'

'Where will you look? It's a big city.'

'I'll start at the Horstelmann Clinic.'

'Yeah. I suppose that . . . makes sense.'

'Ever been there?'

'Where – the Horstelmann Clinic?'

'Yes.'

'Why should I have?'

'I spoke to Nathan Gashry. He told me who paid the Foxtons' bills.'

There was a freighted pause. Then Barney said, 'I should have filled you in on that.'

'Yes. You should.'

'Sorry, Tim. This is getting to be a habit, isn't it? Me

apologizing for keeping you in the dark about something.'

'A habit you promised to break, as I recall.'

'Yeah. Well, that's the last secret blown now, I give you my word.'

'Why did it have to be a secret?'

'Because of how it looks. Which is bad, right?'

'It looks guilty, Barney. You don't need me to tell you that.'

'Does Hayley know?'

'Oh yes. Nathan spilled the beans to her months ago.'

'I suppose that helped convince her I'd murdered Kerry.'

'I should imagine so.'

'And then, to her mind, I murdered Kerry all over again, by cutting off the payments after her parents were killed.'

'Well, you did, didn't you?'

'Shit, what a mess.' Barney sighed heavily. 'OK. Time to face the music. I'll join you in Munich. We'll sort this out together. Once and for all.'

Barney's sudden determination to take a personal hand in resolving the crisis Hayley had precipitated brooked no delay. It was agreed he and Harding would both fly to Munich in the morning. This ruled out Harding's planned visit to Jack Shepherd, but it could not be helped. Tracking down Hayley mattered every bit as much to him as it did to Barney, possibly more so. And Shepherd was going nowhere. He would wait. Harding left a message on his phone, saying he would ring again in a few days to rearrange. What he did not say was that he had no idea what those few days might bring. When they found Hayley, *if* they found her, all bets were off.

He had imagined meeting Hayley alone. Now he faced the prospect of refereeing a confrontation between her and the man she believed had murdered her sister. Worse still, he did not know for certain that she was wrong to believe it. And worst of all, he was unsure what he really felt for her. He should pity her, perhaps, or fear her. He should want to see her only to help her – to save her from herself. But he knew he truly wanted to see her for another reason altogether.

Ann Gashry had not asked what was in the large, flat parcel he was carrying. If he had told her, she would have been incredulous, understandably so. He should logically have left the picture at the storage depot. He did not understand why he had taken it away with him. Or perhaps, he admitted to himself as he removed the wrapping paper in the privacy of his room back at the Great Western and stared once more into Hayley Foxton's eyes, he did not want to understand.

TWENTY-EIGHT

Harding's plane was due to land in Munich a quarter of an hour before Tozer's. It touched down on schedule, giving him just enough time to lodge the carefully re-wrapped painting at the left-luggage office before joining the crowd of people waiting at the arrivals gate.

Tozer was the first Nice passenger to emerge from the customs hall. He looked, if anything, worse than when Harding had visited him in Monte Carlo on Friday – tired, rumpled and preoccupied, his face knotted in a frown that lifted only faintly when he spotted Harding.

They shook hands, Tozer adding a hefty clap to the shoulder as if to confirm their unity of purpose. 'Wouldn't have blamed you if you'd decided to stand me up, Tim. This is all basically my fault.'

'I don't know about that, Barney. I made a few mistakes myself. Let's just try to sort it out.'

'Good lad. Tony said you wouldn't let me down.'

'Tony knows we're here, does he?'

'Couldn't leave him out of the loop, Tim. Matter of fact, he's . . . prepared the ground for us.'

'How d'you mean?'

'I'll explain as we go.'

They could have taken a train into the city centre, but Tozer preferred a taxi. The driver's severely limited command of English ensured the degree of privacy he evidently required.

'It was actually Tony who handled the arrangements with the Horstelmann Clinic on my behalf,' he revealed as the taxi sped along the autobahn towards Munich through the pewter-grey Bavarian morning. 'Using Nathan Gashry as cover was his idea too.'

'Has he had another idea?'

'Sort of. We kept the clinic sweet – and discreet – by fixing up a couple of freebies for the chief administrator. He got to meet some celebs at the Cannes Film Festival – that kind of thing. We run a stable of potentially influential people who owe us favours. Ulbricht, the administrator, is one of them, thanks to accepting our generosity. Tony spoke to him yesterday and reminded him of that. Result: the bloke's interrupting his weekend to meet us this afternoon.'

'Does he know anything about Hayley?'

'He didn't yesterday. But hopefully he'll have found out if she's contacted anyone at the clinic by the time we see him. My bet is she has. That must be the help she told Ann Gashry she was getting.'

'Let's hope so.'

'Yeah.' Tozer rubbed his jaw reflectively. 'I never thought I'd find myself going back to the Horstelmann Clinic, that's a fact.'

'When were you last there?'

'Three years ago. Shortly after Kerry's parents were killed. I spoke to her doctor. Just to confirm there was . . . no chance of a recovery. I did my best for her. I even asked if her sister had been in touch. When I was told she hadn't, I . . . assumed she'd washed her hands of her family. Well, as it stood then, with the Foxtons dead, there seemed no point carrying on. It wasn't actually my decision. But when I stopped paying for Kerry's treatment . . .'

'They stopped treating her.'

'She was already dead, Tim. She was never going to come out of that coma.'

'Why did you pay for her to go to the Horstelmann Clinic in the first place, then?'

'I felt responsible for what had happened to her. I wanted to do something – anything – that might . . . ease my conscience, I suppose. I didn't expect any miracles. But the Foxtons did, of course. And I'd have been happy to pay for them to go on expecting them indefinitely.'

'But you wouldn't have been happy for them to *know* you were paying.'

'They wouldn't have understood. They'd have taken it as proof that I murdered their daughter. So would a good few others. Ray Trathen for one. So, I kept it quiet. I told no one except Tony.'

'Not even Carol?'

'No.' Tozer grimaced. 'I didn't want any . . . bad memories . . . getting between us.'

'Does she know now?'

Tozer nodded. 'I told her straight after you called.'

'How did she react?'

'She wasn't best pleased, to put it mildly. She finished up saying I'd got us into this mess . . . and had better get us out.' Tozer gave Harding a ruefully crumpled sidelong grin. 'Well, she's right, isn't she?'

They booked into a city centre hotel selected for them by Whybrow. The Cortiina was his sort of place – smart, reserved and efficient. After a snatched lunch in the hotel bar, they ordered a taxi and headed for the Horstelmann Clinic.

It was too soon for Harding to have any grasp of the geography of Munich. They were bound for Schwabing, according to Tozer. It looked a nice part of town through the taxi window – quiet and prosperous, an ideal location for the kind of establishment the Horstelmann was.

The clinic was, in the event, hard to distinguish at a glance from the elegant apartment blocks lining the side-street it was situated in. Its double-doored entrance was wider, but not by much. The brass plaque bearing its name was modestly proportioned. And Harding did not notice that the door handles were fashioned in the likeness of medical caducei until he was about to push at one of them – only for the doors to swing open automatically at the last moment.

The reception area had the hushed and wood-panelled air of an exclusive spa, with a statuesque blonde on duty to complete the effect. They were, of course, expected. She directed them to the lift with an orthodontically idealized smile. And they reached Herr Ulbricht's office without glimpsing a single nurse, far less a patient.

'Welcome, Mr Tozer.'

Ulbricht was a neat, fussy little man in occupation of a neat, fussy but by no means little office. His hair was fair, almost yellow, complementing the strange golden hue of his skin. His small, round eyes sparkled opalescently behind small, round glasses. He seemed slightly breathless, if not nervous, though whether their presence was the cause of this remained unclear.

'And your friend . . .'

'Tim Harding.'

'Welcome also.' They shook hands. Ulbricht's palm was clammy, but his grip was tight. 'Sit. Please.'

Harding and Tozer took the chairs arranged in front of the desk. Ulbricht sat behind it, separated from them by several feet of pale, polished wood conspicuously bare of paperwork. At the Horstelmann, less was evidently more in all departments.

'Mr Whybrow explained the . . . difficulty of your situation,' said Ulbricht, his smile of greeting fading slowly.

'Good,' Tozer responded.

'I have made . . . enquiries.'

'We're grateful, Heinz, believe me.' Ulbricht's first name had not previously been mentioned. Tozer's use of it now struck Harding as calculated – a declaration of the extent to which the administrator was beholden to him.

'We have rules . . . of confidentiality.'

'Which we understand. And respect.'

'So, what I say . . . must be . . .'

'Between us.' Tozer squeezed his forefinger and thumb together and ran them across his mouth as if zipping it shut. 'Absolutely.'

'Very good.' Ulbricht cleared his throat and re-assembled his smile. 'It appears . . . Miss Foxton – Miss Hayley Foxton – came into the clinic Thursday. She desired to speak with the doctor who was in charge of her sister's case. This was a big surprise. We had no records of a sister. But she showed her passport. The date of birth and the place of birth matched our records of Kerry Foxton. Also, one of the nurses . . . recognized her. Noticed the resemblance, I mean. This was . . . em-barrassing. As next of kin, she should have been informed of the decision to . . . to . . .' Ulbricht's mouth shaped itself round several possible expressions, none of which made it into speech.

'The decision to terminate Kerry,' suggested Harding, drawing a frown from Tozer.

'Ja,' said Ulbricht, with a slight nod of the head. 'This is so. Procedure required it. But . . . we were not told about her.' There was a hint of reproof in his glance at Tozer. 'We did not know.'

'Did she get to speak to the doctor?' Tozer prompted.

'*Ja*. Friday. Dr Hanckel met with her. There was no problem. She . . . understood. She gave no complaint. She only wanted to . . . speak about her sister . . . and her time here.'

'So, Hanckel filled her in?' asked Tozer.

'He told her . . . as much as he could.'

'And then?'

'She left.'

'That was it?'

'Not . . . exactly. Dr Hanckel gave her some . . . items belonging to her sister. We had kept them after the . . . termination. And he suggested she contact her sister's . . . companion.'

'Her what?' put in Harding.

'We have a . . . *Begleiter Programm* for coma patients. Each patient has a companion who visits them regularly. To talk to them. To read to them. It shows good results. But not always. *Natürlich*. And not for Kerry Foxton. Still, the companion spent longer with her than anyone else, so . . . Dr Hanckel thought it could help Hayley to speak with him.'

'Can we speak with him?' asked Tozer.

'I will give you his name and contact details. I have not contacted him myself. He no longer works for us. It must be a . . . private matter between you.'

'Sure.'

'What about those items Hayley took away with her?' asked Harding.

'Minor personal effects. Nothing valuable. Nothing

important. But our policy is to store those things for five years if they are not removed by the family.'

'What were they?'

Ulbricht slid open a drawer in his desk and read from a note he had presumably left there with this query in mind. 'Some earrings. A necklace. A brooch. Several books and CDs.' He looked up. 'Dr Hanckel would have asked Mr and Mrs Foxton to bring some of Kerry's favourite books for the companion to read from. And her music to play.' He looked back down again. '*Ja*. There was also a . . . *Blockflöte*.'

'Sorry?'

'*Blockflöte*. I have not the English for it. It is . . . a pipe children play.'

'A recorder?'

'*Ja*.' Ulbricht smiled. 'A recorder. This is the word.'

A picture formed in Harding's mind of Kerry Foxton lying in a mutedly lit room somewhere in the Horstelmann Clinic, motionless in her bed, wired, drained and tracheotomized, her eyes firmly closed as the plangent notes of her childhood recorder sounded unheard and unremembered in her ears.

'The companion's name is Gary Lawton. He is English. This is why he was chosen for Kerry. I do not know what he told Hayley. He may have told her nothing. He may tell you nothing.'

'Hayley hasn't been back here, though, has she?' Harding asked.

'She has not.'

'So, it looks like she got something out of him.'

Ulbricht pursed his lips. 'I . . . cannot say.'

'Don't worry, Heinz.' Tozer grinned at him. 'We'll ask the man who *can* say. And we'll make sure we get an answer.'

TWENTY-NINE

Gary Lawton lived with his German wife, Helga, and their three children in a brand-new little semi-detached house of glaring white render, pale brick and orangey terracotta roof tiles deep in newly colonized residential land on the eastern fringe of the city. Harding and Tozer's arrival at their door excited the children – and the dog – but elicited from Gary and Helga only brittle smiles.

'The Horstelmann Clinic sent you, did they?' Gary asked glumly.

'Yeah,' Tozer replied. 'Any chance we could have a word about Hayley Foxton?'

'I suppose. Who did you say you were?'

'Barney Tozer. Tim Harding.'

'Tozer? Don't I remember that name . . . in connection with Kerry's accident?'

'I was the other diver.'

'Ah. You were, were you?'

Helga said something to Gary in German that

sounded anxious and reproachful. He smiled grimly and nodded.

'Maybe this isn't such a good idea, gents.'

'I'm a friend of Hayley's, Mr Lawton,' said Harding. 'You should know she broke into Barney's home last Wednesday night and threatened his wife with a knife.'

Gary grimaced. 'Oh hell.'

Helga contributed another four pfennigs' worth. Gary's response sounded soothing but uncertain. It caused Helga to throw up her hands and stalk away, shooing the children and the dog ahead of her.

'You'd better come in,' said Gary with a frown of resignation.

He led them through to a square, bare-walled lounge dominated by an enormous flat-screen television. The furniture was of the unstructured bean-baggish variety. Patio doors looked out on to a small, immature garden. There were several toys and a large rubber bone lying on the pocket-handkerchief lawn.

'Want a drink?' Lawton asked, taking a swig from a bottle of Löwenbräu standing on the coffee-table. He was lean and round-shouldered, thirty-five or so, with spiky hair and a pasty, small-featured face. There were lots of smile lines round his eyes and mouth and he looked, in his low-slung jeans and sweatshirt, every inch the suburban family man. But his expression was downcast, his glance wary. He was not merely suspicious of his visitors, but anxious about what their journey to his home signified.

Harding and Tozer both declined the offered drink. A fragile silence formed in the room. The cries of the children seeped through from elsewhere in the house. Lawton puffed out his cheeks and took another swig from the bottle.

'When did she come here?' Harding asked.

'She didn't. She phoned. I went into the city centre to meet her. In a beer-hall.'

'When was that?'

'Early Friday evening.'

'After she'd been to the Horstelmann Clinic?'

'Yeah. Hanckel put her on to me.'

'Because you were Kerry's . . . companion.'

'Sounds like you know it all.'

'We don't know what you told her.'

'No. Well, maybe that's between me and her.'

'If she pulls any more stunts like last Wednesday and you turn out to have helped her cover her tracks,' growled Tozer, 'it won't look too clever for you.'

'Worried she might have a go at you, are you?'

'Should I be?'

'Maybe.'

'We're trying to help her, Gary,' said Harding. 'And she does need help. I'm sure you realize that.'

'I don't know where she is. She didn't say where she was staying. She may have left Munich by now for all I know.'

'Just let us in on your chat in the pub,' said Tozer. 'We'll settle for that.'

'We talked about Kerry. That's it.'

252

'Come on, Gary,' said Harding. 'We need to know.'

Lawton cast a sidelong glance behind him into the garden, then sat down in one of the shapeless chairs. Harding and Tozer took up cramped occupation of the sagging sofa opposite him. There was another silence. Gary appeared to be locked in some fierce debate with himself, the darting of his eyes signalling the trading of points. Then, quite suddenly, it was over. He heaved a sigh. 'It really was all about Kerry.'

'What about her?' Harding prompted.

Lawton carefully replaced the bottle on the table and rubbed his forehead. 'The *Begleiter Programm* sounds like a cushy number when you sign up for it. Good money, which I needed at the time. Helga and I had just got together and I didn't have a regular job. The two oldest kids aren't mine, you see. Anyway, it seemed an easy way to earn some dosh. The clinic's an OK place to be if you don't mind the . . . hermetic atmosphere. And working as a companion? Well, it's a doddle. So you think when you start, anyway. Sit by the bedsides of these wordless, motionless people and read to them or talk to them or hold their hand or just . . . just sit. The undead. That's what they are. The gone but not quite departed. Oh, a few of them come back. Part of the way, but never the whole way, if you know what I mean. Must be like being shut up in prison for a couple of decades. The world you return to isn't exactly the one you left. Everything's slightly but crucially . . . *off*.'

'The job got to you, did it?' asked Tozer, with the hint of a sneer.

'Yeah.' Lawton glared at him. 'Big time. You spend long enough with someone like Kerry, young, beautiful, talented, full of . . . spirit . . . and, yeah, it gets to you all right. You read up on her background. You speak to her family and friends. Well, those who show up, I mean. You read her favourite books and listen to her favourite music. You talk to her. About this and that, something and nothing, *her*, *you*. You sit with her. A few hours, every few days. She doesn't say a word. She doesn't so much as open her eyes. She doesn't respond in any way at all. But still, little by little, you get to know her. Or you imagine you do. You wonder what it would be like, what *she'd* be like, really *like*, if one day . . . she sat up in that bed and said, "Hello, Gary."'

'But she never did,' put in Harding.

'No. That's right. She never did. They switched her off. I stood there when they did it. I watched her die. I went to her funeral too. Which is more than any of those many friends I'm sure she had bothered to do.'

'Maybe they didn't know about it.'

'Maybe. But Barney here knew. Didn't you?' Lawton's look defied Tozer to deny it. 'According to Hayley, you paid for Kerry's treatment. And then you stopped paying.'

'I did it . . . for her parents' sake.' Tozer shifted uneasily on the sofa. 'When they were killed, there was no point going on. I checked with Dr Hanckel. There wasn't a hope in hell she'd ever recover.'

'No. But then there never was, was there? Luckily for you.'

'What d'you mean by that?'

'Well, you must've wondered what she'd say – about *you* – if she ever woke up. I mean, as I understand it, we only have your word for what happened to Kerry during that dive.'

'Now just a—'

Tozer was halfway out of the sofa when Harding grabbed his elbow. 'Sit down, Barney,' he urged. 'We're just talking, OK?'

'I've had seven years of people who know absolutely bloody *nothing* insinuating that I murdered Kerry.'

'I know.'

Tozer stared across at Lawton as he slowly sat back down. 'I was careless. But so was Kerry. Which no one ever mentions. It was an accident. They happen. But she's always the victim. And I'm always the villain.'

'What was Hayley's . . . state of mind . . . when you met her, Gary?' Harding asked, endeavouring to steer the conversation into smoother waters.

'Calm. Rational. Curious.'

'Curious about what?'

'Kerry's last days.'

'Which you described to her?'

'Yeah. The switch-off at the clinic. The cremation at Ostfriedhof. I talked her through the whole thing. She seemed . . . glad to hear about it. Like it was . . . the next best thing to being there at the time.' Lawton sighed and looked across awkwardly at Tozer. 'Maybe I was . . . out of line . . . just now. Maybe I . . . went too far. Sorry.'

'That's OK,' said Tozer, with a hint of sarcasm. 'I'm used to it.'

'When you parted,' Harding resumed, 'did she give you any idea . . . what she meant to do next?'

'No.'

'Or where she meant to go?'

'No.'

There was something in Gary's tone – in his manner and his posture – that made Harding doubt this neatly wrapped version of their encounter. He sensed there had been more to it, more said, more imparted, more declared. 'Surely she—'

Harding was cut off by the bleeping of Tozer's mobile. He pulled it out of his pocket and glanced at the screen. 'It's Carol. I'd better take it. Sorry.' He stood up and pointed enquiringly towards the patio doors.

'Go ahead,' said Lawton. 'They're open.'

'Won't be long,' said Tozer, clapping the phone to his ear as he strode past Lawton to the doors and slid them apart. 'Hello, princess. Everything OK?'

Tozer was still absorbing the answer to this question as he slid the doors shut behind him. Harding looked steadily across at Lawton. 'It must have been a shock, learning Kerry had a twin. Then meeting her. Almost like what you said: Kerry waking up one day and speaking to you.'

'Almost.' Lawton dwelt on the thought for a moment, then went on. 'She was wearing a brooch that had belonged to Kerry. One of the things her parents had brought over from England. Hanckel gave it to her, apparently.'

'So Ulbricht said.'

'Yeah. It's a fox cub. Chosen as a gift because of their surname. Nice little thing. Jet and mother-of-pearl, I remember Mrs Foxton saying. I'd seen it dozens of times, lying with the other things where she used to arrange them beside the bed..But never worn. I'd never seen it worn before. That was . . . weird.'

'Did Hayley mention me?'

'No. Unless . . .'

'What?'

'I asked her . . . y'know, if there was anyone . . . in her life.'

'What did she say?'

' "Not sure." I mean, that's what she said. "I'm not sure." Is it you she's not sure about?'

'Could be.'

'Yeah. And you tagging along with Barney Tozer could be the reason.'

'That's not—'

One of the patio doors jerked open. Tozer stared in at Harding, still clutching the phone in his hand, several inches away from his ear, as if the call had not yet ended.

'What is it, Barney?'

'Hayley. She's been in touch. She wants to meet us. You and me. Here in Munich. Tomorrow.'

THIRTY

'Where's Nymphenburg?' Tozer demanded of Lawton the instant he ended his conversation with Carol. Harding was still waiting for some clarification of Hayley's message, including why it had come via Carol. And it seemed for the moment that he would have to go on waiting.

'It's the suburban palace of the old Bavarian royal family,' Lawton replied. 'Out to the west.'

'Ever been there?'

'Once or twice.'

'Is there a park behind the palace?'

'Yeah. Acres of it.'

'And a canal?'

'Er, yeah. I think so. An ornamental affair. Beyond the garden.'

'So, her directions made sense.'

'How about letting me in on them?' asked Harding.

'I'll fill you in on our way back into town, Tim. No

sense keeping our taxi waiting any longer, is there? And we're done here, aren't we?' Tozer looked at Lawton with an expression that suggested their host had suddenly become irrelevant – and that this was a welcome development.

'Hold on,' said Lawton, evidently no less confused than Harding. 'That wasn't Hayley on the phone.'

'No. But she's left a message for me. We'll meet tomorrow. And sort all this out. No need for you to worry about it any more, squire.'

'Are you sure about this? She's going to meet you at Nymphenburg tomorrow?'

'I'm sure. And like I said: you can leave it to us.'

'Was needling Lawton such a good idea, Barney?' Harding asked as their taxi pulled away from the house.

'Tit for tat. He'll get over it.'

'And what did you mean about the message from Hayley? Did she phone Carol?'

'No. Nathan Gashry phoned Carol.'

'*Nathan?*'

'Hayley didn't want to speak to any of us direct, apparently. Not over the phone, anyway. It has to be face to face. She got Nathan to pass the message on. Ten o'clock tomorrow morning, at Nymphenburg. We're to take the path through the park along the north side of the canal. She'll be waiting.'

'How did she know we were in Munich?'

'Maybe Ann Gashry told her. You didn't leave her in any doubt you meant to follow Hayley here, did you?'

'No. But I never said you'd be coming with me. At the time, I didn't know you would be.'

'Guesswork, then. Or a tip-off from someone at the clinic.'

'Something like that, I suppose. Or else . . .'

'What?'

'I don't know.' That was not quite true. The other possibility, in its way the most worrying, was that Hayley knew they were together because she had already seen them together. Which put her very much one step ahead. And meant she was likely to view Harding as Tozer's friend, not hers. He had not abandoned her. But he was going to have his work cut out convincing her of that. 'I just don't know.'

Tozer did not share Harding's disquiet – nor indeed the reasons for it. Over dinner and several drinks in the bar opposite the hotel afterwards he struck a confident note, apparently convinced that Hayley's desire to meet them signalled a willingness on her part to admit she needed professional help in coping with the demons the past had left her with.

'I'm not a monster. Or a murderer. I think she's coming round to understanding that. And she must realize the only reason we haven't shopped her to the police is that we want to do our best for her – and draw a line under this whole bloody episode.'

'I hope you're right.'

'I am. According to Nathan she sounded humble, almost apologetic. She wants to put it all behind her,

Tim. We just have to make it possible. And we will. Tomorrow.'

It was not yet eleven o'clock when Harding returned to his room. Tozer had called an early halt to their drinking session to ensure they both had a clear head in the morning. Harding felt far from sleepy, however. And he needed, for his own sake, to check Barney's optimistic assessment of their situation with Carol. Her number was busy the first time he tried it. And the second. But not the third.

'Nice of you to call,' was her barbed greeting.

'Have you just been talking to Barney?' he asked, ignoring the rebuke.

'Yeah. We've been saying goodnight, like the happily married couple we are.'

'How did he seem?'

'Fine. The way he tells it, tomorrow gets the job done.'

'What about Nathan Gashry? How did *he* seem?'

'Grouchy and grudging. As you'd expect. He didn't enjoy having to call me.'

'Why do you think Hayley went through him?'

'You tell me. You know her better than I do.'

'I have this feeling she may be more interested in confrontation than conciliation.'

'I'm sure you can handle that.'

'I'm doing my best on your behalf as well as my own, Carol. Remember that.'

'I'm trying to.'

'How did Hayley know Barney and I were both here? That's what worries me.'

'Barney thinks she may have a mole at the clinic.'

'I doubt it.'

'What's your theory, then?'

'I don't know. But . . .'

'Got an itchy feeling between the shoulderblades?'

'Sorry?'

'They tell me it's a sign you're being watched.'

Harding sighed. 'Thanks for the advice.'

'Listen, Tim.' She sounded suddenly more serious. 'Maybe Barney's right. Maybe Hayley's willing to come quietly. That'd be fine as far as it goes. But it doesn't get us off the hook with Tony Whybrow, does it? What are we going to do about him?'

'I don't know.'

'No. And neither do I. *That's* what should be worrying you.'

Harding felt, if anything, less drowsy after his conversation with Carol than before. He resorted to Euromush television in the hope it might knock him out. But long before the rules of an Italian game show had become clear to him, his phone rang, only for the caller to cancel the moment he answered. The number had been withheld, which was suspicious in itself. A repeat performance a minute or so later convinced him someone was trying to tell him something.

It was the recollection of Carol's crack about an itchy feeling between the shoulderblades that prompted him to go to the window and check the street outside. He had closed the shutter earlier. A surreptitious peek was hardly possible. There was nothing for it but to open the window and then the shutter to see if there really was anyone keeping watch on his room.

The figure on the opposite pavement was walking away. But Harding's instinctive impression was that she had been stationary until the instant he opened the shutter. Her face was obscured by the brim of a hat. But he recognized the short, belted mac. She was Hayley's height and build. In that moment, there was no doubt in his mind. It was her.

He only realized it was raining heavily when he burst out of the hotel. There were several groups of people making their way along the street, clutching umbrellas, and a couple of taxis dropping off passengers. His glimpse of Hayley in the distance, rounding a corner, was scarcely more than a guess. But he raced in pursuit.

There she was again, surely, rounding the next corner into the main shopping street. He was running head-long now, oblivious to the rain and the traffic and the passers-by. But she was running too, a twitch of shadow implying a backward glance. And the lights of Marienplatz U-Bahn station gleamed ahead. Suddenly, she vanished from sight.

Harding's plunge down the steps to the station was slowed by a collision with a couple coming up. The male half fired some insults after him as he reached the concourse. He did not look back. His eyes scanned the escalators leading down to the platforms. There was no sign of Hayley. She could have taken any one of them. He could hear trains pulling in and out even as he stood there, hesitating. Every line on the system went through Marienplatz, to judge by the number of destinations on offer. He had no idea where Hayley was going. If evading him was her priority, she could have chosen the first train to any-where, or even exited the station at the other end of the concourse.

He checked all the platforms in the end, futile though he knew the effort would be. The clocks of the city churches were striking midnight as he made his way back to the hotel. It had stopped raining and was grow-ing rapidly colder. He was shivering, though whether the drenching he had received was the cause he could not have said.

THIRTY-ONE

By morning Harding had convinced himself he might have been mistaken. Maybe the woman he had seen was not Hayley after all, but someone who merely happened to look like her, someone hurrying through the rain to catch a late train home. Why should she be watching him when they were due to meet soon anyway? And why should she run from him? It made no sense. But what about the phone calls? Who had made them? Who – and why?

He said nothing to Tozer about what had happened. His doubts and suspicions were too vague to put into words and nothing seemed likely to dent the other man's confidence that their rendezvous with Hayley would bring a resolution of their problems. Harding had more problems than Tozer knew about, of course. A resolution of them all was way out of reach. But Hayley had said she wanted to meet them. And he badly wanted to see her again – to talk to her, to make her understand. The circumstances would not be ideal. They would be about as far as possible from ideal. But they were the only ones on offer.

Nymphenburg. The baroque, white-faced palace flung back the clear winter light at them as they walked towards it. A tunnel led beneath the central block to a formal garden, beyond which the park, patched with old snow and fresh frost, stretched its wooded acres into the distance. The sky was cloudless, every shadow sharply etched.

Halfway along the path leading through the garden to the canal basin, Tozer checked his watch and announced they were early for their appointment with Hayley. They diverted to the nearest bench and sat down. Tozer lit a cigarette and gazed back at the palace.

'Know anything about the Bavarian royal family, Tim?' he asked, to Harding's surprise.

'As much as you, I expect.'

Tozer chuckled. 'You underestimate me. Carol and I toured the castles down near the Austrian border the year after we were married. Y'know: the fairytale ones built by Mad King Ludwig. Neuschwanstein and the rest. As King of Bavaria, Ludwig must have whiled away quite a lot of his time here in his day, mustn't he?'

'So?'

'So, we remember him as mad. Which is how a lot of people remember Hayley. I wondered . . . if she chose to meet us here . . . to make some kind of point about that.'

266

'Are you serious?'

'Not sure. But I'm definitely serious about making this meeting work. For all of us. I'm going to follow Lawton's lead. Tell Hayley about her sister. What happened to her the day she died. I mean when she *really* died, not when Hanckel pulled the plug on her four years later. Hayley's never heard my account of the accident, has she? It's time she did.'

'Neither have I, come to that.'

'It really was an accident, Tim. You know that, don't you?'

'Of course.'

'I've thought about it a lot these past few days. I mean, could Kerry's gear have been sabotaged? Not by me, obviously. I *know* I didn't do it. But by someone else?'

'Well? Could it?'

'Only if you're willing to rope in some pretty unlikely suspects. I took all our gear over on the helicopter the day before the dive. Kerry was staying with Carol in Hugh Town. Ray Trathen travelled with me. I sent him off to a b. and b. and stayed overnight with the Metherells. We loaded the gear into John's car and left it there till morning. Then we drove down to the quay first thing and put it aboard the *Jonquil*. The Martyns were waiting for us. I left John with them and went to fetch the girls. We bumped into Ray Trathen on the way back to the quay. Then we set off. It was a perfect morning. Not a cloud in the sky. Not a breath of wind. Like today. Only about twenty degrees warmer.'

'The unlikely suspects, then, are Metherell and the Martyns.'

'John could have crept out to his car during the night and tampered with one of the hoses. But he'd have had no way of knowing which of them Kerry would end up using. Unless I was the target, of course. Or unless he didn't care which of us he was endangering. It's a crazy idea anyway. He set the trip up as a favour to me, but he was keen to go out to the site of the wreck because of his book about the *Association*. He had no reason to want either of us dead. And if he's innocent, so are the Martyns. They couldn't have done anything without him noticing. Besides, they're just Scillonian boatmen who ply for hire. The last thing they'd have wanted was a fatality during a dive from their boat.'

'Alf Martyn said penetrating the wreck on single air supply was foolhardy.'

'He's right. But maybe Kerry didn't realize just *how* foolhardy. Maybe I didn't ram the message home to her.'

'It might help if you told Hayley how much you regret that.'

'I plan to, Tim, believe me.' Tozer dropped his cigarette butt on to the ground and crushed it with his boot, then glanced at his watch. 'It's nearly ten. Let's go.'

They left the garden and headed out slowly along the path beside the ornamental canal, bare-limbed trees to their right, turbid, half-frozen water to their left. The palace had only just opened to visitors and few had

268

made it as far as the park. A woman with a yapping dog was walking along the path on the opposite bank of the canal. But on their side there was no sign of anyone.

'She *is* going to turn up, isn't she, Tim?' Tozer asked anxiously.

'She told us to be here, Barney. And here we are.'

'But where's *she*?'

'Give her—' He broke off. His phone was ringing.

As Harding came to a halt, Tozer went on for a few paces, then turned to look at him. 'Expecting a call?' He arched his eyebrows meaningfully.

'It can't be Hayley.'

'Can't it?'

Harding grabbed the phone from his pocket and answered. 'Hello?'

'Darren here, Mr H. Calling back as promised.'

Harding swore under his breath. He had completely forgotten Spargo's squalid little money-making manoeuvre. He had not so much as mentioned it to Barney. 'I can't talk now,' he said quietly.

'Why not? You've had a couple of days to sort things out with Megabucks.'

'I'll phone you back later.'

'Oh no. I'm not being strung along like that.'

Tozer spread his hands enquiringly. Harding gave him a stalling wave and turned away to avoid his gaze while he dealt with Spargo. 'This isn't a good time. I—'

There was a loud crack, like ice fracturing under

269

pressure, but so close to Harding's ear that he ducked down defensively. 'Caught you at the shooting range, have I?' he heard Spargo ask. Then he looked back at Tozer. And the phone slipped from his fingers.

Tozer was on his knees, clutching at his throat, his eyes wide, staring helplessly at Harding. He tried to speak, but no words came from his mouth, only a trickle of blood. Then there was another loud crack. Tozer's head jerked forward. Bloody fragments of brain and bone burst from the back of his skull. He toppled over, hitting the ground like a falling sack, his last breath forced from him in a dying grunt.

For a second, Harding did not react. Then there was a third crack. He dodged instinctively and saw something that had to be a bullet ping off a pebble a foot or so in front of him. There was nowhere to run to or hide. The only shelter was in the trees, where the shots were coming from. The thought formed in his mind, clear and hard and brittle as an icicle, that he was about to die. A fourth crack snapped the thought clean off. He flung himself to the ground, twisting his head and squinting despairingly towards the trees. Hayley could not be doing this. It was not possible. She had not been able to go through with killing Carol. Surely she—

But yes. It was her. A dark shape detached itself from the cover of one of the tree trunks in his lopsided field of vision. She had stopped shooting and was running hard now, deeper into the woods. This time, she did not look back. A black, fleeing figure, moving fast, threading

270

between the trees, like a deer fleeing the hunter. But in this case the deer *was* the hunter. And she had made a kill.

THIRTY-TWO

For much of the rest of the day, Harding dwelt only half in the real world. Part of his mind – and, strangely, it also seemed to him, his body – was absent, banished to some realm where the events of the past twelve days assembled, dismantled and reassembled themselves slowly and inexorably before him, obedient to a logic he had understood too late. Barney Tozer was dead. Hayley Foxton had taken her revenge. And Harding had been there to witness it happening.

The sluggishness of his reactions posed no problem to the *Kriminal-Polizei* officers who interviewed him at Munich Police HQ for several long, laborious hours. The British Embassy had supplied an interpreter and the translation of the officers' questions and Harding's answers slowed the proceedings to a crawl. He told them as much of the truth as he knew. Tozer's death had rendered any kind of subterfuge or suppression not merely futile, but obscene. Not that the police evinced much interest in the complexities surrounding the case. To them, it was simple. Hayley Foxton blamed Barney Tozer for her sister's death. Tozer had foolishly failed to take the intrusion at his apartment in Monte Carlo as the danger signal it undoubtedly was. He had even more foolishly agreed to meet Hayley in an exposed and isolated location. And he had paid the price.

Harding emphasized that no one could have imagined Hayley would possess a gun – let alone know how to use it. But the police, it seemed, routinely imagined such things. They pointed out that she could have been practising target-shooting for months with this moment in mind. He was, they implied, lucky to be alive himself; unless, of course, she had missed him deliberately, wanting him to identify her as the murderer, needing there to be no doubt what she had done and why.

The search for Hayley had commenced long before Harding's questioning had ended. By the time he was thanked for his assistance and sent on his way, late that afternoon, she might, for all he knew, already be under arrest. There was nothing he could do for her now. If they had not found her yet, they soon would. The future she had made for herself allowed for no turning back.

Tony Whybrow was waiting for him in the station's reception area, a layer of grimness added to his habitual calm.

'I hope they haven't given you a hard time, Tim.'

273

'They just wanted as many details as I could supply.'

'You look all in.'

'Shock, I expect. Delayed reaction. Sorrow most of all. I never saw this coming. Not in a million years.'

'Carol and I flew up here on the same plane. She's at the morgue now.'

'Oh God.'

'You're going to have to go through it all again, I'm afraid.'

Harding sighed. 'We should have contacted the police after she threatened Carol, shouldn't we?'

'Yes. I blame myself for that.'

'Barney was confident he could come to an understanding with Hayley. He was . . . looking forward to meeting her, I think, in a strange kind of way.'

'And she was looking forward to meeting him. In a very different kind of way.'

'Yes.' Harding nodded glumly. 'Apparently she was.'

Carol joined them in the bar at the Cortiina. She seemed numbed by her visit to the morgue, so overwhelmed by what had happened that she was not even visibly upset. Her face was a mask, her gaze barely focused. She listened to Harding's account of how her husband had died with little reaction beyond a few faltering questions, though one of those was in its way more difficult to answer than any the police had posed.

'Do you think Barney knew who'd shot him?'

'Maybe. But he only had a second or so to know anything. It was quick, Carol. That's the only consolation I can think of.'

'It's not much of one.'

'I know.'

'Do they execute murderers in Germany, Tony?'

'No, Carol. They don't.'

'Pity.'

'But they imprison them for life. And I'm sure that's what they'll do to Hayley Foxton when they catch her.'

'*If* they catch her.'

'They will, I'm sure. Soon, probably.'

'How soon?'

'The police will let us know immediately there's any news.'

'I'll have to tell Humph.'

'D'you want me to do that?' Harding offered.

'No. He's not the only one I have to notify. I'd better just . . . get on with it.'

'I'll deal with everybody on the business side who needs to know,' said Whybrow. 'And I'll handle all the form-filling to get Barney back to Monaco.'

'Or Cornwall,' said Carol. 'I'll have to discuss that with Humph.'

'All right. But don't take too much on yourself. We don't need to make any decisions until tomorrow at the earliest.'

'Tomorrow. Yes.' Carol looked at Harding, a spark of her normal self gleaming in her gaze. 'I want to go to

Nymphenburg tomorrow, Tim. To see where it happened. Will you take me?'

'Of course.'

'I'll organize a car,' said Whybrow.

'No need,' said Carol. 'We can take a taxi. And . . . I'd like it to be just Tim and me.' She glanced at Whybrow. 'If you don't mind, Tony.'

Whybrow smiled tightly. 'No problem.'

'That was interesting,' said Whybrow, when Carol had gone up to her room – Barney's room, where his clothes and toiletries were still waiting for him, but which he would never use again.

'Interesting?' Harding dragged his thoughts back to the present once more, away from his memories of the gentle, truth-seeking Hayley he could still not reconcile with the Hayley he had seen running away through the trees at Nymphenburg that morning.

'Carol's a surprisingly resilient person,' Whybrow mused. 'She's already adjusting to the new reality. As I suppose we'll all have to.'

'How d'you mean?'

'Well, I assume Carol will inherit everything from Barney. Including Starburst International. She'll be in charge from now on.'

The point had not yet occurred to Harding. Tozer's death had cut the ground from beneath Whybrow's feet. His hold over them had been his threat to tell Tozer about their affair. Now it did not matter. Carol had become a power in the land. And Whybrow was going to have to accept that she was the boss.

Or was she? Harding's mind grasped a more complex and disturbing possibility in the instant before Whybrow put it into words. 'One should never underestimate the ability of the police to misread situations, of course. If certain information came into their possession, they might think you and Carol had a motive for murdering Barney. And they only have your word for it that it was actually Hayley who shot him.'

Harding took his time before responding. He looked at Whybrow unwaveringly, determined not to rise to the bait by losing his temper. 'A woman walking her dog on the other side of the canal saw the whole thing. The police told me they'd interviewed her.'

'But will she be able to identify Hayley – when they pick her up?'

'I don't know.'

'No matter. I'm sure the police will settle for a straightforward interpretation of the facts. Provided nobody . . . muddies the water.' Whybrow smiled thinly. 'It might be a good idea if you mentioned that to Carol tomorrow, Tim. During your visit . . . to the scene of the crime.'

Harding walked himself into a state of exhaustion that night round the streets of Munich. Horrified by what had happened and sickened by his failure to understand the way Hayley's mind had been working, he could be sure of only one thing. He would have to extricate himself from the affairs of the Tozer family. He would have to start his life afresh, without Carol, without Hayley, without the hope – as well as the anguish – the recent past had brought him. There was no other way. He had done it before. He could do it again. Somehow or other, the future would have to be faced.

THIRTY-THREE

Nymphenburg once more. The weather had changed; a cold wind was blowing across the park beneath a slate-grey sky. A long stretch of the canalside path and a large chunk of the woodland bordering it had been cordoned off. Uniformed police were dotted around the perimeter to ensure the cordon was not breached. The search for evidence continued within, though out of sight from the path on the other side of the canal, where Harding stood with Carol, muffled up against the chill, gazing across at the spot where Barney Tozer had died.

The news of Hayley's arrest, which Harding had half expected to hear that morning, had not come. She had either slipped through the net and fled the city or was lying low somewhere, waiting for the intensity of the search to fade. They would catch her eventually, though. That he did not doubt. Even if Carol seemed to.

'I don't want her to get away with this, Tim. Barney was a nice guy. Maybe I never loved him. But I was fond of him. And I already miss him. More than I'd ever have thought possible.' She dabbed at her eyes with a tissue. 'They've got to find her.'

'And they will.'

'Humph talked as if it was Barney's own fault somehow. Heartless bastard. They were flesh and blood. Though you'd never have known it.' She lit a cigarette, Harding holding her hand for a moment to steady the flame of her lighter. 'Anyway, his attitude settled it for me. He took it as read Barney would be buried in Penzance. But he's got another think coming.'

'It's your decision.'

'Like quite a lot else now, hey? You know, I can't believe Tony thinks he can still push me around. Let him tell the police about us if he wants. Hayley did what she did. There's no way we can be dragged into that.'

'He wouldn't go to the police direct, Carol. I imagine the tape of your message would find its way to them anonymously.'

'He doesn't care that Barney's just been murdered, does he? He only cares about safeguarding his position. One of the first things I'm going to do after the funeral is hire an independent accountant to go through Starburst's books line by line. It wouldn't surprise me if Tony had been cheating Barney.'

'It might pay to keep on the right side of Tony. At least for the time being.'

Carol took a thoughtful drag on her cigarette. 'Yeah. I suppose so. Until they catch Hayley, anyway. She won't try to wriggle out of it. She'll be proud to admit what she did. Then Tony's threats will be worthless. And he'll find out what it's like to have me as his boss.'

'I guess Barney's stake in Jardiniera makes you *my* boss too.'

'I'll write that off as a gift, Tim. You don't need to worry about me trying to run Jardiniera.' She turned to look at him. 'It's probably best if we . . . don't have any reason to see much of each other in future.'

'If that's what you want.'

'It must have been what *you* wanted. When you slept with Hayley.' She let him absorb the point for a moment, then went on. 'Of course, you didn't know she was a homicidal maniac then, did you? But maybe it was a smart move after all. Maybe it's why she didn't shoot you as well as Barney.'

'I didn't cause any of this, Carol. You know that.'

'I guess not. If only Barney hadn't sent you to Penzance. He should just have ignored Humph. Then . . .'

'Hayley would have made her move sooner or later. You know that as well.'

'Yeah. And what will happen to her anyway? Some smooth-talking lawyer will persuade the court she wasn't really responsible for her actions. Tragic death of twin sister. History of mental trouble. Extenuating circumstances by the bucket-load. She'll probably only serve a few years in prison.'

'Just before it happened, Barney was saying . . . how much he regretted not having made his peace with Hayley.'

'So, you think it was his fault, do you?'

'No.'

'Whose side *are* you on, Tim? I'd really like to know.'

'Do there have to be sides?'

'Oh yeah. There have to be. I'm surprised life hasn't taught you that.' Carol looked back across the canal.

Following her gaze, Harding noticed two men in plain clothes walking slowly through the wood, within the police cordon. He recognized the taller and leaner of the two as Streibl, the *Kriminal-Polizei* officer who had asked most of the questions the previous day. The other man was stocky, grey-haired and trench-coated, probably the older, possibly senior in rank. Harding had never seen him before. An animated conversation appeared to be in progress between them, complete with emphatic gestures and energetic nods.

'Do you know those two?' asked Carol neutrally.

'The one on the left is Streibl. He's in charge of the investigation. The other bloke . . . I don't know.'

'So that's Streibl, is it? I'm due to meet him this afternoon. Has he finished with you?'

'He asked me to stay in Munich for twenty-four hours in case there was anything they wanted to check. After that . . .'

'You'll be free to go?'

'I guess so.'

'And will you?'

'I suppose. Unless you want me to . . .'

'No.' She looked at him regretfully but unapologetically. 'I don't think I do.'

*   *   *

Harding opted not to share the taxi for the journey back into the centre. It was impossible to tell whether Carol was grateful for this. More likely, Harding reflected as he set off on foot, she did not care. Barney's death had laid bare her inner strength. She was distressed to lose her husband, but not grief-stricken. She was shocked by what Hayley had done, but not overwhelmed. As heiress to Barney's considerable estate, she would soon control the resources she needed to make her life whatever she wanted it to be. And she had already made it clear that Harding would have no place in it.

He was not a religious man. He had never resorted to prayer during Polly's illness, nor lit candles for her after her death. She would not have wanted him to and, as a good agnostic, he had always respected her atheism. Quite why, after the long, cold walk from Nymphenburg, he went into the Frauenkirche, sat himself down in the rearmost pew in the nave and gazed vacantly along the tunnel of pillars towards the distant altar, he could not properly have explained. There had been a choice of ways to make matters right. But Hayley had chosen a different course. Now Barney Tozer was dead. And her act of revenge, however satisfying in the moment of its commission, was unravelling into the ruin of her life. There was nothing Harding could do for her. And the only thing he could do for himself was to abandon her to her fate. He felt empty of hope and purpose, drained of foresight. Above all, he felt alone.

And solitude, as he knew from previous experience, was a bleak place to be.

But solitude in the literal sense was not destined to last long. He was suddenly aware of a figure looming beside him. Glancing up, he was astonished to see the grey-haired man who had been talking to Streibl out at Nymphenburg. He was smiling down at Harding, a roll of fat around his chin distorted by the upturned collar of his coat, his blue eyes twinkling almost mischievously beneath drooping lids and bushy brows.

'Mind if I sit down?' the man asked, doing so without waiting for an answer. His accent was North Country English. He was clearly not from the *Kriminal-Polizei*. 'The name's Unsworth. Chief Inspector Unsworth. Fraud Squad. On secondment to Europol.' He flourished a warrant-card. 'Ever been to The Hague, Mr Harding?'

'*What?*'

'It's where Europol's based. Boring city, let me tell you. Munich, on the other hand . . .' Unsworth gazed about him, apparently savouring the Gothic architecture. 'More style. More character.'

'Did you . . . follow me here?'

'Ah. You spotted me earlier, did you? No. One of Streibl's men tailed you. They're good at the simple stuff. Whereas what I want to discuss with you . . . is a little complicated.' Unsworth grinned. 'Why don't I buy you lunch?'

THIRTY-FOUR

Harding had little appetite for lunch. Chief Inspector Unsworth, on the other hand, attacked his double order of toasted ham-and-cheese sandwiches with a trencherman's vigour, whilst eyeing the Café Kreutzkamm's cake display with dessert clearly in mind. Acerbic observations on the shortcomings of the Dutch capital and variations on a theme of how much he envied Harding his Riviera existence had delayed an explanation of what he actually wanted so long it seemed it might never come. But with one sandwich swallowed and the second commenced in slightly less urgent style, he came to the point at last, albeit by an indirect route.

'Which way did you vote in the Common Market referendum, Mr Harding – back in 1975?' Harding was too bemused by the question at first even to attempt an answer. And Unsworth saved him the bother by snapping his fingers suddenly. 'Hold on. Of course. You were born in 1958. So, just too young to vote in 'seventy-five'. This, Harding could only assume, was a bizarre method of telling him that Unsworth knew more about him than he might have supposed. 'Well, I voted no. Would again if they gave me the chance. Don't let the Europol credentials fool you. I'd pull us out tomorrow if it was up to me. More corrupt than your average banana republic, that outfit in Brussels. Put a stop to one scam and ten more sprout in its place. What's that stuff you gardening types go in fear of? Bondweed?'

'Bindweed.'

'That's it. Tendrils spreading under the earth faster than you can dig 'em up. That's exactly how it feels fighting corruption in the EU, take it from me. Thankless and hopeless. But . . . we soldier on.'

'I'm sure you do.'

'It can take years to crack just one case. You have to be patient, persistent and pragmatic. The three Ps. I swear by 'em. They've always stood me in good stead. You could say it's the third P we're here to explore.'

'Pragmatism?'

'Exactly.'

Harding sighed. 'I'm not with you, Chief Inspector.'

'No. But you soon will be. Would it surprise you to learn that Starburst International is a conduit for millions of euros in fraudulently claimed EU grants?'

It did surprise Harding, though not as much as he tried to pretend. 'I don't believe that for a moment.'

'Come off it. 'Course you do. You don't think Barney Tozer funded his champagne lifestyle out of timeshares and tourism. That's just . . . window-dressing. Starburst's real business is siphoning cash out of Brussels. And it's a high-turnover business, believe you me. We've been watching them for years. Watching them walk away with a chunk of everyone's taxes – including yours.'

'Why haven't you stopped them?'

'Because proof – in a system where you never know who's on the take – is tough to come by. The sort that would stand up in court, anyway. Whybrow, Tozer's money man, is a smart operator. Too smart for most of my colleagues.'

'But not for you?'

'I wouldn't say that. It's Tozer's death that's given us an opening. See, I'm not two bits interested in why he was murdered. This Hayley Foxton they're looking for? She doesn't figure in my plans. No, it's the *fact* of his death that's important. It creates . . . instability. Which I'm hoping to exploit. With your help.'

'*My* help?'

'Look, I'll be frank.' Unsworth napkinned his lips and leant across the table, lowering his voice as he did so. 'Like I say, we've had our eye on Tozer for years. Which means we've had our eye on everyone close to him, including his wife. As a result, we know all about her relationship with you.'

Harding could not suppress a smile. Apparently, even if Whybrow carried out his threat, he would not be telling the police anything they did not already know.

'Something amusing you?'

'No. Carry on.'

'Your lifestyle suggests you're exactly what you claim to be, Mr Harding. Proprietor of a middling garden maintenance and landscaping business. You probably didn't know the money Tozer invested in it was illegally obtained.'

'Hold on.' The conversation had suddenly taken a disturbing turn. 'What are you—'

'But it's how it looks, isn't it? That's the bugbear. It's how it can be made to appear. If you prove . . . uncooperative.'

'What the hell's that supposed to mean?'

'It's an open question whether Mrs Tozer knows what her husband was up to. But it won't stay open much longer. She's going to find out now, even if she didn't know before. She's bound to. What then, eh? My bet is Whybrow will persuade her to carry on the good work. In other words, it'll be business as usual. I can't think of anyone better placed to stop that happening than you. After all, with Tozer out of the way, you don't have to be so careful any more. I expect you'll be parking your toothbrush in the bathroom cabinet at the apartment in Monte before long.'

'You couldn't be more wrong.'

'Really? You and Mrs Tozer had a tiff, have you? Don't worry. You'll soon patch it up. You'll have to. Otherwise, when we move on Starburst – and, believe me, it is when, not if – Tozer's stake in your lawn-trimming outfit will look very bad for you. Trust me on that.'

'Are you blackmailing me?'

'Certainly not.' Unsworth looked theatrically

outraged. 'I'm actually trying to help you. And Mrs Tozer. Now's the time for a clean break from her late husband's shenanigans. Repaying every last cent would be a painful experience for her. I'd be willing to recommend latitude in that department if information was volunteered to us in the wake of Tozer's sad demise. You see what I'm saying? This is your chance to get out from under – and her with you. You'd be well advised to take it. All you have to do is keep your eyes and ears open. I need documentary evidence. You should be able to lay your hands on some, under the guise of helping out your lady love in her new role as Starburst International's supremo.'

'If what you say is true, if Starburst really is involved in—'

'It's involved, Mr Harding. You're going to have to face up to that. Its principal role is as middleman between the EU grants machinery and false claimants. Agricultural subsidies are the biggest turnover item. You know the sort of thing. Hill farms with a grid reference that if any of those Europrats bothered to check they'd realize was in the middle of the Bay of bloody Biscay. Vineyards various golfing chums of Tozer's built high-rise apartment blocks on years ago. It doesn't stop at agriculture, of course. Recently, they've moved into VAT carouselling. Basically, it's anything and everything, with Starburst taking a fat slice every time. I think Tozer got started in the game when Cornwall was awarded Objective One status back in 2000 and EU money started falling like rain on the land of the piskies. Then he brought in Whybrow – an expert in the field – and things really took off.'

'All right. Say all that's true. Say Whybrow really is pulling the strings. He's clever. You admitted that yourself. He's never going to let me get a sniff of anything *proving* what he's up to.'

'He can't stop you. It's Mrs Tozer's company now. He'll have to let her in on it. And what she finds out you find out. *If* you play your cards right. But remember: I need the kind of material that'll stand up in court. So, we'll see what you can dig up . . . and let you know whether it's good enough . . . or if you need to dig deeper.' Unsworth grinned. 'I'm confident you can get what we want.'

'And if I don't?'

'Let's not be defeatist.' Unsworth plucked a card from his pocket and slid it across the table. 'My number's on there. I'll expect to hear from you within, oh . . . a month. That should give you ample time to get the measure of the situation.' The grin broadened. 'I have a good feeling about this, Mr Harding. You'll enjoy it once you get into your stride. Just think of the public service you'll be performing. You wouldn't let parasites take over a garden, would you? Well, this is no different. It really isn't.'

A phone call summoned Unsworth elsewhere before he could make a move on the patisserie. He left Harding to finish his coffee and stare at the card that was still lying on the table. He had known better than to try to convince Unsworth the state of his relations with Carol meant he stood no chance of being able to burrow into the financial secrets of Starburst International. He did not doubt those secrets were deep and dark. Unsworth's assessment of them had sounded horribly convincing. It seemed entirely possible to him that Carol already knew about them. Not that it made much difference either way. She had made it clear their affair was over. But Unsworth would never believe that. He would simply assume Harding was trying to wriggle off the hook. Which was precisely what he would have to do, somehow, before the month he had been granted was up. Although a month, ironically, seemed to him at that moment an almost unimaginable interval. Where he would be at the end of it – *how* he would be – was a mystery to him.

The ringing of his own phone interrupted his reverie.

'Hello?'

'Tim. Tony here. Is Carol with you?'

'No. We, er, parted at Nymphenburg.'

'I see. Were you able to . . . clear up with her . . . that matter we discussed last night?'

'Oh yes.'

'Good.'

'She's meeting the investigating officer this afternoon.'

'So I believe.'

'Any, er . . . news of Hayley?'

'None. Which is an increasing concern to me. It

would be unfortunate if she remained at liberty for any length of time.'

'Unfortunate?'

'Worrying, perhaps I should say. For Carol. And for you. Unless, of course, you can be absolutely certain she no longer poses a threat.'

'How could I be?' Harding responded, seeking to play Whybrow at his own game.

'True. Absolute certainty in the world of risk assessment is naturally unattainable. Especially if you can't be sure where the risk lies.'

Harding caught himself glancing nervously round the café. For a fraction of a second, he had thought Whybrow might actually be there, smiling at him from a corner table. But no. There were only stolid *Münchners* digesting their lunch.

'When are you planning to go home, Tim?'

'Tomorrow, I . . . suppose.'

'I'll make sure the hotel knows Starburst will pay your bill.'

Starburst will pay. The phrase would never sound the same again. 'Thanks,' said Harding.

'No problem,' said Whybrow. 'It's the least we can do . . . after all you've done for us.'

THIRTY-FIVE

The light was failing when Harding returned to the Cortiina. He had turned off his phone after Whybrow's call and had filled several empty hours sitting on benches in the innumerable galleries of the Alte Pinakothek, gazing vacantly at gloomy yardages of Renaissance canvas. There were no messages waiting for him at the hotel. The police had not been in touch. There was nothing to prevent him doing what he had told Whybrow he meant to do: go home. But home was a slippery concept. He was not sure where to find it any more.

He was in the middle of explaining to the receptionist that he would be checking out in the morning when he heard his name spoken softly from close behind.

'Harding.'

Turning, he was surprised to see Gary Lawton standing at his shoulder, wearing the haunted look of a seriously worried man.

'Gary. Where did you spring from?'

'Bar over the road. I've been waiting for you to get back. We need to talk.' Lawton grasped Harding's elbow. 'We *really* need to talk.'

They did not go to the bar where Lawton had lain in wait. He preferred a beer-hall, piloting Harding round the corner to the Hofbräuhaus, a vast and clearly tourist-oriented establishment where a lederhosen-clad oompah band accompanied the eager guzzling from foaming mugs by its cosmopolitan clientele.

'Nobody local comes here,' said Lawton as they settled at the empty end of one of the farther-flung tables. 'There's not much chance of anyone I know spotting us.'

'Is this where you met Hayley?'

'No. But I wasn't being so careful then.'

'Why are you being careful now?'

'Do you need to ask? For Christ's sake, man, this is a murder case. You were there when it happened, weren't you?'

'Yes,' Harding confirmed, bewildered by the degree to which the memory of the event was assuming a dream-like quality in his mind.

'The police had me in for questioning today.'

'I suppose they would.'

'Helga's doing her nut. She answered the phone to Ulbricht this morning. He quoted a gagging clause in my contract with the clinic that he claims I may have broken.'

'Just covering his back, I imagine.'

'Yeah. But what about *my* back? Helga's got it into her head that Hayley might come after me. She's talking about taking the kids to stay with her mother if Hayley isn't arrested soon.'

'She only wanted Barney, Gary. No one else is in any danger.'

'Are you sure?'

'As sure as I can be.'

'Did you think she might do anything like this?'

'Of course not.'

'Neither did I. That's what—' Lawton broke off as a waitress materialized beside them. Beers were ordered. She vanished. 'That's what worries me,' Lawton resumed. 'I – *we* – obviously hadn't a clue what was going on inside her head. What's worse, the police don't seem to have a clue where she's gone. I got the impression they expected to pick her up without any trouble. But she's outwitted them.'

'It's only a matter of time, Gary.'

'How much time?'

'I don't know.'

'The police wanted me to go through everything she said to me on Friday. Word for word. As if I could remember.'

'Well, you're the last person known to have spoken to her face to face before the shooting, so I suppose—' Their beers arrived. Harding thanked the waitress, but Lawton appeared oblivious to the mug at his elbow and went on staring at some point in the fug-filled middle distance. Harding sighed. 'So, did you . . . recall anything useful?'

'What?' Lawton dragged his thoughts back from wherever they had drifted to.

'*Did you recall anything useful?*'

'No.' Lawton grimaced. 'Nothing the police thought useful, anyway. I actually did most of the talking when we met. That was the whole point. She wanted to hear about Kerry. And I told her. As much as I could. She just . . . asked a few questions. The kind you'd expect in the circumstances.' The grimace was more of a puzzled frown now. 'There was only one thing she said that was . . . odd . . . and that, well . . . didn't amount to much.'

'What was that?' Harding's interest was aroused.

'It was about Kerry's recorder.'

'What about it?'

'She asked if I'd ever played it.'

'And had you?'

'No. I mean, it was there, in the box of stuff the Foxtons brought over. But it never occurred to me to . . . play it, no. Why would I?'

'Why would Hayley care whether you had or not?'

'Dunno.'

'Did you ask?'

'Yeah. I did.'

'And what did she say?'

'A funny thing. "I wanted to be sure," she said. "Kerry would never have expected anyone else but her to play it. Except me. She would never have *wanted* anyone else

296

to." And then she added, "I should have thought of it sooner." '

'What d'you take that to mean?'

'I didn't take it to mean anything. Neither did the police. What do *you* make of it?'

'Same as you. Nothing.'

'Actually . . .' Lawton leant forward, running his thumbnail thoughtfully across his teeth.

'What?'

'While I was in the bar, waiting for you, I tried to work out what she could possibly have meant by "I should have thought of it sooner". Something must have triggered her decision to kill Tozer. Something . . . she'd just discovered. Something that made her regret . . . losing her nerve when she went after his wife.'

'And that something is somehow connected with her sister's recorder?'

'Yeah. Exactly.'

'I don't get it.'

'I think I might, though. It only came to me just now. The recorder. What would've happened if I'd played it?'

'I don't know what you mean.'

'I mean, literally, what would have happened?'

Harding shrugged. 'How good are you on the recorder?'

'Crap. But that doesn't matter. I could've blown a few notes. Right?'

'Right.'

'Wrong. You see, I don't think I could've done. I think I'd have found the holes were blocked. I think that's what Hayley found when she tried.'

'Blocked?'

'By something inside the barrel of the recorder. Something hidden there. By Kerry.'

Lawton intended to inform the police of his supposed insight without delay. Harding doubted they would thank him. It was flimsily reasoned and made their task of tracking Hayley down no easier.

Yet it was undeniably tantalizing. Was it possible Kerry had concealed something – which could hardly be more substantial than a single sheet of paper – inside the recorder? Yes. It *was* possible. But why? And what might be written or printed on this putative sheet of paper?

'*I should have thought of it sooner.*' Hayley's remark, made about the recorder, seemed to hint at an answer that lay in the Foxton twins' childhood. They might have shared the recorder, after all. They *were* twins. As far as Harding knew, there was only one person living who had any close knowledge of their childhood. He phoned her from his room at the Cortiina.

'Hello, Ann.'

'Mr Harding. You got my message?'

'No.' He had still not turned his mobile back on. 'Have you . . . heard the news?'

'Yes. The police contacted me this morning. I was horrified to hear what had happened.' She did not sound horrified. But, as he was well aware, she seldom allowed her self-control to falter for long. 'Nathan had referred them to me as someone with whom Hayley might have been in touch.' Nathan, of course. They would have gone to him first, since Hayley had selected him as her go-between. Harding hoped they had given him a hard time. 'But she hasn't been. I suspect she decided to spare me any involvement in the dreadful course of action she'd embarked upon. Hence she resorted to Nathan to pass her message to Barney Tozer. I'm sorry for what you've endured, Mr Harding. It must have been dreadful.'

'Not as dreadful as it was for Barney.'

'Are you phoning to tell me Hayley's been arrested?' she asked, conspicuously failing to take the opportunity to express any regrets about Tozer's death.

'No. I'm not. The German police are still looking for her.'

'Poor Hayley. They'll show no mercy now, will they?'

'Whatever happens, she's brought it on herself, Ann.'

'I appreciate everyone will think that.'

'Don't you think it?'

'I'm not sure what to think. Especially in the light of this other . . . puzzling development.'

'What development?'

'There was a break-in at the Foxtons' old house over the weekend, Mr Harding. A very strange kind of break-in.'

THIRTY-SIX

'Hello?'

'It's me, Carol.'

'What . . . what time is it?'

'Early.'

'Has there been . . . some news?'

'No. Hayley's still on the run, as far as I know. I just phoned . . . to say goodbye. I'll be leaving shortly.'

'Right. OK.'

It was absurd, in so many ways, to be having a telephone conversation with Carol when her room was a two-minute walk away. But it was an absurdity born of the drastic change in their relationship. Two minutes or two hundred miles made no difference. Their separation seemed to know no limit.

'It'll probably be tomorrow . . . or Friday . . . before we can finalize transport . . . for the coffin. But . . . I'll be in touch when we get back. Or Tony will.'

The use of *we* and the hint that she might

300

communicate with him through Whybrow in future could have been calculated insults, although Harding suspected they were merely all too accurate reflections of the way Carol's mind was working. Either way, he would have preferred to ignore them. But Unsworth's revelations about Starburst International meant he could not. They indeed were why he had rung, when he would have preferred an unannounced departure – as perhaps would Carol.

'I'll say goodbye, then, Tim.'

'One thing, Carol.'

'What?'

'Barney never involved you much in the business, did he?'

'You know he didn't.'

'You should . . . tread carefully.'

'What d'you mean?'

'Tony will only tell you what he wants you to know. Which'll be what he thinks is good for him. Not necessarily what's good for you.'

'I don't need warning not to trust Tony Whybrow, Tim. I'll meet the lawyers. And the accountants. I'll take a long cool look at everything.'

'Even so . . .'

'What is this? Are you worried about me?'

'Maybe.'

There was a brief silence. Carol seemed to have been taken aback by the very idea. But she soon recovered herself. 'Well, you know what, Tim? I'd say it was a bit late for that. Wouldn't you?'

He could have done more to alert Carol to the danger she was in. Harding admitted as much to himself during the train ride out to the airport. But he was not sure she would have believed him. Nor was he *absolutely* sure she was unaware of the dark side of Starburst International. There were too many secrets and grievances between them now for him to risk showing his hand. Though eventually, with Unsworth breathing down his neck, he might have to.

But that threat at least was vague and distant. The lure of an entirely different and more urgent kind of secret was drawing him on. According to Ann Gashry, someone had broken into the Foxtons' old house in Dulwich – now occupied by the Billingsley family – on Saturday night. Or, rather, there had been an intrusion. Nothing had actually been broken. Nor had anything been taken, as far as the Billingsleys could tell. They had not even reported the matter to the police, so vague and puzzling was the evidence that there had been an intruder at all.

But there had been, of course. Harding knew that. There was a strand of logic connecting this with all the other events that had culminated in Hayley's murder of Barney Tozer. It was there, waiting to be grasped. And he could not abandon the search for it. It was, in so many ways, the only thing left for him to pursue.

He did not collect Polly's painting of Hayley from the airport left-luggage office before boarding the flight to

London. He regretted now that he had removed it from the storage depot in the first place. The memory of doing so was a standing rebuke for his foolishness in believing there could be a place for him in Hayley's life. It was not so much that she had deceived him as that he had deceived himself. The knowledge angered him. And only by seeking out the truth could he hope that the anger would die.

It was early afternoon when he reached Dulwich. Ann Gashry was expecting him. He had told her he would come straight there from Heathrow. As he headed along Bedmore Road, however, he saw she had another visitor. Nathan Gashry was hurrying out of the house to his car with the flushed and fretful air of a man with plenty on his mind and none of it pleasant.

He had yanked open the driver's door of the Porsche and was about to climb in when he noticed Harding and froze on the spot.

'Hi,' said Harding as he neared the car.

'What are you doing here?' Nathan demanded, his voice tight with suspicion and hostility.

'I might ask you the same.'

'I was visiting my sister.'

'In the middle of a working day. Spur of the moment, was it?'

'Mind your own business.'

'Could be my business. Considering I was at Nymphenburg when Hayley shot Barney Tozer and you were the source of the message that took us there.'

'I've told the police everything I know. I don't plan to tell *you* anything.' With that Nathan flung himself into the driver's seat, slammed the door and started the engine.

'Hold on,' shouted Harding, rounding the bonnet and standing beside the car so that Nathan could not pull away without driving into him. 'We're not done yet.' He tapped with his knuckle on the driver's window.

Nathan glared at him, then lowered the window.

'I want to know how Hayley seemed when she spoke to you.'

'You do, do you? Well, what I want you to know is this: I'm leaving now. And if you don't want to get run over, I suggest . . . you get out of my fucking way.'

Dora let him in, the King Charles spaniel eyeing him mournfully from behind her. Ann was coming down the stairs as he stepped into the hall. She looked as flustered as he could ever imagine her allowing herself to appear. Nathan's visit had evidently not been an agreeable experience.

'You just missed my brother,' she said, as if it was the most natural thing in the world for Nathan to have dropped in, although the redness of her eyes and the faint tremor in her hands suggested otherwise.

'I didn't miss him. We had a . . . chat . . . outside.'

'Then there's probably no point my pretending we parted amicably.'

'What did he want?'

'Come into the drawing room and I'll explain – as best I can.'

'Nathan's somehow persuaded himself that I'm to blame for the position he finds himself in,' said Ann, when Harding had closed the drawing-room door behind him and she had turned to face him. 'The police evidently contacted him at work, which caused him considerable embarrassment.'

'He could have avoided that by refusing to pass Hayley's message on.'

'I pointed that out to him, for which he did not thank me. He could also have rejected Barney Tozer's original proposition that he pose as the Foxtons' benefactor, of course. I imagine he calculated Tozer might be grateful to him for helping to arrange a meeting with Hayley and would express his gratitude later in tangible form. I fear Nathan's biggest disadvantage is his own mercenary nature. As it is, he's bound to face a good deal of police questioning about his role in events. Further . . . embarrassment . . . may confidently be expected.' There was the quiver of a smile on her lips as she said this.

'You'll be questioned yourself, Ann. When they find Hayley, everything will come out.'

'I'm prepared for that.'

'Some would say you've got what you wanted: justice for the man you believe murdered Kerry.'

'I didn't want a second murder, Mr Harding. I didn't want Hayley to feel she needed to . . . do such a terrible thing.'

'Did you know she'd turned herself into an expert shot?'

'Absolutely not. I'm shocked to learn of it.'

'It means she was planning this for a long time.'

'I realize that. But I assure you it was without my knowledge. It's clear neither you nor I understood the way her mind was working. Yet it's also clear there are aspects to this sad tale we simply have no inkling of. Someone took something from the Foxtons' old house on Saturday night. The question is—'

'I thought you said nothing was taken.'

'Nothing belonging to the Billingsleys, no. But *something*, unquestionably.'

'I don't follow.'

'Something predating their ownership of the house, I mean. The circumstances point to no other conclusion. I know the Billingsleys more as neighbours than friends, but they sought my opinion of what had happened because they're aware I was closely acquainted with the Foxtons and felt certain what was taken must date from when the Foxtons lived in the house.'

'What was it?'

'Let me explain. This house and theirs are laid out exactly the same. When they got up on Sunday morning, they found the carpet had been lifted in this room, over by the window. An armchair had been moved and not replaced. And the edge of the carpet was loose. Underneath, they discovered a removable section that had been cut out at some point in one of the floorboards. It had always creaked, apparently, though they'd never thought to investigate why. There was nothing under the board, but they think – and so do I – that there had been something there. Until Saturday night.'

'I don't understand. How did whoever supposedly took whatever this something was get into the house?'

'With a key. The Billingsleys found the front door had simply been pulled to. They always lock it at night.'

'And you conclude . . .'

'They didn't replace the locks when they moved in, Mr Harding. Who knows how many sets of keys the Foxtons had? But I can certainly think of one person very likely still to have a set in their possession.'

'Hayley.'

'Exactly.'

Harding walked slowly across to the window, thinking as he went. He looked back at Ann. 'It's possible Hayley found a note secreted by Kerry in one of her possessions retained by the Horstelmann Clinic. This would have been on Thursday or Friday of last week. And I suppose it's equally possible . . .'

'That the note told her where Kerry had hidden something in their old home.'

'Yes.'

'So she came back over the weekend to fetch it.'

'Then returned to Munich, her mind made up, apparently, to kill Barney.'

'Because of what she found under the floorboard. Compelling evidence, perhaps, that Barney Tozer murdered Kerry.'

Harding thought of what Unsworth had told him

about Starburst International. And of what Carol had said about Kerry: *'She was always chasing a story of some kind. I had the sense this was bigger than most.'* Yet Unsworth's assessment was that Tozer had not yet strayed into outright illegality by the summer of 1999. So, what could the story have been? And what could Kerry have gone to such lengths to put beyond anyone's reach – except, perhaps, her sister's?

'The authorities might treat Hayley more leniently if they knew she acted in response to some terrible discovery,' said Ann, ever hopeful, it seemed, of finding some way to excuse her friend.

'Maybe,' Harding half agreed.

'And she's bound to tell them what it was. When they finally track her down. Or she gives herself up, as I believe she well might eventually.'

'I suppose so.'

'But perhaps you don't have to wait for that to happen to find out what she discovered.'

'No.' Harding glanced at the clock, calculating as best he could what time it would be when he reached Deal. 'Perhaps I don't.'

THIRTY-SEVEN

It was six o'clock on a raw, dark evening when Harding turned in to Deal Castle Road. A chill wind was barrelling in from the sea and it seemed a good bet that Jack Shepherd, quondam editor of the *Kentish Mercury*, would be at home. Sure enough, the lights were on in his ground-floor flat.

He took his time answering the doorbell, however. When he did, the stick he was leaning on heavily suggested why Harding had been kept waiting so long. He was a big, fleshy sack of a man, with a flushed face that emphasized the whiteness of his hair and a grouchy, thin-lipped expression. He was dressed in a voluminous cardigan, baggy trousers and a frayed shirt. Grey, wary eyes met Harding's through unfashionably large, thick-lensed glasses.

'Jack Shepherd?'

'You must be Harding.'

'How did you know?'

'Oh, voice, age, manner. Or journalist's intuition. I didn't think it'd be long before you showed up, despite crying off on Sunday.'

'Something cropped up.'

'Doesn't it always?'

'Can I come in?'

'Why not?'

Shepherd hobbled back into the flat. Harding followed, closing the front door behind him. There was an aroma of fried food cut with whisky and an immediate impression of learning embedded in dowdiness. The cramped sitting room they entered was long overdue for a makeover, the furniture's second-hand value well below zero. But there were crammed bookcases lining three walls and Shepherd's current choice of leisure reading, standing next to the whisky tumbler on a low table by his fireside armchair, was a biography of Pushkin.

'Want a drink?' Shepherd nodded to a tray on a sideboard. 'There's whisky . . . or whisky.'

'Thanks.' As Harding helped himself to a finger of Johnnie Walker, Shepherd subsided into the armchair and flapped a hand towards the sofa.

'Take a seat.'

'Thanks.' Harding sat down. 'Cheers.'

'Looks like a Scotch evening out there to me.'

'It is.'

'So, what's this all about?' There was no hint Shepherd knew Barney Tozer was dead – or that Hayley Foxton was wanted for his murder. Harding was not entirely surprised. It was hardly the stuff of headlines in Deal. All in all, he reckoned there was no need to rush into announcing the news.

'It's simple enough really. Kerry Foxton worked for you, didn't she?'

'Cub reporter to my sourpuss editor. Yes. She soon moved on, though – on *and* up. But she stayed in touch. I liked her. And I like to think she liked me. She wasn't terribly good at her job, to be honest. Council committee meetings and magistrates' hearings bored her rigid and she didn't hide it well. She was a rotten team player too. But that didn't really matter. She had this . . . dazzling personality . . . that made even a sour-puss editor cut her a lot of slack. Besides, if you put her on to a story with some meat in it, well, she gave it everything. And she got results. She had Fleet Street written all over her. When she left, I never seriously expected to see or hear from her again. But, as I say, she stayed in touch. She liked to get my views on things. I was a little like her when I was her age and I think she sensed that. I was considered a high-flyer in my day. Before I . . . bottled out, you could say, if you were of a punning disposition. But you don't want to hear about my problems.'

'When we spoke on the phone, you said you'd be reluctant to talk about Kerry.'

Shepherd smiled. 'So I did. But that was partly to see how easily put off you'd be. And I thought about it after-wards, especially when I had my daughter and the grandchildren over. Family's important. Probably more important than what I choose to call my principles. Kerry didn't talk much about her sister. But she said enough for me to know she'd want me to do anything I can to help her. So, how's she placed?'

'Oh, she's OK.' Harding winced inwardly at the scale of his misrepresentation. 'Most of the time.'

'And the rest of the time?'

'Well, there's this idea she can't get out of her mind that Kerry may have been . . . murdered.'

'Murdered?' Shepherd frowned sceptically. 'I was going through a bad patch when they held the inquest and wasn't well enough to attend, but I read the reports later. The lead diver may have been sloppy, but it came across as a straightforward accident to me. Tragic. But no one's fault other than Kerry's for entering the wreck. Which sounded to me like the kind of mistake she might make. She always was headstrong. That was part of her appeal.'

'I'm sure you're right. And I think Hayley could bring herself to accept that. If only there weren't so many unanswered questions about what Kerry was working on in the weeks and months before the accident.'

'Ah. I see. You reckon I know, do you?'

'Her friend Carol says she was often on the phone to you while she was staying with her on St Mary's.'

'Yes. She was.' Shepherd drank the last of his whisky and gazed for a moment at the empty glass. 'You couldn't top me up, could you?'

'Sure.' Harding obliged with the Johnnie Walker and Shepherd took another sip.

'After I retired from the *Mercury*, Kerry started using me to do background research for her freelance stories. It was a good arrangement for both of us. Kept me busy and off the booze and saved her having to do all the checking and double-checking she never really had the patience for anyway. She certainly had something on the boil that summer, though she never told me exactly what. She liked to tease me about where the research she palmed off on me was leading and I enjoyed trying to second-guess her. Sadly, I never got the chance to find out where we were heading that time. I kept my files on the work I did for her. I looked through them after you called. Reminded myself what it was all about. And I can honestly say there was nothing in them to suggest Kerry had strayed into . . . dangerous territory.'

'What did you do for her?'

'You're going to be disappointed if you're expecting anything sensational.'

'I won't be disappointed,' said Harding, sticking to his cover story. 'The less sensational the better. For Hayley.'

'OK. Well, it's all pretty obscure historical stuff, actually. There were two strands to it and I think – only think, mind – I know how Kerry hoped to tie them together. The first strand concerns a semi-legendary figure from the fourteenth century called the Grey Man of Ennor.'

'Who was he?'

'To answer that question I need to take you back to the time of the Black Death. Know much about it?'

'About as much as most people, I suppose. A plague

carried by rats that decimated the population of Europe around the year . . . 1350?'

'You've got it. Actually, it was much worse than literal decimation. At least one in three died, possibly more. It spread across Europe, starting in Constantinople in late 1347 and reaching England in the summer of 1348. It was at its height in the West Country between then and the spring of 1349. Which is where the Grey Man comes in. During that period – 1348/49 – an elderly, grey-haired monk from St Nicholas's Priory on Tresco is supposed to have left his cell and wandered through Cornwall, Devon, Dorset and Somerset, miraculously curing plague-sufferers as he went while remaining immune to the disease himself. Ennor was the common name for the Scillies then. Hence the Grey Man of Ennor.'

'Did he really exist?'

'Who can say? It was a widespread enough rumour to warrant mention in the chronicles of the period. But the Church did its best to scotch the rumour. St Nicholas's Priory was under the control of Tavistock Abbey and the abbot's known to have sent letters to the Bishop of Exeter in April 1349 for distribution to his parish priests stating unequivocally that no monk had absented himself from Tresco. Maybe it was just wishful thinking. There was no shortage of people hoping and praying for deliverance from the plague. Basically, there's no hard evidence for *or* against the Grey Man.'

'What about the other strand?'

'How much do you know about King Edward the Second?'

314

'Did Shakespeare write a play about him?'

'No. But Marlowe did. Thanks to which a lot of people know how he's supposed to have died. A gruesome exit involving a red-hot poker.'

'Ah. That was him, was it?'

'Yes. Succeeded his macho-man father, Edward the First, in 1307. Probably gay, though he married and dutifully fathered four children. Certainly no great shakes as a military commander. Widely blamed for defeat by the Scots at Bannockburn in 1314. Court riven with jealousy and rivalry. Civil war constantly threatening. Eventually forced to abdicate in favour of his fourteen-year-old son, Edward the Third, leaving the government of the country in the hands of his wife, Queen Isabella, and her lover, Roger Mortimer. Locked up in Berkeley Castle, Gloucestershire, where, after a couple of abortive rescue attempts, he was murdered, at some point in September 1327. Nasty end to a nasty story. Or was it? Kerry wanted to know just how certain historians were that Edward died in 1327. The answer turns out to be not very. He's got a smart tomb in Gloucester Cathedral, but it took Isabella and Mortimer all of three months to get round to putting him in it. There's a whole host of circumstantial evidence to suggest he wasn't recaptured, as he's usually thought to have been, after he was sprung from Berkeley Castle by a raiding party organized by his former confessor, Thomas Dunheved, in late July of 1327. After searching in vain for him in the Welsh Borders, Mortimer may well have decided it was best to say he'd been murdered, so that he could be dismissed as an impostor if he ever reappeared. But he never did. Perhaps because he didn't want to. Perhaps because he recognized that he didn't have it in him to be a king. So, what became of him? Well, maybe the answer is that the Church gave him sanctuary. Dunheved was a Dominican. Maybe he eased Edward's passage into a remote monastery somewhere on the Continent.'

'You're saying he became a monk?'

'Possibly. Monk. Friar. Hermit. Something like that.'

'Something like . . . the Grey Man of Ennor.'

'It's a tempting thought, isn't it? He was born in 1284. That would make him sixty-four in 1348. The age certainly fits. When he saw the plague rampaging across Europe, might he have decided to return to his homeland in its hour of need? He could have entered the country surreptitiously, via the Scillies. Hence the idea that he was *from* the Scillies. As for the notion that he was able to cure victims of the plague, well, the Royal Touch was a persistent medieval belief. Anointment with holy oil during the coronation ceremony was supposed to confer on the monarch the power to cure leprosy and scrofula in particular by touching the sufferer. This was conditional on the monarch leading a sinless life, which could hardly be said of Edward the Second. But perhaps twenty years in a monastery – or wandering the byways of Europe – could be regarded as sufficient to atone for his sins. Not that I'm suggesting he actually cured anyone, you understand. But the arrival of the Black Death must have felt like the end of the world, so it's small wonder people fantasized about a nomadic healer coming to their rescue. If Edward the Second *was* still alive, he'd be a leading candidate for the role because of the myth of the Royal Touch.'

'So, quite a few historians have identified him with the Grey Man of Ennor, have they?'

'As a matter of fact . . .' Shepherd smiled. 'None at all.'

'But you think Kerry was trying to?'

'It's the obvious conclusion. It's certainly what I concluded at the time.'

'But why? What's there to interest an ambitious freelance journalist in a story like that?'

'Exactly. It's hardly big news today, is it? There has to be more to it. And the more has to be what took Kerry to the Scillies, ostensibly to write about the total eclipse, in the summer of 1999. The research I did for her was just background. There must have been something else – something bigger – she was on the track of.'

'What could that have been?'

'I've absolutely no idea. But a mystery from the mid-fourteenth century doesn't give anyone a plausible motive for murder in the late twentieth. I'm clear about that.' Shepherd squinted at Harding suspiciously. 'Which should be good news for you. But strangely, judging by your expression, it isn't. You look what you said you wouldn't be: disappointed. Now, why's that, I wonder?'

THIRTY-EIGHT

In the end, Harding told Shepherd the truth. There was nothing to be gained by keeping him in the dark about Hayley's murder of Barney Tozer once he had revealed what Kerry was investigating at the time of her fatal dive off the Scillies: not Tozer's suspect finances, but an historical conundrum which by any rational standards could have no connection with her death.

Shepherd deduced Harding's motive for holding out on him swiftly enough and was only briefly angered by it. It was a double tragedy now, he observed, the more so since he did not believe Kerry's accident had been engineered by anyone. There was nothing for Hayley to avenge. And nothing Harding could do to help her.

Nor was there much Shepherd could do to help Harding. Except suggest he top up both their glasses and offer him a bed for the night; as well as proffer some sage advice.

'Go back to France, son. Landscape a few more

gardens. Get on with your life. Let the dead bury the dead.'

'But Hayley isn't dead.'

'She'll be as good as, once the law's finished with her. Not that it ever will finish with her. Prison and/or mental hospital sounds like her foreseeable future to me.'

'I keep wondering . . . if there was something I could've done to prevent this outcome.'

'I wonder that about my entire existence to date. The answer's yes, of course. But it doesn't help to know it. What's done is done. There are no second chances.'

Harding thought of Hayley's apparently serious suggestion that he and Kerry had met in some cosmically real alternative existence. In which case he and Hayley had also met there, with a different result. A happier one, surely. 'Going back to my old life isn't exactly possible.'

'Make it the nearest approximation, then.'

An approximation of life sounded uncannily like what did await him in France. And what he had left behind there when he first set off for Penzance on Barney Tozer's behalf. The truth was that it was no longer enough. He realized now that he had coped with Polly's death by withdrawing from the world he knew. And he had still found no other world to replace it.

'I get the feeling I'm wasting my breath,' said Shepherd, breaking into Harding's thoughts. 'You won't be content until you've explored every last avenue and proved it to be a dead end.'

'Perhaps one of them isn't.'

'Perhaps.' Shepherd eyed Harding over his whisky glass. 'For your sake, I hope so.'

Harding slept poorly, as he had each night since the shooting at Nymphenburg. Whenever he closed his eyes, his mind would replay for him the last few seconds of Barney Tozer's life, over and over again, until eventually it tired and let him sleep – though never for long. He found it restful by comparison to lie awake and hear Shepherd snoring in the adjoining bedroom, to gaze into the darkness and wonder, almost neutrally, what the future held; and to know it had never been less certain.

Shepherd was still snoring away when Harding got up the following morning, made himself a cup of coffee and composed a farewell message for his host on a post-it note he stuck to the toaster. *Thanks for hospitality. Gone to explore those other avenues. Let you know if I find anything. TH.*

Harding could think of at least two leads he could still follow: Nathan Gashry's reluctance to talk to him; and Darren Spargo's claim to know who had stolen the Shovell ring from Heartsease. He would start with Nathan. Ann Gashry had said he worked for an executive recruitment consultancy in the City called Caddick Pearson. That was where the police had contacted him, to his considerable embarrassment. So, why not find out how he would react to an office visit from Harding?

About halfway through the two-hour train journey to London, Harding's phone rang. Seeing the number of the caller, he was tempted not to answer. But he reasoned in the end that Whybrow was a man more safely misled than ignored.

'Hi, Tony. What can I do for you?'

'Where are you, Tim?'

'Oh, in . . . transit.'

'Only I was puzzled when Carol told me the time you left yesterday morning. It didn't seem to fit with any of the scheduled flights to Nice.' So, he had checked, which was worrying in itself.

'I'm in England, actually, Tony. I decided . . . I needed a break . . . after everything that's happened. Thought I'd see the folks and a few old friends.'

'Good idea. Just a little odd you didn't mention it.'

'It was a last-minute thing. No problem, is there?'

'Only that they still haven't found Hayley.'

'But they will.'

'Yes. Of course. But tell me, this break . . . wouldn't be cover for some . . . ill-advised attempt to do the police's job for them, would it, Tim?'

'How d'you mean?'

'Well, you haven't taken it into your head to try and find Hayley yourself, have you?'

'Absolutely not.'

'Glad to hear it.'

'I wouldn't know where to look. Don't worry, Tony. I'll be back next week.'

'Fine.' There was a momentary silence that felt significant. Then Whybrow concluded, 'We'll talk then.'

It was mid-morning when Harding arrived in London, late morning by the time he reached the offices of Caddick Pearson: one floor of a steel-and-glass tower near Liverpool Street station. His plan to catch Nathan unawares in his workaday environment was stillborn, however. Nathan had phoned in sick that morning.

Harding reckoned it was no better than fifty-fifty he would find Nathan at his flat. He did not suppose for a moment the man's illness was genuine; he was up to something. Harding was not discouraged by the thought, however. Quite the contrary. It meant *he* was on to something.

The first warning he had that all was not well came as he approached the apartment block across Vauxhall Bridge. There were assorted vans and cars drawn up in the courtyard area below the flats – at least one of them a police vehicle.

As he drew nearer, he saw a line of police tape, with a constable standing just beyond it, barring access to the courtyard and the adjoining riverside walkway. A small crowd of onlookers had gathered, although they were in the process of dispersing. The incident, whatever it was, had evidently already lost some of its novelty value.

An Asian man dressed in dark-green uniform overalls was among those drifting away. Harding caught sight of the name of the block displayed on his breast pocket. He intercepted.

'Excuse me. Has something happened?'

'A tragedy. Someone has fallen. From one of the flats. They have just taken the body away.'

'Do you know who it was?'

'Oh yes. I saw him. Before the police came. Nasty. Very nasty. Poor fellow. Suicide, I suppose. But who would have thought it? Such a nice man. There was always a joke or a smile from Mr Gashry.'

'*Nathan* Gashry?'

'Yes. You are a friend?'

'Sort of. You're saying . . . Nathan Gashry's dead?'

'Fifth floor. Straight down into the courtyard. You could not survive. He did not want to, I suppose. A desperate, terrible thing. But there it is.' The man spread his hands helplessly. 'Yes. I am sorry. Mr Gashry is dead.'

THIRTY-NINE

Harding waited till dark before presenting himself at Ann Gashry's door. This was not only to allow time for the police to contact her with the news of her brother's death. Harding had needed time himself, to come to terms as best he could with an event that seemed to make no sense in the context of what had gone before – unless, he was coming more and more to suspect, what had gone before was not as he had believed it to be.

Ann's greeting suggested she had been expecting his visit. She invited him in and he found himself once more in the sombre, fustily decorated drawing room, which was thickly curtained and fire-lit against the chill of the evening. There was no obvious sign of distress on her part. She was dry-eyed and calm, though perhaps paler than ever. A photograph album lay open on the table beside her chair. Harding glimpsed faded snaps of seaside holidays long ago: stiffly smiling parents; a teenage girl in an unglamorous swimsuit; a pouty little boy brandishing a plastic spade like a weapon.

'I haven't looked at these photographs in years,' said Ann, gently closing the album. 'They date from before my parents divorced: the brief period when Nathan and I were brother and sister under one roof.'

'I'm sorry, Ann.'

'Thank you. It's a shock, of course. There can be little true grief. We led such different lives. And yet . . .'

'He was your flesh and blood.'

'Indeed.' She picked up a glass from the table and sipped some of the contents. Brandy, Harding assumed. Her tipple, especially at times of stress. 'Would you like a drink?'

'Thanks.'

'Help yourself.'

He poured himself a whisky and tilted the Courvoisier bottle enquiringly towards Ann. She shook her head and sat down. Harding joined her.

She drew a deep breath. 'How did you hear?'

'I went to see him. It had just happened.'

'Was it . . . very dreadful?'

'They'd screened everything off.'

'Did you speak to the police?'

'No. They'd have . . . queried my being there.'

'So you want me to tell you what they make of it.' She looked him in the eye, defying him to pretend his principal reason for visiting her was to offer his condolences. 'Well, perhaps we could start with why you went to see Nathan today. You didn't seem to have it in mind yesterday.'

'I hoped Jack Shepherd – Kerry's old editor – would know what she'd hidden under the floorboards. But he couldn't help me. So, I decided to try Nathan instead.'

'You seriously expected him to know – or to tell you if he did?'

'I was running out of options.'

'Well, you've one fewer left now.'

'Do the police believe it was suicide?'

'They seem inclined to. An accident's out of the question. And murder? There was no sign of a struggle, apparently. Naturally, they wanted to know how he'd been when we last met. Was he distraught at being implicated, albeit unwittingly, in Barney Tozer's murder? Was there any suggestion he was keeping back vital evidence? Was he perhaps not so unwitting after all and prey to remorse? I'm sure you can imagine the direction their questions took.'

'How did you answer them?'

'As frankly as I felt I could. A degree of reticence was essential, for my sake as well as yours. I certainly made it clear I regarded the idea that Nathan had committed suicide as absurd. I gather his girlfriend said much the same. He was planning to go to work today as far as she knew. He wasn't ill. And according to her he wasn't depressed, just angry at Hayley for using him to lure Barney Tozer to his death. None of which I suspect is likely to deflect the police from their suicide theory. It fits the facts better than any other from their point of view.'

'If it wasn't suicide . . .'

'Hayley's not physically capable of throwing a grown man from a balcony, Mr Harding. You know that. It's as absurd as suggesting he threw himself.'

'But something propelled him.'

'Yes. Or someone.'

'Someone other than Hayley.'

'Quite so.'

'Which means . . .'

'Have you seen Sir Clowdisley Shovell's tomb in Westminster Abbey?'

Harding blinked in surprise. 'Sorry?'

'If not, you ought to take a look at it, in view of your involvement in the *Association* story. A grandiose marble monument carved by Grinling Gibbons. Bizarrely, in accordance with the fashion of the day, Sir Clowdisley is depicted, despite his obviously eighteenth-century wig, in a toga and sandals, more like a Roman emperor than an admiral. Most of the thousands of tourists who file past the tomb every year don't pause to read the inscription, so probably have no idea he was a man of the sea. Costume sends a message. And sometimes that message can be misleading, whether by design or not.'

'What are you getting at, Ann?'

'How sure are you that it was Hayley who shot Barney Tozer?'

Harding could not suppress a rueful smile. It was the question he had been asking himself since learning of Nathan's apparent suicide. It was the question that begged all others. He had persuaded himself at one point that the young woman he had pursued through rain and lamplight along the streets of Munich might not be Hayley after all. He had only changed his mind at Nymphenburg, in the seconds after Tozer's death, when he had watched the same young woman run away through the trees, *without* looking back. She matched Hayley in height and build and hairstyle. And she was dressed for the part, in the same kind of mac Hayley had been wearing the very first time he had seen her, at Heartsease, a few days before the auction. But was it her? Was it her beyond the shadow of a doubt?

'If you're not sure, Mr Harding, not *absolutely* sure, then . . .'

'We only have Nathan's word for it she set up the rendezvous in the first place.'

'And if he was lying, for whatever reason . . .'

'He can't own up to it now.'

'Death seals everyone's lips.'

'My God.' Some of the implications of what they were saying flashed through Harding's mind. 'Could this be true?'

'I think it may be.'

'But if it is . . .'

'Then, what do we do about it?' She gazed at him intently. 'What *exactly* do we do?'

With so much unknown, they had to learn as much as they could as quickly as they could. Ann volunteered to contact Veronica and pump her for information about Nathan's activities in recent weeks: where he had been, who he had spoken to, what he had said that might seem more significant now than it had at the time. For his part, Harding could see nothing for it but to chase down the last lead left to him: the identity of the Heartsease thief; which might, just might, be the answer to everything.

Since the call from Whybrow, Harding had kept his phone switched off. He checked for messages as he stood stamping his feet to keep warm while waiting for the next train to Victoria on the wind-lashed platform at West Dulwich station. There was one: from Carol. And it was very different in tone from the last message she had left for him.

Why are you in England, Tim? Tony's told me what you said, but I don't believe it any more than he does. If you're still chasing Hayley, you're as mad as she is. If not, then what the hell are you up to? Explanation please. I think I'm owed one. What are you trying to do?

It was a reasonable question in its way. But it was not one Harding had any intention of answering. He switched the phone off again, shoved it back into his pocket and squinted down the track. Where *was* the train?

The sleeper pulled out of Paddington on schedule at ten to midnight. Harding had secured a berth at the last minute. After dumping his bag in his cabin, he headed for the buffet, where nightcaps were being served. He suspected he would need several.

There were half a dozen or so customers ahead of him in the queue. He paid them no attention. But one of them paid him a great deal.

'Mr Harding,' came a familiar voice. 'This *is* a surprise.'

FORTY

'I've thought about you a lot these past few days,' said Clive Isbister as they settled with their drinks at an empty table in the buffet car. 'I was shocked when I heard Barney had been killed and that Hayley Winter – Foxton, I suppose I should say – was the prime suspect. Then I saw it reported that you were there when it took place. Now . . . what? You're going back to Penzance?'

'Carol asked me to pay Humph a visit and tell him exactly how it happened,' Harding replied. It was a passable cover story. 'She was too busy sorting everything out to come herself.'

'I can imagine. Well, that's good of you. But what a coincidence, hey? I've been up at an ISVA dinner – Incorporated Society of Valuers and Auctioneers.' Isbister's flushed complexion and general loquaciousness suggested he had not stinted himself. 'So, tell me, how *did* it happen?'

There was clearly no avoiding an explanation, so

Harding embarked on one, omitting any mention of his new-found doubts about Hayley's responsibility for Tozer's death – and of Nathan Gashry's supposed suicide. He was in no mood to bare his soul and felt certain there was nothing to be gained by taking Isbister into his confidence.

'Appalling,' said Isbister when he had finished. 'Just appalling.' Which was not, Harding reflected, such a bad summary. 'And there's no question it *was* Hayley?'

'There wasn't much room for doubt.' Which was not, of course, the same as saying there was no room at all.

'But shooting him like that, in cold blood. I'd never have thought her capable of such a thing.'

'Neither would I.'

'But you saw it with your own eyes, so there it is.' Isbister stared thoughtfully into his plastic beaker of whisky and soda. 'It's strange. Ironic, you could say. There's a reunion every decade of my year at Humphry Davy Grammar. *Our* year, I mean. Barney's, mine, Ray Trathen's . . .'

'And John Metherell's?'

'Yes, of course. John's too. You know him?'

'We've met.'

This minor revelation induced a puzzled pause on Isbister's part. Then he pressed on. 'Well, the last was in . . . 1998. Function room at the Queen's Hotel. I remember standing there, chatting with Barney, and . . . yes, actually, I think it *was* John Metherell, now you mention him. Anyway, the do was winding down and Barney said jocularly, "See you in another ten years, then." And John said, "God willing." To which Barney responded, "Don't worry. I'm indestructible." And, you know, in a funny sort of way, I believed him. There was something . . . granite-like . . . about him. Good at rugby, you know? Loose-head prop. Get tackled by him and you remembered it. My God, you did.' He winced in tribute to a long-ago collision. 'Yes. Indestructible. But he wasn't, of course. And he won't be sharing a joke with anyone at the 2008 gathering.'

'Have the police asked you any questions?' Harding enquired, hoping Isbister could be lured away from maudlin reminiscences of his schooldays.

'Not as such. They came to me for the keys to Heartsease, that's all. Wanted to search the basement flat on the off chance of turning up some clue to Hayley's whereabouts. Is she still on the run?'

'As far as I know.'

'Well, they obviously didn't find anything, then. Where do you think she's gone?'

'No idea.'

'There's no mistake, is there? She's Kerry Foxton's sister? I mean, I know there's a resemblance, but—'

'She's definitely her sister.'

'Right.' Isbister nodded. 'I bumped into Ray Trathen in Market Jew Street yesterday, you know.' He glanced at his watch. 'Day *before* yesterday, I should say. He was full of it, as you can imagine. "Told you Barney was up to no good," he crowed. "Now he's got his just desserts." He was drunk, of course. Well, not sober, anyway. But I didn't like the pleasure he took from Barney's death. Or the conclusions he drew. The fact that Hayley evidently believes Barney murdered Kerry doesn't prove he did.'

'No. It doesn't, does it?'

'Barney sailed close to the wind, no question about it. Always did. He was running scams even at school. Started selling Kit-Kats of dubious origin and graduated to reefers. I dare say Ray's right about Starburst International being a dodgy outfit. But the one thing Barney never had was a vicious streak. He wasn't a bully. He was actually a very generous man. He basically wanted everyone to have a good time, preferably in a way that turned him a useful profit. A wheeler-dealer. A barrow boy. A rogue. But a murderer? Especially of an attractive girl like Kerry? Never. It just . . . wasn't in his character.'

'Did you know Kerry?' Isbister's second reference to Kerry's looks had finally caught up with Harding.

'Not really. I met her a couple of times. Once in the Abbey Hotel restaurant. She was dining there with Barney the night my wife and I were celebrating our anniversary. They . . . joined us for drinks beforehand. We . . . chatted . . . about this and that. I remember Janet – my wife – complaining over dinner that I'd been ogling Kerry. Perhaps it was true. Kerry was very attractive, of course. But she had this . . . extra some-thing as well. Glamour. Charisma. I don't know what you'd call it. The wow factor, I suppose. Yes. That's what she had. In spades.'

'What was the other time you met?'

'Oh, much duller. She called round at the office. It

334

can't have been long after we'd met at the Abbey.' Isbister frowned with the effort of recollection. 'Yes. No more than a few days. She wanted my . . . professional opinion on something.'

'What was that?'

'She had a . . . document . . . she wanted me to date.'

'Really?' Harding was now having to exert himself not to push too hard for details.

'Eighteenth-century, she thought. Could we confirm it? I had Julian Mann – our expert on that kind of thing – cast his eye over it. He pronounced it genuine, I seem to remember. It was a single page of handwriting. But clearly part of something longer.'

'Did you read it?'

'Glanced at it. Oh yes.' A jolt of memory animated Isbister's expression. 'I spotted the name Borlase. They were big cheeses in Penzance back in the eighteenth century. So, that was a promising sign in itself. Then Julian gave it the thumbs-up. Right sort of paper, ink, lettering style. That kind of thing. I assumed Kerry had all of . . . whatever it was, so I . . . asked if she wanted us to sell it for her. Antiquarian stuff always attracts a lot of interest. And it looked like there was a local connection too, which was obviously a bonus.'

'But she turned you down?'

'Yes. Just wanted confirmation of the date. Mid-eighteenth-century.'

'Didn't you think it odd, her having this . . . document, but not being willing to show you the whole thing?'

'A little, yes, but . . .' Isbister stared at the night-blanked window for a moment, then snapped his fingers. 'You know, I'd forgotten that.'

'What?'

'Well, she asked me to say nothing to Barney about her visit. Said it was all part of a little . . . surprise she was planning for his birthday. Late August. He was the youngest boy in our year.' Isbister's gaze became distant and unfocused. 'I didn't socialize with Barney. I hardly ever saw him. So, saying nothing wasn't difficult. In fact, I . . . forgot all about it. And Barney never got his present, did he? By late August, Kerry was in hospital . . . on life support.'

'I wonder what happened to the document.'

'So do I.'

'We'll probably never know.'

'Probably not, no.'

In truth, though, Harding thought he *did* know. What it was *and* what had become of it. A complete version of Francis Gashry's report on the Shillingstone affair, stolen by Kerry from a descendant of Gashry's executor, helpfully authenticated by Isbister's antiquarian expert and then concealed beneath the floorboards at Kerry's childhood home in Dulwich, safe from whatever risks she feared she was running in Cornwall. As an additional precaution, she had hidden a note of precisely where the report was secreted in a place where only her sister was likely to discover it, just in case she met with an accident – as indeed she did.

'Kerry's family might have it, I suppose,' Isbister

mused. 'But they're all dead, aren't they? Except Hayley, of course. Perhaps she has it. I wonder . . .'

'What?'

'If it's connected in any way . . . with the theft of the ring from Heartsease.'

'I don't see how.'

'No. Neither do I. Except that . . . everything seems to be connected with everything else.' Isbister was beginning to sound positively philosophical. He lowered his voice. 'I had lunch earlier this week with Gordon Meek.'

'Who?'

'Gabriel Tozer's solicitor. He instructed us to auction the contents of Heartsease in accordance with Gabriel's will. Now the house is to be sold – also by auction. Only then will the estate be wound up. I'd been assuming the proceeds would go to some charity or other. Gabriel obviously didn't want to benefit his nephews, Barney and Humphrey. Otherwise he'd have just left everything to them. Well, that part's true enough. But the rest's a bit more complicated. Gordon was still in a state of shock at the news of Barney's murder. He said to me – in strictest confidence, you understand – that he couldn't help wondering if Hayley might have acted differently if she'd known she was going to become a relatively wealthy young woman. I asked him what he meant and, frankly, I was astonished by his answer. Gabriel Tozer specified in a recent alteration to his will that the proceeds of both sales, contents *and* house, along with his savings, which apparently were considerable, were to go not to various charities, as he let his nephews suppose, but to Hayley Winter, as Gabriel of course believed her to be called, although she wasn't to be told until after the sales were completed.'

'You're sure about this?'

'Gordon Meek doesn't get things like that wrong, Mr Harding. He shouldn't really have told me. And he'd be horrified to know I'd told you, so I'd appreciate it if you'd keep it under your hat. But, yes, Hayley was Gabriel Tozer's heir. She just didn't know it. And it makes no difference now, anyway, does it? She's never going to get the chance to spend the money.'

FORTY-ONE

Isbister caught up with Harding as he was leaving the train at Penzance the following morning – a cold, grey morning, with the fug of slumber still clinging to many of the disembarking passengers.

'Are you going straight round to see Humphrey, Mr Harding?' Isbister asked, grimacing as if his indulgences of the evening and night before had taken their toll.

'Probably not. I'll leave it till a more civilized hour.'

'Could I offer you a lift somewhere? I'm parked on the quay.'

'No need, thanks. I could do with stretching my legs.'

'In that case . . .' Isbister drew Harding aside by the elbow, more or less forcing him to stop and listen. 'Look, I probably shouldn't have told you what Gordon Meek said about Gabriel Tozer's will. But . . . *in vino veritas*; there it is. I'd be *really* grateful if you didn't mention it to Humphrey, though. Or to anyone else, come to that. Not just to spare me some embarrassment, but to avoid ... inflaming the situation. Know what I mean?'

'I shan't breathe a word.'

Isbister smiled in relief. 'Excellent. Good man.'

'Any chance you could do me a favour in return?' Harding asked, sensing an opportunity he would be foolish to let slip.

'Name it.'

'The keys to Heartsease.'

Isbister frowned apprehensively. 'I don't think I can ...'

'Look on it as a favour to Barney. He asked you to help me in any way you could, didn't he?'

'In respect of the auction, yes. But ...'

'Everything's connected with everything else. Remember?'

'I didn't mean—'

'I'd have them back to you within an hour. I just want to ... take a look.'

Isbister's wrestling match with his professional conscience ended in submission. 'I'm not going to regret this, am I, Mr Harding?'

'No. Definitely not.' Harding smiled. 'I'll pick them up later.'

It was pushing close to nine o'clock when Harding reached the Spargo house, still unconscionably early, he suspected, by Darren's standards. His suspicion was soon vindicated when Darren's harassed mother answered the door, or, more accurately, opened it: she was on her way out, young child in tow.

'Darren about, Mrs Spargo?' asked Harding.

'Not up yet. You'd better—'

'I'll give him a wake-up call.' He dodged past her into the hall and made for the stairs.

'Hold on. You can't go up there.'

Patently, however, Harding could. He was certainly in no mood to pay close attention to etiquette. Reaching the landing two steps at a time while Mrs Spargo struggled to reverse back into the house with the child, he spotted only one closed door and made straight for it.

'Come back here,' he heard Mrs Spargo shriek as he flung the door open.

Thin curtains were pulled across the window, admitting an ooze of grey light to the small, cramped bedroom. The bed covered most of the floor space. A shape stirred and groaned beneath the blankets. Harding moved past it and yanked the curtains apart, then opened the window wide in a squeal of swollen wood and a rush of cold air. 'Rise and shine, Darren,' he shouted, turning back to the bed.

'Fucking hell,' came an answering moan. 'What's going on?'

'Ventilation, to start with. It smells like the camel house at the zoo in here.'

'Fuck,' slurred Darren, blearily focusing on his visitor. 'What . . . what are you doing here?'

'I'm phoning the police if you don't leave right now.' Mrs Spargo glared in at Harding from the landing, doing her best to look and sound intimidating while the young child gaped open-mouthed through the banisters from halfway up the stairs.

'Do you want your mother to phone the police, Darren?' Harding countered. 'There are a few things I want to discuss with you they might find very interesting.'

'Shit.' Darren pushed himself up on his elbows, revealing a scrawny torso. He squinted first at Harding, then his mother. A moment of woozy deliberation was followed by a scowl of resignation. 'It's OK, Ma. Mr H and me . . . need to have a chat, that's all. You . . . carry on.'

'Are you sure?'

'Yeah, yeah. I'll be fine. You can . . . leave us to it.'

Mrs Spargo cast Harding a wary look, muttered something inaudible, then retreated down the stairs, dragging the child with her and glancing back suspiciously as she went. 'Who's that man?' the child asked, her high-pitched voice carrying up to the bedroom. But Mrs Spargo's reply did not carry. The front door closed behind them with a clunk. Silence descended on chez Spargo. Darren slumped back on his pillow.

'What d'you want, man?'

'I thought we'd take up that conversation we were having on Monday where we left off.'

'Forget it. Hayley plugging Barney Tozer cancelled all bets. I'm not interested.'

'Frightened she might come after you, are you?'

'What d'you think?'

'I think I might be frightened. In your shoes.'

'Yeah?' Spargo sat up, slid a cigarette out of the open pack lying on the flimsy bedside table and lit it. There was a volley of coughs. Then he said, 'Look, Mr H, I'm sorry I messed you about. It was all Hayley's idea. I just . . . did what she told me. And she really did skip town owing me a grand. Scheming little bitch. So, I'm out of pocket and you're . . . out of luck. Let's call it quits.'

'I want to know who stole the ring.'

'For Christ's sake, why? The ring's Tozer business. And that dies with Barney, the way I see it.'

'Not the way I see it. Who took the ring?'

Spargo coughed out a lungful of smoke. 'You really sure about this?'

'Never more so.'

'OK. The offer stands. Slip me the dosh and I'll slip you the name.'

'I'm not going to pay you a penny.'

'Fine. Don't. You can show yourself out, can't you? Put the kettle on on your way, will you? I'm dying for a cuppa.'

'I'm willing to do a deal, Darren. But it doesn't involve money.'

'Not my kind of deal, then. Since I got burned by Hayley, I've decided to do nothing without cash up front.'

Harding took a step forward and propped one foot on an exposed edge of the mattress. Spargo looked gratifyingly nervous. 'Nathan Gashry, the man who passed on Hayley's message to Barney, setting up the rendezvous, died yesterday.'

'Never.'

'It's true. You'll probably be able to read about it in today's paper. They'll say it was suicide, but it's the old "Did he fall or was he pushed?" problem. Either way, he's dead.'

'Fucking hell.' Spargo had now abandoned all attempts to disguise his anxiety. 'What's going on? What has that bitch got me into?'

'A whole lot of trouble. The fatal kind, potentially. As it is, I'm the only one who knows you helped Hayley. Where did the helping stop? That's the question: the question the police will ask – *if* they're pointed in your direction.'

'What are you saying?'

'I'm saying I won't mention your part in all this to them if you tell me who stole the ring. Provided you genuinely know, of course. Provided what you tell me is the truth. If I check, as I will, and it turns out you've pulled a fast one, the deal's off. You see, conning Barney out of a thousand quid with some duff gen might have been a smart move. But buying my silence with it wouldn't be. Because you need me to keep my mouth shut about your role in Hayley's activities, you really do. Otherwise, who knows what might happen to you? The police wouldn't be your only problem, just like they weren't Nathan Gashry's only problem. So, I hope you know what you claim to know. For your sake.'

'Did Hayley kill this guy Gashry?'

'I don't think so.'

'Then . . .'

'Who? Exactly. Who? And why?'

Spargo shook his head. 'It's not the party who nicked the ring. I can tell you that for nothing.'

'Just tell me who it was.'

'If we're going to get smart, I'd better straighten one thing out. I went round to see Hayley that night – the Sunday before the auction. I was beginning to get the feeling I had a trickier job on my hands than she'd let on. Thought you might give me some serious aggro. I, er, wanted more money up front, like. She talked me out of it with a promise of more later. Only had to open those big wide eyes of hers and you'd agree to any crazy fucking thing. Y'know? Anyhow, she told me to give you your phone back and hang loose till we made our next move. It was supposed to be all about blackmailing you. But I was starting to see there was more to it than that. When I left, I, er, hung about outside. She'd been that keen to get rid of me I thought she was expecting someone she didn't want me to see. So, I, er, kept watch on the place for a while. Just in case, like. Then, all of a sudden, the alarm went off. And I saw this bloke slip round from the back and hustle off down the road. What I'm saying is I can't swear for a fact he took the ring, 'cos I never saw it, but he's your man, sure enough. No doubt about it.'

'And who is he?'

'You don't want to know, Mr H, believe me. Best leave it, hey? If folks are getting themselves killed . . .

the likes of you and me should leave well alone.'

'There are no likes of you and me, Darren. We're completely *unlike*. So, just tell me, OK? Who is he?'

Spargo took a long pull on his cigarette and looked Harding in the eye. 'Have it your way,' he said with a shrug.

FORTY-TWO

'Good morning,' said Harding, stepping into view as Humphrey Tozer approached the stairway that led to his flat.

Tozer was dressed in a shabby mac and flat cap. He was clutching a bulging Tesco carrier-bag in either hand and had obviously just returned from a shopping expedition. For necessities only, it went without saying. He was not a man surrounded by an aura of self-indulgence. He frowned at Harding suspiciously. 'What are you doing here?'

'Why don't we go inside and I'll explain?'

'I'm not travelling to Monte Carlo to attend my brother's funeral. I made that clear to Carol. So, if you've—'

'It's nothing to do with the funeral. Carol doesn't even know I'm here.'

Tozer grunted. 'What d'you want, then?'

'I have an idea you'd prefer to discuss it in private.'

Another grunt was followed by a long moment of deliberation. 'All right.'

Harding tailed Tozer up the steps and into the flat. Tozer set the shopping down in the hall, hung up his cap and led the way into the lounge. Harding had forgotten just how stark and cheerless the man's domestic environment was. As before, the current issue of *The Cornishman*, already well thumbed, lay on the table. **Penzance-born tycoon murdered** blared the headline, above a photograph of Barney Tozer, smiling, wineglass in hand, at some local function several years previously.

'Have they got it right?' Humphrey Tozer asked. He had made no move to remove his coat, which somehow did not surprise Harding in view of the deathly chill gripping the flat. 'You were there? You saw the Winter girl shoot Barney?'

'You mean Hayley Foxton?' Harding asked, neatly skating round the issue of the murderer's identity.

'You know who I mean.'

'I was there, all right. But tell me, why won't you go to Monte Carlo?'

'I don't travel. Carol knows that. She's arranged the funeral there to spite me.'

'I'm sure that isn't true.'

'What would you know about it?'

'Well, I—'

'Barney should be laid to rest in Cornish soil. Like our father and his father before him. Like Uncle Gabriel, come to that. The Tozers belong in Penzance. They belong *to* Penzance. No good comes of them leaving it. I told Barney so when he moved to Monte Carlo. Tax exile, they call him. Well, exile is right enough. In death as well as in life, if Carol has her way.'

'Look, it's—'

'Say what you came to say.' Humphrey Tozer's expression was grim, set and unyielding. 'I don't suppose you're any keener to be here than I am to have you.'

'Very well. I've come about the ring.'

'What about it?'

'You stole it.'

Something flickered in Tozer's gaze. Surprise, perhaps. Or guilt. Whatever it was he soon mastered it. '*I* stole it?'

'You were seen leaving Heartsease the night of the theft.'

'Was I?'

'Do you deny it?'

'I don't have to. If I was seen, this . . . witness . . . would have reported me to the police. They haven't. That says it all.'

'Do you deny stealing the ring?'

'Yes.'

'You may as well admit it. Like you say, the witness hasn't contacted the police. And he isn't going to. This is between you and me. I just want to know. Why did you take it?'

'You accused me of stealing it a moment ago. Now it's *take*. Which d'you mean?'

'Does it make a difference?'

'Oh yes.' Tozer's mouth twitched in what might have

been his version of a sardonic smile. 'You can't steal what's already yours.'

'So, you *did* take it.'

'I'm admitting nothing. All I'm saying is this: Uncle Gabriel stole the ring from our father, whose it was by right as the first-born. So, it wasn't his to sell to the highest bidder, even if that bidder had turned out to be Barney.'

'What would that have mattered once the ring was in your hands? As it would have been straight after the auction.'

'D'you think I was born yesterday?' Tozer took a step towards Harding, who caught a whiff of the strange, bitter smell that clung to the man. The slight tremor of his head had become marginally more pronounced at the same time. 'As soon as you turned up here, I knew what Barney's game was. Buy the ring and keep it for himself. You'd have made off with it, of course. He'd have said you'd stolen it. But you'd have delivered it to him later, in secret. Barney always thought he could outwit me. How wrong he was.'

'That's ridiculous. Barney didn't want the ring.'

'How would you know what he did or didn't want? He devoted his life to taking things other people deserved more than he did. The ring was no exception. I knew how it would be. As soon as I showed an interest in it, he'd take it from me, like he'd taken so many other things in the past. Well, not this time.'

'You're wrong. He didn't care about the ring.'

'I know that.' Tozer looked contemptuously at

Harding. 'Don't you understand? He never cared about anything. Until somebody else wanted it. Grandfather used to show us the starburst box and very occasionally open it, though we were never allowed to touch the ring. *His* father had had the box made specially to hold it. He told us the ring had belonged to an ancestor of ours in the eighteenth century, conferred on him in recognition of some great service he'd done the nation. It was never to leave the family, Grandfather said, *or* Penzance. How Uncle Gabriel could have thought of letting it be sold to a stranger – perhaps even a foreigner – is beyond me. He wanted it for himself. And then he wanted to put it out of our reach. *My* reach, that is. I've reflected on it since Barney's death. I've begun to see how my black-hearted uncle thought it all through. He knew I was the ring's rightful keeper as the eldest of the next generation. I respected what it stood for. But he didn't. He scorned our family name. And he knew I hadn't the means to buy the ring at auction. So, he gave me a choice. See it bought by some dealer or other, or alert Barney and watch him snatch it from under my nose.'

'The ring was stolen from Sir Clowdisley Shovell's body on St Mary's after the wreck of the *Association* in 1707. It never rightfully belonged to any ancestor of yours.'

But Tozer's confidence in his version of history was undented. 'I'll take my grandfather's word for what's rightful and what isn't over the word of one of my treacherous younger brother's errand-boys every time.'

351

It was too late now, far too late, to weigh the rights and wrongs of sibling rivalry between Humphrey and Barney Tozer. As far as Harding could glean, Humph regarded the ring as a symbol of every advantage Barney had somehow stolen from him. Besides, it was his and his alone, according to an ingrained concept of primogeniture which his uncle had tried to subvert and which his paranoid nature inclined him to believe Barney had also been planning to circumvent. In the end, it hardly mattered. His reasons for stealing the ring were locked within his very particular view of the world. Harding had clung to the hope that those reasons would somehow reveal the greater truth he was still seeking. But his hope was failing fast.

'What great service did your grandfather say your ancestor performed?'

'Honour needs not the naming of the occasion.'

'*What?*'

'Whenever Barney badgered him with his questions, Grandfather would say, "Honour needs not the naming of the occasion."'

'And how did he answer *your* questions?'

'I knew better than to ask any.'

Of course. Humph knew better. 'Did Kerry Foxton ever discuss your ancestor with you?'

Tozer frowned deeply, his contempt turning to apparently genuine incredulity. '*Kerry Foxton?*'

'Barney might have told her about him.'

'Why should she be interested even if he did?'

'I don't know. But I think she may have been.'

'You think what you like. I never exchanged a single word with Kerry Foxton. About anything.'

'Maybe she found out what your ancestor did to get hold of that ring.'

'Maybe, maybe, maybe. You can make a noose of your maybes and hang yourself with it for all I care.' Anger was simmering in Humphrey Tozer now. He had said as much as he could be induced to say. A wall was coming down between them. 'I'm not answering any more of your questions.'

'Where's the ring? In a safe-deposit box at the bank? Or here?'

'Didn't you hear what I just said? *I'm not answering any more of your questions.*'

FORTY-THREE

From the pavement, Heartsease looked as it had prior to the auction. But Harding knew it was now an empty shell. The rooms were no longer filled with Gabriel Tozer's innumerable possessions, nor with the voices of those sifting through them in search of a bargain – or an overlooked gem. Like the trees lining Polwithen Road that may once have been part of a local farmer's field boundary, so the house remained, and would remain, long after the going of its latest owner.

The keys had been waiting for Harding at Isbisters' auction rooms. Clive Isbister, who might well have spent the morning regretting his garrulousness of the night before, had been conspicuous by his absence, although his secretary had emphasized how short-term the loan of them was. 'We need them back within the hour.'

That would be no problem. An hour was more than Harding needed. He let himself into Heartsease by the main door, turned off the alarm using the code the secretary had given him and stood in the hall for a moment or two, letting the silence and emptiness of the house declare themselves. There was nothing left. Gabriel Tozer's home had been stripped in accordance with his wishes, every sign of his years there erased.

The third key Harding tried opened the door beneath the stairs marked PRIVATE. He stepped through and went down to the basement flat. This part of the house was still furnished, of course. Theoretically, its tenant might return at any moment, though the certainty that she would not had somehow altered the atmosphere since Harding's last visit. He glanced into the kitchen. Virtually everything had been put away. No tea towels hung on the range. No mugs or plates stood on the worktop. It was as if Hayley had known she might never return there – as if she had foreseen all the events that were to follow her departure.

Harding walked into the bedroom. A sheet had been draped over the entire bed. The memory of the night he had spent there with her was hard to conjure up. So much had been lost, so much altered, since then. It was only last week, but it might have been last year. He opened the drawers in the bedside cabinets, seeking a clue without really knowing what one would look like. But the drawers were empty. So was the wardrobe. Her clothes were gone. Perhaps she had never had many to start with. Perhaps she had always travelled light – the better to flee whenever the need arose.

There was a cupboard in the hall, but all it contained

were spare sheets, blankets, towels and pillowcases. The flat seemed to have been prepared for a new tenant, rather than the return of the existing one. The tracks of the vacuum cleaner could be seen in the pale carpet in the lounge. Hayley had left everything in pristine condition, as if proclaiming the permanence of her going. That, Harding realized, was the only clue he was likely to find there, her absence a statement in itself.

Clive Isbister was pulling into the staff car park in an enormous Saab estate when Harding returned to the auction rooms with the keys. He stopped and lowered his window.

'I'll take those if you like,' he said, smiling amiably – if a touch apprehensively. 'Everything OK?'

'You could say so,' Harding replied, handing over the keys.

'You remembered to reset the alarm?'

'Oh yes.'

'We don't want any more burglaries.'

'There's nothing left to burgle.'

'What did you expect? We pride ourselves on our thoroughness.'

'So does Hayley, it seems.'

Isbister frowned in puzzlement at the remark, but did not query it. 'How's Humphrey?'

'Much as usual.'

'Did he mention the ring? The police haven't made any progress with the case, as far as I can establish.'

'He's not bothered about it.'

'Really? You surprise me. Still, perhaps his brother's death has put such things into perspective.'

'Yes.' Harding allowed himself half a smile. 'That must be it.'

Harding had nowhere to go now. He had arrived where Shepherd had predicted he would have to before abandoning his search for the truth: the last dead end. He was not ready to give up. But he could not see how to avoid it. Nathan Gashry was dead. Humphrey Tozer was the Heartsease thief. And Hayley had fled, he knew not where.

Wandering south along Chapel Street towards the sea front, he saw the doors of the Turk's Head being opened for business. He walked in and ordered a double Scotch.

He had nearly finished his drink, and was seriously considering the merits of another, when a second customer appeared at his elbow.

'Fancy meeting you here,' said Ray Trathen, grinning lopsidedly. 'Having a hard day?'

'Hello, Ray,' said Harding, too worn down by recent events to be riled by Trathen's sarcastic tone. 'D'you normally start this early?'

'Only on Fridays. What's your excuse?'

'Do I need one?'

'Certainly not. In fact, why don't I stand you a drink? Least I can do in the circumstances.'

'All right. Thanks.' Trathen ordered a pint of bitter for

himself and another double Scotch for Harding. 'Which circumstances did you have in mind?'

'Well, you were there when Barney Tozer got what was coming to him.' Trathen lit a cigarette while his pint was being pulled. Studying him as he did so, Harding wondered just how much comfort he would ultimately derive from Tozer's death. Blaming his misfortunes on the local-boy-made-good was one thing; carping endlessly about the supposed misdeeds of a dead man quite another. 'Cheers,' said Trathen, taking a large gulp of beer. 'What brings you back here, then?'

'I had to see Humph.'

'Ah. The grieving brother. Bad luck.' Trathen smacked his lips. 'So, Hayley Winter was actually Hayley Foxton, set on avenging her sister, and now she's been and gone and done it.'

'Is that what they say in the papers?'

'The ones I read, yeah.'

'Must be true, then.'

'Are you trying to imply it isn't?'

'Why would I do that? I was only there when it happened. How should I know?'

Trathen frowned. He nodded at Harding's drink. 'How many of those have you had?'

'Several too few.'

'Blimey. Sounds like it could be a lively lunchtime here.'

'Tell me, Ray,' said Harding, aware that the whiskies were already affecting him, but disinclined to hold back, 'what story do you think Kerry was really working

358

on when she came down here in the summer of 'ninety-nine?'

'You know what I think.'

'The shady secrets of Barney's business empire, right?'

'Right. On the money.' Trathen smiled at his own pun.

'There's no chance you could have got that wrong?'

'She had Barney lined up for an exposé. That's the way I see it. He found out and decided to shut her up. Permanently. He was smart enough to make sure the law couldn't touch him. But her twin sister in full avenging-angel mode was something he hadn't bargained for.' Trathen slapped his hand down on the bar. 'Bang.'

'Ever heard of the Grey Man of Ennor?'

'*Who?*'

'Semi-legendary Scilly Islander from the fourteenth century. Supposed to have wandered the West Country curing people of the Black Death.'

'Bloody hell. Get off with the Nine Maidens, did he? Stony-faced bunch, but biddable, so they tell me.' Trathen's chortlings ended in a quaff of beer. He gave Harding a straight look. 'What *are* you on about?'

'To be honest, I don't know. But *if* Kerry was investigating Starburst International, I'm pretty sure she was investigating something else as well.'

'This medieval healer?'

'Yes. Strange as it may seem.'

'Oh, it seems strange, all right. She was a journalist, y'know. Not a bloody historian.'

'She was interested in the *Association* story.'

'Yeah, but that's bang up to date by comparison with the fourteenth century. And there's a wreck to explore. As she made the fatal mistake of doing. Not to mention divers to interview about the treasure hunt back in the sixties, if she'd had a mind to. Who was she going to interview about the . . . what was he called?'

'Grey Man of Ennor.'

'I take it the old boy's not still around?'

Harding smiled thinly. 'I doubt it.'

'There you are, then. Total non-starter.'

'Kerry never mentioned him to you?'

'Not as I recall. And I reckon I would. Besides, she'd have known better than to ask me about something like that – just supposing, for the sake of argument, she *was* remotely interested.'

'Who would she ask, then?'

Trathen pondered for a moment, then said, 'John Metherell, maybe. She knew him. He lives on the Scillies. And he's a historian – of sorts.'

Trathen was an amused witness when, a few minutes later, Harding phoned Metherell. His call was a surprise, naturally, and Metherell wanted to ask all the obvious questions about Barney Tozer's death, as well as Hayley Foxton's responsibility for it, before he could be induced to focus on the arcane issue of the Grey Man of Ennor.

'I've never heard of him. But then I'm no medievalist. Working on the *Association* story's given me tunnel vision where the past's concerned. I certainly don't remember Kerry asking me anything about the fourteenth century or the Black Death . . . or the Old Man of Ennor.'

'Grey. Not old. Necessarily.'

'Sorry?'

'Never mind.'

'Crosbie Hicks would've been the person to ask. There wasn't much he didn't know about Scillonian history. Used to write a piece in *The Cornishman* every month or so. Might have written about your fellow. Yes, he might well have done. That sort of thing would've been right up his street.'

'*Would've* been?'

'Sadly, he died a couple of years ago.'

'But he was alive in 1999?'

'Oh yes. Very much so. In fact—' Metherell broke off, seemingly struck by a thought. 'Now, that's odd.'

'What is?'

'Well, you've jogged my memory. Crosbie Hicks. I met him once with Kerry. Here in Hugh Town. Nothing unusual about that. It's a small place. You meet every-body sooner or later. But—'

'Hold on. Were you with Kerry? Or was she with Hicks?'

'I was with Kerry. We bumped into old Crosbie coming out of the post office and chatted for a few moments. Well . . .'

'What?'

'It was obvious they knew each other. Again, nothing unusual about that. Crosbie could easily have been a regular customer at Carol's café. But I remember Kerry thanked him for some help he'd given her. So I acted affronted and said, "You've been double-checking what I've told you about the wreck of the *Association* with Crosbie, haven't you?" And Crosbie said, "Don't worry, John. Kerry's asked me nothing about the *Association*. I've been helping her with an entirely unrelated matter." Well, that could have been your Black Death legend, I suppose.'

'Yes,' said Harding thoughtfully. 'It could.'

'Unfortunately, it's too late to ask either of them now. So, we'll never know for sure.'

FORTY-FOUR

Too late. Metherell's description applied to everything Harding had done or tried to do since returning to Penzance. The dead held their secrets too close for the living to unlock. Mere stubbornness had prompted his latest and surely last recourse: a trawl through the public library's microfilmed back copies of *The Cornishman*, in search of some vital clue buried in the roughly monthly offerings of Crosbie Hicks on subjects plucked from Scillonian history.

He had begun with editions from two years prior to the accident and was working his way slowly towards the summer of 1999. So far, Hicks had written about ancient burial mounds, King Arthur, the tin trade, rising sea levels, the Godolphins, Augustus Smith, the daffodil industry, lighthouses, dialect, place names, even the wreck of the *Association*. But none of what he had written seemed to come close to the 'unrelated matter' he had helped Kerry with. And now, as Harding reached the spring of 1999, he began to fear he would come away empty-handed once more.

Hicks's articles appeared, when they did, at the foot of the page of *The Cornishman* devoted each week to specifically Scillonian news. This seldom amounted to anything momentous and Harding had slipped into a pattern of checking at a glance to see if there was a contribution from Hicks that week before scrolling on to the next. He had, in fact, already done so with the Thursday, 29 April edition when some combination of words in one of the headlines belatedly registered in his mind. He scrolled back. And there it was. *Charity Walk to Become Celebration of Miracle Cure*.

The article had not been written by Crosbie Hicks. Yet there, in the phrase *miracle cure*, was the connection with the Grey Man of Ennor Harding had been searching for, the connection that was also a clue.

Charity walk to become celebration of miracle cure

The campaign to pay for a fourteen-year-old St Mary's girl to receive treatment in the United States for a rare form of leukaemia has ended in her complete and unexpected recovery.

A sponsored walk round the coast of St Mary's to raise some of the money that would have been needed was planned for Bank Holiday Monday, 31 May. The walk will still go ahead, but will now be a celebration of the all-clear Josephine Edwards recently received from her consultant at Treliske Hospital. Her parents, David and Christine Edwards, of Guinea-Money Farm, St Mary's, said they were 'amazed and overjoyed' when they were informed that exhaustive tests had confirmed the reason for the sudden disappearance of Josephine's symptoms was that she was now free of the disease.

'We were told a bone-marrow transplant wouldn't be effective for Josephine's particular type of leukaemia,' Mrs Edwards added, 'and that her only hope was a revolutionary treatment being pioneered at a hospital in Colorado. There was no way we could afford to send her there and we're hugely grateful to everyone who offered to take part in fund-raising, including the walk round the island. The doctors can't explain what's happened. They've never known anything like this before. It's not just a remission. It's a total cure. In fact, it's a miracle. We're over the moon.'

Harding went out into the street to call Metherell. His phone rang almost as soon as he switched it on. His first thought was that Metherell had called *him*, perhaps having remembered something more about Crosbie Hicks. Accordingly, he answered without checking the number. And found himself talking to Carol.

'Ah, at last. Mind telling me where you are, Tim?'

'Penzance.'

'Why have you gone back there? What the hell are you trying to do?'

'Tie up some loose ends.'

'Oh yeah? And have you tied up any?'

'For a start, I've learnt Humph stole the ring from Heartsease.'

'Really? Well, I can't say I'm surprised. It's the sort of thing he would do, just to spite Barney.'

'He thinks you're spiting *him*, by holding the funeral in Monaco.'

'He flatters himself. I don't care what he says, thinks or does. The ring means nothing to me. You must know that. Which is another reason why I just don't understand what you're doing.'

'Have you heard that Nathan Gashry's dead?'

'Yes. Suicide, apparently. Good riddance.'

'Is that all you have to say about it?'

'What else is there to say? I never even met the man. But he sounds a nasty piece of work.'

'For God's sake, Carol, don't you see? There's something going on here you're missing.'

'And what might that be?'

'Do you remember Josephine Edwards?'

'Who?'

'A young girl on St Mary's who made a miraculous recovery from leukaemia back in 1999. Just before Kerry went to stay with you.'

'Leukaemia? What are you talking about?'

'Josephine Edwards,' Harding insistently repeated. 'Do you remember?'

'No. Of course I don't.'

'It must have been big news at the time, Carol. Your customers would have discussed it. A lot of them would have known her. Or taken part in the walk round the island intended to raise money for her treatment. Isn't any of this even vaguely familiar?'

There was a brief interval of silence. Then Carol said, 'All right. I do remember. For what it's worth. Yeah. I put a poster up in the café and I signed up for the walk. You're right. She got better spontaneously. Happy ending all round. What about it?'

'Did Kerry take an interest in the story?'

'It happened before she came down.'

'But people must still have been talking about it. You must have mentioned it to her.'

'Probably, yeah. What about it?'

'Did she seem interested?'

'I can't remember.'

'Try.'

'This is crazy, Tim. You're—'

'Did she seem interested?'

Another silence. Then: 'Maybe. Maybe not. I genuinely can't remember. And I really don't see why it should matter. For Christ's sake, Tim, what are you—'

He ended the call there and then. And rang Metherell immediately. 'Why does it matter?' he murmured under his breath as he listened to the dialling tone. 'I don't know, Carol. But it does. I'm certain of that.'

367

'Hello?'

'Mr Metherell. It's Harding again.'

'Ah, Mr Harding. Found what you're looking for yet?'

'I may have. Do you remember a local girl called Josephine Edwards, who made a miraculous recovery from leukaemia? The case got a bit of publicity at the time. This was seven years ago, just before Kerry's accident.'

'Of course I remember. It was a remarkable thing. But I don't—'

'Do you know if she's still living on the island? She was fourteen then, so she'd be – what? – twenty-one now.'

'Certainly she's still living here. In fact, you met her yourself last week.'

'I did?'

'Yes. Josephine Edwards is Josie Martyn now.'

FORTY-FIVE

Harding spotted Metherell's white Honda parked behind the terminal building as the helicopter descended towards St Mary's Airport. It was the last flight of the day, so Harding would not be able to return to the mainland until the following morning. Metherell had offered him a bed for the night, which he had naturally accepted, but he was in truth thinking no further ahead than that afternoon. He was close to the answer now. He could almost touch it.

The Isles of Scilly's famed subtropical splendour was no more in evidence than it had been the week before. The cloud was low, the wind biting. Metherell did not get out of his car as Harding approached, merely raising his hand in greeting.

'And so, here we are again,' he said as Harding climbed into the passenger seat and closed the door. 'My wife thinks I'm mad to be indulging your whims like this, you know.'

'They're more than whims. But I'm certainly grateful for your help. And sorry if I've caused any domestic friction.'

'Don't worry about it. Just put me in the picture.'

Harding did his level best to assemble his surmises and suspicions into a coherent account as they sat watching the helicopter loading for its immediate return to Penzance. The missing segment of the Gashry report; Kerry's interest in the Grey Man of Ennor; Josephine Edwards's miraculous recovery from terminal leukaemia; her marriage to Fred Martyn; and Kerry's fatal diving accident: they were linked, he felt certain. There was a hidden truth that bound them together. Whether he had persuaded Metherell of that, however, he rather doubted. As the tone of the other man's response seemed to confirm.

'What does all this really amount to, Mr Harding? I don't get it. I just don't get it.'

'I can't tell you exactly what it adds up to. But it adds up to something. You told me yourself the Martyn family has lived on this island since the Middle Ages.'

'According to Crosbie Hicks, yes. Since the fourteenth century, as I recall. Which you'll immediately point out to me is the Grey Man of Ennor's century.'

'So it is.'

'But what of it?'

'Barney Tozer talked to me just before he died about the sequence of events on the day of the accident. Mind if I check it with you?'

Metherell shrugged. 'Why not?'

'Barney flew over with Ray Trathen the day before. He spent the night at your house and you drove down to the quay together the following morning with the diving suits and gear he and Kerry were going to use. Right so far?'

'Yes.'

'You and Barney loaded the stuff on to the *Jonquil*, then he walked back into town to fetch Kerry and Carol. You stayed on the boat with the Martyns. Correct?'

'Yes.'

'Were you on board the whole time you were waiting for Barney to come back?'

'Sorry?'

'Did you stay on the boat until Barney returned with the girls – and Ray Trathen, who they met on the way?'

'I . . .' Metherell frowned as he struggled to remember.

'Well, did you?'

'No. Since you ask, I didn't. The harbourmaster wanted to confirm we had proper written permission from the salvors to dive to the wreck. I went to show him the paperwork. I can't have been off the boat more than five minutes, but—'

'You *were* off it.'

'Yes. So?'

'Well, you obviously didn't take the diving gear with you.'

'Of course I didn't.' Metherell looked round sharply at Harding. 'What are you suggesting?'

'The gear stayed aboard. With the Martyns. If they'd wanted to tamper with it . . .'

'Why in God's name would they want to do that?'

'I don't know. I'm not even sure they did. But . . . I just have this . . . feeling that . . .'

'I spoke to Christine Edwards before coming to pick you up, Mr Harding. She remembered the accident, of course. It was big news at the time. Much bigger than her daughter's triumph over leukaemia. She was quite adamant on one point. Kerry Foxton had never contacted them. Which I'm guessing you'd have expected her to, if she made the same connection you seem to be making between Josie's defiance of the medical odds and the Grey Man of Ennor.'

'You believe her?'

'Why wouldn't I?'

'No reason, I suppose.'

'Exactly.'

'Nevertheless . . .'

'I'll tell you what, Mr Harding. Let's go and see the Martyns now. See if you think Josie's lying when she tells us she never met Kerry Foxton. Or if Fred and Alf are holding something back. My bet is you'll sense what I sense: there's nothing to this. You've put two and two together and made five. Actually, a lot more than five. So, how about it? Isn't it time to put up or shut up?'

'OK,' Harding replied, acknowledging with a nod that such a time probably had come. 'Let's go.'

The scene at Pregowther Farm had not altered since Harding's last visit: smoke rising from the farmhouse chimney; chickens scavenging in the yard; a perspective of hazy yellow away through the daffodil fields towards Porth Hellick. He suspected it had probably not altered to any significant degree in centuries. The past and the present were fused here in the thin grey light of late afternoon. Only the future could not be detected.

One of the Martyn brothers stepped into view from the deep shadows of the barn as they climbed out of the car. Harding could not have said with any certainty which of them it was. But Metherell knew. ''Afternoon, Alf,' he called.

''Af'noon, Mr Metherell.' Alf strode across the yard to meet them. 'You've brought your friend with you, I see. Mr . . . Harding, ain't it?'

'Well remembered,' said Harding.

'Still worrying about poor Miss Foxton?'

'In a sense, yes.'

'I read in this week's *Cornishman* her sister was wanted for the murder of Mr Tozer. That right?'

'It is.'

'Sorry to hear that. Folk should let tragedies heal themselves, not go after making them worse. But the gift of leaving well alone is a rare one and that's a fact.'

'Mr Harding just wanted to check a few points about the accident, Alf,' said Metherell.

'Nothing I can tell you I didn't tell you last week.'

'It's the week *before* the accident I'm interested in,' said Harding.

'Can't see how I can help you, then. Mr Metherell here arranged the trip with us. He's the only one of the passengers that day Fred and me had ever clapped eyes on afore.'

'You'd never met Barney Tozer?'

'No more we had.'

'Or Carol Janes?'

'Her neither.'

'Never dropped into her café in Hugh Town?'

'We've got no use for cafés, Mr Harding. There's a hob indoors if we want a cup o' tea.'

'What about Kerry? Did you ever meet her before?'

'That we didn't.'

'Are you sure you can speak for your brother?'

'I am.' Alf gave Harding a long, deliberative look. 'But maybe you ain't. Fred's in the house with Josie. We can step inside and ask him if you want him to tell you himself.'

'Actually, I was hoping to ask Josie the same question, so . . .'

'Come away in, then.'

Alf turned and led the way towards the house. Metherell shot Harding a cautioning glance. But Harding had left caution behind. He would learn nothing by treading carefully. 'How is Josie, Mr Martyn?' he enquired as they crossed the yard.

'Blooming is how she is. Just blooming.'

'Good. Though I gather that hasn't always been the case. She was once very ill, wasn't she?'

'In her girlhood, yes. A long time ago.'

'Did you know her then?'

They had reached the door. Alf pushed it open and

stood back to let them enter. 'Oh, I know all the farming families on this island,' he said quietly.

A narrow hall led straight ahead, past the stairs, to the kitchen and a scullery beyond. A door to the left stood open, while the one to the right was closed. Harding glanced through the open doorway into a simply furnished sitting room, sensing more than observing the immutability that was the dominant characteristic of Pregowther Farm *and* its occupants.

'Fred,' Alf called over Harding's shoulder. 'We'm got visitors.'

Fred's head bobbed into view round the scullery doorpost. 'How do,' he said brightly.

'Hello,' Harding responded, advancing slowly along the hall with Metherell at his shoulder. He heard Alf close the front door behind them. An aroma the sweet side of mustiness disclosed itself around him.

'All well, Fred?' asked Metherell.

'All good, Mr Metherell.' Fred moved into the kitchen, wiping his hands on a towel.

'Josie about?'

'Resting upstairs.' A floorboard creaked above them. 'But . . . sounds like she's coming down.'

Josie appeared above them at the head of the stairs and began a slow descent, her pregnancy looking to Harding even more pronounced than the week before. She smiled down at them. 'Hi, Mr Metherell.'

''Afternoon, Josie.'

'Hello again,' she said to Harding.

'Hello.'

'This is nice. We don't get many visitors.' She glanced at Fred. 'Put the kettle on, darlin'. We'll have some tea.'

It was as she turned, leaning heavily on the banisters, that Harding's eye was caught by a gleam of jewellery on the left breast of her smock-top. He gaped up at it in astonishment. And a fox cub, fashioned from jet and mother-of-pearl, gazed playfully back at him. 'That's a . . . nice brooch,' he said numbly.

'Yeah.' Josie blushed. 'Fred gave it me.'

Harding turned towards Fred. 'Where did you buy it?' he asked.

Fred's mental wrestlings with the question were written on his face. 'That's no business of yours.'

'I think it is, actually.'

'He recognizes it,' said Alf quietly.

'What are you talking about?' asked Metherell. 'What's going on?'

'The brooch belonged to Kerry Foxton,' Harding replied, still staring at Fred.

'No,' said Josie. 'It was her . . .'

'Sister you took it from?' Harding asked, looking back up at her.

'That's torn it,' said Alf.

'You took that from Hayley?' demanded Metherell, rounding on Alf. 'For God's sake, how could you be so stupid?'

'Fred took it. I didn't find out until it was too late.'

'But you knew . . .' Metherell broke off. He had said too much. And the significance of what he had said – the true, terrible meaning of it – was irretrievable. He

376

turned back to face Harding. He seemed to struggle to say something. But no words came.

'You're all in this together, aren't you?' Harding gasped. 'What in God's name have you—' There was a movement behind him, fast and swinging; an impact; then oblivion, as complete as it was sudden, as black as it was total.

FORTY-SIX

Consciousness brought pain, but no vision. At first, he thought he might be blind. The sharpness of the pain, as he moved his head, seemed to confirm it. Then he saw a faint line of light above him somewhere, though how far above he could not tell. The darkness deprived him of all sense of scale. He was lying on a blanket spread on a hard, uneven surface.

He pushed himself up on one elbow, groaning as what felt like the worst headache in the world throbbed through his brain. Then he heard a voice, low and hoarse, from close beside him.

'Tim?'

'Who's there?' He turned towards the sound.

'It's me. Hayley.'

'What?'

'I'm here.' Her fingers touched his hand. They were cold and rough. They were not as he remembered them.

But it was her. He recognized her voice despite the huskiness. 'Are you all right?'

'I don't know. I'm alive. Where are we?'

'The Martyns' cellar. Beneath the farmhouse. They brought you down not long ago, cradled in a blanket. They took me by surprise and I was blinded by the light. Before I could do anything, they were gone again. Not that I could have done much. I'm so weak. Weaker all the time.'

'How long have you been here?'

'What day is it?'

'Friday.'

'Four days, then. Since Monday.' She coughed. 'I'm sorry. It must stink down here.'

'*You've been here since Monday?*'

'Yes.'

She had not killed Barney Tozer. That was certain now. But the identity of Tozer's murderer was for the moment unimportant. They were imprisoned in a cold, dank cellar. The Martyns had done with them what they did with all their secrets. They had buried them.

'There's no way out. The trapdoor is weighed down with a slab of some kind. They heave it into place. The walls and the floor are stone. I've gouged at them, I've pulled, I've prised: nothing gives.'

'Is that light the trapdoor?'

'Yes.'

'I'll have a go at it.'

'You'll be wasting your time.'

Harding scrambled to his feet, the pounding in his

head worsening with every movement. He put his hand to the place behind his left ear that seemed to be the centre of the pain and felt a patch of semi-congealed blood. Then he stepped forward, stumbling against the lowest tread of a flight of steps. He felt his way up, reaching blindly ahead until his fingers touched the wooden trapdoor. There was a wall to his right. Bracing himself between it and the steps, he pushed up against the trapdoor, steadily increasing the pressure until he was at the limit of his strength. The door did not move an inch. He tried again, to no avail, then thumped at it. *'Let us out of here,'* he shouted.

'They're not listening, Tim,' said Hayley softly.

He ran his hand round the frame of the trapdoor and encountered a cable emerging into the cellar. 'There must be a light in here,' he declared in a small surge of optimism.

'But the switch is upstairs,' she responded, almost apologetically.

He patted the pocket where his phone should have been, but it was not there. 'They've taken my phone,' he said grimly.

'There's no way out, Tim.'

'There has to be.'

'No. There doesn't. You just want there to be one. So do I. But there isn't.'

He inched back down the steps and groped his way along the wall. It was constructed of big, roughly worked boulders, unyielding to the touch, solid and ancient. He came to a corner after twelve feet or so, and another, twelve feet after that. Before he reached the third corner, he trod on the edge of the blanket and knew he was back where he had started, their small, dark world all too swiftly circumscribed.

'Sit down beside me, Tim. Please.'

Reaching forward, he felt her outstretched hand and lowered himself to the floor. She had rolled herself in part of the blanket he had been lying on and was shivering with cold and fatigue. He put his arm round her shoulders. She sighed and rested her head on his chest. The shivering abated.

'I wondered if you'd come for me. It was the hope I was clinging to. And you did come, didn't you? But it's done neither of us any good.'

'So much has happened since I last held you like this, Hayley. So much I don't understand.'

'And so much you can't forgive?'

'I can forgive you for wanting to avenge Kerry. It's easy.' He kissed her on the forehead. 'There. It's done.'

'Thank you for saving me.'

'I haven't.'

'I don't mean here, now, today. I mean when I aborted my oh-so-clever plot to kill Carol and frame Barney for her murder. It was caring about you – you making me care about you – that stopped me. And that stopped me taking revenge on the wrong person. Because Barney didn't kill Kerry. I know that now. I guess you do too. It was the Martyns who did it. It wasn't Barney. He's as innocent as he's always claimed to be.'

He was going to have to tell her soon that Barney was dead and that, ironically, she had been framed for his murder. But he could not bring himself to do so yet. 'Why did they kill her, Hayley?'

'The reason's in this cellar with us. Here.' She wrestled something from the pocket of her jeans and pressed it into his palm. 'A miniature torch. The Martyns don't know I've got it. Not that it's done me much good. The battery's nearly dead. But turn it on. Then you'll see.'

Harding rotated the tiny barrel of the torch in his hand until he felt the ribbed surface of the switch. He pushed at it. Hayley's face, hollow-cheeked and big-eyed, was suddenly illuminated. She smiled at him. He stretched forward, holding the torch at arm's length. The rough-hewn walls revealed themselves in vaguely formed shadows. And there, in the centre of the chamber, he saw an old iron chest, about three feet high, four feet long and two feet wide, with an arched lid, mounted on some kind of platform. He glimpsed engraved lettering on the side of the chest facing him. Then the beam of light faltered. And ceased.

'What is that?' he asked.

'An ossuary chest.'

'A *what*?'

'It contains the bones of the Grey Man of Ennor.'

'How d'you know?'

'I drained the battery deciphering the inscription.'

'What does it say?'

'Eduardus Vir Canus Ennoris, MCCCLIV. The Latin version of his name: Edward, the Grey Man of Ennor.

And the year of his death in Roman numerals: 1354.'

'No surname?'

'A monk or friar gives up his surname on taking his vows. But we both know who he was, don't we?'

'I know Kerry was trying to connect the Grey Man of Ennor with Edward the Second. I learned that much from her old editor, Jack Shepherd. How did you find out?'

'Kerry stole the complete version of the Gashry report from Norman Buller, a descendant of Gashry's executor. She hid it under the floorboards in the drawing room of our old home in Dulwich. Then she hid a sketch plan showing where it was in her recorder. She must have been worried from the start that something would be done to stop her and she wanted me to know why. I found the plan when the Horstelmann Clinic handed her possessions over to me. Then I found the report – where she'd put it. That's what I needed the torch for. And when I read the section missing from Herbert Shelkin's copy . . . I understood.'

'What was in the missing section?'

'Everything Gashry uncovered during his investigation here in the Scillies in February 1736, beginning with the Grey Man legend. He was supposed to have returned to St Nicholas's Priory on Tresco after the Black Death and to have died there a few years afterwards. He was buried in the priory church. When the priory was abandoned a century or so later, his bones were removed, placed in that chest and transferred to Old Town Church, here on St Mary's. Godfrey Shillingstone had identified him from his earlier researches and Lord Godolphin had authorized Shillingstone to take whatever so-called antiquities he wanted. So, he excavated the nave of Old Town Church, found the ossuary chest and took it back to Penzance, intending to make his name with his discovery in London. But there were people living here who'd sworn to protect the Grey Man's remains. They followed Shillingstone to Penzance. And they had a valuable ally. Jacob Tozer was a Scillonian by birth. He helped them retrieve the chest, killing Shillingstone in the process and stealing the Shovell ring to put anyone investigating the murder off the scent. But Gashry couldn't actually prove anything. In the end, he recommended supplying Admiral Shovell's family with a specially made replica of the ring and, for the rest, letting sleeping dogs lie.'

'And that's what his boss decided to do.'

'Yes. The incomplete copy of the report aroused Kerry's curiosity and the complete copy convinced her there was a story in it. When she came down here to do some digging, she heard about Josephine Edwards's miraculous recovery from terminal leukaemia. She put a photocopy of a newspaper article about that in with the report for me to find. When I arrived on Monday, I went to see the Edwardses. They sent me here. Stupidly, I thought it might be a coincidence that Josie had married Fred Martyn. By the time I realized it wasn't, it was too late. They overpowered me *so* easily.'

'They believe the Grey Man's bones still hold some of his healing power?'

'I guess. That's why their ancestors were never going to let Shillingstone take the bones to London. They had to be brought back to Scilly at any price. Maybe there's a folk memory of other miracle cures over the centuries. Maybe Josie's was just the latest in a long line.'

'You don't believe a chestful of old bones can conquer terminal diseases.'

'They believe it can. And they have a practical example to back up their belief. That's all that matters. Josie got better, baffling her doctors. Then Kerry turned up, asking all kinds of questions. The way they must have seen it, she was threatening to do just what Shillingstone did. And just like Shillingstone, she had to be stopped. I don't know how they were able to sabotage her gear without anyone noticing, but—'

'They weren't able to, Hayley.'

'What d'you mean?'

'John Metherell helped them.'

'*Metherell?*'

'Yes. He and the Martyns were left on the boat at the quayside when Barney went to fetch the others. Metherell told me he left the boat as well, to speak to the harbourmaster. But then he also told me the Tozers had no Scillonian connections.'

'That's not true. Francis Gashry reported that Jacob Tozer was definitely born here, even though he couldn't prove it because the parish registers for the period had been conveniently destroyed by fire.'

'Exactly. Everything's *very* convenient. Maybe those registers would show Metherell's ancestors were

Scillonian as well. He's been deflecting me and leading me on by turns. He pointed me straight to the Josie connection when I contacted him yesterday. He must have reckoned I'd find out about it sooner or later, so decided to short-circuit the process. Then he could guarantee being on hand to stage-manage my meeting with the Martyns. The plan was obviously to bluff it out and convince me you hadn't been near them. But Josie was wearing Kerry's fox-cub brooch, so that didn't work.'

'She liked it as soon as she saw it. Fred took it from me. But how did you know about it?'

'Gary Lawton described it to me. If he hadn't . . . they might have been able to fob me off.'

'It would've been better for you if they had.'

'Don't say that, Hayley.' He squeezed her hand and she responded, clutching him tightly. 'I don't regret coming after you. Not in any way.'

'I'm sorry for all the lies I told you.' There was a catch in her throat. 'Can you really forgive me?'

'I already have.'

'I felt so sure I'd worked it out. I convinced myself I'd proved Barney Tozer was Kerry's murderer. I was determined to make him pay for what I believed he'd done. And I thought you were just a means to an end. Instead . . .' Her voice sank to a whisper. 'I've never been in love before, you see. Never . . . known what it meant.'

They kissed then, in the closeting darkness. And he gazed into her eyes, or felt he did. Nothing was visible. But everything seemed suddenly clear between them.

Clear and simple. And true. 'When we get out of here,' he began, 'we'll—'

She pressed her finger to his lips, silencing him. 'We're not getting out of here, Tim. You know that. There's no need to pretend you don't for my sake.'

'They can't keep us here for ever.'

'Oh but they can. It's what they intend to do. They wouldn't have put us down here, with the ossuary chest, unless they were certain we'd never be able to tell anyone it's here. Time's on their side. They'll have destroyed the Gashry report by now. As for us, they can wait. As long as they need to. Until the world out there has forgotten us. And there's no more left of us than there is of the Grey Man of Ennor.'

It was true. Every word she had spoken made perfect sense. She and Harding knew too much. They could not be allowed to live. The cellar was their tomb. The damp chill certainty of that closed itself around Harding as he cradled Hayley in the enveloping darkness.

'This is the end for you and me, Tim. I'm sorry. But there it is.'

FORTY-SEVEN

Time became elastic in the sensory vacuum of the cellar. The slow fading of the thin square of light round the trapdoor signalled the coming of night. Hours drifted like a wide, slow-moving river, imperceptibly but inexorably. Harding and Hayley talked, sharing every secret, till there was nothing left for them to guess about each other. Then Hayley fell asleep, wrapped in the blanket, exhausted by the effort of saying so much, her energy sapped by four days of starvation. And Harding lay with her, listening to her breathing, reasoning his way towards an escape from their prison – but finding none.

His renewed efforts to shift the trapdoor had failed. No sound reached him through it and he suspected no noise he made would carry far. Not that the Martyns would respond even if they heard him. They were playing a long game, as was their nature. The cellar would remain sealed for as long as it needed to be. Then . . .

He could not think about that. The grisly realities would unfold in due time. No doubt Hayley would die first, leaving Harding alone with her decomposing body. No doubt the end would be as slow and terrible as he imagined.

He tried to think about other things instead, such as who had been behind Tozer's murder. Only one candidate presented himself, though tantalizingly lacking a motive. It had to be Whybrow, exploiting an opportunity Hayley had created for him. She had never phoned Nathan Gashry. Nathan had been paid – or otherwise obliged – to say she had. And then, perhaps because he had become greedy or had threatened to change his story after discovering he had contributed to a murder plot, he had been eliminated. By the same cool, calm, efficient organization that had supplied a Hayley lookalike to do the deed. Just the sort of organization, in fact, that Whybrow would naturally do business with.

It must have been about money, of course. Everything in Whybrow's world was about money. But that was a commodity so far removed from Harding's present predicament that it seemed colossally absurd for Barney Tozer to have been murdered in pursuit of it. Similarly, Hayley had actually been moved to laughter by Harding's revelation that she was Gabriel Tozer's heir. 'It won't do me much good now, will it?' she had responded. And Harding had laughed with her at the irony of it all.

But their laughter had not lasted long. If Hayley was

right, as Harding knew she was, the Martyns meant to starve them to death. There was no need to harm them directly. That, the brothers must have reasoned, had been their mistake in dealing with Kerry. This time, they would let nature take its slow but certain course. This time, they would ensure their secret could never be uncovered.

Only when Harding woke did he realize he had been asleep, the whirlings of his thoughts having finally worn themselves out. The square of light was back, pale and tantalizing. Morning had come. His head ached less, but the pressure in his bowel and bladder reminded him, though he needed no reminding, that his confinement with Hayley would force them to share every intimacy, until – and including – the end. She stirred beside him. He moved, easing the pain in his back and shoulders. The chill of the cellar had settled on him like a dew. In the fetid, earthy air, there was a primal reek. The past had drawn closer in the night, preparing to claim them. Everything he had ever known felt like a dream he was rapidly forgetting. In its place there was nothing. Except Hayley. And the rest of their time together.

'You're really here,' she said in a gravelly murmur, touching his cheek with her icily cold fingers. 'I thought for a moment . . . I'd made you up.'

'No. I'm really here.'

'Don't leave me.' She was not yet fully awake. But the fuddled sentiment sounded to Harding like a plea he had to answer.

'I won't,' he said, kissing her softly. 'I won't ever leave you now.'

More time passed, invisibly and unmeasurably. Hayley was quieter and weaker than the day before, her voice a whisper, her movements slight. Harding's efforts to sustain a conversation of any length were in vain. Her powers of concentration were sapped, her thoughts unfocused. She did not tell him he was wasting his time, as she previously had, when he heaved at the trapdoor. She did not tell him much at all. Apart from how happy she was that he was there with her. 'Nothing's better alone,' she said to him at one point. 'I know that now.'

She was asleep when it happened. At first, Harding thought the sound had been made by a mouse or some other tiny creature. Then he realized it was coming from above: a scraping, grinding rumble. It stopped and started again several times, ending in a heavy thud and a patter of dust from the trapdoor, the square of light suddenly brighter.

Harding made a lunge for the door, sensing a chance of escape. Before he even reached the steps, however, his prayers were answered. The door creaked open. Light flooded in, dazzling him. He had to shade his eyes to look up. And there he saw Metherell, gazing down at him.

'Come on,' Metherell called. 'We're letting you go.'

Harding did not pause to query what was happening.

This was a chance he had abandoned hope of. He turned back to Hayley, seeing her sallow, hollow-eyed face clearly for the first time since their incarceration. The noise had woken her, but she had not moved.

'Wha . . . What's going on?' she mumbled, squinting at him in the grey light that now filled the cellar, revealing its rough-stoned walls and floor – and the ossuary chest, planted like some dark, crouching beast on a plinth in the centre of the chamber.

'We're getting out,' said Harding, pulling Hayley to her feet as gently as he could, though the urge to drag her up the steps before the door was slammed shut again was strong. She felt so light and frail he suspected he could easily carry her if necessary. But there was no need. She was trembling and breathing shallowly, but she was soon upright. He helped her up the steps, one at a time.

They emerged into the cramped space beneath the stairs, with the trapdoor hooked back against the wall. Metherell retreated into the hall, stepping over a thick granite slab the size of a large paving-stone as he did so. Harding guessed it was what he had heard being pulled clear. Beyond that, guesswork failed him. They were free. For the moment, he did not really care why.

They followed Metherell into the hall, Hayley leaning heavily on Harding's arm. She stumbled as they negotiated the slab, but he was there to steady her. 'It's all right,' he said, as much for his own benefit as hers. 'It's *all right*.'

But was it? He could not be absolutely sure. Metherell

had moved into the kitchen. They turned in that direction and saw Josie standing beside him, wide-eyed and staring. There was no sign of the Martyns.

'Alf and Fred are at the boatyard,' said Metherell, reading Harding's mind. 'I'll drive you to the airport. I've booked you on the four o'clock flight to Penzance.'

Harding stared at him, seeking reassurance that their release was genuine. 'You two set this up between you?'

'Josie phoned me as soon as the coast was clear.'

'Sorry,' said Josie. 'Didn't mean . . . all this stuff to happen.'

'We can leave now,' said Metherell, glancing at his watch. 'We *should* leave now.'

'Why . . . are you letting us go?' asked Hayley, her voice weak and husky.

'You probably won't believe it,' said Metherell, 'but I didn't find out they'd sabotaged Kerry's gear until afterwards. She discovered their secret by befriending Josie and quizzing her about how she'd been cured. Alf and Fred's mother was still alive then. She told the Edwardses to send Josie here so she could . . . touch the royal bones. Kerry thought it was a great story. But I knew it would end in the ossuary chest leaving here. So did Alf. I tried to persuade Kerry not to write the story up. She wouldn't listen. Alf realized . . . something more than persuasion was needed. He actually only intended to frighten her. So he said, anyway. I went along with it after the event because, well . . . a miracle is a miracle. The chest should stay here. The secret

393

should be kept. But I can't force you not to say anything about it. I can only beg you not to.'

'You were willing to let Hayley die down there,' Harding protested, his anger reasserting itself.

'I thought she'd murdered Barney Tozer. When Alf told me yesterday what they'd done with her, I . . .' Metherell's gaze fell to the floor. 'I decided I could live with it. It seemed . . . like some kind of justice. But you as well? That was going too far. And you made me doubt Hayley really had murdered Barney.'

'I never wanted to hurt you,' said Josie. She patted her stomach. 'I can't bring a littl'un into the world with you two on my conscience. Alf said all sorts and Fred agreed, like he always does. But it was wrong. I should have stood up to them. Well, I'm starting now. It's best you leave. What you do – the police and such – is up to you.'

'We won't go to the police,' said Hayley.

Harding glanced round at her in surprise. 'What?'

'I want an end to this. Nothing will bring Kerry back.' She looked imploringly at him. 'Please, Tim. Promise. No police. No more digging. We know the truth. That's enough. Let's leave it there.'

It seemed to Harding that something more – something bigger – was actually being asked of him. It was as if in forgiving the Martyns Hayley hoped to claim her own share of forgiveness. And he could not deny her that. 'All right,' he said. 'It ends here.'

'Thank you,' murmured Metherell.

'You're good people,' said Josie. 'I'm that sorry. I really am.'

'But I want the brooch,' said Hayley. 'My sister's brooch.'

Josie flushed. 'It's upstairs. I'll get it.'

She hurried past them, avoiding their gaze, and headed up the stairs.

'The Martyns have been keepers of the chest for generations,' said Metherell, breaking the silence as they waited for Josie to return. 'I'm grateful to you for letting them go on keeping it. It's . . . as it should be. They'd have died rather than give it up.'

'Hayley needs an alibi for Monday,' said Harding, the demands of the world they were about to return to emerging in his thoughts. 'You'll supply one?'

'Of course. And I'll make the Martyns understand that—'

There were noises from the yard: a revving engine; a crunch of tyres. Metherell's face lost most of its colour. He shot Harding a frightened glance.

'Oh God. We've left it too late.'

The front door was flung open even as Harding turned towards it. Alf Martyn stood on the threshold, glaring in at them. Fred loomed up behind him.

'I knew you were up to summut,' said Alf, looking straight at Metherell. 'You shouldn't have interfered.'

'They've agreed to say nothing, Alf,' Metherell pleaded. 'There's no reason to harm them.'

'They can't leave, knowing what they know.'

'But we *are* leaving,' Harding declared, grasping Hayley by the shoulders and moving towards the door.

'No,' said Alf. His left arm swung out from behind

him. Harding flinched as he saw what he was holding: a shotgun. The stock slapped into Alf's waiting right palm. The barrel was already locked. His finger curled around the trigger. 'You can't leave.'

'*Stop*,' shouted Josie from the head of the stairs. 'Don't shoot, Alf. For God's sake.'

'Stay out of this.'

'No.' She started down the stairs. 'It's my—'

She must have lost her footing. Or tripped. Suddenly, she was falling. Harding saw her rolling, bumping figure as a blur through the banisters. And he saw Fred dodging past his brother, running to intercept. But he was not fast enough. Josie hit the floor with a thump. Fred stopped in mid-stride. And stared, as they all stared, at Josie's face, twisted towards them by the unnatural angle of her neck, her eyes wide and sightless, blood trickling from the corner of her mouth.

There was silence. A frozen moment of horror. Then Fred's wail of anguish began. And did not end.

FORTY-EIGHT

Fred Martyn was like a marionette whose strings had been cut. He sat slumped at the foot of the stairs, gazing vacantly and hopelessly at Josie's crumpled figure. Her miraculous recovery from leukaemia seven years before had led only to this: a snapped neck; a lost child; two lives snuffed out. And the future of the whole family had gone with them. The knowledge of that was written on Alf Martyn's face as he sat at the kitchen table, staring into space. He had broken the shotgun and laid it beside him. Since then, he had not moved.

Hayley was on her knees beside Josie, holding her unresponsive hand. Harding was crouching beside her, one arm round her shoulders, as Metherell spoke to the emergency operator on the telephone. 'Pregowther Farm . . . Yes . . . A pregnant woman . . . She's fallen down the stairs . . . It looks bad. There's no pulse. I think she's broken her neck . . . Yes . . . Come quickly.'

He ended the call and Harding stood up to speak to

him. He dropped his voice to a whisper. 'How long before they get here?'

'Not long. It'd be best if you weren't here when they arrived.'

'I agree.'

'Take my car.' Metherell handed him the keys. 'I'll sort everything out.'

'I'm sorrier than I can say for the way . . .' Harding gestured helplessly towards Josie.

'Me too. And so I should be. For helping create this situation.' Metherell shook his head despairingly. 'But none of it's your fault. Or Hayley's. Get her off the island. Get her far away. I can't put much right. But I'll swear she visited me on Monday if you need me to. You have my word.'

'The Martyns?'

'This has broken them. They'll blame themselves. With good reason. They'll never recover. I don't know . . . what their futures hold.'

'We'll go, then.'

'Yes. Do.'

'Hayley.' Harding coaxed her to her feet. She did not resist. But she did not stop looking at Josie. She was crying, tears coursing down her hollow cheeks. 'We have to leave.'

'Yes,' she murmured.

'Now.'

She nodded her understanding and turned away towards the front door, which still stood open.

'Don't forget this.' Metherell stooped and picked up

the fox-cub brooch that had slipped from Josie's fingers as she fell. He offered it to Hayley. But she did not even seem to see it. Harding took it instead. 'I . . .'

'No more words,' said Hayley, looking sorrowfully at him. Then she walked unsteadily out into the grey afternoon. And Harding followed.

There was time for Hayley to drink some tea and nibble a muffin at the airport before the helicopter from Penzance arrived and was unloaded, then readied for the return flight. Harding kept urging her to sip from a bottle of water he had bought and to eat something more substantial. But she complained of feeling sick and Josie's death was like a black cloud in their thoughts, obscuring almost everything – except the need to leave St Mary's. Even Hayley understood they had to go. Though somehow, crazily, she felt she was abandoning the Martyns in their hour of need.

'They meant to kill you,' Harding reminded her. 'They did kill Kerry. And we're letting them off. Don't you think that's enough?'

'None of it was Josie's doing. And her baby, Tim. God, what a price to pay.'

'It's awful, I know. I only wish I could . . .'

'Put it all right?' She gazed deeply into his eyes and shook her head. 'You can't.'

'No. All I can try to do is . . . stop it getting any worse.'

'How could it?'

'You could be arrested and tried for murder. Remember that. You're a fugitive.'

'Why doesn't that seem to bother me?'

'Because part of you is still in the cellar at Pregowther Farm, slowly dying. And coming back to life is a slow business too.'

'I'm not sure I want to come back.'

Harding smiled ruefully. 'Then I'll just have to make you, won't I?'

They cleaned themselves up as best they could in the airport loos, but Harding suspected they were still viewed with distaste by the other passengers on the flight to Penzance, if only because of their dishevelled appearance. He would not have cared but for the fact that this made them conspicuous as well as memorable. At any moment someone might recognize Hayley as the young woman wanted for Barney Tozer's murder. Every journey they took was risky. But it could not be helped. And he was too drained by what had happened to worry much about it. From now on, what would be would be.

They caught the last London train of the day from Penzance. It drew out past St Michael's Bay through the dusky early evening. They would probably never return to the town. So much they had cared about and striven for and struggled with was slipping away behind them into the retreating day.

Ten minutes later, they reached St Erth, where the St Ives train was waiting at the bay platform. Hayley gazed out at it dreamily. 'Remember our trip to St Ives, Tim?' she asked.

'Of course.'

'How long ago was that?'

'A couple of weeks.'

'It feels longer.'

'A lot's happened.'

'Yeah.' She nodded vaguely. 'I was leading you on then.'

'You had your reasons.'

'I thought I had. Now they seem . . . hardly like reasons at all.' The St Ives train slowly passed from view as they drew out of the station. Hayley turned from the window and looked at Harding. 'What are we going to do when we get to London?'

'Not sure.' He smiled, willing her to be reassured by his words. 'But I will be by the time we arrive.'

It was a pledge Harding was determined to fulfil. He persuaded Hayley to eat a sandwich and drink some water. She fell asleep some time after the train left Plymouth. He wondered, watching her, whether he should have taken her to the hospital in Penzance, but convinced himself she was actually looking better, despite her despondency; there was even a hint of colour in her cheeks. He wanted to sleep himself but instead he forced his mind to concentrate on the problem he knew he would have to solve if Hayley's future was to be a better place than her past; and his with it.

* * *

A couple of hours later, with Hayley still asleep, he closeted himself in a loo and phoned Ann Gashry.

'I've found her, Ann.'

'Thank God.'

'She didn't kill Barney. I know that now for certain.'

'I felt sure of it. Where are you?'

'On a train. Heading your way. Can we stay with you tonight?'

'Of course.'

'I should warn you. She's had a rough time. She'll need . . . gentle handling.'

'She'll get it.'

'Have the police been on to you again?'

'No.'

'So . . .'

'She'll be safe here, Mr Harding. For a while at least.'

'A while is all we need. Did you speak to Nathan's girlfriend?'

'Yes. But she didn't tell me anything valuable. He was worried about something, but she couldn't persuade him to say what. She thinks someone was putting pressure on him. But she doesn't know who. Or why. She doesn't believe he committed suicide, but . . .'

'She can't prove it.'

'Exactly. Can you?'

'No.'

'Then what are we to do? If they catch Hayley, they *will* charge her with Barney Tozer's murder.'

'It won't come to that.'

'How can you prevent it?'

'I think I know a way.'

'Really?'

'Yes.' He confronted his reflection in the mirror on the wall. The expression of the man staring back at him did not echo the confidence of his words. His gaze was wary, anxious, no more than stubbornly hopeful. 'I really do.'

FORTY-NINE

Sunday morning in Dulwich. Ann Gashry's house was a haven of healing silence. Harding woke late and found Ann in the drawing room, sipping coffee and leafing through the *Observer* like a woman pursuing a solitary weekly routine, calmly and self-sufficiently, entirely untroubled by the events he had related to her late the previous night. But she was not untroubled, of course. He knew that well enough.

'Did you look in on Hayley?' she asked, pouring him some coffee.

'Yes.'

'Still sleeping?'

'Like a baby.' He thought for a moment of Josie Martyn's baby, whose life had been snatched away before it had even begun. And then he thought of the baby's father and uncle. For all that they had done to Kerry and been prepared to do to Hayley, the rawness of their loss still gnawed at him. He sighed. 'I think she should stay here today.'

'Of course.'

'But tomorrow, I want you to take her away.'

'*Away?*'

'Wherever you like. It doesn't matter. As long as I don't know where you've gone.'

'I fail to understand, Mr Harding. As long as *you* don't know?'

'It's important I shouldn't be able to tell anyone where you are.'

Ann frowned quizzically at him. Then comprehension dawned. 'You fear you may be . . . forced to tell what you know?'

'The man I'm going to have to deal with . . .'

'Whybrow?'

'Yes. He's a . . . ruthless operator. As we've seen.'

'How do you hope to get the better of him?'

'By playing him at his own game.'

'But he knows the rules better than you. By your own admission.'

'He does indeed.'

'Then . . .'

'It's a gamble, I know. But it's the only way to get Hayley out of trouble.'

'And if it doesn't come off?'

Harding took a sip of coffee. Strong and black, it clarified his thinking, sharpened his certainty. This was the only way. 'I'm going to give it my best shot, Ann. That's all I can do.'

* * *

He phoned the Cortiina in Munich. Whybrow had checked out the day before, along with Carol. So, they were back in Monaco. It would end for Harding where it had begun. One way or another. He phoned British Airways and booked himself on to an evening flight to Nice.

Ann prepared a breakfast tray for Hayley. Harding took it up to her room. The long sleep had done her good. She was looking better, younger, more like herself with each passing hour. But a shadow still lay across her. That too was apparent.

'What time is it?' she asked, sipping her orange juice.

'Lunchtime.' He smiled.

'I wish . . . you'd slept with me.' She blushed. 'I mean, just slept.'

'I did. For a while.'

'I expect Ann's guessed. She's a hard person to keep a secret from.'

'I've asked her to take you away tomorrow.'

'Where to?'

'That's up to her.'

'You're not coming with us?'

'There's something I have to do back home.'

'Home?'

'Where I live. At the moment.'

'You're going to see Whybrow.'

'Maybe.'

'Or Carol.'

'Maybe both.'

'To stop it getting any worse.' She had deliberately echoed his words of the day before.

'I think I can.'

'You're taking a big chance.'

'Not so big.'

'So you say. Either way, it's for me.'

'You have to trust me.'

'I don't have to.' She reached out for his hand. 'I just do.'

'I know.' They kissed.

'When do you leave?'

'Later today.'

'And when do I see you again?'

'Soon.'

'Promise?'

'Promise.'

He left before he strictly needed to, before his resolve could be tested too far. He walked away alone along Bedmore Road, sensing Hayley's eyes on him but not daring to look back. With Metherell's alibi and his own eye-witness testimony, he reckoned Hayley would never be convicted of Tozer's murder even if she was charged. But he wanted a cleaner, swifter end to her troubles than that and believed he could achieve it – and more – by confronting Whybrow. If he was right, they would be reunited within days, free to build a life together. *If he was right.*

* * *

It was nearly midnight French time when he reached his apartment in Villefranche. Never had it felt less like home. He headed straight out to a bar he knew that opened late, but found it already closed, so contented himself with an aimless walk by the harbour before returning to the apartment and trying – with eventual success – to sleep.

He woke later than he might have expected the following morning. By his calculations, Ann and Hayley would already be on the move, destination unknown – to him. He showered and shaved, then went out for breakfast to the bar that had disappointed him the night before. This time it was open. He sat outside with his croissant and coffee in the warm spring sunshine.

He phoned Luc, who assured him Jardiniera was running like clockwork in his continued absence. Harding found himself wondering if Luc might be interested in buying him out. There was money in the young man's family, after all. But that was for another day.

Next he phoned Carol. She did not answer. He left a message, asking if he could visit her that afternoon. He suggested four o'clock. 'I have something to tell you I think you'll want to hear,' he emphasized.

He polished off a *corretto* before his last call. Whybrow's mobile was on voicemail, but Harding guessed he would be at Starburst International's offices in Monte Carlo. So he was. And when Harding gave his name to the honey-toned receptionist, he was put through promptly.

'Well, well. Tim. Where are you? Still communing with friends and family in England?'

'No. I've come back. Like you.'

'Yes. The German authorities were eventually persuaded to release Barney's body. I believe Carol will be fixing a date for the funeral today.'

'Have the police given you any news of Hayley?'

'I'm afraid not. She seems to have vanished into thin air.'

'Worrying for you.'

'More disappointing. We'd all like Barney's murderer to be apprehended, wouldn't we?'

'Absolutely.'

'Heard anything yourself?'

'About Hayley?'

'Isn't that who we were discussing?' An inflexion of irony mixed with mild irritation had entered Whybrow's voice.

'It's certainly who I'd like to discuss with you.'

'Go ahead.'

'Face to face, I mean.'

'That could be difficult. I have a busy day ahead of me.'

'Squeeze me into your schedule, Tony. You won't regret it. And you'll regret it if you don't.'

'Will I?'

'Definitely.'

There was a lengthy pause. Harding could hear the

faint and thoughtful clicking of Whybrow's tongue against his front teeth. Then: 'In that case . . . how can I refuse?'

FIFTY

Whybrow was late for their appointment at the Café de Paris. Harding sat at an outside table, sipping a beer and studying the passers-by drifting aimlessly and affluently between the competing architectural extravagances of the Casino and the Hôtel de Paris. He wondered if both the lateness and the choice of venue were deliberate tactics on Whybrow's part: an engineered opportunity for Harding to consider the realities of wealth and the power that underpinned it. No one dressed scruffily in Monte Carlo. No one had dirt under their fingernails or cause to hurry. The Place du Casino was an arena for the discreet display of material prosperity, tax-free, un-encumbered, unashamed. It was the world Whybrow moved in and was familiar with. Harding was the out-sider, the unwelcome interloper, the fish who did not understand how small he was in a pond only the likes of Whybrow knew the real size of. That he should think twice before issuing any kind of challenge here was implicit; that he should take the easy way out self-evident.

But he was not about to, however long he was kept waiting. And that, it turned out, was not so very long after all.

Whybrow looked as languidly groomed and casually elegant as usual. He greeted Harding with a measured smile and a knowing tilt of the head. 'This must make a pleasant change from England,' he said, casting an appreciative glance around the sun-splashed square.

'And from Munich,' Harding countered.

'True enough.' Whybrow nodded to the approaching waiter. 'Perrier. And . . . another beer for you, Tim?'

'Sure.'

'OK. *Perrier. Une bière.*' The waiter bustled away. Whybrow sat down in the shade, plucked off his sun-glasses and looked expectantly at Harding across the table. 'Not started back to work yet, then?'

'Not yet.'

'Luc reliable, is he?'

'Yes,' Harding replied, cautiously. 'He is.'

'Trustworthy?'

'Certainly.'

'You're lucky. Having people you can really trust around you is the key to success in business. And not just in business, of course. But they're not easy to find.'

'In my experience, trust breeds trust.'

'You think so?'

'I do.'

'Well, it's a point of view.' And it was one Whybrow pondered as the waiter returned with their drinks. He deposited them with a flourish, lodged a second bill under the ashtray and departed. Whybrow watched him go, then said, 'As you can imagine, most of the staff at Starburst are still in shock following Barney's death. My enforced absence last week left matters a little . . . rudderless. So, I have clients to reassure and issues to resolve aplenty. It's a pleasure seeing you, of course, but . . .'

'You want to know why I insisted we meet.'

'Yes. Though I hope I didn't force you to insist.'

'Have you consulted Carol about these . . . issues you need to resolve?'

Whybrow's posture stiffened slightly. He sat forward in his chair. 'Don't take this amiss, Tim, but what have the details of how Carol wants me to manage Starburst International to do with you?'

'Nothing, I suppose.'

'As I recall, you said you wanted to discuss Hayley.'

'So I do. But it's all connected, isn't it? Hayley, Barney, Carol, you and . . . Starburst International. All . . . linked.'

'By what?'

'Ah well, that's the big question, isn't it?'

'It's a question that eludes me, I'm afraid. What are you trying to say?'

'I heard about Nathan Gashry's death while I was in England.'

'I naturally assumed you had.'

413

'What did you make of it?'

Whybrow shrugged. 'Suicide's generally an impenetrable act. I had some dealings with the man on Barney's behalf when we were arranging how to finance Kerry's treatment at the Horstelmann Clinic. For what it's worth, I thought him . . . arrogant but insecure. A little . . . flaky.'

'Potentially suicidal?'

'In retrospect, yes.'

'His girlfriend thinks otherwise.'

Whybrow frowned. 'You've spoken to her?'

'Any reason why I shouldn't have?'

'None. Apart from the obvious.'

'Which is?'

'That you must have better things to do with your time.' Whybrow flattened his palms on the tabletop in a strange, declaratory gesture. 'Carol tells me you've established Humphrey Tozer stole the ring from Heartsease. It's helpful to have that loose end tied up, I suppose, but essentially irrelevant. As is whatever self-destructive impulse drove Nathan Gashry to take his own life. Barney asked you to deal with a small problem for him and you did your best, I don't doubt, but since then it seems to me . . . you've been out of your depth.'

'I have?'

'As confirmed by your failure to anticipate the threat Hayley posed to Barney.'

'But she didn't pose a threat, Tony. That's the point. Not after her aborted attack on Carol. Specifically not in Munich five days later. She posed no threat there at all.'

414

Whybrow's hands left the table. He sat back. 'I'm not with you, Tim. You were there when Hayley murdered Barney. You saw her do it.'

'Not exactly. I saw someone who *resembled* Hayley. Someone *got up* to resemble her.'

Whybrow gave him a long, hard look. 'Surely not.'

'I'm certain of it.'

'Certain . . . it wasn't Hayley?'

'Exactly.'

'You can't be serious.'

'Well, I am. And I'll be telling the German police as much very soon.'

Whybrow glided one hand slowly over the crown of his closely shaven head. Was he nervous? Harding could only hope so. 'What's made you question the evidence of your own eyes, Tim?'

'I've done a lot of thinking in the past few days. A lot of . . . reviewing. I've sorted out what really happened from what I was manipulated into believing happened.'

'Really?'

'Nathan Gashry's death clinched it for me. He knew Hayley hadn't asked him to call Barney. He was paid to say she had. Or blackmailed. Or . . . otherwise induced. It doesn't much matter how or why. What matters is that he was a weak link in the chain. That's why he was taken out.'

'Taken out?'

'Murdered.'

'You seem to be developing a rather elaborate conspiracy theory in the glaring absence of an alternative

415

suspect. Who but Hayley could have had any reason to kill Barney?'

'That's not for me to say.'

'Isn't it?'

'I imagine it's all about money. Maybe Barney wasn't willing to be as . . . financially flexible . . . as someone else wanted him to be. Or maybe he discovered someone was . . . cheating him. Either way, when Hayley attacked Carol, she handed that someone a golden opportunity to get Barney off their back once and for all, with Hayley ready and waiting to take the blame.'

'I see. Well, this is . . . amazing.'

'But true.'

'You intend to tell the police what you've told me?'

'Yes.'

'So, why tell me *first*?'

'Because, once I've convinced them Hayley's innocent, they're bound to cast around for another suspect. I expect they'll start with Barney's business associates. It'd be logical. Money is the root of all evil, after all. That could cause you some . . . embarrassment.'

'Why?'

'You were acquainted with Nathan Gashry. You said so yourself. If Nathan mentioned you to his girlfriend, or his sister; if there's any suggestion he didn't fall to his death but was pushed; if there's any irregularity, however slight, in Starburst International's recent dealings . . . Well, I don't need to spell it out, do I?'

'You're trying to spare me a lot of . . . inconvenience.'

'Something like that.'

'Carol's not going to be pleased by your ... change of heart, you know.'

'I can't help that.'

'And the police may not believe you. They may conclude you were in league with Hayley all along.'

'I'll take my chances.'

'Indeed. A chance certainly is what you're taking. Well, well, well.' Whybrow sipped his Perrier. He had remained calm and softly spoken. Nothing hinted at inner turmoil. Unless it was the knotting of his brow. 'Perhaps you need to make a fresh start in life, Tim. I can see the case for it. Barney's death. Your ... unsatisfactory ... relationship with Carol. A somewhat ... untargeted lifestyle. Yes. Pastures new. A clean break. A change of air. It's probably to be recommended. The only difficulty may be ... funding. If so, I could ... offer to help.'

'No.'

'I'm sorry?'

'I'm not asking you to buy me off, Tony.'

Whybrow looked genuinely surprised, almost hurt. 'What *are* you asking me to do?'

'Back up my change of story with some additional evidence that someone other than Hayley killed Barney.'

'Any suggestions who that might be?'

'Ostensibly, Nathan Gashry had the same motive as Hayley: revenge. Officially, he paid for Kerry's treatment, which could be taken to prove he'd gone on loving her after their break-up. He lured Barney to the rendezvous in Munich. And he committed suicide in a fit of remorse ... about something.'

'Thus denying himself the opportunity to refute authorship of a confessional email sent from an internet café around the time of his death. A hypothetical email, I mean. At this stage.' Whybrow allowed himself the slenderest of smiles. 'What an unexpectedly fertile imagination you turn out to have, Tim. I'm quite . . . impressed.'

'I'm not trying to impress you.'

'Obviously not. Nevertheless, you do.'

'Do we have a deal?'

'We have . . . an understanding.' The smile broadened infinitesimally. Or maybe the sparkle in Whybrow's eyes made it seem to. He offered his hand. Harding had not expected this: a sealing of the bargain. But he was committed. They shook. 'When will you tell Carol?'

'This afternoon.'

'And *what* will you tell her – exactly?'

'That I'm no longer sure it was Hayley I saw at Nymphenburg.'

'She won't take that well.'

'No.'

'And by the time certain other evidence inculpating Nathan Gashry . . . comes to light . . . you'll be gone.'

'Probably, yes.'

'You should expect hard words from her.'

'I do.'

'She may have an opportunity to take them back, of course. If you attend the funeral.'

'Not sure I'll be able to do that.'

'You'll be with Hayley by then, I suppose.'

418

Harding did not respond. Nor did he glance away. He went on looking Whybrow squarely in the eye. Several seconds passed. A silent acknowledgement communicated itself between them. Then the moment was gone.

'Ever try your luck in there?' Whybrow asked, nodding towards the Casino.

'No.'

'Very wise. Luck, of course, has nothing to do with it. But then you don't need me to tell you that, do you?'

'I'm just no gambler, that's all.'

'No gambler?' Whybrow snickered softly. 'I beg to differ. In fact . . . I'd say you were a natural.'

FIFTY-ONE

Carol was not at home when Harding arrived at the apartment at four o'clock. Her texted reply to his phone message had simply said she would see him there, so he was not greatly surprised. He let himself in by the garden entrance and waited by the pool. Twenty minutes or so elapsed while he recollected coming to see Barney less than three weeks before, knowing virtually nothing of the Tozer family and absolutely nothing of the Foxtons and the Martyns and the Gashrys. He had entered a parallel world that day, of the kind Hayley had later told him about: an alternative reality from which he could not escape, even if he wanted to; a land of no return.

A movement caught his eye through the patio doors. He headed over to them and spotted Carol on the far side of the room. She looked at him expressionlessly, almost wearily, then walked slowly across to the doors and slid them open.

'You came, then,' she said neutrally.

'I said I would.'

'You said you'd do lots of things.' She was wearing slightly too much make-up and one of her more obviously couturish outfits. It was a look he had once found searingly sexy. But that, as he knew, had been in a different life. 'Are you coming in?'

He stepped into the room. She moved to the table, where she had dropped her handbag, fished out her cigarettes and lit one. The sigh she gave after the first inhalation suggested it was badly needed.

'Christ, what a day,' she murmured, closing her eyes.

'I'm sorry it's been so rough for you, Carol.'

'Please don't make it any worse, then.' She opened her eyes and looked at him. 'I'm going to have a drink. D'you want one?'

'No, thanks.'

'Please yourself.'

She walked through to the kitchen. Harding listened to the clack-clack of her high-heels on the tiles, the opening and closing of the fridge door, the clunk of ice in a glass, the fizz of tonic; only the gin was silent.

She returned to the room and sat down, taking a deep swallow from her glass before setting it before her on the table. 'Undertaker. Lawyer. Now you. And no one has any good news. You don't, for certain. Right?'

'Not good, no.'

A long draw on the cigarette; a flick of ash into one of

Barney's bespoke giant wooden ashtrays. Then: 'Sit down, for Christ's sake.'

'OK.' He took the chair on the opposite side of the table from her and sat forward on the edge of the cushion, incapable even of pretending to relax.

'Well?'

'I found out who killed Kerry.'

'Are you going to tell me it really was Barney?'

'No. It was all about Josephine Edwards. Last time we spoke, I asked you if you remembered her. The Martyns cured her, Carol. Kerry wanted to write the story up for the national press. But the Martyns didn't want any publicity. Sabotaging her diving gear was intended to scare her off. But . . . it worked too well.'

'The Martyns did it?'

'Yes.'

'To stop people finding out they're . . . faith healers of some kind?'

'Some kind, yes. A very strange kind.'

'Shit.' Another drag. 'That's just . . . so stupid.'

'Stupid?'

'All this . . . mess . . . because Kerry stuck her nose in where it wasn't wanted among the islanders.'

'That's about it.'

'Poor old Barney. I should've believed him all along. I almost feel sorry for Hayley. So much . . . hating in the wrong place.'

'She didn't kill Barney.'

'What?'

'I found that out too.'

Carol shook her head, as if to clear her thoughts. 'What are you saying?'

'She was on St Mary's at the time. John Metherell will swear to that. And I'll swear it wasn't her I saw at Nymphenburg.'

'Not her?'

'No. A lookalike. More of a dressalike, actually. A close enough resemblance at a distance, on the run, but not Hayley. Someone hired, to do the job. The same job they did on Nathan Gashry to stop him admitting Hayley didn't ask him to phone Barney.'

'Who did ask him, then? Who hired this . . . dressalike?'

'Tony Whybrow.'

A long blink. A slug of gin. Carol's hand shook faintly as she returned the glass to the table. She stared at Harding intently. 'Are you serious?'

'Never more so.'

'Can you prove this?'

'No. Which is why I've struck a deal with Tony. For your sake as well as mine – and Hayley's.'

'A *deal*?'

'Nathan Gashry will take the blame. We'll . . . take what we can get. It'd be crazy to accuse Tony openly, Carol. He'll have covered his tracks well. You can be sure of that. And he'd be a dangerous enemy. Look what happened to Barney. You said you thought Tony might have been cheating him. Well, I reckon you were right. Barney must have found out and

423

issued some kind of ultimatum. It was a fatal mistake.'

'Let me get this straight. You're telling me Tony Whybrow had my husband killed. And you're also telling me to do nothing about it.'

'Nothing . . . for the moment.' He took out Unsworth's card and slid it across the table.

'What's this?'

'Unsworth is Scotland Yard's man at Europol. That's his personal number. According to him, Starburst International is a front for big-time EU fraud. The sort of thing you read about. VAT. CAP. Generous slices of Brussels payola. I'm assuming you didn't know. Is that right?'

Carol smiled faintly and shook her head. 'I didn't know.'

'Unsworth's offer is this. Put some hard documentary evidence of illegality his way and you get immunity from prosecution when they move on Starburst. You also get to keep whatever capital you've taken out of the company to date. Tony carries the can. Well, as finance director and the brains behind all the scams, so he should. It'd be the best kind of revenge, Carol. The kind he deals in himself.'

'How do you and . . . Unsworth . . . expect me to get this evidence?'

'You're in control of the company now. You couldn't be better placed to get it. Tony probably plans to let you in on Starburst's trade secrets little by little. His strategy will be to persuade you to turn a blind eye to what he's up to and enjoy your share – Barney's share – of the profits. All you have to do is play along, keep Unsworth advised, then, when the time comes, pull the rug out from under Tony's feet.'

'And when *would* the time come?'

'I don't know. That'd be for you and Unsworth to agree between you. It could be quite a while. But don't they say revenge is a dish best served cold?'

'You'll be long gone, of course. With Hayley.'

'Does that matter?'

'No. It doesn't.' A deep, last draw on the cigarette. She crushed it out in the ashtray with studious emphasis, then looked up at Harding. 'I don't know whether to laugh or cry.'

'What d'you mean?'

'It won't work, Tim. None of it will. I went to see Barney's lawyer this afternoon. There's a . . . wrinkle in the paperwork. It seems Barney signed an agreement with Tony last year giving Tony the right to buy Barney's shares in Starburst International at a fixed – meaning knockdown – price should Barney wish to retire or, in the lawyer's words, "seek otherwise to divest himself of his shareholding". And that, apparently, includes bequeathing it to me. Tony can buy me out. *Will* buy me out. For a sum he's budgeted for. Which won't leave me in the gutter, but does mean I'll never get my feet under Barney's desk at Starburst – or my hands on any Starburst accounts.'

A lengthy, heavy silence settled between them. The significance of what Carol had said ate into Harding's

425

thoughts like acid. Whybrow had known from the outset that he would gain complete and overall control of the company. The agreement was a vital part of his calculations. Maybe there had been no ultimatum, no suspicion whatever on Tozer's part. Maybe Whybrow had simply greeted Hayley's intervention as an ideal opportunity to stage a long-contemplated coup.

'This deal you've struck may suit you and the sainted Hayley,' Carol resumed bitterly, 'but it does nothing for me. Nothing at all. So, thanks, Tim. Thanks a bunch.'

'It can't be—'

'But it is.' The words were spoken by Whybrow, enunciated with all his syrupy precision. For a second, Harding thought he was hallucinating. Then he looked towards the doorway leading to the hall. And there was Whybrow, smiling in at them.

'Shit,' Carol murmured.

'I promised to return those things of Barney's he had with him when he was killed, if you remember, Carol,' Whybrow said softly. 'That parcel from the *Kriminal-Polizei* you asked me to collect. It included his keys, of course. So, I let myself in earlier. I thought I'd wait for you to turn up. Then I decided to take a nap. Well, it's been a stressful day, as Tim will confirm. The waterbed's very comfortable, isn't it? I might buy one myself. I'm not sure how long I slept, but I certainly feel refreshed. Your voices woke me. Sound carries in this apartment, don't you find? Open plan. Hard surfaces. Nothing to soak it up, I suppose. Anyway, the acoustics are remarkable. And revealing. From the landing, I heard every word you said. So, there's no need to worry about losing out under the deal Tim negotiated with me, Carol. Because that's off. As of now.'

FIFTY-TWO

'I don't like people who welch on deals,' said Whybrow, advancing slowly into the room. 'We shook on this one, as I recall, Tim.' He circled round them to the window and gazed out at the city. 'You were going to tell Carol you were no longer certain it was Hayley who shot Barney. That was to be it. Nothing else. No . . . elaboration. Instead, what do you do? Allege I arranged Barney's murder. Explain our confidential agreement. And suggest ways for Carol to betray me. Now, that's not nice, is it? Not nice at all.' He turned to face Harding. 'Of course, I'm grateful to you for drawing my attention to . . .' He picked up the card from the table. 'Detective Chief Inspector Unsworth. Yes. I'm obviously going to have to do something about him.' He slipped the card into his pocket. 'But you've had plenty of chances to tell me about him before and you haven't taken them. So, there's really no way to salvage your bona fides in this situation, is there?'

Harding looked across at Carol. They held each other's gaze. Harding did not doubt that the helplessness he read in her eyes was mirrored in his own. There was nothing he could do now. There was no ploy left to resort to.

'Let me tell you both how we're going to proceed from this point on.' Whybrow moved round the table and sat down on the couch between them. 'We'll forget the idea of fitting up Nathan Gashry. That kite's not going to fly. Hayley remains the prime suspect. Now, I don't mind if she's never actually convicted. I'm a reasonable man. I bear her no ill will. If you can cobble together a workable alibi for her, Tim, or if you still want to withdraw your positive identification of her as Barney's murderer, that's fine by me. Just as long as we're clear nothing's to be said or done that encourages the police to look elsewhere. Because, if that happens, I'll be forced to invoke certain sanctions against both of you. Various documents you signed at Barney's request, Carol, doubtless without bothering to read them, will find their way into Detective Chief Inspector Unsworth's in-tray. They'll convince him you've been a willing party to all of Starburst International's . . . off-balance-sheet transactions. As for you, Tim, a witness will come forward who not only saw you talking to Hayley at Marienplatz U-Bahn station in Munich the night before Barney's murder but overheard part of your conversation. A highly incriminating part, naturally. And then, of course, there's the tape recording that proves you and Carol were lovers. I wonder what the *Kriminal-Polizei* would make of that.'

'You never intended to honour your deal with Tim, did you?' Carol interrupted. 'You were always planning to do this.'

'I can't stop you thinking so,' Whybrow responded. 'The fact remains, however, that it was Tim who vitiated our agreement.'

'Why did you do it?' Carol persisted.

'Do what?'

'Have Barney killed.'

'Oh dear.' Whybrow leant back and clasped his hands behind his head. 'This really does serve no purpose. Accusation and denial merely form a Möbius strip if persisted with. Business is business, Carol. It's not one of those television soaps you spend so much of your time watching. It's a clinical process. When someone loses his edge, his focus, his ... nerve, well, then he has to make way for someone else. He has to move aside. Or be moved. It's as simple as that.'

'Barney trusted you.'

'Yes. I'm glad to say he did. And what he trusted me to do was exactly what I've done ever since he hired me. Keep my eye on the ball. Exploit every opportunity. Look to the future. Plan ahead. Seize the day.'

'He thought of you as a friend.'

'That wasn't in my job description. Tim here was always more promising buddy material. Although he didn't really live up to the billing, did he? Just as you failed in the loyal and loving wife department. Barney

430

never knew how spectacularly you failed, of course. He was spared that at least.'

'You are such a cold-hearted bastard.'

'My ex-wife once told me I was emotionally stunted. It was just about the last thing she ever told me, as a matter of fact. I have the impression you'd agree with her. Well, so be it. The management of money requires a cool head. I've always had that. Fortunately for you, as it turns out. Since the sum I'll be paying you for Barney's share of Starburst International will keep you in Chanel suits and Jimmy Choo shoes for the foreseeable future. Will you be staying here, incidentally? Do let me know if you're thinking of selling the apartment. I might be interested. I adore the view from this room.'

Carol rose unsteadily to her feet. She shot Harding a glance that was at once resigned and despairing.

'Going somewhere?' Whybrow enquired.

'I need another drink.' She picked up her glass and headed for the kitchen.

'You have much less to say for yourself than when we last met, Tim.' Whybrow unclasped his hands and smiled patronizingly at Harding. 'Perhaps you feel you said too much on that occasion.'

'I have nothing to say to *you.*'

'That's a pity. I was hoping you could satisfy my curiosity on one point. This . . . thing . . . you have with Hayley. This . . . *rêve d'amour.* Do you seriously expect it to last? I mean, quite apart from the age difference, there's her psychiatric history to be taken into consideration. Don't you think you might be—'

Harding had lunged at Whybrow before he was even aware of the intention forming in his brain. His need to shut the man's mouth was overwhelming and irresistible, as much a physical reflex as a mental reaction. The blow he aimed would have driven Whybrow's teeth down his throat.

But the blow never landed. Whybrow dodged it with ease, twisting out of reach and sliding off the couch, then countering with a crunching kick to Harding's midriff and a deftly imposed arm-lock. Suddenly, Harding was on his knees, the side of his head pressed down heavily against the glass table top, his left arm scissored up between his shoulderblades, his right anchored to the floor by the weight of Whybrow's foot on his hand.

'Thanks for being stupid enough to try that, Tim,' Whybrow hissed into his ear. 'Your attempt to blackmail me earlier today made me angry. And I don't like feeling angry. It upsets me. It disrupts my sense of order. It *provokes* me.' His grip was tightening, the force he was exerting steadily increasing. Harding's view through the window of the tower blocks of Monte Carlo was blurring as the pressure and the pain mounted. He wondered which would break first: his arm, or the glass his cheekbone and temple were being ground against. He had clenched every muscle and was straining to break free. But Whybrow was too strong for him. In truth, he always had been. 'Do you understand, Tim? This is your fault. This is all your fault.' He grasped a handful of Harding's hair by the roots, raised his head an inch or so, then slammed it down. Harding heard something crack. *'Do you understand?'* Harding's head was yanked up again, higher than before.

And suddenly Whybrow's grip slackened. There was a gurgling noise in his throat. Something hot and wet was flooding on to Harding's back. His head was pushed down almost gently. His left arm was released. Then his right. Whybrow dropped on to one knee. Blood, thick and vivid red, flowed across the table and down on to the floor. Harding raised his head and looked round. He saw Carol standing above him, a long-bladed kitchen knife in her hand, the blade glistening red to the hilt. Then he saw Whybrow clutching his stomach, from which blood was gushing freely, struggling to rise, grimacing with the effort, jaw tight, eyes squeezed into slits, breath snorting in and out, feet scrabbling.

Somehow, he made it. There was blood everywhere now. On the carpet, the table, the couch. On Harding's shirt and Carol's suit. Whybrow tried to speak, but only a strangled slur emerged. He staggered forward, his shoes squelching in the blood pooling beneath him. Three stooping, tottering strides took him to the window. He turned and squinted at Harding and Carol, as if trying to focus on distant, receding objects he was no longer sure were actually still within sight. He stretched out a hand towards them. He opened his mouth. He gagged. Then he fell back heavily against the window. The pane shuddered but did not break. He slid slowly down into a sitting position, blood-tracks smeared on the glass behind him. Still he tried to focus.

Then something went out inside him. His head fell forward. He slumped to one side.

All movement ceased. Time froze. And the only sound was blood dripping on to blood.

FIFTY-THREE

Carol put the knife down on the table with exaggerated care. Harding laid a hand gently on her shoulder. Something between a gasp and a sob escaped her. She took a deep breath and steadied herself, then held up her hands to signal that she was not about to break down; she was in control.

'Listen to me carefully, Tim,' she said. 'I'll have to phone the police soon. You shouldn't be here when they arrive. It would only . . . complicate things. Put something of Barney's on. His clothes will hang off you, but . . . you can't leave looking like that. There's blood all over you. You weren't here when it happened, OK? It was just . . . me and Tony. He admitted hiring Barney's killer. He taunted me. I cracked and let him have it. Crime of passion. They go easy on that kind of thing here, don't they? So, don't worry about me. I'll get off lightly. You see if I don't. I'll need you to testify in my defence, though. You'll do that, won't you?'

'Carol—'

'You *will* do that, won't you?'

'Of course. But—'

'I don't regret it, you know.' She turned and stared unflinchingly at the sagging, crumpled, still bleeding mess of clothing and flesh that was all there was left of the coiled strength and nimble cunning of Tony Whybrow. 'I used the same knife Hayley held to my throat. It was in my hand when the fight started. I'd already decided what to do with it. Barney was a good man. A rogue, of course.' She shook her head in fond remembrance. 'But a lovable one. Except that I didn't love him, did I? Not enough, anyway. Well, I've made up for some of that . . . neglect . . . today.' She looked round at Harding, as if she had suddenly remembered he was still there. 'Go, Tim. Now. Leave me to it.'

'I can't.'

'Don't be stupid. Or noble. Or . . . whatever it is you're being. Just go.'

'There's bound to be lots of forensic evidence that a third person was involved in this, Carol. You'll never be able to cover it up. Once the police realize you're trying to trick them, they'll treat you as a murderer. But it wasn't murder. You and I both know that. Whybrow meant to kill me. Something in him had snapped. He was . . . angry. Like he said. Angry – and dangerous.' Harding touched the side of his face and winced. 'I think he broke my cheekbone. And he wouldn't have stopped there. You had to do it. OK? You had no choice.'

'They'll never believe that.'

'Yes. They will. Because it's the truth. And it fits the facts the way the truth does. I for one have had enough of lies and deceptions and carefully manipulated versions of events. This is where we stop running from the truth, Carol, you and I. This is where we face up to every part of it.'

'What about Hayley? You could go to her now. Take off somewhere. Be free.'

'We're all going to face up to it. Hayley included. And then we'll *all* be free.'

'Is that really how it'll be?'

'Yes. I truly believe it is.'

'And I have to trust you on that?'

'You do.'

'One last time.'

'Exactly.' Harding shaped a smile. 'One last time.'

Several seconds passed. Carol's breathing slowed as she held Harding's gaze and studied him, checking something she saw in him against something she knew in herself. Then she nodded. It was a moment of complete understanding between them; perhaps the very first such moment. 'I'll make that call,' she said softly.

They waited outside for the police to arrive. Carol paced the terrace, chain-smoking, while Harding stood by the pool, staring into the water. When his phone rang, he answered at once.

'It's me,' said Hayley. 'Don't worry. I'm in a call-box. I haven't broken your rules. I just wanted . . . needed . . . to check you were OK.'

'I'm OK. Where are you?'

'Is it safe to tell you?'

'Oh yes. It's safe.'

'We're in Harrogate.' How far away was Harrogate, Harding wondered. A thousand miles? It felt at that moment more like a million. 'When can we leave?'

'Any time you like.'

'So, you've . . . dealt with Whybrow?'

'He's been dealt with, yes.'

'And everything's going to be all right?'

He had planned to return to London after visiting Carol, travelling via Munich in order to alter the statement he had made to the police and to retrieve Polly's painting from the airport. He had been wondering how Hayley would react to her first sight of it. And wondering was all he could do now. He would have to tell her what had just happened – and soon. He did not know how to set about it. But he would have to find a way. There was something else he had to say first, though, something more important, more lasting. The future – their future – began here. He needed her to understand that. He needed her to believe it. 'Yes, Hayley,' he said. 'Everything's going to be all right. For you and me. For us. I promise.'

'I can hear a siren,' Carol called to him.

'What was that?' Hayley asked.

'That?' Harding gazed down into the clear blue water beneath him: a mirror of the sky; a vision of lightness, of liberation, from the past *and* present. He smiled. 'That was nothing. Nothing important, anyway.

Whybrow's dead, Hayley. But that doesn't matter. We're alive. And we're going to go on living. That's what really matters.'

EPILOGUE

The Cornishman, Thursday, 9 March 2006:

Baby's miracle survival after tragic death of mother

A Scillonian family was this week mourning one member and welcoming another after a tragic but life-affirming incident last Saturday, when 21-year-old expectant mother Josephine Martyn died after falling downstairs at her home, Pregowther Farm, St Mary's.

A doctor who attended the scene with an ambulance crew detected a heartbeat in the womb and successfully delivered a baby boy by emergency Caesarean section eight weeks prematurely. The child was later transferred to the special care baby unit at Treliske Hospital. A spokesperson said medical staff were 'amazed' by how well he was doing.

Many islanders will remember that Josephine Martyn, née Edwards, cheated the medical odds herself as a child by recovering from a particularly virulent form of leukaemia.

Speaking on behalf of Josephine's husband, Frederick Martyn, Mr Martyn's brother, Alfred, who also lives at Pregowther Farm, said the baby's survival was a 'miracle' that made Josephine's death easier to bear. 'It's what she'd have wanted,' he added. 'The family line will go on.'

AUTHOR'S NOTE

The known facts concerning the loss of HMS *Association* and three other men-of-war off the Isles of Scilly during the night of 22/23 October 1707 are faithfully represented in this novel, as are the circumstances of the theft of an emerald-and-diamond ring from Admiral Sir Clowdisley Shovell's body when it was washed up at Porth Hellick. There is no evidence either way as to whether this was the same ring later supposed to have been returned to the Shovell family.

Francis Gashry is a genuine if minor historical figure. He thrived under the patronage of Admiral Sir Charles Wager, whose Cornish estate he ultimately inherited. Born in Stepney in 1702, the son of a Huguenot perfumer, he held a number of posts at the Admiralty before securing his most lucrative appointment as Treasurer of the Ordnance. He served as MP for East Looe from 1741 until his death in 1762.

William Borlase, the famous Cornish antiquarian,

was rector of Ludgvan from 1722 until his death in 1772. The construction of an extension to the rectory early in 1736 (to accommodate Borlase's growing family) might well have obliged him to lodge a visiting antiquarian at his brother Walter's house, Castle Horneck, on the outskirts of Penzance.

Historians are increasingly inclined to doubt that King Edward II died, as generally supposed, during his imprisonment at Berkeley Castle in 1327. His son and successor, Edward III, is now believed to have met his father in secret on at least one subsequent occasion and to have been successfully blackmailed by an Italian priest who possessed evidence of the former king's survival. Where, when and how Edward II actually died no one can say.

NEVER GO BACK

Robert Goddard

arry Barnett thought he had left his military career behind, so
e is startled when two figures from his past turn up on his
oorstep after fifty years. An old friend has organised the reunion
end all reunions: a weekend in the Scottish castle where the
x-comrades took part in a psychological experiment many years
efore. They haven't seen each other since.

s they set off on their all-expenses-paid jaunt to Aberdeen, the
ld friends are in high spirits. But the cheerful atmosphere is
uickly shattered by the apparent suicide of one of their party.

Vhen a second death occurs, a sense of foreboding descends
n the group. It appears that the past is coming back to haunt
hem, a past that none of them have ever spoken about. Their
ecollections are all frighteningly different. So what really
appened?

hen when one of them uncovers an
xtraordinary secret, he becomes
onvinced that they will never
eave the castle alive . . .

*Meticulous planning, well-drawn
haracters and an immaculate
ense of place... A satisfying number
f twists and shocks'*
HE TIMES

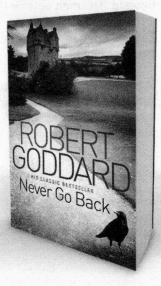

SIGHT UNSEEN

Robert Goddard

It is a hot summer's day in the tourist village of Avebury. A man sits outside the Red Lion pub, waiting. He sees a woman with three young children, two of them running ahead while their sister dawdles behind. A child's voice catches on the breeze.

For want of anything more interesting to do, the man watches. He sees nothing sinister or threatening. Even when another figure enters his field of vision, he does not react. The figure is ordinary – male, short-haired, stockily built. But he is moving fast, at a loping run.

And then it happens. In one swift movement, the running man grabs the youngest child and carries her away. Still the man outside the pub does not react. Suddenly, a white transit van bursts into view, its engine racing, its rear door slamming shut. The child and her abductor are inside. The child's sister rushes forward. The man outside the pub jumps up . . .

The tragedy begins at Avebury. But it does not end there.

'A typically taut tale of wrecked lives, family tragedy, historical quirks and moral consequences'
THE TIMES

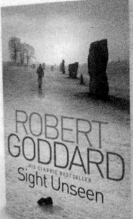

CAUGHT IN THE LIGHT

Robert Goddard

n assignment in Vienna, photographer Ian Jarrett falls assionately in love with the mysterious and beautiful Marian. ack in the UK, Ian resolves to leave his wife for her – only to find Iarian has disappeared, and the photographs of their brief time ogether have been savagely destroyed.

earching desperately for her, Ian comes across a quiet Dorset hurchyard. Here he meets a psychotherapist, who is looking for a issing client of hers: a woman who claims she is the reincarnation f Marian Esguard, who may have invented photography ten years efore Fox Talbot.

ut why is Marian Esguard unknown to history? And who and vhere is the woman Ian Jarrett has sacrificed everything for?

A hypnotic, unputdownable thriller... ne can only gasp with admiration t Goddard's ability to hold eaders spellbound'
AILY MAIL

His best book yet, a sinuous structure f twists and traps leading to an nexpectedly sinister climax'
HE TELEGRAPH

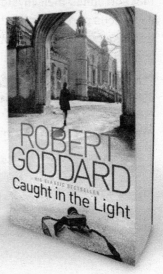

LONG TIME COMING

Robert Goddard

For thirty-six years, they thought he was dead. They were wrong...

Eldritch Swan is a dead man. Or at least that is what his nephew Stephen has always been told. Until one day Swan walks back into his life after thirty-six years in an Irish prison. He won't say why he was locked up – only that he is innocent of any crime.

His return should interest no one. But the visit of a solicitor with a strange request will take Swan and his sceptical nephew to London, where an exhibition of Picasso paintings is the starting point on a journey that will take them back to when the pictures were last seen – on the eve of the Second World War.

Untangling the web of murky secrets, family ties and old betrayals that surrounds their mysterious reappearance will prove to be a dangerous pursuit for the two men.
Because watching their every step is a sinister enemy who will do whatever it takes to stop the truth emerging...

'The master of the clever twist'
SUNDAY TELEGRAPH

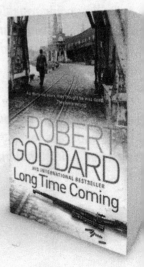